DANGEROUS GAMES

LOUIS SCHREIBER

Prologue

To The Supervisor
Federal Bureau of Investigation
San Francisco, California

Sir:

This is to inform you that a heavy traffic in drugs exists from Vietnam
to the States. I know this because I am personally involved, involved
against my will and under the threat of death. I don't know the origin
of the drugs or how they get to Vietnam, but I am enclosing a map to
indicate where the shipments are given to Americans for delivery to
the States on an air cargo plane company that has its warehouse at
the Oakland Airport. The company knows nothing about this. The
map also indicates where I think the Vietnamese operation has its
headquarters, with radio contact with the source of its supplies. And I
know that sometimes the drugs are brought into the States inside the
bodies of dead Americans. You will have to check that out yourself.

This is how it all came about . . . .

I
Patricia

Chapter One

The loudspeaker on the p.a. system first hummed, then buzzed, then crackled, then coughed, and finally announced, "Pat? Patricia Purney, are you still on the set? Mr. Colby wants to see you in his van right away. Pat Purney, please report to Mr. Colby right away. Anybody, tell Pat Purney to get her ass over to Mr. Colby's van on the double."

Pat Purney was still on the open-air set hidden by some huge scenery props, splitting a joint with two of the grips. Actually, Pat didn't enjoy smoking pot. She got nothing out of it, but when she had first arrived in Hollywood, everybody was smoking, so she went along to make herself one of the crowd.

Now she took a drag on the joint, held it for a moment, exhaled, then passed the joint to one of the grips. She said, "Sorry, guys. Mother has been summoned to Fairyland."

The two men grinned. They knew something.

Pat made her way across the huge set, decorated to resemble a jungle pool on a South Pacific island, including a waterfall. Big bouquets of flowers still bobbed on the water, held in place by weights on the pool floor. Just below the surface was a network of spigots that shot umbrella jets of different colors of water ten feet into the air. Judy Wallace, the star, did her famous backstroke among the clusters of the fifty members of Ted Colby's water ballet. Pat had spent most of the day in the pool; her bathing suit was still very wet.

She allowed herself a fleeting glance at the ledge sixty-four feet up the phony mountain. As a stuntgirl, Pat was assigned to stand in for Judy Wallace to make a swan dive to the pool below. The dive terrified her. It wasn't just the height that troubled her; she had dived from higher places. But she knew that a single wrong move in midair—even a slight blast of wind—could leave her impaled on one of the spigots just below the surface of the water. She knew that a wrong turn on her underwater swim on her way to her position for the ballet could leave her entangled in the chains that connected the floral displays on the surface to the weights on the pool floor. She was always relieved that she reached her place in the water ballet on the surface. At this point, Colby stopped the cameras, Judy Wallace stepped onto a small, flower-bedecked platform and lowered underwater for the few seconds it took for the cameras to start rolling again, then Judy was lifted slowly to the surface, standing, her arms triumphantly over her head, smiling brilliantly, her makeup perfect, not a hair was out of place. And moviegoers were intended to believe that the star herself had made the swan dive.

Yesterday, Pat had made the dive seven times before she finally heard Colby call out: "That's a print."

The cameras had stopped. Pat got out of the pool and went to Colby. She said, "I'm glad to hear it. I wouldn't make that dive again for all the money in Hollywood."

"You don't have to, baby," Colby said. "It was a beauty. Now take your place for the ballet."

Walking across the jungle set, she glanced up at the precipice as though it were a guillotine. The dreaded part of the picture was over. Thank God.

Leaving the set, she made her way to the row of trailers which the bigshots on the film used as offices or dressing rooms between takes. She reached Colby's trailer and tapped on the door, announcing, "Lover boy, are you in? It's Little Red Riding Hood."

"Come in, Pat."

Colby was at his desk. He looked her over and noticed her wet bathing suit. Getting up, he went to the bathroom, fetched a towel. "Here," he said. "Stand on this. No sense making this dump look any dumpier."

"You called?" she asked.

Suddenly he was serious. "Yes, Pat. I've had some bad news."

"Like what?"

"Like we've got to re-shoot your dive."

"The hell with that."

"Something went wrong with the shot."

"But you said we had a print."

"I know. It looked like a print to me."

"So what went wrong?"

"The dailies got here from Hollywood this morning. The big shits looked at them after lunch."

"And?"

"The take I said was a print, isn't."

"Why not?"

"Just before you hit the water, your left tit slipped out of your suit."

"Oh shit," Pat said, impatiently. "So what's the big deal? Just splice on the finish of the dive from another take."

Colby shook his head. "The director insists the dive be one unbroken take, so it looks like Judy Wallace all the way."

She said, "Then let the director do the dive."

"There's something else."

"What?"

"Mr. Kaz got here from Hollywood this morning. He watched the dailies, too. And he wasn't happy. He owns this place, you know."

"What did he say?"

"Well, after the laughing stopped, he said, 'You'll have to re-shoot that dive. This is a family movie. We can't have a naked tit flopping all over the scene.'"

"Then let him do the dive."

"Don't be silly."

She frowned at him. "I told you yesterday I wouldn't dive again."

"I know. I informed the director and he told Mr. Kaz."

"And what did Christ Almighty say?"

"He said to offer you an extra week's salary."

"And if I say no?"

"Then you're off the picture, we'll have to find another stunt-girl, and you'll be finished at LPM studios."

She thought it over. A week's salary? Better than unemployment. She didn't want to lose her job. She had nothing else lined up. And she didn't want to endanger her position at LPM, where she had done all her film work. Yet she couldn't bring herself to surrender. She sighed. "All right, Colby," she said, "but with this understanding. I only do the dive once. If Mr. Kaz doesn't like it, you can look for a new girl."

He smiled. "Good girl. I knew you wouldn't let me down."

"We're working tonight, right?" Pat asked.

"Just a rehearsal. The ballroom number. In the jai alai court. The crew is still building the set. Now get out of that wet bathing suit. Stop off at wardrobe and have them put firmer cups in your bra."

She smiled. "You sound like my mother."

In the large van, which the water ballet girls used as a dressing room and for a rest place between takes, Pat took off the bathing suit and stepped into the shower. Finished, she found herself standing in front of a full-length mirror as she dried off. She appraised her breasts.

Nice. Firm, and not too big.

She said aloud: "Mother, if you could see me now."

Her mother was the reason Pat Purney left home at the age of nineteen. It had been a matter of survival.

Chapter Two

Ellece King Purney used to say, "I don't know about that daughter of yours. I'll never make a lady out of her."

Her husband James would laugh and say, "Now, Honey, don't you worry about Patricia. She's going to grow up to be a perfect lady. She's your daughter, as well, you know."

"I do," Ellece would say, "and I wish you would remember, too. She spends all her time with you. She's turning into a tomboy. You'd think she was a son instead of a daughter."

"Where is she now?" James would ask.

Ellece always thought for a moment, then said, "At ballet class, I think."

"There you are, then," James would say. "You'd never find a tomboy at a ballet class. Stop worrying about her."

There was nothing to worry about. Patricia was the daughter of two strong people, and she absorbed both their qualities totally. If she had a preference, it was for her father. She enjoyed doing things *with* her father. She did other things she enjoyed *for* her mother.

Patricia dutifully studied dance, voice, elocution and the piano to please her mother. Because she enjoyed music, Pat took enough lessons on her own in violin, bass fiddle, trumpet, trombone, saxophone, and clarinet, xylophone and drums. She could play them well enough to fake her way through moderately difficult arrangements. With her father, she learned to shoot skeet well enough to be able to hunt the pheasants and partridge that still remained on the diminished King estate. James taught her how to ride a horse, how to swim and how to use a high dive with some skill and without fear. He gave her lessons in golf, tennis and bowling. He arranged lessons in karate and archery, in both of which Pat won All Girl State championships when she was in her early teens. James also endowed Patricia with a vocabulary of picturesque four-letter words, which they both used freely when Ellece was beyond earshot. They swore constantly on winter weekends when the two of them went in the mountains, where Pat mastered skiing and ice-skating. James and Pat were pals, and, the only real friend each of them had.

To a great extent this was Ellece's fault. She had been born a King, of the Texas Kings, and she had been raised as a princess. At the turn of the century, her branch of the family moved to Colorado and bought a big chunk of the foothills west of Denver as a place to breed horses. In her childhood Ellece had live-in tutors; in her teens she was sent to a convent school in Massachusetts, where she picked up a Boston accent. She was sent to a finishing school in Switzerland, where she learned a smattering of French and Italian, and formed an insatiable appetite for culture in all its forms. Coming home at nineteen, she decided to make Colorado over in her own image.

At that time, horse-breeding was centered in Kentucky, so the Kings did not require such a vast property in Colorado. Piece by piece, parts of the estate—called Evergreen—were sold to wealthy Denverites who could afford a place in the country. Evergreen became the social and cultural domain of the young and beautiful Ellece King, with her teas, her dinners, her balls, her private chapel with Mass occasionally celebrated by the Archbishop. Her entertainments often included performances by world-renowned figures in the concert world.

Ellece King met Captain James Purney, USAF, at the Governor's Annual Ball. Purney was present as an aide to the Commanding General of the United States Air Force Academy at Colorado Springs. For James Purney, it was love at first sight. Before Ellece King let herself fall into marriage, she checked out Captain Purney's heritage. Philadelphia. Old family, both sides. Not much money. Father: retired physician, now doing charity work at Philadelphia General. Mother: former national board member Daughters of the American Revolution. James: only child. Pre-law at Yale. Then the Air Force before deciding on a future career. Handsome. Obviously very much in love with her.

They were married in the private chapel at Evergreen, the Archbishop celebrating the Nuptial Mass. For the next two years, Ellece King Purney suffered the torments of an Air Force wife—there was not a peer in sight. She returned to Evergreen as often as she could. It was there, in the second year of her marriage, that Ellece gave birth to her first child, a girl, Patricia, named after Ellece's mother. And it was at Evergreen where, almost with relief, Ellece waved good-bye to James as he left for a tour of duty in Korea. She could now stay at home.

James Purney had seriously considered the Air Force as a lifelong career. Two things changed his mind. Korea, for one. The horror of it. The pointlessness of it. The other was his wife. He knew how unhappy she always was when she was away from Evergreen. So he resigned his commission, and returned to Evergreen to live with wife and daughter. He read law at the University of Colorado, and three years later opened his law practice in the Evergreen mansion on the very day his second child was born in an upstairs room. A girl. Sandra. Named after his mother. James Purney was a happy man, successful from the start, due in small part to his in-laws in the area, but largely due to his own intelligence, wit, and respect for the law. After four years, he was appointed to the bench. Thereafter, Ellece always referred to him as the Judge. His love for Ellece remained firm and constant. He never lost his amazement at the royal way in which Ellece ruled all of Evergreen. He soon realized that Sandra was almost a clone of her mother. And he had always been crazy about Patricia.

When Patricia was old enough to begin her education, she balked at the idea of live-in tutors, insisting: "I don't want to spend all my time in this house. Why can't I go to a public school like the other kids do?" Patricia and Ellece argued for some time on the subject, until Ellece fell back on what had become her last line of defense: "If it's all right with the Judge, I suppose it will have to be all right with me." Next term, Patricia entered the Catholic school for girls that had recently opened in Evergreen. Each morning, Patricia was driven to school in the family limousine, then home again after school. After a week of this, Patricia developed a scheme to make money for herself. She picked up classmates who lived along the way and charged them a quarter a day to share the limousine with her back and forth to school. She saved every quarter of it, accumulating a small fortune by the time she was ready to move on.

When Patricia was ready for junior high school, she balked at the idea of the exclusive convent school in Boston, insisting: "I've had enough of nuns and hoity-toity girls. I want to got to a school where the teachers are men, and where I can meet some boys." After much argument, Ellece finally fell back to her last line of defense. Next term, Pat was driven every morning to a junior high school in Denver where there were men teachers and boys. She promptly resumed her private jitney service.

Pat balked at the idea of the finishing school in Switzerland. And James said: "I think we ought to let your mother win this one. Besides, you'll get a good chance to improve your ice skating and skiing. You ought to give the place a try."

Patricia's try lasted one year, at which point she returned home, bag and baggage. She explained to Ellece, "The school must have lowered its standards. You wouldn't believe the kind of girls they've got there now. Trash. Just trash. Mother, I know how you feel about trashy people. I didn't have one real friend there." Ellece wondered if at last Patricia was growing up.

But to James she said, "There wasn't one person in that joint who spoke English, even when they knew how. Just French, German and Italian. Chic stuff. I got fed up with all that hoity-toity bullshit."

James nodded, understanding. Then: "Tell me, honey, what do you want to do with your life? What kind of work would you like to do, provided your mother lets you go to work?"

Patricia swallowed hard, then said, "I've been thinking about becoming a lawyer." She had, in fact, been thinking about it since James had put the question to her a moment before. She added, "You know I have always been interested in the law."

That much was true. When James was practicing law, Pat often went to his study after dinner to discuss his cases with him. Sometimes Pat asked an innocent question which provided him with the precise ploy he needed to startle an opposing attorney or deflate an unfriendly witness. When she could, she sat in on his trials, and she was always thrilled when she heard him put forth the tricky question which she had put to him. When James became a judge, she visited his courtroom whenever she could, so proud of him. They also spent many evenings talking shop in his study.

Now, James let a soft whistle escape. "It's a long haul," he said. "And a rough one. I just wish you were surer of yourself than you sounded."

"I'm sure," she said.

"You'll have to prove it before I let myself go to the mat again with your mother."

"What do you want me to do?"

"Are you still up on your typing and shorthand?"

"Yes."

"Okay," he said. "The court provides me with a secretary during the day, but I often need one at night and on weekends to type revisions of my decisions. And I could use somebody to hunt through case books for the precedents I need. Interested?"

"Yes."

He studied her. "I think it might be a good idea for you to get your feet wet for a year or so before deciding on law school. Don't you?"

"If you say so, Dad."

"We'll give it a try, then. You can quit whenever you want."

"I won't quit."

He grinned. "I'll ruin your social life. You'll be working evenings and weekends."

"I don't have a social life."

"What about all those boyfriends who hung around here when you were in high school?"

"They weren't boyfriends. They were just boys."

This was not wholly true. Pat had always preferred the company of boys because boys liked sports. She could beat them at whatever game they played, but she learned early not to win too often because they resented being trounced by a girl. So she let herself lose from time to time. Another problem were her breasts. They developed early. She was amused by the way some boys couldn't keep their eyes off them when they spoke to her. Like most youngsters, she had learned about sex from peers who knew little more about it than she did. She knew about erections and what they meant. She knew that some of her girl friends were having sex with boys. But being raised a Catholic and a King, she never let curiosity go any further than private amusement. But the day came when being a Catholic and a King was not enough.

There was a boy in the Denver junior high school who could, if he were the type, brag to his friends that he had raped the beautiful Patricia Purney, which he hadn't.

The Denver boy—Chick Halloran—had a reputation at the school for never dating a girl he couldn't screw. From the gossip Patricia heard—and overheard—around the school, she figured that Chick Halloran never had any trouble getting a date. She had often watched him approach a girl he scarcely knew, a superficially confident grin on his freckled Irish face, and, focusing his gaze on the girl's tits, he would ask if he could drive her home after school. Then he asked if she would like to go for a ride that night. Pat never saw a girl say no, and she wondered why Chick had never approached her. One reason was the King/Purney limousine was at the curb, the chauffeur waiting to drive Pat and her paying passengers back to Evergreen. Another reason was that Chick Halloran had too much confidence in his technique to drive forty miles to Evergreen on the chance of a piece of ass, even Patricia Purney's beautiful ass.

One day, when there was going to be a basketball game at the school that evening and sure that Chick would be there, Pat told the chauffeur to drop her friends off on the way to Evergreen and then tell her mother she was staying in town for the game and would call home when she was ready for the chauffeur to pick her up. Pat killed the afternoon in the school library until it closed at five. She went to a drugstore and bought a magazine, then took a stool at the fountain and nursed a malted for a long time. The soda jerk kept glancing at Pat's breasts, despite the tight bra Ellece made Pat wear. To kill more time, Pat ordered a dinner of the meat loaf, mashed potatoes and peas. It was cold and tasteless.

When she got back to school, Pat went into a girl's restroom, closed the cubicle behind her, removed her sweater, her shirt and the tight bra, slipped the shirt and the bra into her purse, put on the sweater, and, with a satisfied glance at herself in the mirror, left the restroom and walked down the corridor to the gymnasium. A good crowd was already there, the game just a few minutes away. She looked around for Chick. He was in the bleachers, on the lowest bench, just behind the players. She made a point of passing right in front of him as she made her way to the steps. She caught him surveying her. She went up eight levels until she found a bench where she could sit alone. Before the game began, Chick came up to sit beside her. He talked throughout the game, touching her arm or her back as he cheered or moaned at turns in the basketball game's fortunes.

Their team lost. Surrounded by the disappointed crowd, they made their way out of the building and to the parking lot. Chick said, "I suppose your chauffeur is waiting."

"No," she said. "I didn't know what time the game would end, so I told him I'd call home when I was ready to be picked up."

"You'll have a long wait."

"I don't mind."

"It's a cold night."

"I don't mind."

"Do you want me to drive you home?"

A stab of ice. "Oh, Chick, no. It's so far."

"I don't mind, if you don't mind riding in my beat up old Plymouth."

"Of course I wouldn't, but it's so far."

"C'mon."

They had driven about ten miles, filling silent gaps with efforts about the game, school, teachers, students they both knew.

Then Chick: "You must be cold."

"I'm all right."

"Move over here. I'll warm you up."

She moved to him, their knees touching, and he sent his right arm around her shoulders, pressing her to him.

"Better?"

"Yes."

They had gone about fifteen miles when she became aware of his fingertips approaching, slowly, cautiously, searching, like caterpillars. At twenty miles, the fingertips were halfway to one of her nipples. She stared ahead, waiting. At twenty-five miles, his hand was cupping her breast. A sharp curve made her lean against him. He moved quickly and kissed her neck, his tongue taking a quick lick. Her hand went to his thigh. At thirty miles, he pulled the car to the side of the road, stopped, clicked off the engine, turned to her and took her into his arms and kissed her on the mouth. His tongue on her lips made her gasp, and he sent his tongue into her mouth. She moved her hand to push him away and her fingers brushed against his hardness. She shivered.

His tongue still in her mouth, he pressed against her, pushing her backwards, against the door, his hands at her sweater, pulling it up. She squirmed as his cold hands searched for both breasts. She turned her head away, breaking the kiss. He sent the sweater the last inches to her armpits. He filled his mouth with her right breast. His left hand going down to her skirt and tugging at it. She squirmed again, fighting him. He slid her skirt high on her thighs. His hand went under the dress and tugged at her panties, yanking, ripping. Then she heard the soft metallic hush of his zipper.

Suddenly she was disgusted, hating him. She felt terror explode inside her. She put her hands against his chest and pushed. She could have broken his neck with a karate chop, but he threw himself on her, flattening her low against the door. She felt his hot hardness jabbing at her, banging her belly, her legs, between her legs.

Stunned for an instant, he backed off far enough to look into her anguished face. "Jesus Christ, you're a virgin!" He coughed a loud laugh and thrust his hips forward and jammed full into her in a wild, triumphant stroke.

She screamed. Her whole body went dead.

Then everything seemed to change. She was somewhere else. She was standing alone on a corner on a cold bleak night and she was waiting. She was waiting for something. She was waiting for something to arrive.

She was waiting for the ecstasy that she had expected.

She kept waiting.

She felt nothing.

Only the brutal pounding of him inside her.

Then he collapsed on her and was quiet.

Then he said, "This is gonna be a mess. Why didn't you tell me you were cherry?"

She looked at him and did not know him.

With effort and displeasure, he lifted himself out of her. "Jesus Christ. Blood all over the car. Look at it. Goddam. Gimme a handkerchief or something."

She sat up and lowered her sweater and straightened her legs and arranged her skirt. She opened her purse and handed him her blouse and she moved as far away from him as she could.

He opened up his pants and shorts and tried to wipe the blood from the car seat himself. He kept saying, "Jesus Christ," as he wiped the blood off his pants saying, "Jesus Christ, how am I going to explain this to my father?" He lowered his window and threw out the bloody shirt. Then he started the car and did not look at Pat, did not say a word, as he drove the last ten miles.

He stopped the car at the gates of the King/Purney estate, looking straight ahead, the motor sputtering softly. Pat got out of the car without looking at him, and she heard the car move away as she walked up the long driveway. The only lights she saw in the house were in the windows of her father's office. She let herself in as quietly as she could and went quickly up the stairs to her room. Just inside the door, she stripped, letting her clothes lay where they dropped in the darkness. In the darkness, she went into her bathroom and, in the darkness, filled the tub and took a long hot bath, using a handbrush to scrub herself, scrubbing and scrubbing. In the darkness, she got naked into bed, exhausted but wide awake. She could not think of anything else.

What went wrong? Where was the fun in it? Why did the other girls enjoy it so much and talk about it so much? Why had she felt nothing at all? And the blood, why the blood? She had been menstruating for almost three years now, and one of the maids had explained that to her. She understood it and was not frightened about it, even the first time it happened. But nobody had ever said anything to her about the bleeding when she was being screwed. Was it always like that, the bleeding every time? Why was Chick so upset that she was a virgin? How did he know? If half of what the girls said of him was true, he should be used to the blood. What went wrong? Where was the wrong? Was it in her? Was something wrong with her? That must be it. Something was wrong with her.

Acknowledging this with grim acceptance finally made Pat's tears flow.

In the morning, the first things Patricia saw when she awoke were her discarded clothes on the floor just inside the door. She went to them with guilt and shame. The blood on the panties and skirt was dry and dark. She looked around. On her desk was her briefcase, probably put there by the chauffeur or one of the other servants. She stuffed the clothes into the briefcase. Then she took another hot bath, scrubbing and scrubbing herself. Dressing, she took her bra from her purse and put it on.

When she arrived downstairs for breakfast, she found her mother still at the table, looking through her mail. Ellece asked coldly, "What time did you get home last night?"

"I don't know," Pat said. "I didn't notice."

"How did you get home? You didn't call for the car."

"One of the kids drove me home."

"Who was he?"

"It was a she. Nellie Mason. You don't know her. She drove a bunch of us home."

Ellece sent Patricia a look of quiet rage. "Don't ever do anything like that again," she said. "If you decide you want to stay in town for the evening, call and ask my permission. Or ask the Judge."

That morning, when the limousine arrived at the school, Pat stood aside as her passengers hurried into the building. Pat went around to the parking lot, to Chick Halloran's car. She saw that he had covered the front seat with a blanket. She opened the door. She took her skirt and panties out of her briefcase and tossed them onto the front seat where Chick Halloran would forever think, and perhaps boast, he had raped the beautiful Patricia Purney with the giant tits—and a virgin, no less, can you believe it?

Pat never spoke to Chick Halloran again. She never even looked at him. She never thought about him. As far as she was concerned, Chick Halloran was dead.

Chapter Three

It didn't take Pat long to cease being amused by her job with her father. James not only kept Pat busy evenings and weekends but often weekdays as well. He put her on a salary which she had little time to spend. He bought her a car for her trips around the state to do research in law libraries. The only time Pat felt really free was when she was behind the wheel, breaking all speed restrictions, on her way to somewhere new, to new people, new experiences. Out of this evolved a certain sense of wanderlust that grew within her. Before her year was up, she acknowledged what she had known all along: law was not for her. She needed more freedom.

But how to get it? She began by dropping little hints about being tired and needing a change, gradually expanding this to an announcement that she wanted to get away on her own for a while.

One day, Ellece, exasperated, said, "Patricia, I don't know where I went wrong with you. If I didn't know better, I'd suspect you weren't even a member of this family. Thank God I've never had any problems with your sister."

This was true. Sandra, three years younger than Pat, had welcomed her live-in tutors as though they were old friends of the family. She could serve a proper tea by the time she was ten, she loved wearing gowns to have dinner with her parents, she rode sidesaddle, the way a lady should. Her only other sport was croquet. Her one regret in going to the Boston convent school was leaving her mother. She was fluent in French and German long before she was ready for Switzerland. She had never been on ice skates or skis in her life. She had no knowledge of—or interest in—sex, and when, while at Boston, she began to menstruate, a nun explained to her that it was a punishment imposed by God on women since Eve, along with the pains in childbirth and the burdens of Original Sin. Sandra believed it all. She became a daily communicant and remained one all her life, asking God to forgive her for being female.

"Well, Mother," Patricia had said, "You'll have to take the bitter with the sweet. I don't recall that I've ever given you anything to complain about. If I come home pregnant, you can bitch all you want."

"*Really*, Patricia!" Ellece exclaimed. "That's *shocking*. I haven't heard a woman talk like that since your father was in the Air Force."

There were times when Pat wished her father hadn't left the Air Force. At least then they'd be moving from base to base. She'd be meeting new people, seeing new things, having new experiences. Finally when she reached the point when she could take no more, she announced that she was leaving home and had no idea where she was going or when she would return. Ellece refused to discuss it.

But James said: "All right, honey. I think I understand how you feel. You've always been a gypsy at heart. Okay. Take off. I'll fight your mother on this. Sooner or later she'll get used to the idea. But first you'll have to make a solemn promise to me."

"What, Dad?"

"That the first day you have to go hungry or the first night you don't have a roof over your head, you'll call me and let me send you the money to come home and settle down once and for all."

"I promise, Dad," Pat said.

On her first day away from home, Patricia Purney discovered the motion picture industry—a world that would be her home for the rest of her life.

She had driven forty miles west of Evergreen when a sudden turn in the road revealed a view that first looked like a traveling circus setting up for business on a wide field. When she got closer and saw the cameras, the lights, the reflectors, the covered wagons, the horses, and the many people in costumes at ten o'clock in the morning, she realized what was going on. They were making a movie. LPM Studios was filming one of its last grade-B Westerns, and this field was one of the location scenes.

Intrigued, Pat parked her car, got out, and walked toward the camera crew. Dressed casually in a blouse, beige slacks and sandals, she looked like Hollywood itself, and no one paid any attention to her. She saw that much of the activity was at the foot of a mound at the far end of the field, so she went there. A shot was being set up, dozens of people were waiting.

A young man with a walkie-talkie spoke to an older man sitting in a canvasback chair: "Shall we do a rehearsal, Mr. Romanski?"

Mr. Romanski said, "Yes, Mac. Let's see what it looks like. Does the stuntman know his bit?"

Mac said, "He should. I've gone over it with him a dozen times. Check him out." Mac turned and called, "Stubby, come over here."

A short, stocky man approached, dressed in an Indian costume, his face all war paint, a sheath of arrows slung over a shoulder, a bow in one hand. He asked, "What's up?"

Mac said, "Mr. Romanski wants to be sure you know the bit."

Stubby said, "Of course I know the bit. On one, I come up to the top of the hill. I make the horse rear up a couple times. I do a faraway look. I put an arrow into the bow. I do a coupla war whoops. Then I come tear-assing down the hill and toward the covered wagons."

Mac asked, "Can you do this like an actor instead of a stuntman?"

"Academy Award."

Mr. Romanski said, "Okay, let's try it. Where's your horse?"

"On the other side of the hill."

"Let's go."

Stubby walked away. Mac spoke into his walkie-talkie. "Joey, Stubby is on the way. Are the rest of the Indians ready?"

A voice: "You got it."

Mac: "Remember the bit. I give you the cue. Send Stubby up. After you see him come over the hill, count five and send up the rest of the Indians."

"You got it."

For half an hour, dozens of people—cameramen, lightmen, grips—were making small talk. Then Mac: "Okay, Joey. Now."

"You got it."

Stubby appeared at the top of the hill, looking fierce. He made the Pinto rear three times. The faraway look, hand to brow. He reached for the arrow. And he slid backwards off the horse, hitting the ground with a thud.

Mac: "Joey, hold the Indians." Then bellowing: "Stubby, what the fuck happened?"

Stubby got to his feet and brushed the dust off his costume. "It's the horse. He's slippery. I lost my grip."

"Well, watch it, will you *please*? Try it once again."

Another half hour. Mac: "Okay, Joey. Now."

Stubby reached the top of the hill. The horse reared. The faraway look. Stubby reached for an arrow. A dozen of them flew out of the sheath, scattering.

Mac: "Joey, hold the Indians." Then: "Stubby, what's the matter with you? I thought you knew how to ride a horse."

"Not this bastard," Stubby said. "He's too nervous. Get me another horse."

"We don't have another horse. Go back and let's try it again."

Stubby got off the horse, picked up the arrows and disappeared down the far side of the hill.

Another half hour passed. "Joey, go," Mac said.

Stubby arrived at the top of the hill. The horse reared again. The faraway look. Arrow to bow. War whoops. Stubby galloping down the hill. Halfway down, the horse balked. Stubby went flying over the horse's head, did a flat-out somersault and landed on the ground flat on his back. He screamed.

Mac said, "Hold the Indians." But it was too late. Over the top of the hill came a score of fierce-looking Indians, down the hill, past Stubby's limp body, and off toward the covered wagons, the cameras tracking them. Stubby grabbed his right leg and said, "I think my leg is broken."

Mac walked over to him. "I'll break your thick head. Get up."

"I can't," Stubby said.

Romanski arrived, bent, and ran a hand down Stubby's right leg. "It isn't your leg," he said. "It's your ankle." He pulled back the pantleg of the costume. "Look at that." The ankle was already swollen. "Get the medics out here. This man needs attention."

Mac said, "The medical crew doesn't get here until tomorrow. I didn't think we'd need them before then."

Romanski shook his head. "Well, get somebody to take him into town to a hospital. He may be all right tomorrow."

"This leg won't be all right for a year," Stubby said.

"Ankle," Romanski corrected.

Mac beckoned to two crewmen who were nearby. Mac said, "Help him up. Get him to a hospital. Let me know what they say."

The men slipped hands into Stubby's armpits and hoisted him up. He said to Mac, "I hope you get a good look at that crazy horse. It's his fault, not mine, so don't go around Hollywood mouthing it off that I can't do my job."

Mac said nothing.

Stubby hobbled away, aided by his two human crutches.

Romanski turned to Mac. "Well, genius, what do we do now?"

Mac shrugged. "I guess I'll have to call Hollywood and get another stuntman."

"That will take too long." The Indians had returned from their dash across the plateau and, sheepishly, huddled in a group a short distance away. Romanski indicated them with a nod. "What about one of them?"

"They're extras, not stuntmen. They just know how to ride a horse bareback."

"Ask. Tell them there'll be money in it."

Mac went over to the Indians and talked to them. He returned shaking his head. "They say it's too dangerous."

"Dangerous? I've seen more dangerous tricks by ponies in a circus. Is there anybody else around who can do it?"

Patricia Purney said, "I can do it."

Romanski turned to her. "Who are you?"

"Patricia Purney."

"Are you with the company?"

"No, sir."

"Then may I ask you what you're doing here?"

"I wanted to watch for a while."

"We don't allow visitors on the set."

"I didn't know. I'm sorry."

Romanski studied her. "You think you can do this stunt?"

"I know I can."

"You can ride a horse?"

"Of course."

"Bareback?"

"Any way you like."

"Can you manage a bow and arrow?"

"I won the Colorado state archery championship three years in a row. I competed against some real Indians."

"What do you think, Mac?"

Mac said, "I wouldn't, Mr. Romanski. She's not covered by the insurance. If she gets hurt, she could sue the studio."

"Do you understand that, Miss...What's your name?"

"Patricia Purney."

"If you get hurt, would you sue the studio?"

"I won't get hurt."

"What makes you so sure?"

"I know horses. In a way, Stubby was right. He didn't like that horse and the horse sensed it. When any horse senses that the rider doesn't like him, you can have a lot of trouble trying to control him."

"And you can get this horse to like you?"

"Horses usually do."

"Show me."

The horse was still at the foot of the hill, alone and apart. People were afraid to go near him. Sensing fear all around him, the horse responded with fear, his eyes wide and restless, nostrils quivering. From time to time he snorted and kicked his hind legs defiantly.

Pat approached the horse slowly, deliberately, a smile on her face. When she was still several yards away, she began to talk to the horse. Her voice was soft and warm, almost purring.

She said, "Hello, there, big boy. Are you all right now? They're working you too hard, aren't they? My, you're beautiful. I never saw a more beautiful pinto."

She was close to him now. He watched her keenly, with doubt and suspicion. She said, "Do you want me to scratch your nose? I have a beautiful Arabian at home who likes me to scratch his nose." She raised her right hand slowly. The horse backed away a step. Pat's hand moved forward and her finger touched his snout and she began to scratch in a gentle circle. "There now, isn't that nice? Doesn't that feel good?" She widened the circle. "I'll bet you like to be kissed, don't you? Want me to kiss you? I want to kiss you." She moved in and kissed his snout. A shiver went through the horse. "Want another one?" she asked, teasing. She kissed him again, her hands now massaging his head, his chest. The horse took a step forward and nuzzled against her chest.

A watching crewman nearby said to another watching crewman, "How would you like to be a horse right now?" And the other crewman said, "Yeah, man. Pass the feedbag."

Pat worked her way around to the horse's left side, patting, scratching, massaging, talking. She said, "You must be *very* strong. I sure would like to go for a ride on you. How about that? Would you like to take me for a ride? We won't go far and we'll have a lot of fun. Okay if I get on?" She had her hands on the horse's spine, she bent her knees slightly, leaped up, and she was astride, still talking, still touching. Comfortable, she gave the horse a soft jab with her heels. The horse walked forward slowly to Hugo Romanski and the others.

"There," Pat said. "It's easy."

"What did you do, hypnotize him?" Mac asked.

"Yes," Pat said. "With love. It works on people, too. Can I do the stunt now, Mr. Romanski?"

"Would you?" Romanski almost pleaded. "I want to see what it will finally look like."

"Sure. I'll need the bow and arrows."

Mac picked up Stubby's props where they had fallen on his flight and handed them to Pat. "Just a minute," he said. He flipped through the pad on his clipboard and found a clean page. He scribbled a few words, then passed the board to Pat. "Please sign this, Miss Parnell."

"Purney." She read: *In the event of any physical injury incurred by me on this date, I will not sue LPM Pictures.* She signed and returned the board to Mac. She looked over at the Indians, waiting a distance away. "What about my tribe?"

"I'll send them back," Mac said. "Do you know the business?"

"I've watched it three times."

"Okay, Mr. Romanski?"

"Just be careful, young lady," Romanski said.

"Don't worry. Shall I start?"

"Yes."

She got it right. The first time. Even the Indians raced after her with a fury that seemed real. She brought the horse back and dismounted. "How was that, Mr. Romanski?"

"Perfect, young lady," Romanski said. "Now I've got some idea what it looks like." He turned to Mac. "You'd better call the studio and get another stuntman."

Pat said, "Why? I did the rehearsal okay; I can do the shot."

Romanski looked at her long blonde hair and at her chest. He shook his head. "We'd never pass you off for Geronimo."

"You can try," Pat said. "You've got a makeup department and a wardrobe department, and you're not doing closeups. I can do the stunt, so why send all the way to Hollywood just for another man. You people waste money as it is."

"Mac, what do you think?" Romanski said to the assistant director.

Mac said, "I don't know, Mr. Romanski. There's more than just the stunt involved." He turned to Pat. "Are you a member of SAG?"

"What's SAG?"

"The Screen Actors Guild."

"I never heard of it."

Mac shrugged. "We could get in trouble with the unions, Mr. Romanski. I better get somebody else."

Romanski went firm. "How long are we supposed to be here, Mac?"

"Two weeks."

Romanski looked at Pat. "Can you hang around for two weeks?"

"Yes," Pat said.

"Can you take direction?"

She thought of her mother. "Like a puppet."

"All right, Mac," Romanski said. "We can't afford to waste any more time. Call the studio and have the legal department get this young lady into all the unions. We'll use her." He looked at Pat, at her well-defined breasts. "Get yourself over to wardrobe and see what they can do about those. It'll take a miracle."

The fortnight of work was done in eleven days, thanks considerably to Pat's raw talents. Romanski was satisfied with two takes on the downhill dash, which surprised everyone. Romanski was a perfectionist who didn't care how many takes it took to get the shot he wanted. Three days had been scheduled for the Indian attack on the circle of covered wagons. It was done in two, the cameras mostly on Geronimo as she raced her pinto around and around the wagons, shooting arrows with an accuracy that terrified the actors playing the pioneers. Romanski used Pat as a pioneer woman, too, dressed in a Mother Hubbard, tight bodice, as she hurried back and forth among the pioneer men, reloading their rifles, her blonde hair flowing. For the Indian village shots, Pat wore a black wig, long braids, the skin-darkening was used lightly, her dress cut low. Her business was to pass a gourd of whiskey among the squatting warriors, and Romanski kept telling her to bend forward more. And more.

Pat enjoyed being in a movie. It was like being a kid again, playing cowboys and Indians. But there was a lot about making a movie that puzzled her. So much time was wasted, so much time was spent standing around, waiting for a scene to be set up, the lights and cameras to be placed in the right places, the actors letter perfect, take after take because someone made the wrong move or fluffed a line that was going to be dubbed in later, anyway. Pat also noticed the power of the unions, especially among the crew. No man would do a thing that wasn't specifically within his job profile. More waiting around, more time wasted, more money spent. And it was just a B-movie.

It would have been easy for Pat to return to her home at Evergreen every evening—just fifty miles away. But she knew that, having left home once, returning home nightly would make leaving home again that much more difficult. Because of the crowd from LPM Studios, Pat had trouble finding a room in a motel. She settled for a dingy room in a small motel ten miles west of the location. A light breakfast and a lunch were provided by the studio; she ate dinner at a diner on the way to her motel. On evenings when she wasn't too tired, she visited Stubby at the hospital. They grew fond of each other. He gave her his telephone number in Hollywood.

The last night, Hugo Romanski threw a big party for the whole company. More people gave Pat their Hollywood numbers. Romanski made Pat promise to look him up when she got back to Hollywood. Mac hinted broadly that he would certainly be able to use her on his next assignment as an assistant director. It was another

B movie about Indians and the U.S. Army, to be filmed in Arizona. "You could play Geronimo again," Mac said.

Hollywood. Why not? She had never been there and she felt she now had some friends there. As a next stop it was as good as anywhere else. Why not?

Chapter Four

Money was not a pressing problem for Pat. She had saved most of the money her father had paid her for almost a year. Awaiting her at LPM would be a check for several hundred dollars, minus taxes. And she had brought with her the wills of both Grandpa King and Grandmother King which left her over twenty thousand dollars, payable when she was twenty-one. She could borrow against them if she had to. She also vowed that she would never ask her father for money, not because she was proud but because she was practical. She was determined to make it on her own.

But there was no rush. Pat knew that the movie wasn't finished yet. There would be interior shots to be shot at the studio, dubbing, editing. So she took her time, taking a week to drive to Hollywood. When she reached Los Angeles, she asked a gas station attendant for directions to the Hollywood Roosevelt Hotel, a name she had heard mentioned by some of the Hollywood people in Colorado, and, as far as she knew, the only hotel in Hollywood. She found it and checked in.

She liked it. There was an elegance about it. The swanky men's shop just inside the door, Cinegrill, with photos of the entertainers working there. The airline ticket counters lining the corridor to the lobby. The lobby was small, sedate, and in good taste. She loved her room, large and bright, with a view overlooking Hollywood High, just across the street, and row after row of middle-class homes. This surprised her. Pat's concept of a Hollywood home was lavish houses in Beverly Hills or Belair, in Westwood or the Pacific Palisades, and Malibu. It had never occurred to her that Hollywood included average, middle-class, ordinary people who worked in shops and factories and offices. And she still didn't know that many of these ordinary people, especially the young and the beautiful, had, like her, arrived with the hope of working in the movies. But she soon learned.

Pat spent four days at the Hollywood Roosevelt, most of it devoted to studying greater Los Angeles street maps, and driving around looking for a less expensive place to live. She soon rented a small, furnished apartment on Mariposa, suitable enough, and she gave a day to having a telephone installed and walking around the neighborhood to find shops she would need.

Pat was in Hollywood over a week before she drove out to the LPM Pictures Studio for her paycheck. By then, she had her SAG card and Social Security card. She showed them to the guard at the gate, and he pointed out the long, low building just ahead where she should pick up her check. She had to wait a few minutes while the Social Security deductions were tabulated, and she was surprised by the size of the check. Almost fifteen hundred dollars. Hooray for Hollywood.

She was on her way back to her car in the parking lot when she heard, "*Geronimo*!" It was Mac. He trotted to her and gave her a hug. "So you finally got here."

"Yes."

"Where are you staying?"

"I've got a place on Mariposa."

"Come over to my office. I'll want your address and phone number. And I know Mr. Romanski wants to see you."

He led her to a side street of bungalows, the kind she had seen from her hotel window. In front of one she recognized the limousine Hugo Romanski had used in Colorado. As they went up the stairs, she asked, "Is this Mr. Romanski's office?"

"And mine," Mac said.

Inside, the bungalow was laid out like a typical house, except that each room was crowded with office equipment and secretaries. Leading Pat down a short hall to his own office, Mac explained, "These bungalows used to be used as dressing rooms for the stars, so they could rest before takes or stay overnight when they had an early call. Now that we're into television, the bungalows are used for production staffs and the stars use trailers on the other side of the lot."

Pat nodded. When they reached his office, she noticed his full name on the door. *Loren McKay*. "I hate Loren," he said. "I'm always getting mail addressed to Miss Loren McKay." Pat smiled. She preceded Mac into the office. It was a small cluttered room—a medium-sized desk, two chairs, a sofa. Three walls were lined with books. The fourth, behind the desk, held a huge calendar, the dates heavily marked. Mac sat at the desk and indicated a chair for Pat. He asked, "Want some coffee or a Coke or anything?"

"No thanks. I'm fine."

He picked up a pencil and a note pad. "Okay. Let's have your vital statistics." She gave him her address and phone number. "Okay," Mac said. "Let's see if Mr. Romanski is available." He touched a button on the intercom on his desk.

A woman's voice. "Yes, Mac?"

"Is Mr. Romanski busy?"

"He's in conference with the writers. But he told me to send you in when you got here."

"I'll be right there," he said. "Come, dear. Duty calls."

They went through the short hall, into the reception room, across to an area that was elegantly decorated. In a quiet room at a neat desk sat the woman who, in Colorado, had identified herself as Mr. Romanski's personal secretary. Seeing Pat, she donned a practiced smile and said, "Well, my dear. Welcome to Hollywood."

"Thank you," Pat said.

"I'm sure you'll do well." Then to Mac, "You'd better get in there." She nodded to an open door. "He's in a snit. Writers again."

Pat heard the heated voices in the room beyond. Mac stepped to the door and said, "Mr. Romanski, can you come here a moment? There's someone who wants to see you."

From within came a gruff, "I'm too busy now, Mac."

"It'll only take a moment."

Pat heard the grunt of displeasure as Romanski got up from his desk and made his way to the door. Seeing Pat, a broad smile creased his face. "Well, Patricia, how nice to see you. Welcome to Hollywood." He took her hands and pressed his cheek against hers, his chest pressing hers.

"Thank you, Mr. Romanski."

"Keeping busy?"

"I just got here. There hasn't been time."

"I'm sure we can find something for you to do around here. Keep in touch."

"I will."

"And let's have dinner some night."

"I'd love to."

"Mac, don't ever hire a writer who's published a novel. You can't get 'em to change a *word* they've written. I've got three of them in there now and they're all shits." He turned and went back into his office without another glance at Pat.

Mac said, "Honey, I've got to go into combat. Keep in touch, okay?"

"Okay."

"And listen. In about a month we'll be going to Arizona for the curtain call of the LPM great Westerns. Would you be interested?"

"I think so."

"I'll call you."

"Right."

"And let's have dinner some night."

"I'd love to."

Mac went into Romanski's office.

Pat found her way out of the bungalow and along the narrow sidestreets to the main gate. The guard recognized her and let her pass with a nod. She went to her car in the parking lot and, having nothing to do, drove home.

It turned out to be a long day. She planned only to pick up her paycheck, but having run into Mac and then Romanski, and being greeted so warmly, made her feel like an insider. But being so abruptly dismissed made her feel like a naughty child who had been sent to her room without dinner. She couldn't decide what to do next.

Noon came. She was not hungry, but to kill time she went into her tiny kitchen and prepared a grilled cheese sandwich and a chocolate milkshake. She sat in front of the television while she ate. There were game shows on station after station. She kept getting up to change channels. The PBS station had a documentary on endangered species, so for almost an hour she watched bald eagles, whooping cranes, sea lions and millions of minnows whose lives were being threatened by a dam to be built across some Southern river. The soap operas followed. She turned off the set. What to do?

She remembered the list of names and phone numbers the Hollywood people had given her in Colorado as the work ended. But when she went over the list, she couldn't recall a face to go with a name, so, rather than risk being stuck for an evening with a stranger, she put the list away. She thought of Stubby. He was a safe bet. She called the number he had given her at the hospital. A machine that sounded like Stubby announced that he was out of town and would return the call when he got back. Leave a short message and a number. Pat's message was several war whoops. Where was Stubby? Still in the hospital in Colorado? She considered calling him there, but then she worried about the phone bill. Stubby could talk your head off. She decided on a note, instead.

In case you are in my part of the country, this is just to let you know that I am now in yours. Got here a couple of days ago and busy settling in. Not much happening. Ran into Mac and

Romanski at the studio today. Mac wants me for another Western, this one in Arizona. I may take it. But am I being type cast? Let me know when you are back in town, in case you need a babysitter or somebody to teach you how to ride a horse.

Love, Geronimo

She added her address and phone number.

She searched through her purse for a postage stamp and didn't have one, so she left her apartment and went around the corner to a drugstore and bought a few. She noticed the rack of magazines and paperbacks and bought one of each. As she was paying for them, she saw the display of picture postcards. She bought one showing Hollywood Boulevard at night. She addressed it to her father. *Just passing through. All fine. I'll keep in touch.* She spent the rest of the day reading, with a break for dinner. Tuna fish salad and a malted.

Two days of loafing in her apartment made her stir crazy. She opened a bank account, depositing her paycheck and some traveler's checks she had purchased in Colorado, and she took a long time at it. She went swimming in the ocean—her first swim in salt water. She loved it but stayed out too long. She was getting a sunburn. She went over to Graumann's Chinese Theatre and gave an hour to inspecting the footprints of stars in the sidewalk. She bought a ticket and went inside to see the movie. The vast theater was almost empty; there were more ushers wandering about than customers in the seats. The movie wasn't very good.

One night, she had dinner at the Brown Derby at Hollywood and Vine, but she didn't see any stars. Another evening, dressed in her finest, she had a late dinner at Chasen's. Since she was alone, and because she was not known, she was given a table in the rear, off to one side. No stars.

Then one day she received her first piece of mail in Hollywood. It was from LPM, signed by Romanski's secretary, who wrote:

Mr. Romanski wants you to have these so that you can visit the studio whenever you wish. He will be calling you about dinner as soon as his schedule allows.

The envelope contained two identifications—one wallet-sized for her purse, the other a sticker for the windshield of her car. These were to change her life more than she realized.

Her second letter arrived a few days later, this one from Stubby.

Don't think you can teach me anything about riding a horse.

*That fucken horse hated me, and you said so yourself. But I
probably will need a babysitter for a while. The doctors want
me to stay here a couple more weeks, until I learn to get
around on crutches. And they say I will need an operation
sooner or later, get some pins stuck into me, so that I can get
around on my own. I don't expect to get to work for a long
time. Talking about work, take that job in Arizona. Take anything that comes along. There are dry spells for everybody in
Hollywood, so work when you can and save your money. I'll
call you when I get home. Come and have dinner with me.
Bring your boobs.*

Love, S

Pat waited a few days before using the studio passes. She wasn't
sure what she would do when she got there. Driving to the studio,
she made up her mind that she would not try to see Mac or Hugo
Romanski, both of them evidently too busy to see her regardless of
what they said. Pat parked her car in the visitors' parking lot. At the
gate, she showed the guard her pass. He said, "Lady, with this pass
you can go inside to the employees' park."

"I'll do it next time," she said.

"New here?"

"Yep."

He nodded, looked at her figure and said, "Have a good day."

Inside, she reached the intersection that led to Romanski's office
and went the other way. She found herself in another world.
Really, several other worlds. The buildings on both sides of her
were the size of airplane hangars. Red lights glowed at some of the
doors, and Pat assumed they were filming on the sets inside. Here
and there were people in all kinds of costumes, just chatting and
smoking. *Between takes*, Pat decided. She wandered on. Trucks
with scenery and camera equipment passed her in both directions.
When she came to a hangar without a red light glowing, she
showed her pass to the guard at the door and went in. In one
studio, she watched carpenters and electricians putting up a set,
too incomplete for her to determine what it was. In another studio,
she watched carpenters and electricians tearing down a set, too
much of it gone for her to determine what it had been. In yet another hangar, she saw scores of people milling around on what appeared to be a Victorian set. Moving closer, she recognized an
actress she had seen in pictures a few times. She looked older than
Pat would have guessed she was. The woman's hair was speckled
with gray; makeup put a few lines on her forehead and cheeks; she

was wearing a black Victorian gown, high at the neck, with a lace collar. She was standing next to a man, short and stocky, in shirtsleeves, listening to him intently as he spoke softly to her, at times nodding with understanding. Pat could not hear them. Then the man touched the actress's elbow and stepped back into the shadows.

He said, "All right, Charlie. Call it."

From the sidelines: "Lights."

The set lighted up like Hollywood Boulevard.

"Sound."

A boom microphone was lowered, inches from the actress's head.

"Camera."

A camera was rolled into place, a foot away from the actress. The actress bowed her head, her hands clutched in front of her.

"Action."

A pause. The actress slowly looked up, her face distorted in anguish, tears filling her eyes. In a soft, throaty voice, full of bitterness, she said, "I can't stand this any more. I'm leaving you. I just wish I knew why, why you hate me so. Go away. I never want to see you again." She brought her right hand to her face, almost biting it. She was sobbing now, the tears flowing. Then she turned sharply and walked quickly to a door, opened it, then slammed it behind her.

A pause.

"Cut."

The tension broke. People began to talk. The actress came back on the set, smiling now, laughing at herself a bit, dabbing her eyes with a kerchief. "Was it all right this time, Joel?"

"Great. Just great, Bette. It's a print."

"Good. It's an exhausting scene."

From the audience, a woman's voice: "On the master, she opened the door with her other hand."

"No problem," said the man in shirtsleeves. "We can fix it at editing. Bette, why don't you get some rest? We'll do David's closeup now, and we probably won't get back to you till after lunch."

"All right, Joel. I can use it after five takes. I'll be in my dressing room." The actress left the set, another woman following close behind her. They passed Pat without looking at her, but a practiced smile still lingered on the actress's face.

Pat decided to leave, too. As she made her way to the door, she said to herself, *Just think. All those people, all this time, all this money, for ten seconds on film.*

Outside, Pat resumed her investigations. She came to another hangar, this one with a sign over the door: MUSIC DEPARTMENT—AUTHORIZED PERSONNEL ONLY. There was no red bulb at the door, so Pat went in. She showed her pass to the guard.

He glanced at it. "Who are you here to see?"

"Nobody," Pat said. "I'm just checking the place out."

He had no idea who she was. She could be someone important. "All right. Mind the red lights."

This hangar was different from the others. Instead of being an enclosed football field, it was more like a regular office building with corridors and doors here and there, some with red lights on. The place was, too, strangely muffled. Pat could hear sounds—music—but they seemed to be far away, subdued. Each door had a glass pane at eye level. Pat stopped at a red light and looked in. There was an orchestra—forty, fifty musicians—playing away, the conductor, wearing headphones, on a pedestal in front of them. Pat tried to hear the music but couldn't recognize it. Probably an original score for a picture. Two doors down the hall, Pat observed a woman banging the hell out of a grand piano, headphones covering her ears. Then she must have made a mistake, leaned back, laughed and put her hands to her cheeks. She talked to somebody Pat could not see, turned back the score in front of her a few pages, sat there for a moment, hands poised over the keys, then, with a nod, she was off on another rampage. Pat wondered which movie star would fake playing the piano in a concert hall when the actual scene was shot. Further down the hall, Pat saw five vocalists—two men, three women, each at a separate microphone, each wearing headphones, each holding the score. Pat could not hear them, but when they sang they moved their mouths, their bodies swayed, their facial expressions changed as they flipped the pages of the score. By now, Pat knew that the rooms were soundproofed, not just to keep the sounds in but to keep out sounds from other rooms.

At the end of the hall, Pat went up a flight of stairs. The second floor was quieter. There were no red lights on the doors. Nothing was going on. Then she heard a piano, slow, pronounced, firm. She went to a door and looked in the window. Five young women, dressed in practice clothes, were limbering up at a barre. Someone off to one side was calling: "Plie...Tendu...Round de jambe..." The five dancers followed the calls with confidence and skill. It reminded Pat of the many hours she had spent at the barre in dance school in Evergreen, always finishing with a fine, loose body, ready to move out on the floor for complicated combinations. For a moment, she was tempted to go in and take part. She smiled.

Down the hall, a door burst open, and out stormed a tall, burly man, bald, paunchy. He blurted at her: "Can you play piano?"

"Yes, I can," Pat said.

"Can you sight read?"

"Yes."

He calmed. "Maybe you can help me. I hired a rehearsal pianist for this morning, but the bastard never showed up. I've gotta rehearse my number for a couple of hours. Otherwise it will mean a hundred takes. Have you got time?"

"Yes," Pat said.

"Good," he said. "Come on in here." He led her to an upright piano in the rehearsal hall, took some sheet music off its top and handed it to Pat. "Can you manage that?"

The musical notations were in pencil, like a lead sheet, and without chord indications. After every dozen bars or so, this was written: (Patter). The man said, "At 'patter,' you stop and I do my bits. Okay? I'll let you know when to pick up the music again."

"Okay."

The man went to one end of the studio, leaned against the wall for a moment, shrugged his shoulders several times, wiggled his hands. A dazed smile came over his face. He was turning himself on. Finally he said, "Go!" Pat began at the piano, fattening the slender melody line with full chords that would have horrified her piano teacher in Evergreen. The man went briskly into the middle of the room, his arms swinging, his knees high, looking at himself in the mirrored wall, watching an audience that did not exist. He went into an outrageous dance, arms flailing, legs unhinged, leaping, doing knee bends, his expression blank in concentration. Pat came to patter and stopped. The man didn't, constantly moving, now mumbling to himself, watching himself in the mirror, punctuating every few words with an upward thrust of his arms and a loud, "Boom! Boom!" After some six frantic minutes, he let out his loudest booms and went trotting back to where he had begun, leaning against the wall and catching his breath.

Then he said, "That was great, honey. What's your name?".

"Pat Purney."

"That was fine, Pat. Let me catch my breath and we'll do it again from the top."

"Okay."

After they had done four run-throughs, Pat knew the music well enough not to have to look at it every moment. She glanced frequently at the man. He would have looked like a fool if he hadn't been very funny. She asked, "What happens during the patter?"

"My jokes."

"And the boom boom?"

"That's the drummer."

"You mean you're working to a live band?"

"No. The music has already been recorded. I'm just worried about the timing when the camera starts rolling. I've never done my act the same way twice. Now I gotta. You ever see my act?"

"No."

"I've been around a long time. Fats Mulligan. Vaudeville. Television. Broadway."

"I guess I've missed you."

"Where're you from?"

"Near Denver."

"I've played Denver lots of times."

"I lived out in the country, a place called Evergreen."

"I'm surprised I didn't play there. I've played everywhere else."

"Will you let me hear some of your jokes?"

"I usually don't do the jokes during a rehearsal. Takes the bite off them. Besides, in my act I always heckle the audience. Big laughs. I won't be doing that this time—everything by the clock. Too bad."

"It is."

"Y'know, Pat, I hate these Hollywood bastards. Once at the Oriental in Chicago I did over an hour. Big smash. Held me over three weeks. Not here, though. Here I have to work to a record, and if I miss a beat somebody hollers 'Cut' and I have to start over. If I didn't need the money and the exposure, I'd have stayed in the Catskills. Screw this Hollywood crap."

"I'm sure you're right."

"Ready for more?"

"Any time. But how about letting me hear the jokes? It might help with your timing."

"Maybe. All right. I don't have to worry about *this* audience, though. They're a bunch of jerks who get paid for laughing every time the drummer goes boom boom. Hollywood!"

"Let's go."

They tried it. Hearing the jokes now, Pat found herself breaking into guffaws again and again, something she had rarely done. And she caught Fats Mulligan glancing at her from time to time, pleased, wondering if she was for real. Again and again they went over it, and each time Pat found something more to laugh at, even his outrageous dance.

At last, Fats glanced at his watch. "I've got to get moving. It takes those fairies in makeup and wardrobe two hours to get me ready."

Pat got up from the piano. "I enjoyed it very much, Fats. You're a funny man. I wish I had been at the Oriental when you did over an hour."

"I wish so, too," Fats said, beaming. "With that laugh of yours, I could have done two hours." He took his wallet out of a hip pocket, fished through it, found a fifty-dollar bill and handed it to Pat. "Here, honey. Thanks a lot. You're terrific."

Pat's surprise showed clearly on her face.

Fats said, "What's the matter? Not enough? It's the going rate for rehearsal pianists around here. Twenty-five dollars an hour?"

Pat said. "I didn't expect to get paid at all."

Fats shook his head and gave her a sympathetic chuckle. "Oh, *honey*," he said, "You must be new to this business. Get paid for *anything* you do, even for laughing."

"I'll remember."

"Hey," Fats said. "How about coming over to the set and watch me strut my stuff? I need a friendly face. I've got enough enemies around here."

The set was an old-time burlesque theater in a small town somewhere, years ago. Small stage. Footlights that flickered like candles. Backdrop of ads for local stores. A pit for piano and drums. Several rows of seats for extras who would appear to be the audience. The lighting was set. The camera crew practiced dollying up and down the aisle. Dozens of people were loitering, watching, waiting. A young man, casually dressed and carrying a briefcase, saw Fats.

Fats bellowed, "Where have *you* been?"

The young man tried to smile. "Right here, waiting for you for two hours."

"I told you be in the rehearsal hall," Fats said.

"I forgot. There's still time. Want a quick run-through?"

"Forget it, too," Fats said. "I've already rehearsed. This young lady rehearsed me. She's the best piano player I ever worked with. And I'm going to see that everybody around here knows it."

He did.

Within a few days, her telephone began to ring. Most of the calls were from LPM, but other studios called occasionally and so did recording companies. Pat became known as the "Can Do" girl around town. If a replacement instrumentalist was needed they called on Pat. If some star needed a back-up singer, Pat handled it. If a dancer required a stand-in, Pat was there. When LPM casting called for a female Karate Black Belter, Pat announced that she would be ready by the time the part was ready for shooting. She was busier than she had ever been. Her checks were small but there were a lot of them. She was meeting lots of people, and she had regular dinner dates with men, most of them married, who spent the evening staring at her body. None of them tried to get her into bed. Her confidence, her outgoing charm, her ease with man talk, kept most men at the threshold, secretly fearful of rejection. Some of them waited patiently for the right moment.

Then she got a letter from LPM, saying, "We have been instructed by Mr. Loren McKay, of this studio, to inform you that you have been cast as a featured extra in "War Clouds Over Apache Pass," scheduled to begin location work at Tucson, Arizona, on the 23rd of this month. Please have your agent call us to discuss terms if you are available."

Pat still did not have an agent. Besides, she wasn't sure she wanted to leave town just when her freelance work was beginning to roll. But she remembered Stubby's advice: "Take anything that comes along." She called the studio. She was more than satisfied with the terms, and accepted the job. She agreed to report to a representative of the company in Tucson for further instructions two days before shooting began. Pat also got an answering service to take her calls while she was out of town.

The month in Arizona went quickly. Though Hugo Romanski was listed as the director, he was tied up in Hollywood on another picture. Mac was in charge, with Joey as his assistant. The dailies were flown to Romanski every night for comments and suggestions. Pat played various roles. This time, she played Geronimo, since the actor playing Geronimo was afraid of horses and was adamant in his refusal to mount a horse even when it was standing still. In this Western, the good guys were Army troops stationed at the fort the studio had built in the middle of the desert. Pat sometimes wondered if there would ever be a movie in which the Indians were the heroes, as surely many of them must have been. Once again Pat was an Indian on the attack, trick riding while shooting flaming arrows at the fort. Once again she played a young maiden in an Indian village, as bare-chested as the code in those days allowed. She also played an Army wife inside the fort, boldly dashing back and forth on a narrow ledge twenty feet up, reloading rifles. She wondered what her mother would have thought of her.

Pat rented a room in a small hotel in the foothills outside of town where, as it happened, many of the technicians were staying. She spent most of her evenings with them, talking shop over dinner, joining them for hours in the bar. To be sociable, Pat sampled scotch and bourbon and rye and found them all bitter, burning and unpleasant. She could nurse a small glass of wine throughout a long dinner or for hours at the bar. When the bartender found out that Pat liked malted shakes, he got the ingredients. She taught him how to make them.

The last night, when the stars had returned to Hollywood, the remaining crew and the extras threw a big party in the bar. Everyone, except Pat, quickly got drunk. When it was late, Pat announced that she was tired. Then a sudden rainstorm broke. Jake, one of the grips, offered to let Pat use his jacket for an umbrella as the two of them ran across the courtyard to her door. At the door, the two of them laughed as Jake untangled his jacket from her hair. Then he slipped his arms around her waist and drew her to him.

He kissed her mouth. She let it last. She felt his tongue on her lips and opened for him. He pulled her closer and she felt him hardening against her.

He whispered, "How about a little nightcap?"

"Sorry," she said.

He stepped away and she took her key out of her pocket and opened the door.

He whispered, "Just a quickie?"

"No."

She was too afraid, remembering Chick Halloran.

Chapter Five

It was early afternoon in Hollywood. Pat had just returned from Arizona. There were several letters in her mailbox—checks from LPM, a check from Paramount, one from a recording company, a telephone bill, her rent bill, a letter from her father, a note from her sister, and a note from Stubby saying he was on his way home. She called her answering service and was given a list of dated messages. Pat noticed that as the month had unfolded the number of calls dwindled. Had going to Arizona been such a good idea? She called Stubby, who had called her three times.

He recognized her voice immediately. "Where the hell have you been?"

She let out a war whoop. "Guess."

"Did you have any fun?"

"Some."

"When can you come over?"

"I just got back, Stubby. I've got a lot of things to do."

"Anybody I know?"

"Probably."

"How about dinner tonight?"

"Wonderful. Where do you want to meet?"

"It'll have to be here. I can't maneuver the stairs on these horrible crutches."

"All right. What do you want me to bring, anything?"

"You'll have to. There's not a crumb to eat in this joint."

"Nobody's shopped for you?"

"Hell, no. When you're up in Hollywood, you're fighting people off, but when you're down you're a leper. You'll never find out."

"What can I get you?"

"Everything. I don't even have coffee."

"Jeez. Tell you what. I've got to unpack and unwind. I've got some calls to return and some bills to pay. It'll take a couple of hours. Then I'll go over to the supermarket and load up. Anything special?"

"Yeah, booze."

"Scotch, isn't it?"

"Get a case."

"I'll see you later."

Returning the calls proved dismal. Jobs that had been offered her were filled by somebody else or canceled. Nobody had any offers. People asked how long she would be in town this time and told her to keep in touch. So she had nothing to do. She decided to rest for a couple of days and then start making rounds. Something was bound to come up.

At the supermarket, she spent almost a hundred dollars stocking up Stubby's cupboard, buying him everything from bread to toilet paper, an assortment of steaks and chops, two pounds of coffee, fresh vegetables and fruit, a case of scotch, a package of ice cubes—just in case he couldn't maneuver his refrigerator, either. For herself, ice cream, chocolate syrup and milk. A boy helped her carry the bags to her car. Stubby's apartment was upstairs in a frame, four-flat building off Hollywood Boulevard and a few blocks from the Roosevelt, with a steep flight of stairs on the outside. No wonder he was stranded. Pat needed four trips to carry her purchases to his apartment, taking time on the first trip to kiss Stubby, fix him a scotch-on-the-rocks, and to notice that he was in a wheelchair, his right leg in a cast from the knee down. By the time she had hauled up the groceries, the place looked crowded.

Stubby asked, "You planning to open your own supermarket?"

"Sure," Pat said. "It'll give you something to do."

"It won't work," he said. "I don't know how to make change."

"Don't give any," she laughed. "How about steaks tonight?"

She put small glass jars of shrimp cocktail in the refrigerator to chill. She left two steaks out to thaw and stuffed everything else away in the limited space.

Stubby said, "Jeez, what do I owe you for all this?"

Pat said, "We'll add it up when you learn how to make change." She put two large potatoes into the oven.

"Fix yourself a drink," he said.

She made herself a chocolate shake.

As they waited for the potatoes, they talked shop. She told him about Arizona and the freelance jobs. She told him about the calls for her when she got home.

Stubby said, "You'll do all right."

"What about you?"

"I'm okay. The bill at the hospital in Colorado was seven thousand dollars, but all I had to do was sign it. The studio paid. The workman's compensation checks started coming in a few weeks ago. I haven't been able to bank them yet."

"Let me know when you want to. I'll drive you. How's about your ankle?"

"It's bad, Pat. It'll never be right again. The doctors in Colorado told me about an operation where they use pins that work like hinges. I suppose I'll have to go that route. But it'll never be right. No more stunts for me."

"What'll you do?"

"I dunno."

"I haven't seen much television lately," Pat said, "but every show I see ends up with a car chase. You could do that, couldn't you?"

"It depends on my ankle. I could do extra work. If there is any. Europe is the place. You've been away a while, but you'll be surprised how much things have changed in a short time. A lot of producers have started shooting pictures in Europe. It's a helluva lot cheaper. Few union problems. And they can sign extras for a dime a dozen. So it's slowing down here."

"Something will come up."

"I hope."

"Me, too." She meant that for herself as well as for Stubby. "How do you like your steak?"

"Cooked."

"I'll put yours in now, then," she said. She made a salad. It was still early when she told Stubby she had to leave. She had lots to do.

Stubby asked, "When do I get a reprise? When the cupboard is bare?"

"Don't whine. I'll keep in touch. Call me, too. And if things are as bad as you say, maybe you'll find a roommate."

"Anytime. So long as it's your beautiful body."

Things had gone bad in a surprisingly short time. The studios were dropping Westerns. Some studios were aggressively bidding for and buying Broadway plays, with small casts and few sets. Important roles for women (even unimportant ones) were vanishing. Men were taking over, dazzling handsome men, who almost invariably played young men with mental disorders.

Pat made calls and did the rounds. Everyone was cordial, and now and then somebody would take her to lunch in the studio commissary. They all said that nothing was happening at the mo

ment, but they would keep her in mind. In a month, she got two
jobs: an extra walking along a crowded street and an elevator operator in a department store. The street job lasted two days, the store
job one morning. She got worried, not so much about money as
much as about herself. She felt she was losing her optimism.

At Stubby's one night, she suddenly announced, "Stubby, I'm
thinking about going home."

"So early?"

"I mean to Evergreen."

"Back to the warmth of the family hearth?"

"You can put it that way."

"I warned you there would be dry spells."

"I know."

"A lot of the big stars aren't working. They've gone to New
York, London, or Rome."

"I know."

"Have you tried Romanski or Mac?"

"They're in Europe."

"Okay. What can you do besides war whoops?"

"What do you mean?"

"A lot of the kids are taking jobs outside the industry. Why don't
you?"

"I wouldn't know where to start."

"Well, for Chrize sake, read the want ads. What did you do for
a living before you became a movie star? You never told me."

"Not much. I was at school mostly. And then I worked for my
father for almost a year."

"The Judge?"

"Yes."

"As what?"

"Part-time secretary."

"You can type?"

"Yes."

"And shorthand?"

"Yes."

"Hell, check out the temp employment agencies. You should be
able to find something."

"I never thought of it."

"Everybody needs a secretary one minute after he gets his name
on a door. Check it out."

Driving home, Pat stopped at a newsstand and bought a copy of
the next day's L.A. *Times*. At home, she immediately began to
check out the temporary employment agencies. Many of them

were seeking secretaries, but usually not in fields for which Pat had the required technical knowledge. She found two ads for legal secretaries. In the morning, Pat called an agency on Wilshire and was told to come in for an interview. She was there in an hour. The waiting room was crowded and Pat had to wait another hour before her name was called. She was interviewed by an elderly woman in an office the size of a telephone booth. Then she was given a long form to fill out about herself and her business experience. She wanted to list more than her father as an employer, so she added the names of a few of his friends for whom, she said, she had done part-time work. Sent to another room, she took a typing test. In another room, she took a shorthand test. Another hour in the waiting room. Finally she was summoned by the elderly woman who had first interviewed her.

"This looks very promising," the woman said. "We'll call you when we have something. When is the best time to reach you?"

"I have an answering service," Pat said.

"Good. Tell me something. Why did you move to California when you evidently could find work so easily in Colorado?"

"I moved here for my health," Pat said.

"Not the movies?"

"Oh, I've done some extra work, just for the fun of it, but my work usually ends up on the cutting room floor."

"Most girls do. We are a temporary employment agency, Miss Purney, but we prefer reliable people, not somebody who will go running off to a movie studio at the drop of a hat."

"Never fear," Pat said.

Two days later, Pat went to work in the secretarial pool of a law firm that occupied two floors of a new building on Wilshire Boulevard. It was more of a secretarial ocean, one entire floor given over to row after row of women and men of all ages clacking away at electric typewriters, some working from tapes, some from dictation, all of them busy every minute, none of them really understanding what they were doing. Pat had been told that the job would last three weeks and, because of her legal background, she would love it. The three weeks unfolded into three months, with no end in sight. Five days a week, nine to five. Boring. Boring. Boring. For Pat, the only good thing about it was that the income was enough to keep her from spending her savings.

She hated the routine. Getting up at the same time every morning, going to the same place, doing the same thing all day, then going home without any sense of having really achieved anything.

Thank God there was Stubby. She had him to shop for, cook for, and to look the other way when she held him up at the bathroom sink to take a sponge bath. He was great about being able to talk to, to bitch to, to chew her out.

Stubby taught her that she could find out more about what was going on in Hollywood from the grapevine than from the trade papers. At least two evenings a week, she was on the telephone with people she had met through her studio work, and picked their brains. Then they picked hers. She knew they were on the same hunt.

One night she got a call from a dancer she had met during the three days it had taken to shoot a ballroom sequence at Fox. The dancer said, "Your mother sure is pooped tonight, honey."

"What you been up to?" Pat asked.

"I spent all day auditioning for the new Ted Colby musical at LPM. It was a *killer.*"

"Ted Colby?"

"The choreographer."

"I don't think I know him."

"He's spent the past two or three years in Rome, doing television crap. Somebody at LPM obviously thinks musicals are coming back, so they sent for him. They're still working on the script, but they plan to start shooting the musical numbers in a week or so."

"That sounds good. Did you make it?"

"No, dear. I got through the ballet and the modern and the jazz okay, but I flunked out on the tap."

"You don't tap?"

"I can do a time step, but that's it. If I could do the tap combinations that little bastard gave us, I'd go to New York and get into the Rockettes."

"Rough, huh?"

"Murder. I'll bet five hundred gals showed up for the audition, and I'll be surprised if a dozen got through the tap."

"Did Colby do the audition himself?"

"No. Some Guinea assistant of his from Rome. He could barely speak English. It was a disaster area."

"Well, you don't know," Pat said, consoling her. "You still might get a callback."

"I wouldn't bank on it. But I think I'll take some tap classes. You're in pretty solid at LPM, aren't you? You've done a lot of dubbing for them, haven't you?"

"I wouldn't bank on that, either," Pat said. But she was ready to bank on something else. Pat had studied tap in Evergreen but hadn't used it much since, usually just after the dinner parties when the wine made her a little giddy. She had decided what she was going to do. *Tap classes, here I come.*

She started taking three tap classes a day—beginners, intermediate, advanced. Her footwork was a bit rusty at first but quickly improved. She was thrilled by how easily she could pick up a tap combination from the instructor, no matter how difficult. This was the trick of dance auditions—not skill but skillful faking, a good eye and a quick memory.

At Stubby's one evening, she asked as airily as she could, "Do you think you can find out when Ted Colby will schedule the callbacks at LPM?"

"Sure I can. But why Colby? He's a choreographer."

"I know. I want to watch. I might learn something."

His eyes read right through her.

"All right," she said. "A job is a job."

Stubby reached for his telephone. "I don't know why you want to be a hoofer when you've got the makings of a fine actress. You don't know what you want."

"Right," Pat said. "I *don't* know what I want. But I'm going to keep looking until I find out. Then I'll get it."

He studied her for a moment, quite calmly, and then said, "That's the one thing I hate about you. You *will* get what you want."

"What's so awful about that?"

"Nobody out here gets what he wants without paying a big price for it. And they don't keep it for long."

"I'll pay the price," Pat said. "And then I'll pay a higher price to keep it."

He sighed. He picked up his phone and dialed. "Terry? How are you, baby? Good. It's Stubby. Oh, I'm okay. One of these days I may even be able to stand up. Right. No, everything's fine. Hey, Terry, listen. A friend of mine wants to know when Ted Colby is holding callbacks on that musical at LPM. Have you heard? Oh, did you? Yeah, I hear the auditions didn't go too well. Well, tap, y'know? Who taps these days? Right. When? What time? You will? Terry, how about I tell my friend to say hello to you? No, she just want to watch. Right. Her name is Pat. A beauty. Okay. Thanks, Terry. Come up and see me sometime, as they say. Good. See you."

He hung up. "The callback is Thursday morning at nine. LPM. Building six. Terry will be at the piano."

"Terry who?"

"Molino. I've known him for years. Nice guy. He worked a lot with Busby Berkeley."

"He played for the auditions?"

"Yeah."

"What did he say?"

"A mess."

"How come?"

"It was mostly tap," Stubby said, "Most of the kids never studied tap. And those who did study tap hadn't used it for years. They were rusty. Did you study tap?"

"Long ago."

"Good luck." He sighed again. "Terry said that another problem was that little Guinea who gave the combinations. He hardly speaks English and nobody could understand him. And even when he demonstrated steps, most of the kids couldn't get it."

"Why didn't somebody complain?"

"The word is that he's Colby's current boyfriend. Addio! You speak Italian?"

"No."

"Why don't you run over to Berlitz for a crash course?"

"I'm just an onlooker, Stubby."

"Bullshit. Fix me a drink."

Next morning, a Wednesday, Pat parked her car in the LPM employees' lot and then hurried through the narrow streets. It was eight a.m. The place was already busy.

Pat headed for the Music Department building, showed her pass to the guard inside the door, and went upstairs. She chose a sizable rehearsal hall. That morning, she had put on slacks and a sweater; she carried a small canvas zipper bag that contained her tap shoes (high heels) and her lunch. She wasted no time. She put on her shoes, circled the hall, knees high, loosening up. She did twenty minutes of stretch exercises, squatting, reaching, twisting, kicking, until her body went supple and felt controllable. She sat on the floor, again reaching, twisting, bending. She went flat on her back, her legs high, ankles on hinges, pumping a bicycle, her breathing steady and subdued.

Finally, she placed herself in front of the mirrored wall and put her body into the ballet first position. Okay. Good lines. Watch the arms. There. Better. She went into a time step, watching herself in the mirror. Head up. Tilt. Smile. Arms moving. She listened to herself. Her right foot was better than the left, the taps firmer, louder, sharper. She concentrated on the left foot, over and over again, until the sounds of her taps were equally firm, loud, sharp. She began to move out, doing riffs, her toes in rapid fire, her heels quick thunder. Leaps. Turns. She noticed that her butt was protruding slightly. She tucked it under. Good lines. On one turn, she almost lost her balance, her right leg extended straight out. Her left heel clicking, she brought the right leg down slowly, her shoulders forward a bit, the right foot gently to the floor. Tapping. Good. Sexy. Keep it in.

By late morning, she felt hungry and ate an apple. At two, she broke for a sandwich and a malted shake. At six, she ate a candy bar, watching her every step in the mirror. At eight, she saw that sweat had caused rivulets in her makeup. She muttered, "Fuck it." She changed shoes, lighted a cigarette but snuffed it out after two drags, took her zipper bag and left the building.

At first, the lot seemed very quiet, but as she walked along Pat could pick up sounds in the distance, people like her headed for the parking lot. Some technicians stood at the vast sliding doors of a sound stage, talking to each other as they worked.

Two men, walking quickly, one carrying a briefcase. "If that son of a bitch thinks I'm going to rewrite that scene again, he can shove the whole script you know where."

The guard at the gate. "Working late, Miss Purney?"

Her telephone was ringing as she entered her apartment. She locked the door. The telephone rang twice more and stopped. Probably Stubby wondering where she had been all day. But what she wanted now was a long hot bath. She turned on the water in the tub. In her bedroom, she undressed and put on a negligee. She checked her answering service. Four calls from Stubby, the last call a few minutes ago. Universal.

Pat asked, "Did Universal leave a message?"

"They want you for a recording session on Friday. You're to call a Mr. Lewis before noon tomorrow to confirm."

"All right. I don't want to take any calls tonight, so will you please plug in if my phone rings?"

"Yes. Good night."

Pat luxuriated in her tub for an hour. The phone rang. Just once. Surely Stubby again. No sense checking on it. Most likely Stubby could guess how she had spent the day, and she didn't want to have to lie to him. Later she had an English muffin and a cup of tomato soup. Then she went to bed, setting her clock for five A.M. In the morning, she examined her meager wardrobe and chose a cream-tinted dress, trim in the bodice, short sleeves, a narrow belt of the same material, a flared and pleated skirt. First she put on black pantyhose, the silky material fitting her long legs snugly. She debated whether she should wear her hair up, which a dancer would do, or let it all hang out. She let it hang. She was careful with her makeup. Not much; just enough. After all, she was supposed to be on the set to watch, not to compete. Quickly she downed a cup of tea, picked up her zipper bag from the chair where she had left it the night before. It was almost seven o'clock when she got into her car.

When she reached Sound Stage Six at LPM, she was surprised to see about a dozen girls, obviously dancers, at the door, digging into their purses or their zipper bags for their callback passes. Pat showed her permanent pass to the guard and went inside. At the far end there were more dancers, more than Pat could count at a glance, undressing down to their work clothes. Leotards, some with the French cut, cotton padding at the crotch to enlarge the bulge. Shorts. Swim suits. Jeans. Khakis. Pat noticed that practically all of them were wearing low-heeled tap shoes. Okay for work but not for show. High heels give a better line—provided you could dance in high heels.

Pat heard a piano and went to it. "Terry?"

Middle-aged. Lean. Thinning brown hair. "Yeah?"

"I'm Pat Purney. Stubby's friend."

"Hi. How is the little bastard?"

"Improving."

He looked her over, hands still softly playing. "You one of the callbacks?"

"No. I missed the audition. I was at Universal for a recording session."

"Harry Lewis?"

"Yes."

"Nice guy."

"I've never seen Ted Colby work, so I thought I'd come and watch. Which one is he?"

Terry nodded toward a cluster of four or five men on the far side of the stage. "The fruitcake with the hairnet."

Pat located him. Oh, yes. A dancer. He had acquired a slight paunch and he was no longer young, but his gestures, his confident gait, the body tense but relaxed all clearly marked him as a dancer. Pat said, "And the assistant I've heard so much about?"

"The Italian elf in the pink pants and all the jewelry. I'm surprised he can stand up with the excess luggage."

Pat located him. He was cute, but he was playing the dancer too dramatically. Pat surveyed the scene. "I didn't expect so many people. I had heard the auditions were small."

"Chaos. But Roberto can't speak much English, so a lot of kids got callbacks who shouldn't've."

"Roberto?"

"The elf."

"Well, they're an early crowd—I'll say that for them."

"The word got out," Terry said. "We're doing it the Italian way. Early start, five hours for lunch, work late."

Ted Colby broke from the cluster and went center stage. He waved a signal at the sound booth, and a boom mike was swung to him, just over his head. He cleared his throat.

"All right, everybody, calm down," Colby announced. The place went calm. "I've got something I want to say to you, so gather around me." There was a loud clatter of tap shoes. Quiet. "In case you don't know who I am, I'm Ted Colby. You'll be doing my dances. In case you don't realize it, I have a reputation for being a slave driver." Some titters. "So if you aren't willing to work hard for me, you can go home now." Nobody moved. "As you may know, this picture is about the Thirties, so there will be a lot of tap. I hear some of you never had tap shoes on before these auditions. That's probably your fault, or your mother's fault for not making you study tap. Either way, get ready for a lot of eliminations." Murmurs of fear. Colby: "Now, in case you don't know, I've got a reputation for bringing in a picture under budget. This picture will be no exception. There must be a hundred of you here; I can use only thirty: that's budget, too." Murmurs. Colby: "Now, we couldn't get Fred Astaire or Gene Kelly for this picture, so we're bringing out Buddy West from Broadway. You know what they say about Broadway people. But there's one thing you've got to say for Broadway people. They learn quick: they pick up fast. On our way here, we stopped off in New York and spent four days with Buddy in a rehearsal hall. He's already got his routines down. We've got to be ready to start shooting when he gets here in two weeks because he's got to get back to that heap of junk he's doing now on Broadway. So if you don't learn fast, if you don't pick it up quick, go home and blame your mother." Murmurs and titters. "Okay, now," Colby said. "Line up in rows of ten, counting from the left. Some space between the rows. I want to see what you can do. We'll start off with a time step, a simple time step. Roberto?" The elf was quickly at Colby's side, clipboard in hand, and Colby prattled at him in Italian.

Terry chuckled softly. Pat asked, "What's so funny?"

"Colby's Italian. I've heard better Italian in Brooklyn."

"You speak Italian?"

"With a name like Molino? I speak better Italian than Colby, and I've never been east of Coney Island."

"What did he say?"

"He wants the kid to stay with him while he looks over the girls."

Colby announced: "Everybody ready? Okay. Terry, how about some time steps?"

Terry went into "Tea for Two."

With that, Patricia Purney had her first involvement with the lowest level of show business: a chorus call. It was cruel. Ted Colby walked slowly along the row of dancers, giving each girl one full glance, then watching her feet for a few moments. If he passed a girl without any indication of being aware of her, she knew she had a chance. If, after watching her feet, he glanced at a girl's face and shook his head, she was out. She stopped dancing and left. It was humiliating, this instant-coffee evaluation. Years of study, hours of practice, a life of dreams, dismissed in seconds because, at the moment, you didn't look right or move correctly.

When Colby finished his tour, there were about forty girls left. He said, "All right, gather around. Roberto is going to demonstrate a combination from one of the numbers in the picture. See if you can pick it up."

The girls gathered around. Roberto stepped into the open, his elfin face serious, thoughtful. He snapped his fingers a few times, giving himself the beat; then he went into the combination. It was brief: twenty seconds. Pat watched closely. The kid was good. His footwork was fine, his taps sharp; his body lithe and graceful; his gestures specific. He demonstrated it again. Again.

Then Colby: "All right, children, that's it. Line up and let's try it."

Terry called, "You want some music, Mr. Colby."

"No," Colby said. "I want to hear the taps." The girls lined up. Colby: "All right. On the count. Just keep repeating so I can see. Ready? Five, six, seven, eight!" It was a mess. Colby screamed, "Cut! Cut! That was awful! I thought you were dancers. You move like pregnant cows. Jesus." He said something in Italian to Roberto. Roberto did the combination again, twice. Pat moved closer, watching intently, her mind a camera. Colby: "All right, let's try it again. Five, six, seven, eight!" It was worse than before. Colby screamed, "Hold it! Hold it! Stop! Jesus H. Christ! What's going on here? Didn't you watch? Didn't you see? You're supposed to be dancers! What do you have to have? A blueprint? Isn't there anybody here who can do this simple combination?"

Pat found herself moving toward Colby, slowly. Simple? Fred

Astaire couldn't do it. Nearing Colby, she said, "I think I can do it, Mr. Colby."

He looked at her. "Who are you?"

"Pat Purney."

"Are you one of the callbacks?"

"No, sir. I missesd the audition. I was working in Vegas and couldn't make it."

"Where in Vegas?"

"The Ritz."

"Do you know Ray Jarvis?"

"I know who he is. He's the choreographer in the main room."

"Did you work for him?"

"No, sir. I worked in the lounge. I did my act."

"Dance?"

"Yes, sir."

"Tap?"

"Mostly. Some jazz. A little modern. A bit of ballet."

"Well, what are you doing here?"

"I've heard a lot about your work, Mr. Colby. I just came to watch. I was sure I'd learn something." Bull's-eye.

He smiled. "And did you?"

"You know dance, Mr. Colby. You know dance."

"Stop with the 'mister' shit. You think you can do that combination?"

"I'd like to try. It's a beauty. I may steal it for my act."

"Before you steal it," Colby said archly, "let's see if you can do it. Okay?"

"Sure."

Colby looked around and announced to the world, "All right, everybody. Miss er—ah…"

"Pat."

"Miss Pat here is going to demonstrate the combination you seem unable to grasp. Watch closely. You might learn something. Go ahead, Miss Pat."

The place went quiet. Pat walked to the spot where Roberto had begun the combination. She took first position; then, counting half aloud, she began to move on eight. Head high. Eyes bright. Smile. She saw nothing around her, heard nothing, but in her mind she saw Roberto, and she matched his every step, every move, every gesture, finishing with the double turn.

Silence.

Then Colby said, "Very good, Miss Pat. Very good." To the world, "There, you see, you ninnies. It can be done. Miss Pat, you told me that you have a nightclub act."

"Yes, sir."

"Do you work alone?"

"When I work in a big room, I have a couple of boys with me. When I work a lounge, I work alone."

"Have you something from your lounge act that you can show us? I'm sure we'd all like to see it."

Pat pretended to be surprised. "Oh? I dunno...Let me think..." She put the fingertips of her right hand to her forehead, thinking. She smiled. Then: "Yes, I do have something."

"Good," said Colby. "Let us see it."

"I've got my tap shoes with me: I was going to work out this afternoon. It'll take a moment."

"Go ahead."

She went to her zipper bag at the piano, and, as she changed, Terry knowingly whispered, "I thought you came here just to watch."

"I did watch, didn't I?" Her glance at him was also knowing. She went center stage.

Terry called, "Do you want some music?"

"Yes," Pat said. "Let's try the *Beguine*. Upbeat."

"How upbeat?"

"Like this." She did a brief combination from the middle of the routine she had put together the day before, taps rapid, loud, firm.

"You got it."

Terry struck two opening chords, then went into the Cole Porter tune. Pat began, quiet, subtle, graceful, building. By the tenth bar, she knew that it was good, that the routine was working for her. She was glad she had chosen the dress she wore. The dress seemed to dance with her, the skirt flaring out on her turns and leaps. When she came to the combination where she thrust her right leg out sharply and then brought it down slowly, right on the beat, she saw Colby's approving nod. Terry matched her every move, sometimes like bold brass, demanding, sometimes like violins, softly backing off. Then the big finish.

Applause.

Colby, Roberto, Terry, the callbacks, the technicians.

Smiles and applause.

Colby walked toward her. Glancing at his wristwatch, he called, "Everybody take ten. Miss Pat, I want to talk to you."

"It's Pat. Pat Purney."

"Come with me, Pat Purney." He led her away from the others, to the far end of the vast building where it was quiet and they were alone. He said, "That was very good, Pat."

"Thank you."

"A regular Eleanor Powell."

"She's always been my idol."

"It shows. Who did the choreography for you?"

"I did it myself. I always do my own routines."

"Well, it was good. Tell me, where do you go from here?"

"Today?"

"No. Work. What's your next job?"

"I don't have anything lined up right now. After that Vegas job, I'm worn out and I want to rest for a few weeks. They murder you in Vegas. Two shows a night and no nights off. I'm bushed."

"I can understand that. Then there's nothing on the horizon?"

"Well," Pat said, "When I worked in New York recently a Broadway producer came back and said he wanted me for his next show."

"Who was it?"

"Davidson." She had seen the name in *Variety*. "I met him at a cocktail party while I was in New York. He's supposed to be pretty good."

"So I hear."

"Where did you work in New York?"

"The Rainbow Room." She had seen that name, too, in *Variety*.

"Good spot. We had dinner there one night. Are you going to take the Davidson offer?"

"I don't know. I've got a couple of months to decide. It would mean going on the road again, and I'm not too crazy about that idea."

"I don't blame you. Who's your agent?"

"I don't have an agent. I handle my own deals."

"Who does your bookings?"

"People call."

"I'm sure they do. Tell me something. How did you manage to pick up that combination this morning?"

"The one Roberto demonstrated?"

"Yes."

"I watched him. And when he did it the second time, I counted it out with him."

"Smart girl. Could you break it down?"

"Break down the combination?"

"Yes."

"I suppose I could, after I do it by myself a few more times. Why?"

"I need somebody like you, Pat. I need somebody who can break down a combination so that maybe those birdbrain callbacks can pick it up. Pat, you seem to have some time on your hands. How'd you like to go to work for me?"

"As what?"

"My assistant."

"But you've got an assistant. What about Roberto?"

Colby sighed heavily and looked away. "That boy. I adore him, of course. He's got a charming personality, he dances well, his face is pure Dresden, and his body looks like something Michelangelo would have carved out of butter. But the dear boy doesn't have a brain cell in his head. At times, he is of no help to me at all."

Pat said, "Well, he sure did that combination well enough."

Colby said, "Oh sure. He's quick. He's a fast learner. He can pick up a whole routine faster than a Roman hustler can pick up a trick on the Spanish Steps. But he's never really studied dance. He hasn't learned the language. He doesn't know the difference between a tour jete and a pratfall. He can't break a combination down. He can *do*, he can *demonstrate*, but he can't *teach*. In Rome, I had someone else do that, but I couldn't get her to come to the States. So I'm stuck. Will you take the job, Pat?"

"I'll have to think about it."

"While you're thinking about it, will you help me out, at least for today?"

"What do you want me to do?"

"Stay here and practice the combination by yourself a few times. When you're ready, come on back to the mob and try to break it down simply enough for those lulus to catch on. It'll mean a lot to me, Pat. And I'll see that you get paid for it."

"Don't worry about that. Okay, Ted. I'll do what I can."

"Thanks, Pat."

"Ted, if you knew about Roberto, why did you bring him to Hollywood with you?"

"Now, that's a silly question," Colby said, scolding, and he walked away.

It turned out to be a long day. But a good one. The combination clear in her mind, Pat worked with five callbacks at a time, demonstrating each move, each tap, each gesture. When she felt they were ready, she told Ted Colby, and then she walked to the far end of the soundstage, leaving it to Colby to decide which thirty of the forty callbacks would get the job, a cruelty she could not bear to perform herself. Then the long lunch, Italian style. After lunch,

Colby began rehearsing the full routine of the audition combination, a routine he and Roberto had already worked out, with Pat now the intermediary between Roberto and the dancers.

It was almost seven when Colby called it a day. He said to Pat, "Let's go to my office. I want to talk."

They walked along the narrow streets, quiet except for the night sounds, here and there, of preparations for the morning. As they neared Colby's trailer, he took some keys out of his pocket and handed them to Roberto. They gargled briefly in Italian, and Roberto hurried away.

Pat asked, "What was that all about?"

"I told him to take the car and go home and get dinner ready."

"How will you get home?"

"You'll drive me. You can stay for dinner, if you like."

"Roberto can cook, too?"

"On top of the rest. Get ready for five different kinds of pasta. That's all he can make."

"Did you tell him about your idea?"

"Yes. I talked to him about it at lunch. I guess with my fractured Italian I didn't get the message clear. He thinks you're going to be *his* assistant. Feels like a big shot now. No problems."

They reached the trailer and went in. Pat settled in a wicker love seat, the fabric all blue flowers and birds.

Colby went to a cabinet. "Want a drink?"

"Thanks, no."

Colby fixed himself a drink and settled in a wing chair opposite Pat. He said, "You're a good dancer, Pat."

"Thank you."

"And a good teacher. Frankly, I wasn't sure you'd pull it off."

"It helps if you know the language."

"Where did you study, Pat?"

"In Evergreen."

"Where's that?"

"In Colorado."

"Where's that?"

"You probably flew over it on your way here from New York."

"Oh. One of those places." He took a sip of his drink, then studied her. "Have you thought it over, Pat?"

"Your idea?"

"Yes."

"I've thought it over. I have some questions."

"Ask away."

"How long is this job going to last?"

"This job? I've got a budget for eight weeks, but I want to bring it in in six."

"What has to be done?"

"Well, there's the number you worked on today. Buddy West does that one with the girls. Then there's a number he does with the girls and the boys."

"The boys?"

"Yes. Their callback is next Wednesday. Then Buddy has two solos. He'll choreograph them himself. And there's the big finale with the whole cast."

"And you expect to get all that done in six weeks?"

"It can be done. Try television some time. You've got five days to put together a whole show."

"What comes next?"

"Vegas. Caesar's Palace wants me for their new show. Give it a month."

"And then?"

"Tell me, who the hell is Thelma Swift?"

"She won a Gold Medal last year in the Olympics."

"For what?"

"Skating."

"Roller or ice?"

"Ice. She's a figure skater. She skis, too."

"I've heard. Do you ice skate?"

"Yes. And ski."

"Good. LPM wants me to do a musical with her. I'll need you for that."

"Okay. And then?"

"Who knows? A Broadway show, maybe. Television. Something is always coming up, Pat. It's a steady job. Do you want it?"

"Yes. But I've got to tell you something first."

"Tell away."

"I lied to you this morning. About my experience."

"I know you did."

It was like a slap in the face. "You knew?"

"Certainly. I knew it while you were standing there in front of me, lying in your teeth."

"Oh, God. What gave me away?"

"Well, for one thing, Ray Jarvis is not the choreographer in the big room at the Ritz. Gino Lopo is. He worked for me in Rome. I taught him everything he knows. I even got him his job at the Ritz."

"Oh, God. What else?"

"The Rainbow Room. The Rainbow Room hasn't had a show in years. The show is in the Grill, and it's usually a name band or some name vocalist."

"I feel awful."

"Don't. Everybody has to lie to get anywhere in this business. God knows how many lies I had to tell to get my ass out of the chorus and into choreography. Forget it. All I had to do was watch your *Beguine* number to know I needed you for this picture."

"I lied about that, too. The choreography wasn't my own. It's Eleanor Powell's old routine."

"I know that, too. I recognized it. She did it in a picture with Fred Astaire. But the leg extension bit, that was your own, wasn't it?"

"Yes."

"I thought so. I've never seen that before. Very pretty."

"Thanks."

"Tell me something else," Colby asked. "Have you ever really worked in Las Vegas?"

"Where's that?" She said. And they laughed. she said, "Now you tell me something. Who is Ray Jarvis?"

Colby said, "Where's that?" And they laughed.

She drove him home, a house he had rented in Brentwood. Roberto was waiting to serve five kinds of pasta. Colby prepared the veal. Pat made the salad. They talked and talked. About dancing. The conversation cut in half by Roberto's need for translations.

When Colby and Roberto walked Pat to her car, Colby said, "We haven't discussed money."

"I'll leave that to you," Pat said.

It was after midnight when Pat got back to her apartment. The answering service had two calls from Stubby. It was late, but she knew he often stayed up late watching television. She had to tell somebody the good news. Stubby's phone rang several times before he answered it. Pat said, "I hope I didn't wake you up."

"No," He said. "A phone rang in the movie at the same time mine rang. I could't tell which was which."

Pat said, "I've got some wonderful news for you."

"I already know it," Stubby said.

"You do. What is it?"

"You're going to be Ted Colby's assistant."

"Who told you?"

"Terry. He called me when he got home. He says you're a sharp operator." His voice had a bit of a bite.

"Who told Terry? I'm sure Ted Colby hasn't mentioned it to anyone, except that Italian kid with him."

"Oh, Pat, people here have a way of finding these things out. By now, all of Hollywood knows it."

She didn't like his tone. "Stubby, did I do the right thing?"

"Well, it wasn't *my* idea," he said. Silence. "Who knows? It might be your first step to stardom. After all, this is the way Gwen Verdon began."

"I'm no Gwen Verdon."

His heavy sigh was loud and clear. "Well, I suppose that as long as you're working for Ted Colby you'll be set for life."

She let it sink in. Finally, "I suppose I will be."

But she knew it wasn't true.

There was still too much to learn. Life was just getting really interesting. Any deal she made now would be short term.

Chapter Six

Pat learned fast.

She met Steve Ehlers through Stubby. Like Stubby, Steve was a stuntman, who had been working in Europe for two years. He said, "I could have stayed and kept busy. But I guess I just got homesick."

Steve was often at Stubby's when Pat dropped by. Stubby was now using a cane and was mobile. Now and then, the three of them would go to a nightclub for the evening, Pat and Steve dancing. Or, they would spend a weekend in the mountains, Pat and Steve ice skating or skiing, the three of them in the lounge for the evening, before a roaring fire, amused by the stumbling efforts of the younger singles to make out. But lately Pat spent her weekends at the studio with Roberto, learning combinations and routines, preparing for the next week, making the work easier and go faster. On these weekends, Pat spent Saturday evening at a cookout at Colby's house in Brentwood.

Steve began to phone Pat at the studio, suggesting dinner. Sometimes Pat said yes. She enjoyed Steve's company, but something quietly gnawed at her during their dates. Something was missing. Stubby.

The Buddy West picture finished, Pat loafed for two weeks. Then she and Colby and Roberto chartered a small plane and flew to Las Vegas to do the new show at Caesar's Palace. The Palace had its own choreographers, but getting Ted Colby, of Hollywood, Rome and London, to do a show was a coup and ads proclaiming this appeared in major cities across the country. Most of the dancers and show girls were regulars, but they were good. They worked late and partied long and usually slept until mid-afternoon. This limited rehearsals, with luck, to three hours late in the afternoon. Big as it was, the stage at the Palace was not the size of a Hollywood sound stage, so Colby had to work smaller and tighter. Colby's routines were clever, sophisticated, witty, and just sexy enough. Pat suspected that Colby was reviving routines he had used on the smaller sets of Rome television. If so, they were good.

Pat had a lot of time on her hands. Before rehearsals, she worked out with Roberto for an hour. During rehearsals she rarely had to demonstrate a combination more than twice. The dancers, having done the routines of the current show for several months, enjoyed doing something new, something different. Secure in their jobs, they laughed at their mistakes; and after three or four tries, there were no more mistakes.

After rehearsal, everybody scattered. Colby and Roberto were busy with music arrangers, set designers, and costume designers. The dancers were a clique; Pat never got to know any of them well. An early riser by Hollywood habit, she usually went to the pool alone. She played golf alone. She hung around the tennis courts hoping for another loner to show up, and she usually ended up playing with the pro, always remembering a good tip when they finished. Her evenings were also empty. Colby seemed to know everybody in Las Vegas, or got to know everybody. His late evenings were often spent at private parties in somebody's suite, and lasted until dawn. Twice he took Pat along. She was uncomfortable. The other guests were gay, both men and women, and their elitist exuberance smothered her. She usually begged off, telling Colby she had to work.

To occupy herself evenings, Pat took up going to other hotels along The Strip to see the shows. At first, she walked for the exercise, until she found out that nobody walks in Las Vegas and strollers were stopped and questioned by the police. Obviously if you couldn't afford a car or a cab in Las Vegas, you shouldn't be there. Pat started using cabs. When she had seen every show, Pat watched television in her room. Dinner was sent up.

Pat was therefore delighted one evening when her phone rang and a man's voice asked, "What the hell are you doing in your room? This is Las Vegas. Go out and lose some money."

"Stubby!"

"Yes."

"Where are you?"

"We're in the casino."

"We?"

"Steve. He's got a few days off from his Paramount job. We drove over this morning to keep you company."

"Thank God. I'll be right down."

Gambling had never appealed to Pat so she had not spent much time or lost money in the casinos.

The Palace casino was crowded that night. Pat searched for

Steve and Stubby for a few minutes before she spotted Stubby seated at a 21 table. She went to him, slipped an arm around his shoulders. He looked up, grinned at her, and gave her a social kiss.

"How are you doing?" Pat asked.

"Holding my own," Stubby said. "How you doing?"

"Holding my own. Where's Steve?"

"Losing his shirt at a crap table."

"I'll say hello and be right back."

"Don't hurry. I just won three straight hands. Thanks to this little lady here."

Pat looked at the dealer. Woman in her thirties. Red hair. Subtle makeup. Slight smile. Intent on the game. Pat said, "Let him win. He's miserable when he can't have his own way." She went to look for Steve.

She found him in a crowd, pressed against the table, a pile of chips in front of him. He was sweating. Pat forced her way to him and softly asked, "Why don't you quit while you're behind?"

He looked at her, grinned , kissed her quickly, and concentrated on the table. "Doesn't anybody leave here winners?"

"No."

Pat said, "I thought you guys were going to keep me company."

"One last bet." The dice flew. Steve's chips were swept away. "Damn!" He picked up his chips and stuffed them into his pocket. "Where's Stubby?"

"Making out with the dealer."

"I knew he would. Had dinner?"

"I was just about to."

They moved away from the table. "Where's a good place?"

"Here. But I have to say that. I work here."

They saw Stubby coming toward them, his cupped hands full of chips. He asked Steve, "How'd you do?"

"I dropped a couple of hundred."

"I picked up a couple of hundred. Dinner's on me. Where we going."

"Pat says this place is all right."

"Christ. Hotel food. I'm sick of it."

Pat said, "There's a Trader Vic's somewhere around here."

Steve said, "Let's go someplace where we can dance."

"Shit," said Stubby. "Alone again."

"Let's eat here," Pat said. "Stubby, want to cash in your chips?"

"No. I'm going to play some more later, while you guys are dancing."

"Come on, then."

She led them through the casino and across the lobby to the door of the main room. A long line of people were already waiting for the first show. With a gesture, Pat indicated that they should wait for her. She went alone to the door, to the maitre d'. "Evening, Carl."

"Hi, Pat. Coming in?"

"Yes, if there's room."

"Sure. I'd think you'd be sick of the show by now."

"I've got a couple of friends here from Hollywood."

"No problem."

Pat returned to Stubby and Steve. "No problem. Just somebody slip the man a twenty." Steve took a twenty out of his wallet. They went to the head of the line.

Carl said, "Good evening, Miss Purney. Your table is ready." He stepped aside and let them pass; Steve slipped him the twenty. "Evening, sir."

The captain was at the head of the stairs, and he smiled recognition at Pat. Stubby whispered, "How much does he get?"

"A ten," said Pat.

"Will he take it in chips?"

"No chips. Evening, Henry."

"Hi, Pat."

"I've got some friends from Hollywood. They want to see the show."

"Fine." He led them down the stairs and turned them over to the head waiter. Stubby slipped him the ten. "Enjoy the show."

The head waiter led them down the rest of the stairs and around to a center booth. As he pulled away the table, he said, "I caught some of the rehearsal this afternoon, Pat. Looks good."

The waiter: "The usual for you, Pat?" Stubby and Steve ordered scotch. The waiter put menus on the table and left.

A combo started playing. Pat and Steve got up and danced. After dinner they watched the show, Pat announced she was tired and went to her room, knowing Steve and Stubby wanted to get back to the casino.

Next morning, Pat and Steve met for tennis; the three of them had lunch in the coffee shop; Pat went to work and Steve and Stubby headed for the casino. They spent the evening at the Sahara. The next morning, Pat and Steve played a round of golf; lunch again in the coffee shop; Pat again to work, and they spent the evening at the Riviera. In the morning the three met at the pool. Stubby lay in the sun while Pat and Steve swam. They spent the evening at the Golden Nugget.

Pat and Steve were dancing, when he said, "Stubby and I head back for L.A. the first thing in the morning."

"I know," Pat said.

"There's still time," said Steve.

"For what?"

"For you and me to drive out to one of those little chapels at the edge of town."

Pat fought the slight tension that rose in her. "You in the mood to pray?"

"I'm in the mood to get married."

"Happy hunting."

He waited a moment. "Think about it."

They kept dancing.

Pat did not sleep well that night. When she awoke in the morning, she was aware of a certain disquiet inside her. It wasn't until she realized that Steve and Stubby were gone that she recognized it. She tried not to think about it. She tried not to think about it all day. She tried not to think about it for the week she remained in Las Vegas working on the show.

Opening night went well. After the first show, Colby and Pat went backstage with the notes they had taken during the performance and gave the cast a few instructions. The second show went much better. After it, the customers gone, the Palace management threw a big party for the cast and the performers from other hotels who poured in for the free booze.

At one point, Colby took Pat aside and said, "I'm ready to go home. Are you?"

"Whenever you say."

He looked around. "I don't know what time this shindig will end. What about tomorrow afternoon?"

It was already two in the morning. Pat asked, "*This* afternoon or tomorrow?"

"This. Around three?"

"Okay."

"I'll have a car at the door to take us to the airport."

At three-thirty, Pat was at the main door, waiting for Colby, knowing he would be late. A cab pulled up. Roberto hopped out, dressed as she had last seen him at the party, in a tux, his bow tie hanging open around his neck. As he hurried past her, she called "Where's Ted?" He turned and shrugged and trotted to the elevators. At four, the doorman told her that Ted's limousine had arrived.

It was a quarter to five when Pat saw Colby step from an elevator, obviously troubled, followed by Roberto, changed and obviously troubled, followed by a bellhop pushing their luggage on a cart.

Colby said, "The little shit was out whoring all night."

Pat said, "He's young."

"I'm not. Did you pass out the tips?"

"Yes. I feel like Santa Claus."

"I'm glad somebody does. Where's your luggage?"

"In the car."

"Let's go."

They went outside. Roberto was helping the bellhop fit all the luggage in the trunk. Colby muttered something to him in Italian. Roberto tipped the bellhop and the doorman and then got into the front seat with the driver; Colby and Pat sat in the back. Nobody said anything until the airfield came into sight.

Colby said, "We're using the hotel's plane."

The Gulf Stream II was parked a short distance from the terminal, other private planes lined up in rows behind it. The pilot was waiting. Colby went aboard immediately.

Pat said to the pilot, "Sorry we're late. We got tied up."

"Okay," the pilot said. He glanced at his watch. "There may be a little delay getting into L.A. But we'll get there."

Pat watched Colby sitting at a window, staring out. Roberto and the driver brought the luggage aboard; Roberto tipped the driver. The pilot came aboard, pulled in the steps, locked the door and went into the cockpit, shutting the door behind him. They taxied out to a runway and took off.

It was seven-thirty when they finally landed at Los Angeles, held up over the sea for thirty minutes. Heavy traffic. Colby debarked quickly and disappeared into the terminal, Pat tracked him. Roberto went to find help with the luggage. Colby stopped and said to Pat, "We'll be taking a cab home. Can we drop you?"

"I go the other way," Pat said. "I'll get my own."

He looked at her as though he was seeing her for the first time. He seemed almost humble.

"Thanks, Pat," he said. "I couldn't have done the show without you. I know that."

Pat's mailbox was stuffed with envelopes. She flipped through the mail quickly, noting only the return addresses. Bills, mostly. Junk mail. A letter from her sister Sandra. She dialed Stubby's number.

"I'm home," she sang out.

Stubby said, "Pat?"

"The one and only."

"When did you get home?"

"One minute ago."

"And how did you leave Las Vegas?"

"Bored. Where's Steve?"

"Right now, he's probably being chased by the cops down the Santa Monica Freeway. Television."

"Have you seen much of Steve?"

"Every night. He stops by after work. We eat something and play cards."

"Have you had dinner yet?"

"No."

"Have it with me, Stubby?"

"Come on over. Steve can shift for himself when he gets here."

"I don't want to see Steve, Stubby. There's something I want to talk to you about. Let's go somewhere."

"Okay. What's up?"

"We'll talk later. Can you be in front of your place in fifteen minutes?"

"Sure."

She hung up.

This wasn't going to be easy. She had a problem. Something was wrong. For once in her life she didn't know how to handle it. Her only confidant was Stubby, and even he was not close enough to reveal what had nagged at her for over a week. For a moment, she considered calling back and proposing a raincheck. Instead, she found herself leaving her apartment.

Stubby was sitting on the steps of his building. When he saw her, he got in the car. "No cane?" she asked.

He gave her a peck on the cheek. "Not any more. My right leg is still weak and still I limp a lot. Otherwise I'm okay. I should be ready to go back to work in three weeks."

"Wonderful, Stubby."

"Pat, did you say goodbye to Gwen?"

"Gwen?"

"My 21 gal at the Palace."

"I didn't have time to say goodbye to anybody. She wouldn't have known me, anyway."

"Yes, she would. I've called her a couple of times since we got back. She knows who you are. Too bad you didn't get to know her."

Pat glanced at him. "What did she do, deal you only winners?"

"No. She couldn't do that. The house watches the dealers like vultures. But she could count the deck, and she'd let me know when the odds were against me."

"Sounds crooked to me."

"So what? The whole town is. You don't think Vegas is run by the Salvation Army, do you? Where are we going?"

"A little place in the Valley. It's quiet and the food is good and they don't rush you."

"Okay. What did you want to talk to me about, Pat?"

"Over coffee."

They were over coffee, both of them smoking cigarettes. Having covered all the Hollywood gossip. Stubby said, "Okay, lady, what's eating you?"

"Nothing's eating me."

"Something is. So far, I've done most of the talking. You must have something on your mind. Spit it out."

She took a drag on her cigarette, let it go, and then: "Steve asked me to marry him."

"I know that."

"You do?"

"Yes. He told me on the drive back to L.A. So what's the problem?"

"I wasn't sure he was serious."

"He was. Steve is crazy about you, Pat."

"I think the world of him."

"Christ, don't ever say that." Stubby said. "Don't-call-us—we'll-call-you."

"I don't really know him, Stubby."

"You want his resume?"

"I'd want to know more about him, that's all."

"Well, he's been one of the best stuntmen in Hollywood for twenty years. He's honest. Decent. And he's a good friend. What more do you want to know?"

"Why didn't he ever marry."

"Didn't he tell you?"

Pat closed her eyes against the shock. "No. What?"

"He was divorced."

"Where's his wife?"

"Back East somewhere. I don't know."

"Children?"

"Two. They're with her. Steve supports them."

"Why were they divorced?"

"She didn't like his life style, I guess. Traveling. Risking his life everyday. He doesn't talk about it. I think she wanted him to get a nine-to-five job so she could pick him up every night on the six-fifteen."

"Did you know her?"

"I saw her a few times at parties. She was all right. I didn't see much of Steve during the three or four years he was married. Nobody did. Maybe she wanted it that way. She had him on a short rein, that's for sure. I thought it was doomed from the start. It's the same old story."

"What old story?"

"Never try to change people into something you want them to be, just for your own sake. And never try to change yourself into something you will never be, just for somebody else's sake. Either way, it won't work."

"I wonder why Steve never mentioned his marriage to me?"

"Why should he? He probably will, sooner or later, I expect, but what difference does it make? How would you feel if Steve expected you to tell him the story of every man you've been to bed with?"

"It would be a short story," Pat admitted.

He looked at her. "Really?"

She looked at him. "Yes. Really."

He shook his head. "I can't believe it."

"Why not?"

"With your body and boobs, I figured you'd be picking up a parade of hornies every time you set foot out of the house."

"Well, I don't."

He was having fun now. "Are you fighting 'em off?"

"No."

"Are you turning 'em down?"

"No."

"Are you a virgin?"

"No."

"Don't you enjoy it?"

"No."

"Are you a dyke?"

"Stubby!"

"Well, there has to be a reason."

"Let's talk about something else."

So they talked about something else.

But she could not think of anything else.

She was sure of this: She would have to avoid Steve until she made up her mind whether she was willing to risk marrying him and having him find out that she was both inexperienced and possibly frigid, or turning him down and hoping the friendship could survive as it now was, and she wanted at least that. To avoid Steve, she had to avoid Stubby as much as she could without diluting her friendship with him. If Steve arrived at Stubby's when Pat was there, she quickly announced a fictional early appointment, and left. If Steve was there when she arrived, she dropped off whatever groceries she had picked up for Stubby or his laundry, then said that she had to get home to wash her hair or write some letters. Stubby began going to Las Vegas on weekends, to be with Gwen and to gamble. Dodging Steve, Pat didn't answer her telephone on weekends. Occasionally, she drove down the coast and checked into a motel, and spent the weekend, playing miniature golf, riding horseback and watching television. Whenever Stubby questioned her about her absent weekends, she simply lied and said she had a gig somewhere.

One day, Ted Colby called Pat saying it was time she went Las Vegas to see how his choreography was holding up. Pat got an afternoon plane, took a cab to Caesar's Palace, checked in, and stayed in her room until showtime. She caught the first show from backstage, gave the dancers some notes during the break, then caught the second show from the back of the house. She realized the dancers needed some rehearsal and set it up for the next afternoon. She stayed in her room until rehearsal time, returned to her room immediately after, caught the first show from backstage, and was satisfied. Then she managed to hitch a ride on the hotel plane flying some high rollers back to Los Angeles.

Home, she checked her answering service. Stubby had called. It wasn't too late to call him.

As soon as he heard her voice, Stubby demanded, "Where the hell have you been?"

"Vegas."

"What for?"

"I had to check on the show. Why?"

"Steve had tickets for the Dodgers' game tonight and he wanted to take us."

"Sorry. Ted's orders."

"Well, you ought to let people know. Did you see Gwen?"

"I didn't go into the casino. I was tied up with rehearsals."

"You could have called her."

"I didn't know her number."

"I could have given it to you. Listen, wench, in case you haven't figured it out, I'm not just playing 21 with that girl. I like her. And I want you to get to know her. She always asks about you, and more than once she's said she'd like you to stay with her when you're over there."

"Oh? I'll remember that."

"I wish you would. Neither one of you two seems to have any talent for making girl friends. Maybe you were meant for each other."

"I'm not a lesbian, Stubby."

"Neither is Gwen. Believe me."

Later, when Pat was getting ready for bed, the thought struck her that now she had to talk to somebody about sex and why she was so bad at it. She didn't have a woman friend in Los Angeles she could talk to. It was too late for her to turn to her mother. Her sister Sandra wouldn't understand her worry. It had to be Gwen.

Three weeks later, when Ted Colby scheduled another spot-check at Caesar's, she called Stubby. "I'm heading back to Vegas tomorrow," she said.

"Would you call Gwen?"

"Give me her number."

"Got a pencil?" He gave Pat Gwen's number. Then: "I'll call her right now. She should be home. I'll tell her she'll hear from you in a few minutes. Give her your flight time and she can pick you up when you get in."

"Thanks, Stubby, but I'll call her from the hotel."

"Why the hotel? You can stay with Gwen."

"That would be inconvenient. I'd have to rent a car."

"Gwen's got two cars. Her daughter uses one."

"Her daughter?"

"Didn't I tell you? Gwen's been married and divorced. She's got a daughter. Vicky. The kid's in high school and needs a car to get around. She wants to be a dancer, poor thing."

"I'll try to talk her out of it."

The first few moments were awkward. Pat didn't recognize Gwen, having seen her only briefly at work. But before they reached Gwen's car in the parking lot, Pat relaxed when Gwen said, "Let's go to the house so I can show you where it is. Then you can drive me to the hotel. I've got to go to work early today. There's a convention in town. I've drawn the shit detail."

At the house, Pat put her weekend bag in the bedroom Gwen assigned to her. At the hotel, Pat decided that, being there, she might as well hang around. A rare experience for her, she went into the casino and spent over an hour feeding quarters into a one-armed bandit, winning a few back, then feeding her winnings into the machine and losing it. Showtime was nearing, so she went into the coffee shop and had a malted with pralines. When she got to the dancers' dressing room, some of the dancers were already there, a few doing warmups, others just chatting over cigarettes and coffee. She watched the first show from backstage, was satisfied with it, called Ted Colby and told him so. She said she'd probably catch a morning plane back to Los Angeles.

Returning to the casino, she was surprised to find it so quiet. She went to Gwen's table. "Where is everybody?"

"They're on a package," Gwen said, glumly. "They've just piled onto buses and gone over to the Desert Inn to catch the second show. It's probably the last we'll see of them tonight."

"Too bad. It must be boring for you."

"It is," Gwen said. "Let me see if I can get off. I've put in my time." Gwen was gone for just a minute, returning with a young man in tow. She said to Pat, "Jerry's taking over my table. Let's go."

At Gwen's house, Pat noticed another car in the driveway. She asked, "Vicky home?" She hoped not.

"Looks like it," Gwen said as they got out of the car. "She's probably in bed already. She's on the early shift at school so that she can take class in the afternoon."

"What's she studying?"

"Ballet."

"It's a tough life."

"I know," Gwen said, unlocking the front door. "But I'd rather have her go into ballet than become a Vegas chorus girl. At least I'll know that she'll be on her toes most of the time, not her back."

There were lights on in the living room. Then Gwen said, "I usually don't eat this early. How about a drink?"

"No, thanks."

"A malted. I've got your pralines for you."

Pat laughed. "You know about me and pralines?"

"Stubby told me about it. When you called yesterday, I went out and stocked up."

Gwen was back from the kitchen in a few minutes, the malted with pralines for Pat, a bourbon and ginger ale for herself. They both lit cigarettes.

Pat said, "Stubby tells me that you see to it that he wins when he plays your table. Is that kosher?"

"No, it isn't," Gwen said. "I'd be murdered if I got caught at that. Feeding a player is the only mortal sin in Las Vegas. I just see to it that Stubby doesn't lose too much. The house makes enough in the long run, anyway."

"Stubby thinks the world of you."

"That's nice. I like him, too."

"I think he's getting serious about you."

"I think I am serious about Steve, Gwen. but I am also worried about marrying him. I don't think it will work. Not his fault, but mine."

"What do you mean, your fault?"

Pat took a deep, even breath. "I want to confide in you, Gwen. I have no one I can talk to. I have never had a girlfriend, so I am counting on your friendship with Stubby. I mean because of Stubby, you might be willing to hear me out."

God, Pat. Of course."

It was difficult and embarrassing for Pat to begin. "Okay," she said. "I have had only one sexual encounter, and it was a disaster."

"When?"

"In high school." Pat lowered her eyes. "I wanted to find out what it was like. A lot of girls in school were making out, and it seemed they all loved it. I was a virgin. It was a *horrible* experience."

"That was the *only* time you got screwed?"

"Yes."

"Didn't other men try?"

"Well, a kid in Evergreen, Colorado. And a key grip on location in Arizona for an LPM western."

"And?"

I was afraid. I was convinced that something was the matter with me. Maybe anatomically." Pat winced. "But I love men. I don't have a lesbian problem. Just fear of being condemned to a non-enjoyment of what everyone else thinks is ecstasy." Pat's eyes went out of focus. There were tears filling them.

"Oh, Pat," Gwen said. "It's nothing to worry yourself sick about." She laughed. "In Vegas, you would be considered a virgin." Gwen became serious. "Look, there are two things to do. First, I will make you an appointment with my gynecologist. He will tell you whether it is a physical problem, which I am sure it is not. Then I think you should see Hyman Bates. He is first rate psychiatric counsellor. Non analysis. Practical advice. He specializes in psycho-sexual hangups."

"I hope I'm not beyond help."

"Pat, baby," Gwen said. "You could scarcely judge the sexual experience by a fumbling macho teenager with zero technique, obsessed only with conquests, like trophies. I mean he was *nothing*."

Gwen made the appointments for the next afternoon, before she went to the casino to work. When she left for Los Angeles late that very afternoon, she sent two dozen roses to Gwen's place. Her note read:

A friend in need, is a friend indeed.
Love and thanks
    Pat

Chapter Seven

Because of the rush hour traffic at Los Angeles, Pat didn't reach her apartment until almost eight. Nothing interesting in the mail The answering service said Stubby had called a few minutes before. She called him.

He said, "You're late. Gwen said you had a four o'clock flight."

"The traffic was bad, in the air and on the ground. I just got in."

"How did things go in Vegas?"

"Okay."

"What do you think of Gwen?"

"I think she's great."

"So do I."

"Do you need anything, Stubby, before I get undressed?"

"If you're going to get undressed, I'll be right over."

"Behave yourself. You can't beat what you've got in Vegas."

"I know, but I can try."

"Have you been seeing Steve?"

"Oh yes. He stops by on his way home or calls when he gets there."

"How's he doing?"

"Okay."

"Where is he now?"

"Probably roaring down the Santa Ana Freeway with the fuzz at his ass."

"A job?"

"Yeah."

"I thought he already did that bit."

"He did. This is a different show. Same bit. Different freeway. That's television."

"I know. Will you see him tonight?"

"He'll either come by or he'll call."

"Tell him I'm back."

"Okay."

"And tell him I said yes."

"Yes to what?"

"If he doesn't know, tell him to forget it."

"Okay. Tell me about Vegas. What did you do there? Did you see any shows?"

"I'm too bushed, Stubby. Some other time. I'm going to bed."

"I'll be right over."

"Go to Vegas."

She was too tired to eat anything. She took a bath and went to bed. On her night table she saw an Agatha Christie novel she hadn't finished and had forgotten. She began to read it from the beginning. She fell asleep before she reached the part where she had left off the last time through, unaware as she reached for the lamp.

She could hear bells. Struggling out of her deep sleep, she realized that her telephone was ringing. The room was still in darkness. With effort, she got up and headed for the living room, noticing the luminous face on the alarm clock. Six. Six in the what? She found the telephone; it sounded so loud. She managed a hello.

She heard, "So where will it be? Las Vegas? Tijuana? Johannesburg?"

"Steve?"

"Yes."

"Are you all right?"

"I'm fine. I didn't get home from work until one o'clock this morning, and I didn't want to call you at that hour."

"What hour is it now?"

"Six."

"Six in the what?"

"Six in the morning."

"Steve." It was a scold.

"I'm sorry, honey. It's better than calling at one, isn't it?"

"Never mind."

"I called Stubby, though. He gave me the good news."

"What good news?"

"That you told him yes."

"Yes to what?"

"To Las Vegas or Tijuana or Johannesburg. You did, didn't you? I couldn't make much sense out of Stubby. He said he was recovering from a miserable hangover."

"What brought that on?"

"I don't know. Pat, did you say yes?"

How could she put it? She said, "I don't want to go back to Las Vegas so soon. And Johannesburg is such a long trip."

"Tijuana, then?"

"If you're sure you want us to go there."

"I'm ready to go to Pluto."

"Where's that?"

"Who cares? Let's do it right away, Pat."

"Like when?"

"Let's see. It's six now. Can you be ready by nine?"

"This *morning*?"

"Sure. Why not? It'll take a few hours to drive to Tijuana. A couple of hours there. On the way back, we can stop off for a few days for the honeymoon."

"Steve, I can't be ready in three hours."

"Why not?"

"In the first place, I don't have any clothes."

"Who needs clothes for a honeymoon? Just throw your toothbrush into your purse and you'll be all set."

"Steve, this is silly."

"Let's be silly, then. It's high time. Pat, I'm very happy."

What the hell. "All right, you nut."

"Great. I'll pick you up at nine."

"Yes."

Pat hung up the phone. She burst into tears, the purple morning touching her windows.

There was so much to do, but Pat did little. She got out a suitcase, threw in some underthings, a couple of skirts and blouses, slacks, sweaters, hankies. There were only two dresses left in her closet. One was a black cocktail dress; the other was the Eleanor Powell dress she had worn the day she got her job with Ted Colby. It had brought her luck then; it might bring her luck now. She decided to wear it to Tijuana. She took a quick bath, did her hair and makeup, tossing paraphernalia for these things into the suitcase.

It was eight-fifteen. What to do for forty-five minutes? She dressed. She made her bed. She had a coffee, washing the cup immediately. Eight-forty-five. She couldn't stand it. She closed her suitcase; she left the apartment, double-locking the door; she went downstairs and outside, standing guard at her front door. Promptly at nine, she recognized Steve's car as it rounded the corner. Somebody was in the back seat.

As Steve pulled up, Stubby leaned out the window of the back seat and called, "What's the matter, you wench? Couldn't you wait?"

Pat quelled her surprise and her annoyance. Steve got out of the car and hurried to Pat. They had a quick kiss. Steve took Pat's suitcase and put it into the trunk. Pat got into the front seat. She stretched back to accept Stubby's kiss on her cheek. Steve settled behind the wheel, slipped the car into drive, and they moved away.

Pat asked, "How's your hangover, Stubby?"

He said, "I got cured fast enough when this monkey called me at six o'clock this morning and said he wanted me to come along for moral support."

Steve said, "Well, Stubby brought us together, so I thought he ought to be there when we got tied together. Besides, he can be my best man."

Pat said, "I didn't have time to think about a maid of honor."

Stubby said, "I'll be that, too, if I survive. I need a hair of the dog."

"In Tijuana," Steve said. "Tequila. At the reception."

"I won't survive to Tijuana," Stubby said. "At least get me some coffee."

"Next stop," Steve said.

Just before they turned onto the southbound freeway, Steve saw a coffee shop and pulled up to it. "Want anything, Pat?"

"No. Nothing."

"Be sure the coffee is strong," Stubby said. "And black."

Steve went into the coffee shop and came back carrying the top half of a cardboard box that held paper containers. Pat said, "Looks like he bought enough for the trip to Johannesburg."

Stubby said, "Huh?"

Steve was at the car. "Here, Stubby, take this so I can get in." He passed the box to Stubby and got back behind the wheel. "Stubby, there's enough coffee there for you to sober up the Marine Corps."

"So you're a Marine," Stubby said. "Big deal."

Pat asked, "You were in the Marines, Steve?"

"Yes. In Nam. I got something for you, too, Pat."

"I told you I didn't want anything."

"You'll like this. It's your favorite. Malted shake. Stubby, pass Pat the big container. And a coffee for me."

Pat had to laugh.

They got on the freeway and headed south, far exceeding the speed limit, Steve sipping his coffee as he drove.

Pat said, "Steve, you're not making a movie now. Slow down."

"I can't," he said. "I've got a big date in Tijuana."

"Then slow down," she said, "so that you make it."

He laughed and slowed down a mile or two.

Before long, the road signs indicated San Diego, Stubby said, "Steve, turn off at the airport exit, okay?"

Steve glanced at him in the rearview mirror. "What for?"

"I want to make a reservation."

"What for?"

"For Los Angeles, of course. I want to get back there tonight."

"Hey, Stubby," Steve almost moaned, "we were expecting you to spend a few days with us."

"Bullshit," Stubby said. "I agreed to come along on this jaunt to give you moral support and be your best man. I'll even be Pat's maid of honor. But I'll be goddamned if I'll turn into a mother-in-law and spend your honeymoon with you. Now, turn off at the airport exit or I'm jumping out of this car right now."

Pat said, "The last time you tried a trick like that you broke a leg."

"So I'll break it again," Stubby said. "If I hadn't broken it the last time, none of us would be here this moment."

Steve looked at Pat and shook his head. He turned off at the airport exit. They were at the terminal building in minutes.

Stubby got out. "Keep her running. I'll be right back." He went.

Steve shook his head again. "That's a shame. We would have had a lot of fun together."

"We could," Pat said. "But Steve, after all, it is our honeymoon."

"Yes, but we're not kids and—" Steve stopped and stared. "I'll be damned."

Pat looked. It was Gwen.

Stubby and Gwen reached the car, and, as they got into the back seat, Stubby said: "Surprise!"

Gwen said, "Anything I hate is impulsive people who rush into things. Patricia, you didn't say a goddam word about this when you left the house yesterday."

Pat said, "I didn't have anything to say. I'm as surprised as you are."

Steve turned to Stubby. "How in hell did you pull this off?"

"Easy," Stubby said. "After you woke me up at six o'clock this morning, I decided to wake Gwen up just for the hell of it. When I told her why I was up at that hour, she insisted on joining the party. Voila."

Steve looked at Gwen. "You're a dream walking, baby."

"That's funny," Gwen said. "I said that about you to somebody just the other day."

"Anybody I know?"

"I don't remember."

Stubby said, "C'mon, Steve, move your ass while we're still feeling horny."

Steve said, "Stubby, tell us the truth now. Are you really going back to Los Angeles today?"

"No," Stubby said. "That was part of the surprise. I'm going to Las Vegas."

"Vegas? What for?"

"I have to work tonight," Gwen said.

Stubby said, "You're damned right, lady. And remember, you'll be working for me. How else am I going to pay for all these airline tickets?"

Gwen put a scold in her voice. "Careful what you say, Stubby. These two might be send-ups."

They all laughed again.

In ten minutes they were at the border, and, as they passed through the gates, Steve asked the attendant, "Where do people get married around here?"

The man said, "If they've got any sense, they don't get married."

"We don't have any sense."

"Straight ahead three blocks, then. Weddings on the left; divorces on the right."

"We'll turn left this time," Steve said. He drove ahead.

Mexico gave them a sullen welcome. Blatant poverty everywhere: old buildings, dirty streets, shabby bars, rundown shops with windows full of worthless jewelry, prostitutes at every door, people in rags. They watched it all in silence.

Stubby asked, "Steve, where's the ring?"

"I couldn't get one," Steve said. "All the stores were closed. I brought along the only ring I could find." He fished in his pocket, extracted a ring, and passed it to Stubby. It was a gold ring, heavy, with a chip of ebony at the crown with a small diamond, some lettering etched along the edge.

Stubby looked at it. "What's this?"

"My high school graduation ring."

Stubby looked at the date. "Jeez, Steve, how old *are* you?"

"I was a smart kid," Steve said. "Ten years younger than the rest of my class."

"Even so," Stubby said, "you're just about ready for your Social Security."

Steve looked at Pat. "You don't mind, do you?"

"Of course not."

"I'll get you a better ring when we get back to L.A."

"This one will do. I can tell our kids I was your high school sweetheart."

"Do that," Steve said.

They made a left at the third intersection and moved slowly along the bustling street. At the next corner, they came upon a shop that had a red neon cross aglow in the window, and a sign: WEEDINGS.

Steve said, "Shall we get 'weded' here?"

"Why not?" Pat said. "It'll be something else to tell the kids."

They parked the car in a vacant lot next to the shop, where they noticed three other cars with U.S. license plates. They went inside and were led down a narrow corridor to a small room where an elderly Mexican, holding a Bible, was sitting alone at a desk. It was all over very quickly.

When they came out, there was a certain quiet about them. It had not been a glamorous affair. Stubby said, "Okay, where's the tequila?"

Steve looked around. "I don't think I'd like to have the wedding reception anywhere around here."

Gwen said, "I noticed a place just before we crossed the border. It looked nice. I think it was a Howard Johnson's."

"There are better places in San Diego," Steve said. "Let's go to the El Cortes."

"I don't care where we eat," Stubby said, "but I'm not leaving Mexico without the tequila I was promised."

There was a bar across the street. They went there and, standing at the bar, had tequilas all around, Pat studying her wedding ring, heavy and loose on her finger.

At the border, an attendant asked, "Where were you born?"

They all answered, "The United States."

The attendant nodded. "Have you anything to declare?"

Steve said no, but Stubby said, "I have something to declare. I declare that tequila tastes lousy and I can't wait for some good scotch."

Small laughter.

In San Diego, they went to the El Cortes Hotel, set atop a hill, and they took the elevator to the restaurant on the top floor, with a beautiful view of the city and the bay. Steve and Stubby ordered Scotches, Gwen her bourbon. Pat ordered a malted shake, downed it quickly and ordered another, washing the taste of tequila out of her mouth.

Over coffee, Gwen asked, "Pat, if it isn't a secret, where are you spending your honeymoon?"

Pat shrugged. "I don't know. Ask Steve. I just came along for the ride."

They smiled at it. Steve said, "There's a nice hotel right on the cove in La Jolla. We could stay there. I haven't made reservations, but they should have a room at this time of the year, and especially in the middle of the week."

"If not," Pat said, "we can always sleep in the cove."

At the airport, as Stubby and Gwen were getting out of the car to catch a plane to Las Vegas, Gwen kissed Pat and said, "I hope you read that book."

"I memorized it by the numbers," Pat said.

Kisses and handshakes all around. Steve drove to La Jolla. There was a room for them, but it wasn't ready yet. Steve and Pat went to the bar to wait, Steve for a Scotch, Pat a Coke.

Steve said, "Did I ever tell you I was married before?"

"No, you didn't."

"Long ago. You want to hear about it?"

"Not particularly."

"I thought you'd be curious. A pause. "Did you bring along a bathing suit?"

"I think I did. I'm not sure. I packed so fast I don't know what I brought along. We can always pick one up."

"Yes."

"The ocean may be a bit chilly, won't it?"

"There's a pool. Didn't you notice it when we came in?"

"I wasn't thinking about swimming."

He laughed a little. "We ought to get out of the room once in a while, darling."

A bellhop approached and told them their room was ready. As Steve signed them in, the clerk asked: "How long do you expect to be with us?"

"The weekend," Steve said.

The clerk said, "I'm sorry, but we'll need the room Friday morning. We're booked for the weekend."

"Okay."

The bellhop, carrying their two suitcases, led them to their room; Steve tipped him and the bellhop left. It was a small room, most of the space occupied by a vast, king-sized bed. Steve said, "It's all ours, for forty-eight blissful hours."

Pat looked at the bed; she looked at Steve. "You want to go swimming?"

Steve moved quickly to the bed and yanked away the coverings.

This time, it was different. This time, it was the way she had imagined it would be the first time. This time, there was no rush, no painful discoveries, no bewilderments, no questions, no doubts. There were many kisses, tongues probing; many caresses, fondlings, Steve long and full at her breasts, his mouth touring her full length. She spread her legs for him, her fingernails digging into his neck and shoulders as he sipped the tastes of her. Gusts. Gusts. Gusts. When she could bear no more, she drew him up on her; and after more kisses drenched their faces and necks, she gave his shoulders a gentle push, putting him on his back. She toured him, then, as he had toured her, his nipples, the hairs on his chest, on his belly, filling her mouth of him, slow, long, deep. Then she ascended him, straddling. She took hold of him and aimed him. He watched her intently, unbelieving. She took all of him and rotated on him until his eyes closed in ecstasy.

Chapter Eight

Los Angeles gave them a smoggy welcome. Steve said, "Your place or mine?"

She had to smile. "I've never seen your place."

"It's like Stubby's. Small. A dump. It needs a woman's hand. I've never seen your place."

"It needs a man's hand. Let's go there first. I need some clothes."

"What for?"

They went to her place. In the lobby, she picked up her mail. At her door, Steve asked, "Aren't you going to carry me across the threshold?"

Pat said, "Listen, after forty-eight blissful hours with you, I'm lucky I can carry myself."

They went inside. Steve said, "Very nice."

"It's home," Pat said offhandedly.

"Where's the john?"

"Through the bedroom."

"Meet me there in five minutes." He went.

Pat flipped through her mail. The only envelope of interest was from Caesar's Palace. She opened it and found a check for almost three hundred dollars. When Steve got back, she said, "Look at this." He looked at it. She said, "I wonder what it's for?"

"Your paycheck?"

"I got my last paycheck the day before the show opened and I mailed it to my bank. I'd better ask Ted Colby about this."

"Don't ask," Steve said. "Cash the thing right away before somebody finds out there's been a mistake."

"I can't do that. I'll call Ted." She went to the phone.

Steve sank into a chair. "Oh, the woes of having a working wife."

Pat dialed Ted's number and prepared herself for Roberto's usual "Pronto!" Instead, she heard a male voice she did not recognize. "Mr. Colby's residence."

She asked, "Is he in?"

"May I ask who's calling?"

"Pat Purney."

Steve muttered, "Forty-eight blissful hours, and she's still Miss Pat Purney."

Pat heard, "Patricia, dear girl, where the hell have you been?"

"Hi, Ted. I went on a little vacation."

"Well, that's fine, of course, but you ought to let people know. I've been calling you all week."

"I just got in. What's up?"

"We've got a lot of work to do, young lady."

"Work?"

"Yes. You did say that you ice skate, didn't you?"

"Yes, I do."

"Well, the studio wants us to get going right away on the musical for Thelma Shit—or whatever the hell her name is. I've never been on ice skates in my life, so I'm going to need you to help me work out some routines for her."

"Okay. When do you want to start?"

"Monday?"

"Okay. At the studio?"

"No. Later on, LPM is going to build us a real winter wonderland somewhere on the lot, but for starters we'll have to work at some ice rink somewhere. Are there any around here?"

"I'm sure there are, but I don't know where. I'll ask Steve. He might know."

"Who's Steve?"

"My husband."

Long pause. "Your *husband*?"

"That's right."

"When did this happen?"

"On my vacation. I had to do something with all that free time."

"Thank God you didn't have more time or you'd probably come back pregnant."

"Maybe I did. Ted, actually I called you about something else. I got a check in the mail from Caesar's Palace."

"Yes?"

"What's it for?"

"It's your cut of my cut for doing the show. You'll get one every week as long as the show runs."

"How nice."

"Isn't it?"

"How's Roberto doing?"

"Well, if I know the dear boy at all, he is at this moment cruising the Spanish Steps, looking for his next Sugar Daddy."

"He's in Rome?"

"Yes."

"On a vacation?"

"A permanent vacation."

"Oh?"

"Oh, don't fret about Roberto, my dear. He'll do all right for himself until he's thirty, and then, with all that pasta in him, he'll balloon out into a Goodyear blimp."

"Then who answered the phone just now? Your new assistant?"

"No. That was Buzz, my new butler."

"You've got a butler now?"

"That's what I write him off as, but he's got all kinds of talent. Why don't you two come over tomorrow evening? We'll have a cookout, the four newlyweds."

"I'll talk to Steve about it and call you back tomorrow."

"All right. Happy fucking."

"Same to you."

Without discussing it, Pat and Steve kept their separate apartments. Some of Pat's clothes eventually found their way to Steve's apartment, and some of his clothes found their way to hers. They both had unpredictable schedules, they would never know where they might end one day, or begin another. They were often separated for days and be lucky to reach each other by phone.

It was like that from the beginning.

That first night at Pat's, she had hung up the telephone after her talk with Ted Colby and turned to Steve. "Ted wants us for a cookout tomorrow night. Shall we go?"

"Why not?"

"And where can we find a place to ice skate?"

"He wants to go ice skating?"

"Well, no. Ted is going to choreograph the Thelma Swift picture—the Olympian—and he doesn't know anything about ice skating. I have to show him. We need a rink."

"Where does he live?"

"Brentwood."

"I don't know of any ice skating rinks in that neck of the woods. Let me check around."

"Didn't you say you needed the john?"

"Oh yes. But let me check my answering machine."

"And I'll check the john."

With the bathroom door closed, Pat could not hear what Steve was saying on the telephone, but she could tell that he was angry. He opened the bathroom door on her, a burst of familiarity she had not adjusted to as yet.

Steve said, "I gotta go to work."

"Now?"

"Yes."

"For God's sake."

"I know. There was a message from the studio. Urgent. The stuff we shot on the Santa Ana Freeway the other night didn't come out. Something was wrong with a camera on one of the helicopters. We have to shoot it again."

"Tonight?"

"Yes."

"But it's Friday. It's the weekend. Can't they shoot it on Monday?"

He shook his head. "Honey, this is television. We don't have all the time in the world, like you movie people."

"Damn. How long will it take?"

"Who knows? You know this business."

"Damn."

"Have you got an extra key to this place?"

"Yes."

"Give it to me. All I can say is that I'll get back as soon as I can."

"All right. May I finish here, please?"

"Oh." He went into the living room and waited for her to come to him. She gave him a key. They kissed. He left.

Pat felt a sense of abandonment she had never experienced before. Bang, he was gone. She stood there looking at the door for a long time. Standing there, mind blank, loneliness slowly seeped into her. This was going to happen again, she knew it, again and again. And it would happen to him. She would be rushing off somewhere, too. She might as well learn to live with it. It was as though some director had hollered, "Cut!" Pat shook her head and came out of it.

What to do?

She did little things. She unpacked. She went through her closets and dresser drawers, piling up things to take to the tailor and the laundry. Pad and pencil in hand, she checked her cupboards and her refrigerator, her shopping list long now that she had two mouths to feed. It was after ten when she prepared a cup of tomato soup for herself, enough for the moment. If Steve came home in time, they could sent out for Chinese.

Now what?

Somehow the television set was like a stranger in the house. She ignored it. She found some magazines and, cozy in her favorite chair, flipped through them, not reading, part of her waiting for the telephone, part of her waiting for a key in the door. Around midnight, she took the magazines to bed with her. The Agatha Christie novel was on the night table. She put the magazines aside, reached for the novel, and began to read it from the beginning again. When she awoke in the morning, her reading lamp was still on, the magazines were strewn at her side, where Steve should have been, and Agatha Christie was on the floor. It was almost eight. No Steve.

She got up, annoyed and a little worried. She knew that the car chase and crash Steve was shooting was supposed to take place at night. Here it was morning; certainly the job was done. Could he have gone back to his own place to freshen up and perhaps had fallen asleep? She called him, and a machine told her to leave her name and number and a short message after the beep. She hung up. No sense in calling Stubby; Stubby wouldn't know anything.

She got dressed. She informed her answering service that she would be out for a couple of hours, and she left the apartment. She drove to the shopping center and dropped off her clothes for the tailor and the laundry. A men's store was open, so she went in and bought pajamas and socks for Steve. She would have bought him shorts, shirts, suits, everything, but she did not know his sizes. She went to the supermarket. She was known there and had no trouble cashing the Palace check. She stocked up. At the liquor store, she bought a quart of scotch.

At home, the first thing Pat did was call the answering service. Nothing. Then she made two trips to bring in her purchases. The answering service. Still nothing. She put her purchases away. In the bedroom, she emptied a couple of dresser drawers, for Steve's things. She rearranged the two closets to make room for Steve. She called Steve again. The machine. Unable to bear the idleness, she located a chamois cloth and some Pledge, and she polished every piece of furniture in the apartment until the place sparkled. She changed the bed.

Around one, her phone rang. She grabbed at it. She heard, "Pat? It's Steve."

"Where the hell are you? I've been worried sick."

"I'm sorry, Pat. I couldn't call before."

"Are you home?"

"No. I'm at L.A. General."

"The hospital?"

"Yeah."

"Oh God! What happened? Are you all right?"

"I'm all right. It's Mark Hamlin, one of the other stuntmen."

"What happened?"

"We were doing one more take, to be sure. Mark lost control of his car and went flying over the embankment. A thirty-foot drop. He's a mess."

"Oh God."

"A bunch of us came over to the hospital to see if we could do anything. We all gave blood."

"Has he got a family?"

"Yeah. I got stuck with the job of going over to his house and telling his wife. She's here now."

"He's bad, huh?"

"The doctors are still patching him together. Even if he lives, he's through in this business."

"I wish you were."

He went sharp. "Jeez, Pat, don't *you* start that. I've been through all that with my first wife."

"I'm sorry. What time can you get here?"

"I think I'll go home and get some sleep."

"You can sleep here."

"Are you kidding? Is that thing still on at Colby's tonight?"

"I haven't talked to him yet, but I suppose it is."

"What time does he expect us?"

"He likes to have people there around six."

"Okay. Call me at my place around five. I'll pick you up."

"All right."

Again she had a feeling of abandonment. Something had happened to someone who was important to Steve, someone whom she did not know and perhaps would never know. Not knowing was another kind of separation, a gulf, a gulf, she realized, she would never be able to bridge. There would be other gulfs. The fact that she knew people Steve did not know, and perhaps would never know, did not enter her mind. This was the first time in her life that her world was not *the* world, and she was suddenly lost in it.

She inched through the afternoon doing little things, deliberately and very slowly.

At five, she called Steve, his phone ringing several times before he answered. He sounded tired.

Pat said, "Look Steve, I can call Ted and cancel out for tonight if you don't feel up to it."

"No, let's go," he said. "It'll take my mind off this morning."

He picked her up at six, his fatigue still showing. He said, "I called the hospital and talked to Mark's wife. He's in intensive care, still unconscious."

"What a shame. Is there anything we can do?"

"Did you send flowers?"

"To where? The hospital or a funeral parlor?"

"What a thing to say."

"That's show biz, honey."

At Colby's, Buzz answered the door. Pat measured him with a glance. Young, but not as young as Roberto. A bit tall. Lean athletic body. Nice face. Pleasant Southern drawl. He led them through the house to the pool, where Colby was struggling to assemble the barbecue stove. He kissed Pat on the cheek and shook hands with Steve.

Colby pointed to a serving table nearby. "There's the booze, if you want any. Pat, I told Buzz about your silly malteds. They should be good. He says he used to be a soda jerk back home."

"Where's home?"

"Tabor City."

"Where's that?"

"North Carolina."

"Where's that?"

"Christ knows. Steve, can you help me with this goddam machine? I'm no good at gadgets."

"Sure," Steve said, and put the stove together.

Buzz came from the house with a metal container. "Here's your shake, Miss Purney. I had trouble finding pralines in this town."

Pat said, "Bless your Tar Heel heart."

Buzz to Steve: "Can I fix you a drink, sir?"

"Yes, please. Scotch on the rocks. Heavy on the scotch."

Colby said, "And stop making with the formalities, darling. We're family tonight. And do take off that jacket. You look like a busboy at MacDonald's."

Soon the four of them were sitting around, chatting, joking, laughing, Buzz quick to fix fresh drinks or bring Pat another shake. When it began to grow dark, Colby said, "Buzz, is the salad ready?"

"I'll make it now," Buzz said, getting up.

Steve said, "Why don't I get started on the steaks?" He followed Buzz into the house.

Colby turned to Pat and asked, "What do you think of Buzz?"

"He seems very nice."

"He's a treasure. I think he'll be around for a while."

"Where did you find him?"

A half-smile of smug content came upon Colby's face. "In the Yellow Pages."

"You're kidding."

"No, I'm not. After Roberto left, I needed somebody to help me take care of this place; so I looked in the Yellow Pages and there, under 'Maintenance—House & Apt. Cleaning,' were several agencies that supplied houseboys. I called and said to send someone over for an interview. The doorbell rang an hour later; I opened the door and—voila!—there stood Buzz. He's been here ever since."

"Is he another struggling Hollywood actor?"

"Not any more. He started out as a professional golfer, believe it or not, but he never won enough to pay his travel expenses. Then somebody suggested that he come out here and try his luck in pictures. He didn't know anybody in Hollywood, but he had the sense to read the trade papers and make rounds. Every casting director he read for told him he couldn't act for shit."

"That's usually the case."

"I know. It's sad, isn't it? Anyway, the only work Buzz could find was with an escort service, but he didn't like many of the people he had to go to bed with, so he quit and turned domestic."

"Is Buzz gay?"

"Let's say he's informed. Not all of the dates at the escort service were with women. He seems to be enjoying himself here, and so am I."

"Well," said Pat pointedly, "is he doing the job or is he just sponging off you?"

"See for yourself," Colby said with a broad sweep of his arms. "The house is spotless, the garden has never been in better shape, the pool is always clean, my clothes are always immaculate, and he's clever around the kitchen. No more pasta, thank God."

"I'm glad you're happy, Ted."

"It's easy to be happy, if you know how to manage it."

She gave a small laugh. "How can anybody manage happiness?"

He looked at her for a long moment, then turned away. "Take a word of advice from your old auntie, my dear. As I understand it, in all the thousands of years the Great Sphinx has squatted there in the Sahara, she has said only four words. 'Don't...Expect...Too... Much.' I have tried to live by that all my life. It's the key to my survival. No matter how happy you might be, no matter how much in love you might be, no matter how glorious a relationship might be—even you and Steve, the moment inevitably comes when Christmas is over. That's when the hell can set in."

"What hell?"

He cleared his throat of memories that choked him. "If you have expected too much—worse, if you have given too much of yourself—you have nothing to sustain you when the ax falls. And the ax will fall, sooner or later, in one way or another. The trick is: Always hold part of yourself back. Don't give anybody everything that you are. That way, you have something left to support you, something to prevent you from committing a form of suicide. You can go on. Do like the squirrels do, Pat. Hide autumn acorns in a safe place. Winters can be long."

Pat wondered how many winters Ted had suffered. She asked, "Ted, why were you so upset about Roberto that last day in Vegas?"

"I wasn't upset about Roberto," Ted said, slightly piqued. "I was upset about myself. I had broken my own rules. That wasn't the first time Roberto had gone carousing; I knew it and I didn't care. After all, I was nearly three times older than Roberto, and I could understand why he would want someone his own age once in a while. But that night was different. That night was my first real triumph back in the States in years. I was ecstatic, I was in a rare heaven, and I expected Roberto would want to share it with me. Well, I expected too much. I waited for him all night. I was furious. Then I realized what I was doing—breaking the rule—and I became furious with myself. The ax had fallen, and I didn't know it. Well, I'm not the kind to commit suicide. The only way out was to get rid of Roberto as soon as possible."

"And so to Rome."

"Yes."

"What about Buzz? Has he gotten the acting business out of his system?"

"Apparently it was never there. But don't worry about Buzz. That boy is never going to see the inside of a movie studio until the day I am lying in state in the lobby of the executive building at LPM."

"And if you're wrong about him?"

"There's always the Yellow Pages."

Steve came from the house carrying a platter of steaks and ears of corn. He put a match to the charcoal and said, "Let me know how you like your steaks."

Buzz came from the house, pushing another serving cart. Huge salad. Assorted china. Silverware. Napkins. He said, "Want another shake, Pat?"

"Maybe later, Buzz. Thanks."

Later, when they were driving to Pat's apartment, Steve said, "Ted Colby is okay, isn't he?"

"Yes, he is."

"I've never had much to do with faggots. You don't find many of them in my end of the business. I wonder what I'd do if one of them ever made a pass at me."

"Smile, probably."

Steve laughed. "The kid's okay, too, isn't he?"

"He seems to be."

"That's a set-up, isn't it?"

"Everything is, at the beginning."

In Pat's apartment, Steve said, "I don't suppose you have any booze in the house?"

"It so happens that I do," Pat said. "I guess I know when I've married an alcoholic. It's on the kitchen table. Glasses in the cupboard."

He went into the kitchen and returned in a few moments with a tumbler of scotch with a few ice cubes.

Pat said, "Steve, scotch doesn't go bad."

"I know," he said, "but maybe I will. Let's see if there's anything on the news about Mark." He turned on the television set and settled in front of it.

Pat went into the bedroom and got the pyjamas she had bought for him that morning. Returning, she dropped them in his lap.

He looked at them. "What's this?"

"Pyjamas. I bought them for you this morning."

"You wasted your money. You know I always sleep in the nude."

"Supposing you walk in your sleep some night? I wouldn't want you strolling down Mariposa stark naked."

"Let's try that together some night," Steve said. "It might be fun."

There was nothing on the news about Mark Hamlin. Steve finished his scotch, then announced, "I'm tired. Let's go to bed." And he went into the bedroom.

Pat went into the bathroom and brushed her teeth. She undressed in the living room. When she joined Steve in bed, he was already asleep. Resigned, she rolled over on her side, her back to Steve, and she found herself thinking about what Ted Colby had said about autumn acorns. Now was a good time to start saving them.

In the morning, they made love. When he got up, Steve took a shower and put on the pajamas. Pat put on a house coat. She knew

Steve liked a big breakfast and she fixed him one, coffee and toast for herself.

Steve said, "I think I'll stop by the hospital some time today. Want to come along?"

"No. Not at this point. But you go. Maybe I'll go with you when he's feeling better."

"If he ever does. You've got things to do today?"

"Yes."

"What do you want to do tonight?"

"Whatever you want."

Actually, she had little to do. The subject of the skating rink had not come up at Ted's on Saturday night, but she knew it would. She had to find one. She checked the Yellow Pages and called a few places, but they were closed on Sundays. Then she went through the sports section of the Sunday *Times* and came upon an ad for a rink at the beach that had Sunday matinees. When she called and explained who she was and where she worked and why she wanted to rent the rink, the manager had visions of a massive LPM musical filmed at his rink, with all that money and all that publicity. He said that Pat could rent the rink any weekday from nine until one, at which point the work crew came in to prepare the rink for the public at two. He added that he would close the rink to the public whenever LPM was ready to start shooting the production numbers. Pat did not tell him that eventually the studio would build a rink of its own on the lot. She called Ted and talked to Buzz and gave him the news.

Buzz said, "Listen, I've just taken a beautiful loin of pork out of the freezer. Why don't you kids come over for dinner?"

"I don't think so," Pat said. "Steve's at the hospital. His friend, you know."

"Oh, yes. How is he?"

"Still in a coma, Steve says."

"Oh, dear."

"So I'd better not make any plans."

"Of course. A raincheck, then?"

"Yes. And tell Ted I'll pick him up at eight in the morning. We're due at the rink at nine."

"He'll hate that. He's spoiled, sleeping late, with all this time off."

"Well, it's time he got back to work. It's time we all got back to work."

"Right. I'll be glad to get him out of the house. I've got other things to do around here besides him."

Steve called at five. "He's still in a coma," he said. "It looks bad, Pat. Some of the guys are here. I'd better hang around."

"Of course. Is there anything I can do?"

"No. There's nothing anybody can do."

"You've no idea when you might come home?"

"No. It's touch and go, Pat. I could be here all night."

"All right." She decided not to mention Buzz's invitation, but she told Steve about the rink. "I'll be out of here early in the morning. If you need me, tell the answering service or call Ted's. Buzz will be there."

"Okay."

At eight, Stubby called from Vegas. "I just heard about Mark Hamlin," he said. "The series shoots out here a lot, so people know him. I heard about it at the hotel. How is he?"

"In a coma, Steve says. He's at the hospital. He said several of the other stuntmen are there."

"Sounds like a death watch. I'd better get back. Which hospital?"

"Los Angeles General."

"All right. I'll take the first plane I can."

"Stubby, will you do me a favor?"

"Sure."

"Will you keep in touch with me? With all this on his mind, Steve is apt to forget."

"They were very close," Stubby said. "Mark was the head stuntman on the series. He hired the rest of us when we were needed. He used Steve a lot, here and in Europe. They were very close."

"I'm sure. I'd just like to know what's going on."

"Of course. I'll keep in touch. Gwen says hello."

"Hello to Gwen."

The gulf widened. Pat searched for acorns.

She filled the hours with little things. Her riding pants were the heaviest she had. Two light sweaters to a heavy one. Two pairs of golf socks. She found a snow cap she had bought one weekend when she and Steve and Stubby had gone to the mountains when it was unusually cold. Her only gloves were the white ones she had worn the night Ted Colby took her to the premiere of the Buddy West picture. In the fridge was the barbecued chicken, quartered, she had purchased at the supermarket. She put a quarter in the broiler and opened a small can of yams. She went lightly through the *Times*. She watched the ten o'clock news. Nothing about Mark. She went to bed, setting the clock for six, and leaving a lamp on in the living room for Steve. Morning. No Steve.

As she pulled up at Ted's door, Pat tapped the horn a few times. Ted and Buzz came to the door. Ted was carrying one of the sketchpads he used to calculate his choreography. He was wearing pale blue slacks and a Hawaiian shirt.

Pat called, "Put something on. You'll freeze in that place."

Ted looked up at the warm sun. "On a morning like this?"

Pat called, "Buzz, make him put on a coat. And a hat. Give him a shawl and a blanket. Is there any coffee? Give him a thermos."

The two of them went into the house obediently. Minutes later, they approached the car, Ted wearing a jacket and a beret; Buzz carrying the shawl and the blanket and the thermos.

Ted said, "Where the hell are we going? Little America?"

Pat said, "You'll think so after you're there a few minutes."

Buzz said, "Let him freeze. We can use him to chill the wine at lunch."

The skating rink was vast and dark and threatening. An attendant turned on a few overhead lights, then took Pat to the supply room where she chose a pair of figure skates. Ted took a seat in the front row of the stands, sketch pad open on his lap, marker in hand. Pat was cautious on the ice. She had not been on skates since Switzerland.

Comfortable, Ted said, "Okay, show me what you can do." To warm up, Pat made a few round trips of the rink. Ted called, "Is that all there is to it?"

She called back, "I get clever in a minute." But she knew she could not be clever. She had done little figure skating, and then only for her own amusement, never competing. But the ballet classes in Vegas now gave her some ideas. She did jetes and turns and pointe, sweeping waltz glides, some tap.

After a half hour, Ted called, "Did you leave the coffee in the car? I'm getting cold."

"It's on the seat next to you," Pat called. "And put on the shawl. Use the blanket."

In another half hour, Ted called, "My hands are getting stiff. I can't draw. Give me your gloves."

She tossed them to him as she passed him.

And in another half-hour, he called, "Let's cut this shit. I've just caught pneumonia."

She went to him. "This won't work," she said. "We'll have to try something else. Did you see any of the Sonja Henie pictures?"

"One. I walked out on it."

"Why?"

"If there's anything I can't stand, it's a saccharine Scandinavian with a silly, smile on her Kewpie-doll face all the time."

"You didn't see her production numbers?"

"No. I didn't know she did any."

"She did. And they were wonderful. We'll have to get some of her pictures so you can see what can be done."

"I don't steal."

"You don't have to steal. But at least you can see what can be done on skates and what can't."

"Oh, Christ. Just get me out of here."

In the car, Ted kept the shawl around his neck, the blanket over his lap, and he finished the coffee. As they neared the house, he said, "Buzz will enjoy this. He loves watching me suffer. You'll have to defend me."

"I can't stay," Pat said.

"Why not?"

"I've got to get home. Steve's friend is still in bad shape. Steve may need me."

"Yes. All right." As he got out of the car, Ted said, "You'll see about getting some of that Swede's pictures?"

"She was Norwegian."

"They're all the same."

As she pulled away, Pat saw Buzz at the door, laughing as he watched Ted stumble to him.

At her apartment, Pat went directly to the phone and called her answering service. Nothing. She put water on for coffee, then went into the bathroom and took a steaming shower. She had just finished when the telephone rang. It was Stubby.

He said, "He's gone. Mark died a couple of hours ago."

"Oh, Stubby. I'm so sorry."

"We all are."

"Where are you?"

"At Steve's."

"Oh? Let me talk to him."

"Don't try. He's smashed."

"He's drunk?"

"They're all drunk."

"He's got people?"

"The guys. They're having the farewell party.'"

"That's a strange way to say goodbye to a close friend."

"They're not saying goodbye to Mark. They're saying goodbye to the next one of us who gets it."

"Stubby, that's dreadful."

"It's the tradition. In this business you never know, so say goodbye while you can."

"That's terrible. When's the funeral?"

"Tomorrow."

"So soon?"

"Yes. I suppose Maude was expecting it. She had everything arranged."

"Maude?"

"Mark's wife. Widow."

"Is there going to be a wake or anything?"

"No. Just the funeral tomorrow."

"Do you know where?"

"No. But some reporters were at the hospital. It might be on the news later or in the papers."

"All right. Steve can't talk to me?"

"Steve is in a stupor. They all are."

"So what do I do about Steve?"

"These things usually last a few days. Leave Steve to me. I'll take care of him. I'll send him home as soon as he sobers up."

"All right, Stubby. Thanks. And keep in touch with me."

"Sure, as long as I'm sober enough to keep in touch with myself."

She called Ted. Buzz said, "He's in the tub. He's got me pouring buckets of boiling water on him. I've almost got him cooked."

Pat said, "Tell Ted I won't be able to see him tomorrow. I've got to go to a funeral. Steve's friend died."

"I'm sorry. Is there anything we can do?"

"No. Just tell Ted I'll get back to him as soon as I can."

"All right. Let us know if we can do anything."

"I will."

She could not wait for the news or the papers. She called the hospital and said she was a friend of Mark Hamlin, and could anyone tell her where the remains had been taken. She was given the name of a mortuary in Riverside. She called there and said she was a friend of Mark Hamlin, and could anyone tell her what the funeral arrangements were. She was told that services would be held at eleven o'clock the next morning at a Catholic church in Riverside, with interment to follow at the Catholic cemetery outside the city.

She inspected her closets. She had nothing to wear to a funeral. Dressing, she drove to the women's shop in the shopping center and bought black shoes, a black dress, a black hat, and black gloves. There was a movie theater in the center. Pat went in and sat through two showings without any idea of what was happening on the screen. Home, she pressed the dress and brushed the hat and washed the gloves. She put another quarter of the chicken in the broiler.

She was uneasy and restless and expectant. Reading struck her as somehow improper. Television was out of the question. She was aware that she was in mourning, but she was not sure for what.

Next morning, she was awakened by crashes of thunder and bursts of lightning, the wind and heavy rain battering the trees outside her windows. She dressed, concealing her mourning costume under a raincoat and an umbrella. She drove to Riverside, got lost twice, but still arrived at the church early. She took a place in the last pew, far to one side of the church. Around eleven, the activity began. Stubby and Steve were two of the pallbearers. Stubby looked all right, but Steve looked still in his stupor. It was a low Mass, over quickly, the coffin blessed, the small crowd out of the church and off to the cemetery. Pat waited until the church was quiet again, everybody gone, the scent of incense fading away. Without decision, she went to her car, turned it around and headed home. On the long trip through the downpour, all she could think about were autumn acorns.

Home, she changed into slacks and a blouse. She went to the telephone and dialed a number.

She heard: "LPM Studios."

She said: "The film library, please."

"Thank you."

She heard: "Film Library."

She said, "This is Patricia Purney. I'm calling for Ted Colby."

"Can I help you?"

She said, "I hope so. Is there any way we can get our hands on a few of the old Sonja Henie movies?"

She heard: "Who?"

Chapter Nine

Friday, after another long day of staring at the Scandinavian Kewpie-doll, especially her production numbers, over and over again, and then after another dinner at Ted's, talking shop, Pat got home around eleven. As she opened the door, she noticed that the lights were on. As she came into the living room, she saw Steve, sitting in her favorite chair, watching television, a drink on the end table at his elbow. They looked at each other for a moment, unsure, both putting half-smiles on their lips.

Pat said, "Hi."

"Hi."

"How are you?"

"Pretty good. You?"

"Okay, if you're hooked on Sonja Henie."

"Is she making pictures again?"

"No. It's Thelma Swift. Ted's never done any choreography for an ice-skater, so he's learning from Sonja Henie." She was close to him now. He stretched and kissed her cheek.

Steve said, "I didn't think Ted Colby had to learn anything from anybody."

"He does now. When did you get here?"

"Around eight."

"Have you had dinner?"

"I found some cheese and crackers."

"I'll fix you something."

"It's all right. I had a late lunch."

"Let me know if you want something."

"You eat at Ted's?"

"Yes. Thanks to Sonja, we're inseparable."

"I figured you'd be there."

"Why didn't you call? You could have joined us."

"I don't know his number. And Information says it's unlisted." He tried. He tried. "It was shoptalk, anyway."

"How's Buzz?"

"Fine. Where's Stubby?"

"Vegas, I suppose. Gwen's."

"When did he go?"

"I have no idea. I have no idea of anything much, until I woke up this morning. I'm sorry, Pat."

"Please. I understand."

"I saw you at the church. Thanks."

"How's Maude?"

"I went over there on my way here. She's okay."

"What's she going to do now?"

"She's got a lot of things to clear up. Then I think she'll take the two kids and go back home."

"Where's home?"

"Savannah."

"A long way."

"Mark was from Savannah. They were high school sweethearts."

Pat looked at her wedding ring. "How's your drink?"

"Okay. You'd think I would have had enough of the stuff by now."

"It helps. I'll get myself a Coke. I've got some chicken in the fridge. I'll make us some sandwiches. I'm a little hungry."

"After one of Buzz's dinners?"

"Buzz made the mistake of making pasta tonight. Ted threw a fit and wouldn't touch it. Poor Buzz couldn't understand why. We ended having grilled cheese sandwiches."

"I don't get it."

"It's a long story."

A long story. Story. Would it be like this now? Stories. Filling each other in? Sharing what?

Pat got her Coke and took a chair on the other side of the room. "What's on for you now?"

"I wanted to talk to you about that. When my head cleared this morning, I played my answering machine. There was a call from the studio. Mark's outfit. I had lunch there. They offered me Mark's job."

"As what?"

"Chief stunt."

"What's the deal?"

"Steady job. A lot of money. A lot of travel."

"A lot of danger?"

"No. Oh, I'll probably have to demonstrate a bit for the guys now and then. But I'll have my own crew. I'll be like the director of the stunts. I won't be doing any of the stunts myself. The other guys will do that."

"So you took the offer?"

"Yes. Of course, if you don't want me to—"

"Don't be silly. It's your career."

Around midnight, Pat made the sandwiches. They talked until two. It was Sunday afternoon before they made love.

Thelma Swift turned out to be a bitch. She was also a nitwit. A routine screen test done of her in New York while she was appearing in an ice show at Madison Square Garden sent shudders through the LPM lot when it arrived on the Coast. Thelma Swift could not act, she could not sing, she could dance only on ice skates, and she had no chin. Thelma Swift had won her Olympics Gold Medal mostly on the basis of her excellent performance in the school figures, done on a small square of ice, with five judges watching her every move like vultures. No other competitor came anywhere near her. She could have done a nondescript free skating on her ass program and still won the gold medal.

But what horrified the LPM staff was the fact that Thelma Swift had a severe lisp. After her test had been screened at the studio a few times, people walked around saying to each other, "Have you theen Thelma Thwift'th thcreen tetht? Thenthational!" It was hopeleth.

After Ted Colby watched three screenings of Thelma's dance routine in the Olympics—the same routine she was doing in the ice show, he leaned to Pat and whispered, "What is that music she's using?"

Pat said, "The Lord's Prayer."

Colby said, "Well, the Lord will have to go. We're doing a Hollywood musical, not having a revival meeting."

The LPM writers, who had just about finished the script for "Heaven On Ice," were called in by the producer and told: "You'll have to rewrite. We can't have any words with s's in them." Three of the five writers on the job quit.

Making matters worse, and despite the fact that Thelma Swift knew she had signed for a picture that was scheduled to take five months, she had nevertheless entered into a two-year unbreakable contract with the producers of the ice show, requiring her to perform in the show whenever it played major cities where the higher prices of tickets would cover the huge salary she demanded. As a result of this, the LPM production had to be put on ice repeatedly, and a picture scheduled for five months took thirteen.

One day, Joel Steirman, the LPM producer on "Ice," called his section heads together and said, "We're up thit creek. The studio has already sunk over a million in the winter-wonderland set, we've signed up a dozen expensive actors for the duration, and we've rented all of Sun Valley for the entire winter. Somehow we've got to find a double for Thelma, somebody who can double for her on everything except close-ups, and somebody who can double for her on everything that requires vocal cords. That means somebody who can act, sing, dance, talk, ice skate, and has a chin."

The director said, "It means skiing, too. The script calls for skiing up at Sun Valley. Thelma can't thki."

Steirman said, "Oh Chritht."

Ted Colby said, "I think I've got somebody for you."

Steirman said, "Who?"

"Pat Purney."

"Who's he?"

"It's a she. She's my assistant."

"Can she sing and dance and skate and all that crap?"

"She can do anything."

"How is she built?"

"Like a brick thithouth," Ted said.

Steirman turned to the director. "Look her over and see what can be done."

Everything was done. Pat became the star behind the star and, now and then, the star in front of the star. And the star never knew it. As Ted's assistant, Pat auditioned the battalion of dancer/skaters, both boys and girls; she rehearsed them, and, as the choreography shaped up, skated Thelma's part. Pat recorded the four songs Thelma was to sing. For the sake of appearances and the sake of peace with an ice skater who turned out to have a hellish temperament, Thelma recorded the songs, too. When the scenes were shot and Thelma mouthed the words for the camera, she evidently had no idea that the voice on the playback recording was not her own.

When it came time for Thelma to rehearse her scenes with other actors, the actors bolted from the set, got sick somewhere in a corner, and refused to return for more rehearsals until they were assured that when the scenes were filmed they would not be recorded but would be dubbed later, with Pat doing Thelma's lines.

It was up to Pat to rehearse Thelma Swift. Ted Colby would have nothing to do with the Olympics queen. Pat took Thelma to the skating arena where she and Ted had gone to rehearse the film's production numbers. Knowing that Thelma would be on screen

only for close-ups, Pat rehearsed Thelma mostly for close-ups, trying again and again to teach the star to keep count during her spins
so that she would finish up facing the camera. It was hopeleth.

Thelma Swift went on location with the company at Sun Valley
only to film the exteriors in which she had lines. Now and then,
Thelma was required to act while holding up a pair of skis, Thelma
holding them fearfully, as though they were pythons. Now and
then, Thelma had to wear skis, eventually poling herself the few
feet on a flat surface necessary to get her out of the frame. But it
was Pat who, as Thelma Swift, was filmed racing down the slopes
and through the trees, maneuvering herself with other skiers
through the designs Ted Colby had choreographed and which,
later in Hollywood, in an editing room, would be spliced into a
stunning ballet, music added. But when Pat, as Thelma, was supposed to go soaring off cliffs and into somersaults and dives, it was
a young man in a Thelma Swift costume who risked his neck. Pat
was becoming too valuable to take any chances.

She was becoming valuable in more ways than she ever expected. So involved in the on-camera aspects of the picture, she
became involved in the off-camera aspects as well. She sat in on location sites discussions, script-revisions arguments, the costume
and lighting and set debates, even on budget battles. Pat became involved in all sides of the picture business simply because it was the
only way the nitwit bitch could be duped as well as dubbed and
her highly inflammable temperament kept on ice, as well as her ass.
Nobody ever told Thelma Swift about the dailies the production
staff watched every afternoon, in pain, and so she never saw the
movie until it was released, released so successfully that she gave
up movies and made a fortune doing television commercials for a
product that prevented chapped lips, chapped hands, and chapped
buns, and, although she had a lot of screen-time in the picture, nobody at LPM ever found out whether Thelma ever realized that all
of the sounds of her and most of the sights of her in the picture
were somebody else.

During the shooting of "Ice," Pat realized that she was learning
the motion picture business from the outside in. She was becoming party to most of the important decisions made on the picture,
decisions usually preempted by the star. In Thelma's case all the
star worried about were her percentages of the gross. The more Pat
became involved in the various aspects of the picture, the more
she enjoyed her work. Gradually it dawned on her that she was
probably more involved in the various aspects of the picture than
anybody except the producer, even more than he in some aspects.

One day in Idaho, Pat went to Ted Colby and announced: "I've got a complaint."

Ted said, "Oh Jesus. You too? What now?"

Pat asked, "What is my job on this picture?"

"You're my assistant," Ted said. "You know that. That's what you're getting paid for."

"That's my point," Pat said.

"What's your point?"

"I'm your assistant, and I'm getting paid for that. But I seem to be everybody else's assistant, and sometimes I'm actually doing their jobs for them, and I'm not getting paid for that. I think I should be." Pat then went into a fifteen-minute harangue about everything she was doing on the picture besides the job she was being paid for, and then she said, "I don't care if I have to pay dues to a dozen different unions to get what's coming to me. Either I get paid or I quit doing it."

Ted Colby listened with a half-smile of amusement, recognition, growing respect, and a touch of apprehension. When she finished, he said, "You're turning into a real cunt, aren't you?"

"Sticks and stones," Pat said. "Either I get paid for what I'm doing around here or I stop doing it."

Ted shrugged. "Joel called me last night from Hollywood. He's coming up for the weekend. I'll talk to him."

Two weeks later, when the paychecks arrived from Hollywood, Pat was pleased with the increase on her check, even after taxes, and even though she had to start paying dues to a dozen different unions.

But what pleased her more than the money was what the money represented, the responsibilities it imposed on her, the sense of authority these responsibilities gave her. And above all, authority. She found herself thriving on authority—like a crown princess who had finally gained the throne.

Pat continued her Las Vegas assignment, with the Las Vegas checks. Every third weekend, whether she was in Hollywood or Sun Valley, Pat boarded a plane and flew to Vegas on Friday evenings, staying with Gwen. Saturdays, Pat caught both shows, taking notes. Usually the notes were enough to get the dancers back into shape. Sometimes Pat had to call a rehearsal for Sunday afternoon. New stars opened at the hotel every few weeks. Some of them wanted to show off by getting into one of the production numbers, expecially the finale. Often this meant that Pat had to reorganize Ted Colby's choreography so that the star could show off without lousing up the whole number. When this happened Pat had to stay in Vegas a day or two longer.

Late one night, Gwen asked, "How's the honeymoon going?"

Pat asked, "Which one?"

"Steve."

"Oh. Oh, that's all right," Pat said. "Of course, we don't see each other much, we're both so busy and travel so much, but we're good about staying in touch. It's all right."

It was just all right.

They seldom saw each other. Both of them kept their separate apartments. Sometimes Steve would be in town for two or three days at his own place before Pat found out about it. Sometimes Pat was out of town for two or three days before Steve found out about it. But they kept in touch, mostly by telephone, and this mostly by Steve's calls from wherever he might be, Pat usually unable to call Steve because she was never sure where he was, what time it was where he was, or even if a telephone was within miles. They sent notes to each other, to each other's apartments. And there were Steve's gifts from wherever he might be. A tapestry from the South Pacific. Drums and carved animals from Africa. A walrus tusk from the Arctic. Whatever, wherever. When they were together, there was never any great rush for a bed. And when they did go to bed, it was all right. Just all right.

Gwen said, "Stubby sees Steve once in a while. Steve uses Stubby on jobs here in the States. Stubby doesn't want any more of those long jaunts overseas."

"I know," Pat said. "Steve mentioned it."

Gwen said, "Stubby said Steve has changed."

"He has?"

He had. Ever since Mark Hamlin's death, Steve had lost much of the abandon that had made him such a charming suitor and persistent honeymooner. Since then, when they were together, Steve seemed to be restrained, preoccupied, withdrawn. Pat took it as concern about his job, his responsibilities, and he had a lot of responsibilities now.

Gwen said, "He has. Stubby says it's Mark Hamlin."

"What does that mean?"

"By now," Gwen said, "you should know about stuntmen. Every stunt has its dangers: the more dangerous the stunt, the better the pay; the better the pay, the more a stuntman is aware that his next stunt may be his last."

Pat said, "But Steve tells me he's not doing any of the real dangerous stunts any more. He's the boss."

Gwen shrugged. "When you're the boss, if it isn't your life, you're the one who decides whose life it's going to be. It must be a terrible thing to live with."

"How awful."

"Yes. Stubby says that he gets the feeling these days that Steve is like the little kid who has been warned not to touch the hot stove and yet he knows he's going to touch the hot stove someday and he's trying to prepare himself for the pain. Nobody gets close to Steve any more. He won't let them. They might touch the stove first, I guess."

Pat nodded. And she thought: autumn acorns.

It was hard to believe.

At last the filming was finished, months late and millions over budget. Everybody was bored, tired and uptight. They were ready for the bisexual frenzy that erupted after the last wrap.

Before it began, Ted Colby said to Pat, "Let's get the hell out of here. I'm thick of the whole thing."

Pat said, "Thay when, thweetie."

Ted became the naughty boy. "Let's help ourselves to one of the limousines and drive back. We can spend a few days in San Francisco. I haven't been there in ages, and Buzz has never been there. I'll call him and have him meet us at the Mark Hopkins. We can go wild on great seafood."

"And not a Thelma Thwift in thight." ·

"Let'th thcram."

So they phoned Buzz and quickly packed and helped themselves to an LPM limousine and, with Pat at the wheel, drove all night arriving at the Mark Hopkins just as Buzz arrived by cab from the airport. They spent a week in San Francisco, eating at seafood restaurants and working off the calories by walking up and down the hills, touring gay bars at night, Buzz brushing off the men, Pat brushing off the gals, and Ted bribing the guys and gals with drinks and assuring them that Buzz and Pat were great in the hay and were just playing hard to get.

They drove to Los Angeles, on the coast highway, Buzz at the wheel, driving at top speed, skidding around the sharp curves on the cliffside road. Ted and Pat were in the back seat, speechless with fright. They spent the night at a seaside motel near San Luis Obispo, and went for a naked midnight swim in the freezing bay. The remaining drive to Los Angeles was quiet and monotonous. They left the limousine in the LPM parking lot and took separate cabs, Ted and Buzz to their house, Pat to her apartment on Mariposa.

As Pat's cab pulled up at her building, she saw Stubby standing at the door. Getting out, stiffly, clumsily, still a bit foggy, she said, "Well, I wasn't expecting a welcoming committee."

"I'm not a welcoming committee," Stubby said. "I've been hanging around this door so much for the past few days that your neighbors have started calling the police."

"What's up?" Pat asked.

"You don't know, do you?"

"Know what?"

"I thought so. I tried to call you at Sun Valley but they said you'd already left."

"What is it, Stubby?"

He could not look at her. "There's been an accident."

She waited.

Stubby said, "Steve."

She waited.

Stubby said, "Steve is dead, Pat."

Pat closed her eyes.

II
Ron

Chapter Ten

A t first he did not know where he was or how he got there or what had happened to him. Slowly he became aware of a certain heaviness upon him, crushing him like a ton of bricks. Had he somehow died and been buried? He tried to move; savage pains shot through his body. He waited. He opened his eyes. A blur. He forced himself to blink several times. And then he saw the rash of stars in the dark sky. He must be lying on his back. Again he tried to move, but the heavy pain held him down. He put a hand to his face and felt the moisture. Blood? Sweat? Water? Piss? He took a deep breath and forced himself to roll over, prone. Pain weakened him. He lay there, breathing deeply, waiting. He raised his head and saw in front of him a solid object. He looked at it for what seemed a long time before he realized it was the door of his car. He took another deep breath, closed his eyes, and with great effort raised himself to his hands and knees. Then he placed his hands against the car door and, putting what strength he had into his legs, hoisted himself up.

He looked around. A parking lot. He looked at the gaudy building a short distance away. Caesar's Palace. Then it all came back to him.

Those two guys. Those two bastards. He had tried to fight them off, but there were two of them, and they kept pounding him and pounding him, until a sudden blackness engulfed him. He had no idea what happened after that.

He put a hand to his chest and felt his wallet still in his breast pocket. Had they taken the money? Who cares? He glanced at his left wrist and saw the expensive gold watch, one of the few luxuries he had allowed himself. How had they missed that? Amateurs. Probably casino losers panicked for a few bucks to get out of town.

Then he heard the siren in the distance. Cops? An ambulance? For him? Had there been a witness? Had somebody seen the fight and sent for help?

He fished his car keys out of his pocket, got into his car, and started it up. He was just pulling out of the parking lot as the ambulance pulled in. Close call. He drove to his apartment.

In the darkened living room, he took off his jacket and dropped it on a chair. He tugged at his black bow tie, loosening it. He opened his short collar. He went into the bathroom and clicked on the light and looked at himself in the mirror.

Christ, what a mess. Blood was still oozing from his nose. His right eye was beginning to go purple. Blood on his chin. His teeth hurt. He ran his tongue around his mouth. No missing teeth. He looked at his hands. A few of his knuckles were slightly skinned. Well, at least he had evidently got in a few good licks of his own. He turned on the hot water in the sink and let it run. Looking at himself in the mirror, something strange happened. He saw the face of a woman, a beautiful woman, a beautiful blonde woman, and superimposed on her face, was an image of the same woman, but in the distance, and she was swinging her arms and kicking her feet, fighting something off. Then she vanished. Ron caught himself staring at himself without seeing himself, as though his mind had wandered. He shook his head and blinked his eyes a few times, and then moistened a face cloth and applied it to himself. As he washed himself, he happened to glance into the mirror, looking himself in the eyes. Suddenly the whole thing seemed so stupid, so dumb, so silly, so ludicrous, that he let loose a laugh, wincing at the pain it caused.

And he said aloud to the mirror, "Oh, Shad, if you could see your boy now. If you could see me now."

He had seen Shad Grady for the first time over ten years before at a small airstrip in Northern California, seeing him for the first time from the air. He had been cropdusting some farms up north and was on his way home. He was coming in low, banking into the wind, when he noticed another cropduster parked on the ramp at the small hangar, a man standing beside it. He came in steady and firm, touching down softly. He taxied to the ramp, turned off the engine and hoisted himself out of the cockpit. The man walked over to him.

He was older, stocky, brown hair turning gray, wisps of it blowing in the breeze. He said, "You work pretty low, don't you?"

"What do you mean?"

"I saw you a couple of hours ago, up north. I couldn't tell if you were spraying a crop or planting one. I never saw anybody work so close to the ground.''

"Well, you're supposed to spray dust *on* the fields, aren't you?"

"Yeah," said the man, "but if you keep spraying so low, one of these days you're gonna be spraying yourself on a field."

"I know what I'm doing."

"I hope you do."

"How come I didn't see you?"

"I was at twelve o'clock at seventy-five hundred, over you. At first I thought you were my shadow. Where you from?"

"Around here. You?"

"L.A. I haven't been up this far north for a couple of years. Used to be a lot of work around here."

"There still is."

"You getting it all?"

"We try to keep it in the family."

"You Turks are all alike."

"We're not Turks. We're Armenians."

"I know. Same thing."

"Like hell."

"I got a job up in Oregon tomorrow. Is there a motel around here for tonight?"

"Got a car?"

"Does it look like it?"

"There's not a motel around here for miles."

"Shit. I don't want to fly all the way down to Sacramento. Isn't there anything?"

"Not that I know. Maybe my mother knows somebody that can put you up. Let's go to my place."

"Swell. What's your name?"

"Ron Kazurian."

"It figures," the man said, nodding at the Armenian name. He added: "Shad Grady. Shanty Irish.".

Ron said, "It figures."

They both laughed.

They shook hands.

It was a handshake that would become worth millions.

It was his grandfather who turned Ronald Kazurian into a crop-duster. Omar Kazurian often said, "Never pay somebody to do for you what you can do for yourself." He had lived by that all his life, and it had made him a rich man. He had come to America from Armenia at the turn of the century and had spent two years working his way across the country at odd jobs, eventually reaching his destination: the Armenian farm community in Northern California. Another three years at odd jobs and a passion for accumulating land of his own by saving every penny he earned led to the day when Omar could buy a small farm. He worked it himself, building the house himself and acquiring more land as he could afford it, becoming in time the largest landowner in the county. Along the way, he also acquired a wife, a son—Jacob Kazurian, a daughter-in-law, and three grandchildren, Ronald being the first of these, and every one with chores around the house and on the farm.

Ron Kazurian loved the farm, because he knew one day he would own it, the ownership passing down to the first son, generation after generation, the Armenian way. Knowing this, he made no other plans for his life. At school, he was an average student. He had only a little interest in sports, his work on the farm keeping him in good physical condition. He had only a passing interest in girls, knowing that one day his parents would choose a wife for him. The Armenian way. He had no close friends: there was no time for friends. Evenings, his chores done, his homework finished, he would watch television for a while or go out on the front porch and listen to the grownups talk.

Ron was still in high school when, one Sunday after church, Omar Kazurian invited several of his neighboring farmers home for lunch. As the farmers and their families ate the Kazurian food and drank the Kazurian liquor, they listened to the plan they all knew Omar would have for them. Omar always had a plan.

Bugs. For the past few years, the entire area had been invaded by hordes of insects of all kinds that were causing great damage to the crops. Every farmer had bought cropspraying equipment, towing the tanks back and forth on the fields, but to little effect. It was expensive in time and money and in frustration. Omar told his neighbors about an ad he had seen in a farm journal. Down at Bakersfield were pilots who had special airplanes they used to spray crops from the air, covering a large area in a short time and doing a much more thorough job of killing the bugs. Omar admitted that he was thinking of hiring a cropduster, as they were called, but what good would it do him to have his own fields sprayed if his neighbors' fields remained infested? Would his good neighbors be interested in joining the crop-saving project with him, if the price was right? They would.

Ron wrote the letter of inquiry. The price was not quite right but worth a try because of the danger. Omar's friends joined the project. The first season the results were fair because the invasion was massive. The second season, results were better, and the third season even better. But something troubled Omar Kazurian. Each year the price went up, the pilot explaining that the prices of pesticides were going up. But something else bothered Omar even more. That pilot was taking Armenian money with him out of the county and spending it down at Bakersfield. Omar didn't like that at all. Something had to be done.

One evening, the family on the front porch, Ron's high school graduation a few weeks away, Omar tested, "Ronald, do you want to go to college?"

Ron said, "No, Grandpapa. I've had enough of school."

"Then what do you want to do with your life?"

The question surprised Ron. "You don't know, Grandpapa? This farm is my life."

"Yes, I know that, Ronald," Omar said. "But with all this equipment we've been buying, there is less and less work to do. We even have machinery to milk the cows."

"I know. But the land still takes much work."

"That is true," Omar said, "but you can work for the land without working on the land. I've been thinking maybe you should go into business."

Ron braced himself. "What business, Grandpapa?"

"Cropdusting."

In the Armenian way, coming from the head of the family, the suggestion was an order.

Omar paid for everything. The flying lessons, the airplane maintenance studies, the plane, the supplies. On a parcel of land he owned four miles away, he paid for the airstrip, the small hangar, the warehouse. When everything was ready, Omar had only to invite his neighbors for lunch again to present Ron with his first dozen customers.

One day, Ron asked, "Grandpapa, I've been wondering about something. Whose business is this?"

Omar was ready for that. He said, "I have put a lot of money into this business. I expect you to pay me back, so we are partners for now. You pay all operating expenses. Out of your profits you pay me thirty percent, to return my investment. When you have paid it all, the company is yours."

Ron thought about it. "That sounds fair, Grandpapa. So what do we call the business?"

"I've thought about that, too," Omar said. "It is the Ronald/Omar Kazurian Airlines. R.O.K."

The first year, R.O.K. ended in the red, so many bills to pay, so much to learn. The second year Ron toured surrounding counties and signed up more Armenians. The red was turning pink. The third year saw more expansion and better methods. Black was on the horizon.

But something else was on the horizon.

Vietnam.

When Ron had turned eighteen he registered for the draft. Nobody worried. All the members of the county draft board were Armenian farmers with sons suddenly classified as essential to the national economy and security. Nobody was drafted. But as the war worsened and more and more young men were being drafted, the members of the California Draft Board in Sacramento noticed there was not an Armenian in the crowd, and began to wonder what he was doing up there. Investigations were made. The young Armenians began to go.

Ron's status, therefore, became the most critical matter in the Kazurian family. Omar often said, "It's the war itself. I don't understand it. We were not attacked, like Pearl Harbor. Why are we in it?"

Omar did all he could to keep Ron out of it, but he knew his efforts were hopeless unless something happened.

Something happened.

Shad Grady.

Chapter Eleven

Natalie Kazurian was adamant about it. "Mr. Grady," she said, "you will stay here tonight. We will be glad to have you. You will stay with us Mr. Grady."

"Thank you, Mrs. Kazurian."

"It is no problem at all," Natalie said. "My son Stewart is at the flying school at Sacramento. He will not be home tonight. You can use his room."

"Thank you."

"Do you like lamb?"

"Yes."

"We are having lamb for dinner tonight."

"Yes, I like lamb."

"Good." She turned to Ron. "Ronald, maybe Mr. Grady wants to wash up before dinner. Why don't you take him upstairs and show him where everything is?"

"All right, Mama."

Upstairs, Ron led Shad into Stewart's room. "The bathroom is right across the hall. I think you'll find everything you need."

"Thanks. This is great."

"Armenian hospitality."

"Your mother is quite a woman."

"I think so, too."

"She really takes over."

"Usually my grandmother runs the house, but once in a while my mother asserts herself, especially when she has a reason."

Shad glanced around the room. "She's got reasons?"

"She'll let you know sooner or later."

"I don't like surprises," Shad said. "Give me a hint."

"It's probably Vietnam."

"Vietnam?"

"Yeah. Uncle Sam is nipping at my heels."

"The draft?"

"Yes."

"How old are you now?"

"Twenty-one."

"How come you haven't been drafted already?"

"The county draft board is full of Armenians. But the review board is making all the guys One-A, and we're beginning to go. I could go any day."

Shad asked, "What does your mother have in mind?"

"She's a mother," Ron said, making a point of it. "What do you think?"

Shad shook his head, not sure.

Ron said, "Come down whenever you're ready. We'll be on the front porch. It's booze time."

Ron went down to the front porch. Grandfather Omar and Jacob were already there, each in his rocking chair, both with goblets of wine. Nearby was a small table with bottles of whiskey and wine, an ice bucket, some glasses, and the metal container with Ron's milk shake. He took it and went to the chair where he usually sat as the men waited for dinner. Then Shad Grady came out on the porch.

Ron asked, "Care for a drink, Shad?"

"Yes, I would."

"What would you like?"

Shad looked at Omar and Jacob and their wine, at Ron with his shake, at the small table. "Got any scotch?"

"Yes. How do you like it?"

"On the rocks."

Ron went to the table, put some ice cubes into an old fashioned glass, filled it with scotch, then carried it over to Shad at the chair he had taken.

Shad downed a gulp, glanced at the neat fields in front of him, then looked at Omar and said, "You've got a fine place here, Mr. Kazurian."

Omar said, "We work hard. It keeps us all busy. We need all the help we can get."

They talked about farming.

Then Omar asked, "How did you get into the cropdusting business, Mr. Grady?"

"It was a job," Shad said. "I have always been into flying. I couldn't stand one of those indoor, nine-to-five jobs. This way, I get around. I am my own boss. I set my own hours."

Omar asked, "And do you make a good living at it?" Ron frowned a scold at his grandfather.

Shad said, "I do all right. I pay my bills. I enjoy the life."

Jacob said, "Before we went into the business ourselves, we hired a man from Bakersfield. Howard Peterson. Do you know him?"

"Yes, I know Pete," Shad said. "He told me once that he was hoping to build up a good business around here, but I guess you people took care of that."

Omar said, "Our neighbors wanted it. We were just trying to help."

Shad looked at Ron. "Is your brother going into the business, too?"

"Yes," Ron said. "He'll take over if I get drafted. Otherwise, we'll buy another plane and expand."

Natalie came to the screen door. "Dinner is on the table," she announced.

The four men stood up. Ron said, "Freshen up your drink, Shad?"

"I'll do it," Shad said.

Ron noticed that Shad put only one ice cube into the glass, then filled it with scotch, so Ron picked up the bottle and carried it to the table and placed it near Shad.

Natalie waited until dessert was on the table. Then, without looking at him, she asked, "Were you in the war, Mr. Grady?"

He looked at her. "Which one, Mrs. Kazurian?"

"Which war were you in?"

"I was in Korea."

"In the Army?"

"I was a civilian."

Now she looked at him. "A civilian in the war? How could that be?"

"I was working for an air transport company," Shad said. "The company got a contract from the Defense Department. We flew in supplies."

Ron asked, "What did you fly, Shad?"

"Helicopters." Shad poured more scotch into his glass.

Natalie asked, "Was it dangerous, Mr. Grady?"

Shad took a sip. "Well, Mrs. Kazurian, flying over a combat zone is always a little dangerous. I got shot at a few times, but I never got hit."

Omar lit his pipe. "Mr. Grady, why didn't the Air Force pilots do that flying?"

"They were too busy flying combat," Shad said. "We got into Korea in a hurry, you remember. Somebody had to make the deliveries until the Air Force caught up enough to take over."

Natalie again. "What do you think of Vietnam, Mr. Grady?"

"I think it's a shame."

"Why do you say that?"

"Because we're going to get in over our heads, and for nothing."

"For nothing, Mr. Grady?"

"For what, then, Mrs. Kazurian? It's going to end up just like Korea. We'll keep sending more and more of our kids over there, until the next thing you know we'll be doing most of the fighting ourselves. But we won't go all out because we don't want to start a bigger war, maybe with China or Russia. So after enough of our kids have been killed and we realize we can't win, we'll sign another phony truce agreement and pull out, and the Communists will take over the country, anyway. What's the sense.?"

That silenced the table for several beats. Ron waited, wondering where the conversation would go next. Then Jacob cleared his throat. "Mr. Grady, if you got a notice tomorrow to report for the draft, would you do it? Or would you go to Canada?"

Grady thought about it, then: "I don't know. I couldn't say. It's something I won't have to decide. I'm too old. I'm forty-one."

Omar then. "Mr. Grady, that company you worked for in Korea, are they doing the same work now in Vietnam?"

"No, sir. After Korea, they sold out to a big air freight company down in L.A." He reached for the scotch.

"Is that company making the deliveries in Vietnam now?"

"I don't know. I haven't heard anything."

"If they were, would you go to work for them, even though you feel the way you do about Vietnam."

"In a flash. The pay is terrific."

A light clicked on in Ron's mind. He clicked it off. The thought was too farfetched.

Natalie again, testing. "Where is your home, Mr. Grady?"

"Wherever I park my plane." He laughed at it; he sipped the scotch.

"You don't have a home?" She couldn't believe it.

"I don't stay any place long enough to set up a home," Grady said. "I've got a post office box in Los Angeles, and I check it whenever I'm in the neighborhood. But that's it."

"You're not married, then.'

"Not any more. It didn't work. She said I drank too much." He laughed at himself.

Natalie let that go. She pushed her chair back from the table. "Why don't you men go into the parlor, so Mama and I can clean up?"

Omar said, "Let's go out on the porch. It's a nice evening."

Everybody stood. Natalie said, "Ronald, bring the ice bucket." When Ron took the bucket into the kitchen, she filled it with cubes from the refrigerator. Then she handed him a fresh bottle of scotch, and she said, "His wife was right."

So the men sat on the porch for a couple of hours and talked of many things. When Natalie and Grandmama Kazurian finished their kitchen chores, they came out on the porch and sat on the swing, listening, not saying much. Then Ron noticed that Shad was fighting yawns.

Ron asked, "Didn't you say you go to Oregon from here?"

"Yeah. I've got a couple of small jobs up there tomorrow."

"And then where?"

"Idaho, I guess. The potatoes should be ready by now. I'll call from Oregon to find out."

"You can call from here."

"Okay."

"Do you need anything? Fuel? Spray?"

"I can gas up in Oregon if I go on to Idaho. Otherwise I'm okay." Shad yawned.

"Ready to hit the hay?"

"Yeah. It's been a long day."

The two of them stood up and said their good-nights and went upstairs. At the door to Stewart's room, Ron said, "Listen, I hope you didn't mind the way the family picked your brains at the table."

"Was that what it was?"

"Yes. They're trying to find some way to keep me out of the Army."

"I don't blame them. But tell them to stop calling me Mr. Grady. Mr. Grady is my father."

Ron pretended to be surprised. "You've got a father?"

Shad shrugged. "I must have had one at some point. He took off shortly after I was born."

Ron said, "I don't blame him."

In his room, Ron could hear the voices of the four still on the porch. He could not catch what they were saying, but he was sure they were talking about him. He fell asleep to the muffled sounds.

When Ron awoke in the morning, he heard the shower running in the bathroom. He glanced at his clock. Seven-thirty. Everybody else was up. It had to be Shad in the shower. Ron got up, put on a robe and slippers and went down to the kitchen for coffee.

Natalie was there. "Is Mr. Grady up yet?"

"Yes. In the shower. And he wants you to stop calling him Mr. Grady. His name is Shad."

"All right. He goes to Oregon this morning, doesn't he?"

"Yes."

"And then?"

"Idaho maybe. He isn't sure. He's got to call there. I told him he could use our phone."

"And if he doesn't go to Idaho?"

"I don't know."

"See if you can get him to come back here."

"What for?"

"We want to talk to him."

"We?"

"Yes. After you went to bed last night, we talked about something. We want to ask Mr. Grady about it. Shad."

"What is it?"

"Never mind. If he doesn't go to Idaho, invite him to come back here tonight."

Ron heard Shad Grady coming down the stairs. "In here, Shad," he called.

Shad came into the kitchen and said good mornings. Natalie asked, "Want some coffee? Shad?"

Shad shot Ron an amused glance. Natalie caught it and lowered her eyes, amused. Shad said, "Yes, Natalie, I'd love a cup of coffee."

As she poured the coffee, Natalie said, "Ronald, get dressed. I'll fix breakfast."

Upstairs, Ron took a quick shower, dressed, and when he returned downstairs he found Shad in the living room in front of the television set, watching the Today Show. Ron asked, "Anything interesting?"

"I'm waiting for the weather report," Shad said.

"I usually have to call Sacramento for that."

"It should be on in a few minutes."

"Did you call Idaho?"

"Yeah. They don't need me this week. The following week."

"So where do you go from Oregon?"

"I guess I'll fly down to Bakersfield and see if I can pick up some work for next week."

"How about stopping off here for tonight?"

"Oh? That's a nice idea. I wouldn't want to wear out my welcome."

"You wouldn't. It's my mother's idea. She told me to invite

you."

"Tell her I'll be glad to."

"I think you're in for some more brain-picking.'

"There isn't that much to pick from."

"Don't worry. If there's anything there, an Armenian will find it."

Natalie came to the door. "Breakfast is on the table," she announced. She almost added "boys," but she realized Shad Grady was as old as she was, so she stopped herself and went back to the kitchen.

Awaiting them on the dining table were a platter of six fried eggs, a platter of bacon, a platter of ham steaks, a bowl of home fries, a mountain of buttered toast, a pot of coffee, and small jars of homemade jams. As they settled down to it, Natalie looked in from the kitchen.

She asked, "Do you need anything else?"

"Yes," said Shad. "Two more people to eat most of this food before it goes to waste."

"No waste," Natalie said. "What you don't eat goes to the pigs." Shad laughed.

Ron said, "Mama, Shad is coming back here for tonight. Isn't that nice?"

"Yes. Very nice." She looked at Shad. "What time do you think you'll be back?"

"I'm not sure. Probably late afternoon."

"Then I'd better pack a lunch for you," she said, and she went into the kitchen.

Shad shook his head. "That woman. If I hang around here long enough, she'll have me weighing a ton."

"Just watch yourself. She'll have you working it off, one way or another. It's one of her tricks."

Ron drove Shad to the airstrip and stood by as Shad checked out his plane. Ron said, "When you get back in the neighborhood, buzz the house. I'll come and pick you up."

Shad said, "Roger."

Ron said, "Roger yourself."

Late that afternoon, the four men were again on the front porch of the house, the nearby small table again filled with the bottles and the glasses and the bucket of ice cubes.

Omar Kazurian said, "Shad, tell me something. What does it take to get a contract with the Defense Department?"

"To do what?"

"To deliver the supplies by air in Vietnam."

"Well, for one thing, it takes a lot of money."

"What else does it take?"

"It takes a lot of bullshit."

Chapter Twelve

With little specific experience to draw on, they proceeded with their plan in a childlike innocence that bordered on fantasy.

They changed the name of the company to R.O.K. Air Transport Corporation and Associates, Inc. The associates were Shad Grady. Not by vote but by acknowledgment, Ron became president and treasurer of the corporation. Shad Grady became vice president and secretary, and he labeled himself the Bullshit Veep. Directors of the board were Omar, Jacob and Natalie. Granmama Kazurian, being old and wise, gave the project her blessing but wanted no part of it for herself. Daughter Helen who, though still considered a member of the family, had married and was living in town with her husband, a schoolteacher, was excluded from the corporation as an officer but would be awarded some stock when the time came to issue stock. Son Stewart, who would also receive some stock, was still working on his pilot's license and would probably take over the corporation's cropdusting division after he qualified. Also by acknowledgment, Shad Grady abandoned his vagabond life as a tramp cropduster, moved into the Kazurian home, and occupied the room that had been Helen's, which Natalie had turned into a retreat where she could do her sewing and ironing and simply escape from the family whenever she felt the need. The Kazurian living room became the corporation's headquarers; its equipment a card table and the portable typewriter Ron had bought. The corporation had no stationery, but the stationery could be printed up when stationery became necessary. The corporation's rolling stock: Ron's plane, still considered new, and Shad's plane, already considered old.

All this was established Saturday evening, before they went to bed. During the long and enthusiastic discussion, Shad Grady had knocked back a quart of scotch. Natalie decided not to offer him another bottle, and that put an end to the evening.

As they parted at Stewart's door, Shad said to Ron: "Listen, if I'm

going to hang around here any length of time, there's something
I have to find out."

"What's that?"

"Where can I get laid around here?"

"Try Sacramento."

"Where in Sacramento?"

"I'm sure Stewart can tell you."

Sunday morning went to turning Helen's room from Natalie's retreat into Shad's bedroom, the furniture retrieved from the attic
and the barn. Then church, an experience that startled Shad Grady
and from which he quickly recovered when they returned home
and Shad found a bottle of scotch on his own. Then a big lunch.

After lunch, Omar gathered together all the legal documents he
had pertaining to his financial status. Counting the land he owned,
the farming equipment, the barn and its animals, the house and its
furnishings, the four family cars and two trucks, three insurance
policies on which he could borrow, and the cash he had in the
bank, Omar had a financial potential of close to two million dollars—on paper. Ron had eleven thousand dollars in the bank, but
he still had to make the final payment on his plane and he still had
to pay for the pesticides that were stored in the hangar at the airstrip. With the jobs he had for the remainder of the season, he figured he could clear another three or four thousand, but only if the
weather remained good and the invasion of insects bad. Shad admitted that in a Los Angeles bank he had a savings account of a few
hundred dollars, but in a safe deposit box he had savings books for
five other banks across the country, banks where he had deposited
part of his local earnings so that he could cover his living expenses
whenever his job-searching took him back into the area.

He said, "I guess I have always lived a hand-to-mouth existence.
My wife didn't like that, either."

Natalie thought: I don't blame her.

Omar said, "Well, Shad, how much would we need to start?"

Shad said, "I was thinking about that in church."

Natalie frowned. Church was for prayers, not business.

Shad said, "If we can get all the equipment we need to start—
and even if we can find some bargains, we'll need a bankroll of
about ten million dollars."

Ron gave a low whistle. "Jeez, Shad, can't we start out small and
build as we go along? That's the way it is in business, isn't it?"

Shad shook his head. "Not in this business. If the war in Vietnam
gets much worse—and I'm sure it will—the giants in air cargo will
go rushing to Washington to get some of those juicy contracts for

themselves. Unless we can hold our own against them, we're kaput."

Ron shook his head and whistled low again.

Shad said, "Omar, how's your credit rating at the bank?"

"Excellent," Omar said. "How do you think I got what I've got?"

"Then let's all go to the bank tomorrow and see if they still love you."

Ron said, "I can't go to the bank tomorrow. I've got three jobs to do, and I can't put them off."

Jacob said, "Papa, you know what Mondays are like around here. So much work. I'd better stay here."

Omar said, "Stewart will be home tonight, won't he? He can do the chores."

Jacob said, "Whenever Stewart comes from Sacramento, he is so screwed out that he is not much good for a couple of days."

Omar nodded, understanding.

Natalie closed her eyes against what she knew was the truth about her younger son. No Ronald, that one.

Omar said, "Very well, Jacob. You stay home. Shad, we need everybody, do we?"

"I don't think so," Shad said. "Tomorrow we should get some idea whether we are going ahead or we can forget it."

When Stewart returned home late that afternoon, he was stunned by the development in his family. He said to his brother, "But, Ron, I thought everybody was trying to keep you *out* of Vietnam."

Shad said, "He'll be a civilian. If he gets shot at, it won't count."

Stewart shook his head. "I couldn't be more surprised if the family had decided to open a whore house in the barn."

"You'd be happier if we did," Jacob said, accusing.

After dinner, the family gathered on the front porch again. The evening was warm, with no breeze, and, tired from so much talk and planning and dreaming, one by one the members of the family excused themselves and went to bed, until at last just Stewart was there, with Shad and his bottle of Scotch. Ron could hear them in his room, their voices low and muffled. He was quite sure that Stewart was telling Shad where in Sacramento he could find some cheap—if not free—pussy.

Ron was out of the house before dawn, off to his day of cropdusting. Jacob went early to the barn, to milk the cows and turn them out to pasture, to feed the chickens, to empty the buckets of yesterday's leftovers into troughs for the pigs. Omar and Shad had a long breakfast, discussing their strategy at the bank, Natalie hovering nearby to fetch more toast and more coffee. Grandmama Kazurian slept late. Stweart slept much later.

As the bank manager listened to Shad's account of the creation, development, and plans for the R.O.K. Air Transport Corporation and Associates, Inc., his face went more and more pale. And when he heard how much the corporation wanted to borrow, he had a coughing spell.

He looked at Omar and helplessly announced, "Mr. Kazurian, I don't have enough authority even to discuss this kind of loan with you. You'll have to go to San Francisco and talk to our people in the main office."

"We have to go to San Francisco?"

"I'm afraid so," the manager said. "Even if I forwarded your application, they would want to see you. Ten million dollars is a lot of money, Mr. Kazurian."

Shad said, "We'll go to San Francisco. Can you arrange a meeting for us?"

"I can do that."

"Can you do it today?"

"I don't know if I can do that. First I'll have to find out who you have to see about a loan of this size."

Omar said, "We want to talk to the president of the bank."

The manager said, "I don't know if I can arrange that."

Omar said, "Then somebody who can tell us yes or no right away."

"I'll let you know."

Shad asked, "When do you think that will be?"

"I'll call you as soon as I have something definite."

When Omar and Shad got back to the house, Stewart was sitting down for breakfast. Omar challenged him with: "You up already?"

"Just. How did things go at the bank?"

Shad told him.

Stewart said, "San Francisco, huh? I hear San Francisco is a pretty good town—if you like boys."

Omar said, "Sometimes I wish you did. Eat, then get out to the barn and help your father."

Omar and Shad went to the corporation's office in the living room, to the card table to plan further strategy. Natalie brought coffee for Omar and scotch for Shad. After lunch, they were back in the office, still plotting, when Ron returned from his day's work. He listened to their report about the meeting at the bank, nodding now and then, shrugging his shoulders, as though he hadn't expected much, anyway. Then he went into the kitchen to fix himself a malted. He was there when the telephone rang, and he answered it on the kitchen extension. He stepped into the living room and said, "Grandpapa, it's for you. It's the bank."

Omar took the call on the wall phone in the hallway. Shad, Ron and Natalie came close to hear, Omar holding the phone slightly away from his ear. They heard:

"Mr. Kazurian?"

"Yes."

"I've been able to get you an appointment in San Francisco for Thursday at ten o'clock. Can you be there?"

Omar glanced at Shad; Shad nodded. "Yes, we can be there. Who do we see?"

"You see a Mr. Covington. Morley Covington."

"Is he the president of the bank?"

"No, but he's close to it. He's the one who makes the final decision on transactions of this size."

"Does he know how much we want to borrow?"

"Yes."

"What did he say?"

"Nothing, really. He's used to dealing with such figures."

"And he's the one who says yes or no?"

"He's more likely to say no or maybe. These things aren't easy to pull off, Mr. Kazurian. They take time. Be sure to take all your papers with you so that Mr. Covington can see what you've got for collateral."

"We'll do that. Did you put in a good word for us?"

"I sure did, Mr. Kazurian. I told him you are a very prominent family in these parts and that you are very influential in the Armenian community."

"Did you tell him that I always pay my bills on time?"

"I did. The main office has records of your dealings with the bank, Mr. Kazurian, and Mr. Covington said he would take a look at them before you get there."

"Thank you. I'll let you know what happens."

"Please do that. I'll be interested. I've never been involved in anything this big before."

Omar hung up, then regarded the coterie or eavesdroppers around him. He said, "Let's go out on the porch." The small table was already there, waiting. As they prepared their first drinks, Jacob and Stewart came in from the fields. Omar told them about the call from the bank.

Ron said, "Thursday is bad for me. This whole week is. I've got a couple of dusting jobs every day."

Jacob said, "Can't you call these people up and put them off to next week?"

"I could, Papa," Ron said, "but I don't like to. These people are money in the bank. Why put them off for money we may not get from a bank?"

Omar said, "You have to go to San Francisco, Ronald. You are the president of the corporation."

Shad said, "Hell, Ron, I can help you out on the dusting. My plane is sitting at the airstrip doing nothing."

"That's a good idea," Ron said. "Between the two of us, we should be able to get most of the work done."

After dinner, Ron took Shad to his room and went over maps of the farms to be sprayed the next day. They would each spray two. Then they went back to the porch for a night cap, Ron to the lemonade, Shad to the scotch. When, around ten o'clock, Ron saw Shad reach for the scotch for the third time in twenty minutes, he said, "Shad, we have a lot of work to do tomorrow. I don't want you with a hangover."

Shad gasped as though he had been struck. "When did you ever see me with a hangover?"

"Not yet," Ron conceded, "but I've never seen you sober, either."

"Christ, you sound like a wife."

"I hope I have better luck with you than the last one did."

Shad downed the inch of scotch in a gulp. Then he stood up. "Okay, Mr. President, I'm ready for beddy-by now."

Upstairs, on his way to his room, Ron stopped at Stewart's door and opened it. Stewart was stretched out on his bed in his shorts, one hand massaging his groin as he paged through a girlie magazine.

Ron said, "I want you to get up early tomorrow and bust your ass helping Papa with the chores around here or I'm gonna bust your ass for you."

Stewart gave a snappy salute. "Yes, sir, Mr. President!"

Shad said, "Mr. President, you haven't even started working yet. From now on, you're into it up to your own ass."

Chapter Thirteen

They were in over their heads.

Going through the revolving door of the San Francisco bank building, they entered a world where they did not know the language, did not know the rules, did not know the risks and did not know the rewards. But, going through that revolving door, they entered the lives of three men who would be part of their lives as long as they lived, men who knew the language and knew the rules, who knew the risks and were wiling to take them because they knew what the rewards could be, rewards not only for themselves but for the world they inhabited, the world of Big.

Had Ron and Omar and Shad gone through that revolving door with a recipe for making chocolate popcorn, these men would have listened to them, considered whether the rewards were worth the risks, and, if deciding yes, would have applied the language to exercise the rules, using the tools of money, power, influence, connections, and, above all, intuition, snap judgments and self-interests, not only their own self-interests but the self-interests of anybody who, in any way, could protect, defend and expand their own self-interests in chocolate popcorn.

The three men.

Morley Covington, banker, head of the department of industrial loans and investments at one of the biggest banks in San Francisco, one of the biggest banks in California, one of the biggest banks in the United States, one of the biggest banks in the world.

David French, attorney, the most senior of the four senior members of one of the most powerful law firms in San Francisco and, up the ladder, in the world.

Bert Bernstein, attorney, Dave French's son-in-law and head of French's dynamic staff in Washington, D.C., where legal success was more a matter of lobbying than of law and where the tools of self-interest determined law more than the Constitution, the city that was both the Mecca and the Vatican of the religion of Big.

Even before Ron and Omar and Shad had gone through the revolving door of the San Francisco bank building, Morley Covington had checked them out and knew almost as much about them as they knew themselves. He also checked out the background of civilian ferrying companies in other wars—Korea, World War II and the worldwide uprisings in which the United States was not supposed to be openly involved but was nevertheless supplying one side or the other, using civilian ferrying companies as the cover-up. And he checked out the aircraft industry, checking it out so well that, without looking at his notes, he could tell you the price of any aircraft being built and its operating cost per mile.

As he waited for the three men who had been announced from the reception desk in the lobby and were on their way up to him, Covington already knew they were virgins in the world of Big, but he also knew what the rewards could be in a field that, as yet, was still wide open, in a war that, as far as the United States was concerned, had still to come to a boil. All he had to find out now were the risks as far as these three virgins were concerned.

As the three virgins were being ushered into his spacious office, Covington put labels on them at a glance. Omar: money, age, wisdom, caution. Ronald: youth, brains, drive, leadership. Shad: brawn, charm, booze, women, Irish bullshit. Covington met the three of them halfway between his huge desk and the cathedral-like double doors of his office, and instead of leading them back to his desk, he guided them to one side of the vast room where there was an island of leather furniture surrounding a coffee table. Before they had settled in the soft, submitting chairs, a secretary who was the secretary to Covington's secretary came in with coffee.

Settled, Covington gave them a smile and asked, "Well, gentlemen, what can the bank do you for?"

Shad Grady did most of the talking, as Covington had expected, and Covington listened attentively to what he already knew. Then he turned to Omar and said, "Well, Mr. Kazurian, all this sounds very interesting, but I think I should point out to you that you have a problem. According to the figures I've seen, you have assets of about two million dollars, and you want to borrow ten million dollars against that. I'm afraid that's not enough. Where would the bank stand if you defaulted on the loan?"

Omar said, "You could have my farm. You could have any airplanes we buy."

Covington gave that a patient nod. "The bank would consider your property, of course, but we certainly don't want to end up with any used aircraft on our hands. We're not in the business of peddling secondhand airplanes. Is there any way you can find more property?"

Omar thought about it. "Maybe," he said. "My neighbors own their farms. We are all Armenians; we are like brothers. Maybe they would be willing to put up their property if I asked them."

"They would have to put that in writing, of course," Covington said.

"Of course."

"Do you have an attorney?"

"A lawyer?" Omar said. "Yes, I have a lawyer up home. I have been doing business with him for years."

"Does he have representation in Washington?"

"Pardon?"

Covington went patient. "Mr. Kazurian, in order to get your business off the ground, you will have to get a government contract. This is a very complicated procedure. If I were you, I'd get myself a first-rate law firm in Washington, somebody who knows how to battle through all the red tape. You see, Mr. Kazurian, if you already had a government contract, if you could show the bank that your business is a going operation or about to become one, we wouldn't be too concerned about the collateral. You need top attorneys for that."

Ron asked, "Where do we find one?"

Covington made a call.

That afternoon, the three virgins passed through another revolving door, another set of cathedral-like double doors, and settled in soft, submitting leather chairs around another coffee table, the coffee there in a moment. Four hours later, Omar wrote a check for ten thousand dollars, a retainer to Dave French, and the three of them walked back to the St. Francis Hotel, not knowing whether they would get the loan, not knowing whether they would get a government contract, not knowing what they had achieved during the day except that it had cost ten thousand dollars.

At the hotel, Omar said, "Let's call Natalie and tell her what happened."

Ron asked, "What have we got to tell her, Grandpapa?"

Omar said, "People drink a lot of coffee in San Francisco."

Shad said, "You tell her about the coffee. I'm ready for something else." And he headed for the bar.

Three weeks passed before there was any evidence that the trip to San Francisco had been anything more than a day away from the farm. Then Dave French called, Omar taking the call on the hall phone, Ron on the kitchen extension, Shad on the line upstairs.

Dave French said, "We've been busy. I've had your company incorporated; we should have stock certificates in a few days, but we can talk about that later. Can you be in Washington on Monday?

Omar said, "What for?"

Ron said, "We can be there, Mr. French."

French said, "Good. Come into San Francisco first. Can you be here Sunday morning?"

Ron said, "We can be there, Mr. French."

French said, "Good. I've got some papers for you to sign. And I want to give you a rundown on what to expect in Washington. You're in for some rough weather, but Bert will be there to help you."

"Bert?" said Omar.

French said, "Bert Bernstein, my son-in-law. He runs our Washington office. He's been through this a hundred times with all kinds of government contracts, so he knows where the potholes are. Just do what he says. Is Mr. Grady there?"

Shad came on. "Right here, Mr. French."

"Okay," French said. "Have you got any friends in Washington? Anybody in the Pentagon?"

"Not that I can think of," Shad said. "I didn't know any of the big shots in Korea, and I haven't even seen any of the military people from Korea since I left there myself."

"It would help if you had some connections high up," French said. "Now, Mr. Grady, I hope you don't mind my saying this, but you are a pretty good bullshitter. I think so, and so does Morley Covington. You people are going to have to go through a lot of meetings with a bunch of Washington blockheads who don't know their own jobs, let alone yours, so lay it on thick."

Shad said, "Thick as I can."

French said, "See to it that you do most of the talking at those meetings. Don't get discouraged by any flack you run into at the lower altitudes. But if you survive to the top, you'd sure as hell better know what you're talking about."

Shad repeated, "Thick as I can."

French said, "Mr. Kazurian?"

Both Ron and Omar said, "Yes, Mr. French?"

French said, "Take along your checkbook."

There was flack all over the place.

Bert Bernstein told them, "The first thing you've got to learn in this town is never lose your temper. You're going to run into a lot of chicken shit, mostly from crapheads who don't have anything to say about anything, anyway. It makes them feel important, so shut up and grin and suck ass, and you'll survive. Now, I've got some people waiting for us in the conference room. They're going to give you a sample of the treatment waiting for you at the Pentagon so you can be ready for it."

An hour through the treatment, Shad banged his fist on the table and bellowed, "Jesus Christ, we're not trying to overthrow the government. What's going on here?"

The sudden silence, then Bernstein's soft, "Suck ass, Mr. Grady."

A few days later, after the first meetings with the lower echelon at the Pentagon, at dinner one evening Shad announced, "Everything I eat in this town tastes like shit."

Bert Bernstein said, "You're getting the hang of it."

It was near the end of the second week of meetings that Bert Bernstein told them: "Today you hit the big time—the second rung on the Air Force ladder. How these guys feel about you decides whether or not you get the contract. They're the ones who advise the Chief of Staff what to do; and if there are any mistakes, they're the ones that get shipped to Timbuktu. Is your tongue, ready, Shad?"

Shad stuck out his tongue and wiggled it.

An hour later, as the three of them and Bernstein entered the cavernous conference room in the Pentagon, they saw a dozen men standing about, chatting, waiting for them, several of them in uniform. Shad took a few steps into the room, stopped in his tracks, and exclaimed, "Son of a bitch! Chuck Nygren!"

A two-star Air Force General, startled, turned around, looked at Grady, studying his face, and then burst into a grin and a loud laugh. "Jesus Christ! Shady Grady! Scotland's best customer!"

The two of them moved to each other quickly and went into a hug, pounding each other on the back and laughing. Shad said, "How the fuck did you ever get two stars in the Air Force? You couldn't fly a plane for shit."

"I did it on charm," the general said. He turned to the three-star general. "Shad and I were together in Korea. We had some wild times, didn't we, you little shit? Two things Shad could always find for the fellas, even at the front lines. Booze and broads."

Everybody was smiling. Omar was puzzled. Ron was relieved. Bernstein was grinning.

The two-star general said, "Are you in on this deal, Shad?"

"Yeah. I'm Vice President in charge of Bullshit."

"You're qualified. Let's meet your friends and get down to business."

Shad introduced Omar and Ron and Bernstein; the General introduced three-star General Milland. They all sat down at the table. General Nygren said, "I'm glad that you're in on this, Shad. We've been getting a few nibbles from other companies, but nobody with any combat experience."

Shad tested, "Any contracts yet?"

"No. Vietnam is going to be a big show, Shad. I hope we can convince the shitheads on the Hill about that before it's too late. Anyway, we don't want any weekend flyboys fooling around over there. I've been waiting for a pro to show up."

Shad said, "We're ready to go as soon as we get the green light."

Nygren said, "Okay. Let's hear the bullshit."

They talked for over two hours, Shad and General Nygren doing most of the talking. When the meeting broke up, Shad and General Nygren stepped aside.

Shad asked, "What do you think, Chuck?"

"I don't see any problems. You've got the experience, and it sounds like you've got the setup. Who've you got on the Hill?" Shad named a California Congressman and two California Senators. Nygren said, "They're okay. Tell them to put on the heat."

"Okay. How long do you think it will take?"

"It depends on the heat."

"We've got a lot of money riding on this."

"I'm sure. Don't worry. How long will you be in town?"

"I don't know. We want to get back as soon as possible."

"I'm sure. But if there's time, try to have dinner with me. I want you to meet the Chief. We're buddies. I married his bitch of a daughter and got her out of his house while he still had some sanity left. How the hell do you think I got these stars?"

Shad said, "You get us this contract, Chuck, and I'll see to it that you get a couple more."

"I don't need any more stars," Nygren said, sadly. "Just take me with you to Vietnam. I've got to get away from that woman."

In the limousine heading back to Bernstein's office, Bert kept saying, "Holy shit! Holy shit! Holy shit! Shad, why didn't you tell me you knew General Nygren? We could have saved a lot of time."

Shad, "I didn't know he was still in the Air Force. He was the only pilot I ever met who could crash a plane without getting it off the ground. He's lucky he married the boss's daughter."

Bernstein said, "So are you."

Ron asked, "So what do we do now?"

Bernstein said, "First thing, Shad, you have dinner with your buddy and his boss. That ought to wrap things up good." He looked at Omar. "As for you two, tomorrow you start going up to the Hill and pass out some campaign contributions to the people who can put the pressure on the Defense Department. Then we all pray."

Three days later, the four were in a limousine headed for the airport. Ron said, "What do you think, Bert? Have we got the contract?"

Bert Bernstein said, "Right now, I'd say that if you don't get the contract, I'm going back to ambulance chasing. But this is a crazy town. You can think you're in business, and then some giant shows up with more money and more power and more influence, and you're up shit creek."

Omar put in: "But the other night the Chief told Shad not to worry."

Bernstein said, "That depends on how solid the Chief is in with the Joint Chief and how solid the Joint Chief is in with the Secretary of Defense. That's Washington: The Up-The-Ladder Club."

Shad said, "The Up-The-Ass Club, you mean. I saw it in Korea. The military is the only racket in the world where a tube of K-Y is required equipment in a survival kit."

Omar asked, "What's K-Y?"

They had flown tourist to Washington and Omar, in his guarded optimism, insisted they fly tourist back to San Francisco. Having applied for seats at the last minute, they were assigned to the back of the plane, the three of them sitting abreast. The 747 took off, achieved altitude, then leveled for the four-hour flight to San Francisco. An attendant worked her way down the aisle with newspapers and magazines.

Reaching the back seat, she asked, "Care for anything to read?"

Shad asked, "What have you got?"

"Just the *Wall Street Journal* and *Sports Illustrated*."

Shad said, "Does the *Wall Street Journal* have any comics?"

"All over the front page."

"I'll take it."

She looked at Ron. Ron said, "I'll wait for the movie."

She looked at Omar. Omar was asleep.

Nothing on the front page of the *Journal* interested Shad, and he began to page through the paper. Suddenly he stiffened and gasped. He shoved the paper at Ron and pointed to a headline. "Look at that."

The headline:

TRANSCONTINENTAL SEEKS
VIETNAM CONTRACT

The first sentence was enough.

"Transcontinental Freight, the nation's third largest air cargo carrier, has applied to the U.S. Department of Defense for a government contract to ferry U.S. aid to South Vietnam, a spokesman for the company announced in Los Angeles this morning."

Ron looked at Shad, waiting.

Shad was boiling. "We're screwed," he said. "I know that company. They're the outfit that bought out the company I worked for in Korea. They're the giant Bert Bernstein warned us about. We're fucked. Wake up, Omar."

Ron sank low in his seat. He said, "No. Let him sleep. Let him dream. Maybe we've all been dreaming all along."

Chapter Fourteen

Seated where they were, they were the last passengers off the plane. As they were passing through the waiting area, Omar said, "Look. There's Mr. Covington."

Ron looked. Morley Covington. And Dave French. Faces full of anxiety. Eyes full of questions.

Omar said, "Isn't it nice for them to meet us."

Ron said, "Yes. Very nice."

Shad said, "I wonder where they parked the hearse."

As they were all shaking hands, Covington turned to Ron and asked, "Did you see today's *Wall Street Journal?*"

"We saw it on the plane."

Dave French said, "Bert saw it when he got back to his office. He called right away."

Covington said, "We've been on the phone with Transcontinental ever since."

Omar said, "What's going on?"

French said, "Let's talk about it in the car."

The five of them crowded into the back seat of the limousine, Ron and Shad in the jumpseats.

Dave French was saying, "I know I should have waited to consult with you people, but I didn't want to lose any time."

Covington said, "Transcontinental has its account with the Los Angeles branch of our bank. I was able to get through to their vice president in charge of government contracts."

French said, "And I got in touch with their lawyers. I had to bullshit them. I said we already had the contract and that you were flying back with it. That cooked their goose, and they knew it. That's why they bit when I said we'd be willing to renegotiate the contract to bring them in on the deal as partners."

Omar said, "So we've got partners we don't even know yet."

Covington looked at him. "Omar, let me tell you something. Before you people came into my office for the first time, I already knew that the ten million you wanted to borrow wouldn't add up to a drop in the bucket. But I figured that if you could get a firm government contract, the bank would go along with whatever amount you needed."

Omar asked, "Would the bank still be willing to go along with that?"

Covington gave Omar a level stare. "Omar, you are talking to the bank right now."

Ron said, "A fifty-fifty deal, huh?"

French said, "Yes."

Shad said, "That's a pretty good bite. We do all the work and they get half the profits without moving their ass."

"Right," Covington said, "and for half the profits they save you from going millions and millions of dollars into debt to buy the equipment they already have."

French turned to Omar. "As I've said, Omar, Transcontinental uses its big planes to fly the stuff from the States to Saigon, and now all R.O.K. has to do is buy a dozen helicopters to make the on-site deliveries inside Vietnam."

Shad said, "And get our asses shot off."

Ron said, "Don't say anything like that in front of my mother, Shad. She started all this crap just to keep me out of the Army."

French said, "You are out of the Army, Ron. Bert told me. When he got back to his office, there was a call from the Pentagon. You're off the shit list. You've been reclassified. You've got a permanent deferment."

Omar asked, "What does that mean?"

Ron said, "It means that if I get my ass shot off in Vietnam, it won't count. I'm a civilian."

What, in a sense, shot them down at first was the heat. The humidity. Even the nights were brutal. American involvement was still simmering, gradually working its way to a boil. Most of the fighting was still being done between the Vietnamese themselves, South and North, the American observers participating more and more with the South. And more and more the troops began to arrive, Army and Marines, by air and by sea, the Navy building strength offshore.

At first, the R.O.K. people were housed temporarily in Bachelor Officers' Quarters, with the understanding that they would seek residences of their own as soon as possible. Without discussing it, Ron and Shad did not live together. Shad found an apartment in the city; Ron found a small house on what had been the plantation of a Frenchman who had left the country after the French defeat. It was about a mile from the airport, and Ron used part of it as an office.

The mornings were devoted to practice flights by the R.O.K. helicopter pilots, short trips into the nearby secured bush country, learning how to land a helicopter in a small clearing just big enough to park a car. Afternoons went to studying maps, memorizing them until the pilots could identify a delivery site from the air by means of a nearby mountain or stream or village or rice paddy.

The pressure began to mount. The dozen pilots, including Shad, started making one combat-zone delivery a day, then two, then four or five.

Shad insisted that Ron stay at his desk and not do any flying. He said, "You've got the lousy job—trying to keep everything in order. Nobody else can do it. What would happen to us if something happened to you?"

But Ron was adamant. "Damn it," he said, "I'm going to make a delivery whenever I can get away from this fucking desk. Jesus Christ, I don't want to feel like a complete draft dodger." So Ron made deliveries, sometimes at least one a day, sometimes having to go a few days without one. Each delivery gave him a sense of nervous tension he could feel in his crotch, a kind of pleasure he enjoyed every time.

The lousy part of Ron's job was the paperwork. As the war increased, the paperwork increased, and there were times when Ron made a delivery or two just to get away from it all. Each time a Transcontinental giant arrived, Ron had to be there to check the cargo against the bill of lading. Then he had to supervise the distribution of the cargo to designated warehouses at the airport. Thefts were rampant, both by the military and the civilians. Ron had to hire guards to keep an eye on the guards already hired, and even then supplies kept disappearing. Each time a delivery was to be made, Ron received a bill of lading of the cargo to be flown to some remote spot in the jungle. Ron had to check to be sure the cargo reflected the bill of lading, nothing more, nothing less. Procedure required that the ranking officer at the delivery site sign a receipt. Sometimes there was no ranking officer; sometimes there was nobody at the site, the troops moving on; and then the pilot had to return the cargo to the airport. More paperwork. After each arriving Transcontinental giant had been emptied, seats were installed for the passengers on the return flight. Space had to be arranged for the wounded. Space had to be arranged for the dead. More paperwork. At the end of each week, Ron accumulated the bills of lading for the week, made an itemized list of them, sending the bills to Morley Covington in a pouch aboard one of the Transcontinental giants, the list to Morley by military mail. This way, Covington could check the bills against the list and see that nothing was missing and nothing had been tampered with. Covington then prepared an invoice and, adding it to the stack of bills of lading, sent everything across the street to Dave French, who, having power of attorney, signed the invoice and sent it to Bert Bernstein in Washington, who sent everything on to the Pentagon. The Pentagon checks made the return trip to Covington. He banked the checks. At the end of each month, he prepared a statement of accounts, a copy to Ron, a copy to Transcontinental, half the profits to Transcontinental. To Ron, Covington also sent a supply of cash, which Ron turned over to Shad Grady to pay the men.

Little of the paperwork made much sense to Ron. He knew that the project was succeeding, but he was never sure how much R.O.K. was making or how much of the profits was his. He didn't care. He had complete trust in Morley Covington and Dave French, and, since his interests were their interests, he knew he was in safe hands. Ron had the same feeling for the Vietnam project that he had for the Kazurian family farm at home: Everybody did his chores and then took from the family coffers what he needed for himself.

Ron's needs in Vietnam were few. Because he worked in the house where he lived, he had the place included in operating expenses. An elderly Vietnamese couple worked for him, the man keeping the house and grounds in order, the woman doing the cooking and laundry. The woman's efforts with American menus were so dismal that Ron told her to cook Vietnamese, and he developed a taste for it. Evenings went mostly to paperwork. Ron didn't have a television set, so usually he unwound at the end of the day by reading paperback novels he bought at the commissary. The longer the novel, the better he liked it; the more intricate the plot, the more involved he became; the larger the cast of characters, the more fascinated he became by them. As he read, he would envision the story as a movie in his mind, and he enjoyed this because it took him away from himself, away from the boredom his job gradually became for him. As the war expanded, Ron had to work every day. He welcomed this. It gave him something to do. He had never been able to make friends easily, and he was not making any in Vietnam.

Ron knew Shad Grady's apartment in the city had quickly acquired a flamboyant reputation. There were parties every night. The men were mostly from the American military and the civilian sector arriving more and more in the country, a few Frenchmen, a few Vietnamese, a few Chinese. The women were mostly Vietnamese, a few French, a few Chinese, more and more American civilian women arriving in the country. Booze flowed. The pungent scent of marijuana grew thicker as the evening unfolded. Occasionally someone ducked down a hall for a snort or a needle. Most of the women usually got fucked at least once before morning. When Shad heard there was a little homo hankypanky going on, he announced that as long as the participants were from San Francisco it was okay. Otherwise, do that shit elsewhere. As he always had, Shad made friends easily, and he was soon a celebrity in Saigon, greeted by name wherever he went.

Ron had been to a couple of the parties but then stopped. The fury gave him a headache. The stench of booze and marijuana made him nauseous. The determined progression toward orgies depressed Ron and put him close to a vow of chastity.

Ron saw Shad, then, mostly in spurts, sometimes at the office, sometimes at the airfield, sometimes running into him in the city. When Ron knew Shad was on a dangerous delivery, he did not leave the airfield until Shad safely returned.

One night, Ron was at home alone, reading, when there was a knock at the door. He answered it. He looked at a Vietnamese man he did not know. Without speaking, the man handed Ron an envelope. Ron opened it and extracted a small piece of paper. He read:

Ron—if you ever want to see me alive again, do what this man tells you.

Shad

P.S. It's serious.

Chapter Fifteen

The Vietnamese said, "You are to come with me."

Ron followed him to a waiting car. He was told to get into the back seat. Another Vietnamese was in the car. When Ron was seated beside him, the man took a black cloth out of his pocket and blindfolded Ron. He heard the car being started. The familiar potholes of his driveway faded as the car moved out to the highway. The driver turned left. Ron tried to keep track of the turns the car was making, the speed it was moving, but he soon became confused and dropped the effort. He tried to keep track of time by counting the seconds slowly to himself, but this, too, soon became hopeless. The journey went on and on.

Then, suddenly, potholes began again. The car stopped. Still blindfolded, Ron was helped out of the car. He was walked a few steps, then led up some stairs and across what sounded like a porch. He was led through a door which he heard slam behind him. A screen door. Then a long hallway. Then another door. His blindfold was removed.

He saw Shad Grady. He was sitting in a wooden straightback chair, smoking a cigarette. Beside him stood a Vietnamese holding a revolver. Ron glanced at the man who had brought him in. He was the man who had come to his door.

He looked at Shad. "What's going on?"

Shad said, "We're in trouble."

"For what? What have we done?"

"It's not what we've done. It's what they want us to do."

"What?"

"Dope."

"Dope?"

"Yeah. They're in the business. They want us to get their stuff into the States."

"They're crazy. How could we do that?"

"They've got it all figured out."

"Yeah?"

"Yeah. They know what business we're in."

"So what? A lot of people know that."

"They've been watching us ever since we got here, Ron."

"Then they ought to know that we can't help them."

"They think we can."

"How?"

"I don't know where the heroin is coming from, but they've got 'drops' all over this country. They want us to pick it up in our helicopters and get it to the Saigon airport."

"And then?"

"Get it on a Transcontinental flight to the States."

"That's crazy. That's impossible. You know the paperwork. Nothing gets on or off a plane without being checked against a bill of lading."

"They know that, too. And they know that you do the checking. They expect you to figure out the way to get the stuff on the plane. They've got their own ways of getting it off once it gets to the States."

Ron shook his head. "I can't do it."

Shad smiled sadly. "They don't like those words. They said they'd make it worth our while."

"Like what?"

"A hundred thousand each time we get the package through."

"What if we get caught? We'd spend the rest of our lives in jail."

"That's better than the alternative."

"Which is?"

"They've already said they'd kill me if I didn't get you out here. And they said they'd kill you if you said no."

"Fuck 'em."

"Ron, they *mean* it. They've already got some stuff through, but it's not enough for them."

"How?"

"Well, if the folks back home could open up some of the dead boys we're shipping back, they'd be in for a big surprise."

"Jesus Christ!"

"It's big money, Ron."

"Yeah?"

"Yeah. If you could have the take these people make off one delivery after it hits the streets, you could make Morley Covington very happy in a minute."

Ten million. Ron turned to the Vietnamese who had come to his door. "Who is in charge of all this?"

"Not your business."

"I have to talk to him."

"Is not possible."

"Well, I can't say yes or no right now. I've got to figure it out. I've got to have time to think about it."

"When you know?"

"Tomorrow night."

"I come to your house."

"What about Mr. Grady?"

"He stay here, until we get your answer."

Ron looked at Shad. "Will you be all right?"

Shad said, "I'll be all right as long as you come up with the right answer."

Ron said to the Vietnamese, "All right. Tomorrow night. Take me home now."

The blindfold was put back in place. Ron was led back to the car. He was driven home. On this trip, he did not try to play cops and robbers. This time his only thought was how to figure out some way to say yes. Some way to save Shad Grady's life. And his own.

The lights were still burning in Ron's house when he was let out of the car. He glanced at his watch. About two hours had passed. Inside, Ron turned off the lights except for a lamp in the living room. In a cabinet was a supply of liquor Ron kept handy for Shad and the rest of the staff whenever their business brought them to the house. He poured a couple of inches of scotch into a glass and sat down to sip and think. Each sip was bitter in his mouth and burning in his throat. He thought. He thought. He fell asleep. He was awakened shortly after dawn by the elderly Vietnamese couple, returning to the house for their day's work. He got up and freshened himself with a shave and a bath, there being no shower, and he had a breakfast of *cafe au lait* and French bread, heavily buttered. He drove to the airfield.

The day passed as the days had passed for almost four months now. Three Transcontinental giants arrived from the States. Ron, bill of lading in hand, checked the cargo before it was unloaded. He stood by, supervising, as the cargo was sent off to the warehouses. As the giants were being prepared for the return flight, Ron gave his time to assigning R.O.K. pilots to their deliveries into the bush, checking their cargo before they took off.

Just before a giant took off, Ron went aboard, as he always did, to check his documents against the list of pasengers, the wounded and the dead, knowing now what some of the bodies of the dead probably contained in their bellies. And he noticed something he had not considered before. The only food aboard the returning giant was a couple of large urns of coffee and a couple of boxes of sandwiches. He looked into the electric ovens where, on a commercial flight, meals would be stored, frozen, until mealtime, when attendants would turn on the ovens, heat the food, and serve it to the passengers. Ron saw that the ovens were empty. And the only attendants aboard were the medical corpsmen who spent all of their time with the wounded. Whenever a passenger wished, he could help himself to coffee and a sandwich.

Ron made this same inspection of the ovens just before the second giant took off. And the third.

At the end of his day, all the R.O.K. pilots back safely, Ron went home. He had dinner. Then he waited. It was around ten, the elderly Vietnamese couple sent home early, that Ron heard the knock at his door. He opened it. There stood the Vietnamese from the night before.

Ron asked, "Do I go with you?"

"No," the man said. "You write your answer."

Ron nodded. The man followed Ron through the house to the office. Ron sat at his desk, placed a plain piece of paper in front of himself. He wrote:

It is possible that we can cooperate on what you want. But only under these conditions:

1. You are to release Mr. Grady immediately into my custody.
2. You are to inform us in plenty of time of the place for the first pick-up.
3. Mr. Grady and I will fly there in separate helicopters. After we receive the product, we will leave one of the helicopters with you as collateral.
4. By our own means, we will arrange delivery of your product to our hangar at the Oakland Air Freight Terminal, Oakland, California, our port of entry into the U.S. We will inform you in advance of the estimated time of arrival, and where the product can be found on the plane. It will be the responsibility of your people to remove the product from the plane.
5. When you receive confirmation of a completed delivery, you will arrange a meeting with us at the place where our helicopter may be. At that time, you will pay us $250,000 in U.S. currency for the delivery. We shall also reclaim the helicopter. If there are any more deliv-

eries, the time and place will be set by you. On the
pick-up, you will pay us the $250,000 in advance. We'll
inform you of arrival time of the product at Oakland.

6. We will not be responsible if any delivery is intercepted
    by others at Oakland or en route.

7. I will know that you accept these conditions the next
    time I see Mr. Grady.

Ron signed his name. He folded the piece of paper, placed it into
an envelope, sealed it, then, picking up his pen, asked, "Who gets
this?"

"I do," the man said and took it.

"When do I get the answer?"

"When I do." The man left.

Ron's trip the night before had taken about two hours. Now, he
figured, if his conditions were accepted, Shad should be back in
two hours. He wondered if his conditions were too severe. He
couldn't have cared less about the money, but it seemed to him
that if some bastard was going to end up making ten million dollars
on the deal he ought to be willing to pay more than a fraction of
it to get his hands on the stuff. But most important was Shad. Ron
would have been willing to make the transshipment free to get
Shad released. Anything.

Ron was too nervous to do any paperwork. He shut off the lights
in the office and went into the living room. He glanced at the
liquor cabinet but decided against it. He went out to the kitchen
and got himself a Coke, then returned to the living room, sitting
there and watching the door, when the room went dawn purple.
Aching with fatigue and despair, he took a hot bath, shaved and
dressed, and drove to the airfield. Near the warehouses was a small
frame building, about the size of a one-car garage, which Ron used
as an office at the field. It had a telephone. When Ron was sure the
Vietnamese couple were at the house, he called them and said he
wanted to be notified the minute Mr. Grady showed up.

The day began. A giant arrived. The R.O.K. pilots drifted in. Military planes took off on their regular reconnaissance flights. A few
of the commercial planes still serving Saigon came and went. Suddenly it was noon. Usually Ron went home for lunch; sometimes
he lunched at the officers' mess at the field. But he wasn't hungry
now, concern for Shad simmering in his gut. He sat at his desk in
the shack and stared at papers but could not focus on them.

Another giant arrived. Ron picked up his clipboard and headed
for the plane. He heard behind him:

"Hello, Mr. President."

Ron turned.

Shad.

Shad looked very tired. He badly needed a shave. His clothes were disheveled. His smile was sad and weak.

With a few quick steps, Ron took Shad in a hug. He said, "You son of a bitch. Why can't you stay out of trouble?"

Shad said, "You've got balls, Mr. President. I'll say that for you."

They stepped apart. Ron asked, "What do you mean?"

Shad said, "They made me read your conditions and sign them. Christ, here they've got a gun at our heads, and you give them orders. That's class."

"What did you expect me to do? Kiss their ass?"

"I would have eaten their shit, I was so scared."

"Are you all right?"

"Yeah."

"They didn't hurt you?"

"They didn't touch me. But they would have. They were serious. And they still are. We know too much now, Ron."

Ron dug in his pocket for his car keys. "Here," he said, handing Shad the keys. "Go to my place. Get some sleep, clean up, eat something. I'll be there in a couple of hours. We've got a lot to talk about."

Shad asked, "You keep the booze in the same place?"

"Yes. And don't drink too much. I want you to be able to make sense."

"I always make sense," Shad said, and he walked away.

The giant was emptied and the cargo stored and Ron had one of the maintenance men drive him home. He found Shad asleep on the sofa in the living room, washed, shaved, wearing one of Ron's robes, an empty glass on the nearby coffee table, the liquor cabinet door open. Ron went out to the kitchen and told the Vietnamese couple they could go home now.

The woman asked, "But dinner, sir?"

"I'll fix dinner," Ron said. "Do we have any steaks?"

"The freezer, sir."

"All right. You can go now. I'll see you in the morning."

They gathered their things and left. Ron took the steaks from the freezer compartment of the refrigerator and put them on the table to thaw. He filled a bowl with ice cubes, got a Coke for himself, and returned to the living room. He took the scotch bottle out of the cabinet and half filled the glass on the coffee table. Settling in a chair opposite the sofa, he had a couple of cigarettes as he watched

Shad sleep.

Finally Ron said softly, "Bullshit Veep?"

A low moan from Shad.

"Are you awake, Bullshit Veep?"

Low moan. "What smells so good?"

"Open your eyes."

Shad opened his eyes and saw the glass. "Ah, mother's milk."

"Sit up. We've got a lot to talk about."

Shad swung his feet to the floor and sat up. He put a few ice cubes into the glass, took a sip, then looked at Ron. "What's on your mind?"

"What do you want for Christmas?"

"A gorgeous redhead with big tits. There are no redheads around here, and Vietnamese women got tits like boys."

"How come you know about boys?"

"I was a boy once myself."

"Then tell me, boy, how the hell did you get into this mess?"

Shad took a sip. "I don't know."

"How did it get started, then?"

Shad took another sip. "Well—when was it—three nights ago? I was in my apartment, waiting for people to show up for a party. You know how life is at my place."

"Yes. So does everybody in Saigon."

"Anyway, the doorbell rang and I answered it. There stood these four goons."

"Vietnamese?"

"Yeah."

"Did you know them?"

"I never saw them before. But that doesn't mean anything at my place."

"I know. What then?"

"I thought they were there for the party. So I invited them in and offered them a drink. Then this one little guy pulls a gun on me."

"Then what?"

"Then the bastard with the gun said they want me to go with them. I said where to. He said never mind. Then one of the other men tied a blindfold around my head and they took me out of the place and put me in a car and we drove off."

"Where?"

"Who knows? I didn't think I should ask."

"Was it the place where I saw you last night?"

"It had to be. We didn't stop any place."

"Where is that place?"

"Who knows? All I could tell was that it must have been way out in the country. They didn't have a john."

"How'd you find that out?"

"Because I needed one. I told them. I told them let me go to the john. So some bastard with a gun took me out in the backyard. That's when I heard the generator."

"A generator?"

"Yeah. That's how I figured I was out in the boonie's. They make their own electricity. And they've got a radio transmitter."

"How do you know that?"

"I was at that place three days, remember? I had to go outside more than once. Once it was during the daytime. That's when I saw the antenna. Didn't you notice it?"

"How could I? I was blindfolded."

"Well, they got one, believe me."

"When did they tell you what they wanted?"

"The first night. I wasn't surprised that it was heroin. They're pouring the stuff into Saigon already. Half the G.I.'s here are hooked. A lot of the kids push it."

"What a way to win a war."

"What can you do? The stuff is everywhere. It's big business, the biggest business in the world. And they don't screw around."

"How did you find out about the dead bodies? Did they tell you?"

"No. I heard about it in town."

"How the hell do you pull it off?"

"They must have connections. Figure it out. Some of the kids get killed in the bush. Some of them die in hospitals. At some point, the military has to turn the bodies over to some outfit that puts the bodies into boxes. Somewhere along the line, somebody is doing some surgery."

"That's sickening."

"Sure."

"How do they get the shit back?"

"Somebody must be tipping them off. Like you're going to be tipping them off, which plane has the stuff aboard when they land at Oakland. It's up to them to get the stuff out of the dead before the bodies get shipped home."

"Now that I've got you back, I'm not going to go through with this."

"Oh, no? How long do you think it will take them to kill you? You know too much. So do I. So how are we going to work this?"

Ron told Shad about the unused electric ovens on the Transcon tinental giants.

"You think that's safe?" Shad asked.

"It's the only way I can think of."

"How are you gonna get it on board? Everything is checked out, isn't it?"

"Yes. But I'm the one who does the checking."

"Okay."

"Now, about once a week I send a pouch to Morley Covington. The last thing I do after I check out the plane is give that pouch to the co-pilot."

"Okay."

"The plane makes a stopover at Guam for a couple of hours. It makes a stop at Hawaii for a couple of hours. The co-pilot calls Morley and gives him an E.T.A. at Oakland. Then Morley sends a messenger from the bank over to Oakland to pick up the pouch from the co-pilot when the plane gets in."

"Okay."

"Now, if we go ahead with this deal, I'll take two pouches aboard the plane when I give it the final check. One pouch I'll give to the co-pilot; the other one I'll slip into the oven. I've got a pretty good idea of the E.T.A. at Oakland. I tell the goons. They take it from there."

"Suppose something goes wrong?"

"Like what?"

"Bad weather. Mechanical snafus. Change of flight plan."

"Look, if those bastards can figure out how to get the stuff out of a dead body, they can figure out how to get it off a plane."

"Okay, Mr. President."

"All right. Now I want to ask you something, and don't bullshit me."

"Shoot."

"Are you on heroin or have you got more sense?"

"I've got more sense. Oh, I smoke pot once in a while. But it doesn't do anything for me, so I don't use it much. Besides, it makes the scotch taste bad." He took a sip of his.

"How long have you known about the action in town—the G.I.'s, dead or alive?"

"Oh, I heard about that right after we got here. People talk. You hang around. You listen. You learn."

"How come you've never mentioned it to me before?"

"Oh, I hear a lot of things I don't mention to you."

"Like what?"

"Like there are some people in Saigon who think you are a

queer."

"How come?"

"Because there is not a broad in town who can brag that she has slept with you."

"What do you say when you hear that?"

"I tell them I don't know you well enough."

"You're a real pal, Shad. You know that?"

Chapter Sixteen

Two days later, when Ron unlocked the door of his shack at the airfield, he saw an envelope on the floor. It was addressed to him. Inside was a piece of a map that had been torn out of a larger map. On the back was written: "Tuesday, 12.0700." He put the paper into his pocket.

A few minutes later, Shad came in for the day's assignments for his pilots. Ron said, "Look at this."

Shad looked at the piece of paper. "What is it?"

"What does it look like?"

"Like a piece of a map."

"Yes. But where is it on the map?"

"I can't tell." Shad said. "I'll check it out."

They went to the wall map Ron had in the office. Starting Saigon, they moved the piece of paper in tight semicircles on the map, looking for similarities. They had moved it several inches, when Shad stopped.

"Here it is," Shad said. "Let's see. Yes. Here's the mountain. Look, the river. And there's the village."

Ron asked, "Do you know the place?"

"No. We've never sent anybody there. It's further west than we go."

"How far?"

"Oh, fifty, sixty miles, I'd say."

"It's from *them*."

"The pick-up."

"Yeah." Shad glanced at the back of the paper again. "When's the twelfth?"

"Next Tuesday."

"Seven o'clock in the morning."

"Right."

"We could get into a lot of trouble."

"Can you think of another option?"

"Yeah. Leave the country."

It had rained most of the night. The clouds were just lifting as the two helicopters approached the rendezvous. Ron and Shad had kept radio silence on the short flight. Shad wobbled his copter when he recognized the meeting place. Shad went down first. There was just enough space for Ron to land nearby. As they got out of their copters, several Vietnamese men came out of the surrounding woods, all of them armed. Ron recognized the man who had come to his house. The man was carrying a package wrapped in brown paper and tied with a string. He went directly to Ron and handed him the package.

Ron asked. "How do I let you know when it reaches Oakland?"

The man said, "Tell your cook."

Son of a bitch. Everybody was in on it. Ron asked, "How do you let us know that it is delivered?"

"Your cook will tell you."

"Okay. That's the helicopter you keep for now," Ron said, nodding at it. "Let's go, Shad."

The Vietnamese said, "He stays."

Ron said, "What?"

"He stays until you come back."

"Like hell he stays," Ron said. "That's not one of the conditions."

"Is new condition."

"Okay," Ron said, and he tossed the package at the man.

The package fell to the ground and the watching Vietnamese gasped, as though a sacrilege had been committed. Ron watched uncertainty come over the man's face.

The man said, "All right. He goes. No delivery, you die." He muttered in Vietnamese to one of his accomplices, who picked up the package and handed it to Ron. Ron and Shad got into Ron's helicopter and took off.

Aloft, Shad said, "You've got balls, Mr. President."

"Tell your lady friends in Saigon."

At the end of the week, as Ron was preparing a pouch of paperwork for Morley Covington, he took a second pouch and inserted the brown package. Later that morning, as he was finishing the final check on a departing Transcontinental giant, he stopped at the coffee urn and poured himself a cup. When he was sure nobody was watching, he slipped the second pouch into the unused oven. Then he went forward and gave the Covington pouch to the co-pilot.

Ron asked, "When do you get in? My people want to know."

The co-pilot said, "Sunday morning. Around noon."

"Do you go on from Oakland?"

"No. We turn around Monday night."

Back home, Ron wrote a note: "Sunday, 17th. Noon. TC638J Pouch in oven." He put the note in an envelope, sealed it, and took it out to the kitchen. He said to his cook: "You know a Vietnamese man who knows me?"

The woman looked away. "Yes, sir."

"Give him this," Ron said, and he gave her the envelope.

"Yes, sir."

Ron went back to his office.

Because of the time difference and the International Dateline, Ron had to figure out when, if everything went well, the package would arrive in Oakland in terms of Vietnam time. He estimated that Sunday noon in Oakland would be sometime Monday midday in Vietnam. Yet he had no idea how long it would take for Oakland to tell Vietnam that the delivery had been made safely.

Early on Monday morning, Ron was staring at the ceiling in his darkened bedroom. He got up, shaved, and spent an hour at his desk. It was still dark when he drove to the shack at the airfield. When he opened the door, he hoped there would be a message on the floor, or some indication of how things were going. Nothing.

Shad and two other pilots arrived around seven. Shad came into the shack. "Anything?"

"No. Too soon, I guess."

"I'm scared stiff."

"So am I."

"What's on the books for today?"

"Five trips. How many men have you got out there?"

"Two. Pete Lavel had to stop at the motor pool for some gas. He should be here in a few minutes."

"I'll take one of the trips myself."

"Do you think you should? You ought to hang around here, just in case."

"I'd go crazy. Let's load up."

Ron checked the cargoes as the five helicopters were loaded. He gave each pilot a map showing his destination; the pilots began to lift off. Before Ron could take off, a Transcontinental giant arrived, which meant a two-hour delay while the plane was unloaded, the cargo checked, and stored in the warehouse.

Aloft, Ron felt as though he had escaped from a prison. Just getting away for a few hours, and having something else to think about, gave him a sense of freedom. There were moments on the flight that he forgot that he had a care in the world. His destination was a small Vietnamese field hospital and a couple of American doctors. His cargo: medical supplies, food, fresh water, ammo, mail. Returning, he carried two wounded American observers, a list of items for the next delivery, mail.

It was early afternoon when Ron got back to the Saigon airfield. Hungry, he went directly to the officers' mess to eat. Later, approaching his shack, he was surprised to see the Vietnamese couple waiting for him.

He looked at the woman. "Yes?"

"You go early today."

"Yes."

"The man you know—he come to our house very early."

"My house?"

She shook her head. "Our house."

"What did he want?"

"He say tell you: tomorrow: same time: same place."

"All right. Thank you."

"You come to dinner?"

"Yes. And Mr. Grady, too. Be sure there's scotch."

"Yes, sir."

Ron kept glancing at his wristwatch, then at the sky, then his watch, eager for Shad's return. Shad was late; and with the slow passing of time Ron grew more and more worried. The other pilots returned. Only one of them had been shot at. Since Shad had gone into the same area, Ron's concern deepened. He couldn't sit at his desk. He stood outside the shack and kept watching the sky.

Then, around four, he heard the chopper before he could see it. Suddenly, there it was, coming in low and fast. Ron went to the ramp in front of the hangar and waited. Shad got out of his copter with a grin and a wave.

Ron said, "You bastard, where the hell have you been?"

"I stayed for lunch."

"Don't do that again, dammit. You had me worried. Joe Reilly got shot at."

"So did I. That's why I had to take the long way home."

"Did you get hit?"

"They broke a window."

"Have your guys fix it. C'mon. You're going home with me."

"I can't. I've got a date tonight."

"You've got a date tomorrow morning, too. Same time. Same place."

"Our buddies?"

"Who else?"

"How'd you get the word?"

"My cook. They went to her house early this morning. She was waiting for me here when I got back."

"Can you trust that woman?"

"I don't know. Just let's be careful what we talk about around the house."

"All right. I wonder if the stuff got through?"

"How could they know so fast?"

"That fucken radio they got. Listen, Mr. President, these guys play rough, and they don't fool around with any penny-ante shit. Whoever's running this show probably already knows which hand you wipe your ass with."

"I don't use my hand. Let's go home. We've got an early day tomorrow."

"My date will kill me for standing her up tonight."

"Call her up and tell her you'll screw her tomorrow night."

"If I'm still alive."

They could see below them the helicopter they had left behind. As soon as they touched ground, the several Vietnamese again came out of the woods, again armed. Among them was the man who had come to Ron's house. This time, he was not armed. He carried two packages, one in each hand, both wrapped in brown paper and tied with string. As he approached Ron, there was less of a threat about him. He seemed almost to be smiling. He held out one of the packages to Ron.

"This is the money," he said. "And this is the next shipment."

Ron pointed to the shipment. "Is the money for that with the money in there? That was our condition."

"The money is there."

"Then the first shipment got through?"

"You are still alive," the man pointed out.

Ron accepted the two packages. "I do the same thing? I tell the cook?"

"Yes. And I will tell the cook when you come back."

"When will that be?"

"I will tell the cook."

Ron looked at Shad. "Rev up that chopper and see if it works."

Shad climbed into the second copter. In moments, the huge overhead blades began to rotate, creating a wind that bent the trees and made the Vietnamese move back. He lifted the craft slightly into the air. He gave Ron the okay sign.

Ron said to the Vietnamese: "I will tell the cook." He got into his helicopter and ascended, Shad joining him on the rise. They were back at the Saigon airfield just as the R.O.K. pilots were arriving for their assignments.

Shad went with Ron into the shack. Ron put the two packages on his desk. Shad asked, "Gonna count the money?"

"I don't even want to look at it," Ron said.

"What are you going to do with it?"

"Send it to Morley."

"How are you going to explain it?"

"I'm not. He's our banker. All he has to do is bank it."

"Won't he think it's a little funny?"

"Let him."

"You're getting mean in your old age, aren't you?"

"I'm learning. Somebody wants to fuck me, I fuck him first. I can play rough, too."

"Yes, Mr. President. But what are you going to do with all that money?"

"I'll think of something."

"I'm sure you will. Include me in."

"Fifty-fifty, ole buddy."

"Thanks. And when these goons get enough of us, they can bury us side by side."

"Right. Now, why don't you head into town and fuck your head off for the rest of the day?"

"You got no jobs for me today?"

"So far, we've got only three trips. The other guys can make them. Anyway, you've earned your day's pay."

"Yeah. A quarter of a million. Jesus H. Christ."

"Don't spend it yet."

"I still think we ought to skip this fucken country."

"At these prices? Let's fuck these bastards good. Scram now. The President has work to do."

Later that week, as Ron was preparing a pouch for Morley Covington, he added this note:

Dear Morley:

In this pouch you will find some cash. It has nothing to do with our government contract. Don't mention it to anybody—not to Dave, not to my family, not to the people in L.A. Don't even mention it to me. Just open an account of some kind in my name and Shad's. If something happens to either of us, the money goes to the survivor. If something happens to both of us—well, buy yourself a cigar.

Ron

So it began.

And so it went on, week after week until it became so routine that it also became monotonous. At least once a week, Ron or Shad would fly to a rendezvous to pick up the shipment and the payment. At least once a week, Ron put the cash into the pouch for Morley and the shipment in a pouch in the oven of a departing Transcontinental giant. Then he would give the E.T.A. to his cook. Every few days she would tell him when and where again. Every several weeks, the rendezvous was changed, the change indicated as before, by a piece of a map Ron found on the floor of the shack when he arrived some morning.

This went on for over a year, a year which saw the steady increase of American troops and American materiel in Vietnam. More and more, the military took over the delivery of supplies and men to the pockets of fighting within the country, the R.O.K. flights becoming fewer and fewer.

One day Ron said to Shad, "Do you think you can run this show on your own for a few days?"

"Sure," Shad said. "What's up?"

"I think I'll make a quick trip home."

"Anything wrong?"

"No. But it looks to me like our job here is winding down. I want to check out a few things about what we do next."

"Okay. When do you want to go?"

"I think I'll fly back with the next shipment."

"Okay. And when do I see you again?"

"A couple of days."

"Going to see the folks?"

"If there's time."

"Why the rush? Things are getting pretty quiet around here."

"I know that. I just don't want to wait until they get too quiet."

"How will I know if a shipment comes up?"

"Check my house. The cook will know."

"Roger."

"Yeah. Roger."

A few days later, the Morley pouch and the shipment pouch ready, Ron notified the military to add his name to the passenger list on the next Transcontinental flight to Oakland. When the flight arrived, Ron helped Shad check the unloading of cargo and passengers, then check the loading of both. When the flight was ready, Ron and Shad shook hands, and Ron went aboard. He went through his usual routine. A paper cup of coffee. Pouch into the oven. Forward to the flight deck. Pouch to co-pilot. As the plane

taxied out for take-off, Ron took a seat where he could see the galley. There was a two-hour stopover at Guam, mostly for refueling
and fresh coffee and mail. There was a three-hour stopover at
Hawaii for the same. Then Oakland. Ron did not sleep at all on the
long flight. He kept an eye on everybody who went near the galley.
At Oakland, he stayed in his seat as everybody else got off.

The crew came out of the flight deck. The co-pilot saw Ron and
said, "This is as far as we go, sir."

"I know," Ron said. "I'm just waiting for the others to clear Customs." He got up and followed the crew off the plane. He said, "I
have to make some calls. Is there a phone around here?"

"In the office. I'll show you."

Ron was the last person off the plane. He walked with the co-
pilot to the hangar office, big windows overlooking the ramp. The
co-pilot pointed to the phone. Ron watched as the man handed the
Morley pouch to a messenger from the bank. Ron went to the wall
phone and took the receiver off the hook, but he kept watching
the giant on which he had arrived.

And then it happened. He saw the small plane arrive and taxi
close to the giant. A door was lowered on the smaller plane. A man
came down the few steps and hurried over to the giant. He went
aboard. In seconds, he was back in sight, moving quickly to the
smaller plane. Ron made a mental note of the identifying numbers
on the plane's tail. The door of the plane was pulled up. The plane
moved off. Ron watched until it had gone too far down the runway for him to see it any more.

Ron replaced the phone and looked around. "Where can I get a
cab?" A clerk told him cabs were usually waiting at the main gate.
He found one and told the driver to take him to the St. Francis
Hotel in San Francisco.

At the hotel, the desk clerk told him, "I'm sorry, sir, but we're
pretty booked up. All I have is a two-bedroom suite."

"I'll take it."

"All right, sir. For how long?"

"Two nights."

"Very well." The clerk slid the registration card to him. "Will
you fill this out please? I'll have a bellhop get your luggage."

"No luggage," Ron said. "Just this." He held up his canvas weekend bag. He picked up the pen and wrote Ronald. Then he caught
himself. He wrote Avakian, his mother's maiden name. For an address, he wrote 1600 Pennsylvania Avenue, Washington, D.C.

He went up to the suite by himself. In the living room he found
the telephone book and looked up an address and wrote it on the

hotel's pad next to the phone. So that he would remember what the address was for, he added "F.B.I." Then he called Morley Covington.

Covington was surprised. "Ron? Ron, where are you?"

"At the St. Francis."

"Here in San Francisco?"

"Yes."

"Well, for Christ's sake, what a surprise. When did you get in?"

"A few minutes ago."

"What brings you back to civilization?"

"I thought I'd better have a talk with you about my next move."

"You're going to make a move?"

"Soon, I figure. Things are slowing down over there."

"I noticed."

"Yes. The military choppers are taking over our job."

"Well, you knew something like that would happen when the war hotted up. How long are you going to be around?"

"Just a couple of days. I made the trip just to see you and maybe Dave French. Then I'd better get back."

"You're not going up to the farm?"

"I don't think so. Anyway, I'll be back for good soon enough. When can I see you, Morley?"

"Come right over."

Covington was waiting at the door of his office as Ron came down the hall. "What a surprise," Morley said. "Why don't you let people know?"

"It was a last-minute decision," Ron said. They went over to the island of leather furniture and sat opposite each other.

Covington asked, "Want some coffee?"

Ron was about to say no when the secretary to the secretary came in with coffee. He waited until she was gone, then he said, "I wonder if you can check something out for me?"

"What's that?"

"When we landed at Oakland, I noticed a private plane at the ramp at Transcontinental's hangar. I'd like to find out who owns it. Have you got any way of doing that?"

"I can ask. What's up?"

"Nothing special. I liked the plane, and now that Shad and I will be coming home soon, I may want to buy something like that if I can afford it."

"I'm sure you can."

"Maybe I can buy this one from the owner and get it a little cheaper. You know us Armenians, always trying to save a buck. I got the number of the plane. It must be registered somewhere. Let me write it down before I forget it." On the coffee table were pencils and pads of paper. Ron jotted down the plane's identification number and handed it to Morley. "If you can…"

"If I can," Morley said. "Now, you said something about your next move."

"Yes. Where do we go from here?"

"Where would you like to go? Got any ideas?"

"No. I've been out of touch for a while. What financial shape are we in?"

"Very good, Ron. Very good indeed. Your share of the earnings from the government contract have just about paid off your loan to the bank. And that special account I'm not supposed to mention— well, Ron, you're a wealthy man. A very wealthy man."

"Enough to move around?"

"Any direction you want to go. Of course, your credit rating here is tops. I'm sure the bank would back you up no matter how much you want."

Ron nodded at that. He said, "It makes sense that we ought to stay in the business we're in now."

"Air cargo?"

"Yes. Have you heard any talk about how that's doing?"

"No. But I can find out. I have heard that the postal service is thinking about starting something like air express. I can check it out."

"Okay. And anything else that looks interesting."

"Are you going to be around for a while?"

"A few days."

"How about having lunch with me? I want to hear all about Vietnam."

While they were having lunch, Covington asked, "How long do you think you and Shad will stay on in Vietnam?"

"It's hard to say. Not more than a few months, I guess. I'm thinking of letting some of my pilots go. There's not enough work any more. Why?"

"Well, Transcontinental is involved in this, you know. They ought to be informed so they can make their own plans. Maybe they'd want to take over your part of the operation."

"Maybe so. Do you think they'd be willing to buy the equipment we've got over there?"

"They might. Or they might get somebody else to take over that end of it."

"Could be. But you'd better warn them that the gravy train is getting slower and slower."

"I'm sure they know that. They get copies of everything. Even so, they may want to take over the whole deal themselves. That was their original idea, remember?"

"Well, okay. Let me talk to Shad about it. I'm sure he's ready to get out, too. By now, he's screwed all the broads in Saigon, and from what I hear the place is running low on booze. Why don't we leave it at that for now?"

"You're the president."

"Will it be complicated?"

"What?"

"Phasing out of Vietnam?"

"I don't know. That's Dave French's department. I suppose with you out of the picture, the government contracts have to be changed somehow. You'd better talk to Dave about that."

"Do you think I could see him today, just in case the thing does turn out to be complicated?"

"Dave's in New York. He gets back tonight."

"Tomorrow maybe?"

"I'll try to line it up. I'm surprised you're not going to see the family. You've been away a long time."

"I know," Ron said, "and by now they're used to it. I'd only be home for a day or so, anyway, so it's better to postpone family reunions until I know I won't be rushing off again before they get used to having me around."

"Whatever you say. What are you going to do tonight?"

"I'm going to loaf," Ron said. "I'm going to stuff myself with good American food, I'm going to get a good night's sleep on a good American bed, and I don't want to hear a fucken word of Vietnamese."

Covington said, "I'm surprised you didn't say you want some good American pussy."

"I can get that in Vietnam," Ron said, knowing full well that he had not even tried to get any pussy at all.

For the rest of the day Ron loafed, as he said he would. Next morning he slept late, and he would have slept later but the telephone woke him at ten.

It was Morley Covington, and he said, "Ron, when I got back to my office yesterday after lunch I decided to make a call to Transcontinental and maybe sound them out about their own plans in Vietnam."

"What did they say?"

"They said they wanted to hang around for a while. Well, hearing that, I dropped a little hint that maybe you wanted to get out."

"What did they say to that?"

"Just what I figured. They asked if you'd be willing to sell out your operation to them. In fact, Dave French just called me. The Transcontinental lawyers have been on the phone to him already this morning. Ron, I think we'd better have a meeting with Dave before you head back to Vietnam."

"Okay. When?"

"Dave said any time."

"Okay. I just woke up. How about in an hour?"

"All right. Pick me up here first. I'll let you know."

An hour later, descending in the bank's executive elevator with Morley Covington, Ron asked, "Have you had a chance to check out that plane I told you about yesterday?"

"I've put my secretary on it. I mentioned it to Dave, too. He'll be talking to Bert Bernstein about it and have Bert find out what he can in Washington. But, dammit, Ron, with all this going on, what the hell's so important about some fucken airplane?"

"Maybe someday I'll tell you."

In Dave French's office, they got right down to business. French said, "It's definite that Transcontinental wants to take over your operation in Vietnam. But they have a problem."

Ron asked, "What is it?"

"Not expecting the R.O.K. offer, Transcontinental was in advanced negotiation to buy a small air cargo airline operating in Orange County, serving smaller cities in the Southwest where the Transcontinental jumbos could not land. The company—FreytFlite—had been owned by one man. He died. His heirs were anxious to get rid of a company whose business they knew nothing about. Transcontinental was ready to buy FreytFlite because its equipment would give Transcontinental access to grassroots cities not only in the Southwest but all over the country, FreytFlite would become a feeder line. In fact, the deal was just about to be closed. But out of nowhere comes the R.O.K. offer, which Transcontinental wants. The problem was that Transcontinental did not have enough cash on hand to go along with R.O.K. and FreytFlite at the same time, and there was no way they could go ahead with R.O.K. without getting out of the FreytFlite deal, facing a lot of lawsuits for welshing at the last moment.

Ron took all of this in, thought about it, then asked, "So what do we do?"

Morley leaned at Ron across the table. "You buy FreytFlite. You said yesterday that you wanted to stay in the air cargo business anyway. Here you are. A going concern, in good shape and ripe for expansion."

Ron asked, "Can we afford it?"

Covington took some papers out of his attache case and passed them to Ron and French. He said, "This is your financial statement as of yesterday. As you can see, you've been making a very healthy profit on the Vietnam project. You can also see that you've taken a big bite out of your bank loan. You're in excellent shape. Now, Transcontinental pays you for your equipment in Vietnam, and we'll try to get a bit more for your good will. You use that money to buy FreytFlite. If you need more, just come to the bank."

Ron asked, "The bank will give us another loan on top of what we already owe?"

Morley sent Ron an impatient look, and, jabbing his thumb against his chest, slowly and deliberately said, "You are talking to the bank." He relaxed, but added pointedly, "Besides, you have your own financial resources, don't you?"

French held up his hands helplessly. "That's for you to decide."

Ron said, "I can only make decisions on the basis of the advice I get from you two." He turned to Covington. "Is it a good deal?"

"It is," Covington said.

"Okay," Ron said. "We go. What else has to be done?"

French said, "There'll be some red tape in Washington. I've already talked to my son-in-law. He's waiting for the word from you."

"He's got it," Ron said. "What does he have to do?"

French said, "He'll have to go over to the Pentagon and have your government contract renegotiated, turning everything over to Transcontinental."

"Okay."

"And Morley says he's heard that the post office is going into the express-mail business. Private companies seem to be walking away with it all. My son-in-law thinks the post office will go ahead on this. There'll be contracts and sub-contracts on that."

"Tell him to go ahead."

French said, "Yes, let's tell him." He looked at his secretary. "Get Mr. Bernstein on the line, will you? Make it conference."

The woman went to the phone on French's desk and put through the call. In a few moments she said, "Mr. French, I've got Mr. Bernstein on the line. Gentlemen, the other phones are tied in." She pointed to a telephone on the coffee table and one at the far end of the conference table. Morley moved down to the one on the conference table; Ron went across the room to the island of leather furniture.

They all said their good-mornings. Then Dave French: "Bert, we've talked it over and Ron wants to go ahead."

"Okay. The whole shebang?"

"Yes. So you send somebody over to the Pentagon and clear that up."

"Will do. What about the post office?"

"That, too."

"I'll need some facts and figures on that."

Morley said, "Bert, just break ice over there. We can fill in the blanks when we know what they want."

"Okay. I'll get the ball rolling and get back to you when I can."

Ron said, "Hold it, Bert. Were you able to find out anything about that airplane?"

Bert said, "Not much. All I know is that the plane is registered in Florida. It's owned by some real estate company in Palm Beach. A friend of mine in Miami drove up there, but he said the door was locked, and the neighbors say nobody is around there much. I'm sorry, Ron. That's all I can find out. Is it any help?"

"Not right now," Ron said. "Maybe some day. I'll let you know."

He added to himself: If I live so long.

Chapter Seventeen

Next morning, after breakfast, Ron called the Transcontinental hangar at Oakland, identified himself, and had his name put on the passenger list for the next flight to Vietnam. The flight was at eleven that morning. He called Morley Covington and Dave French, to say goodbye, but they were both in conference. He took a cab to Oakland.

He was standing at the large window of the hangar office as the giant slowly taxied up, its cargo already stored at the far end of the field. A few minutes before eleven, the passengers were told to board, just five of them. Ron did not keep an eye on the galley. He dozed now and then on the flight westward. He stretched his legs at Hawaii. He stretched his legs at Guam. As the plane pulled up near the warehouses at Saigon, Ron saw Shad Grady standing there, waiting, clipboard in hand, looking very officious. The plane stopped, the door was opened, the flight of stairs pushed into place. Shad came aboard and went first to the flight deck to get the bills of lading and passenger list.

Then Shad came into the passenger section and, looking at his clipboard, said, "All right, gentlemen. If you will show me your travel orders, I'll check you off my list and you can deplane." He looked up and saw Ron. He said, "Shit. What are you doing back so soon?"

Ron said, "I missed you."

Shad said, "Shit. I was just beginning to enjoy this new sense of power. Get off."

Ron laughed and got off the plane, waiting at the bottom of the steps as Shad checked off the other passengers, then inspected the rear cargo against the bills of lading. Ron stood aside as the cargo was unloaded and Shad had ground crews truck it to the warehouses.

Finished, Shad stepped to Ron and asked, "What's the good word from home?"

"It's very good. I've got a lot to talk to you about."

"Make it short. I've got a heavy date."

"Has she got a friend?"

Shad gave Ron a slow look, waiting for the punchline. "You kidding?"

"No. The trip was frantic. I'm on a high. I need some relaxation."

"I'll be damned. Sure she's got a friend. I'd pay to watch this."

"Maybe you'd better. I may need some coaching."

"Naw. It comes natural. I was doing it before I was old enough to know what the hell it was."

Finished for the day, Shad locked the shack door and gave Ron the key. They went to Shad's car and drove out of the airfield. Shad asked, "You want to stop at your place?"

"No. I don't want the cook to know I'm back yet. Her friends will find out soon enough."

"That reminds me. There's a pick-up tomorrow. I'll make it."

"The cook?"

"Yeah. I've been stopping off every day, like you said. What's the big news?"

"How'd you like to go home?"

"The States?"

"Yes."

"I'd love to. I'm getting tired of these Oriental pussies. They always smell of rice. We're going home?"

"Yes. Transcontinental is taking over the government contract."

"When's this?"

"A few weeks. A couple months."

"What happens to our outfit?"

"Transcontinental is buying the equipment. They want the guys to stay. Do you think they will?"

"Probably. The pay is good. Not me, though."

"Me neither."

"So what happens to us?"

"We're buying an airline. Cargo."

"Where?"

"Out of L.A."

"Great. We got the money?"

"I saw our financial statement. The bank loves us. Shad, you're a rich man."

"How'd I do that?"

"You've got a date to make some more tomorrow morning."

Shad nodded, understanding. "I'll be glad to get rid of that shit, too. I haven't felt safe since we got into that crap."

"You'll be safe as soon as we get out of this country. Just don't tell anybody that we're going. Not a word to anybody."

"Yes, Mr. President."

"Right, Mr. Veep Bullshit."

"Goddam you, you fucken Armenian. Sometimes I wish you had a pussy."

"You can get all of that you want when you get back to San Francisco. The town is full of it. Even Armenians, I'm sure."

When he looked back on it much later, Ron was amused by his clumsiness, his ineptitude, his terror at the moment. She was so young, so small, so pretty in the way Vietnamese women had when they were young and so quickly lost because they were so quickly old. He didn't know if the lights should be on or off. In his uncertainty, he turned them off. He stepped away from the bed and undressed. He moved to the bed, tentatively, bashful and afraid. He could see her silhouette, naked, waiting for him. He stretched out beside her. She moved into his arms, her mouth searching for his. Kisses. Kisses. Her tongue entered his mouth, and he jerked back, surprised and puzzled. She straddled him on hands and knees. She licked his eyebrows, his eyelashes, his upper lip, his neck, his shoulders. She munched on his nipples. He felt himself harden, and was embarrassed as the tip of him brushed against her body. Her tongue found her navel, his groin. She lifted a ball into her mouth. His body flinched in a new pain. He lifted her head away. She returned, licking the thick vein, up and down, up and down. Then she rose slightly and zeroed in, her lips, her tongue, her suction devouring him. A familiar dawn he had learned from his hand began to rise in him. Not yet. He put his hands on her shoulders to stop her. He drew her up, guiding her beside him, taking her into his arms, his hips held away. He did what she had done to him, his tongue on her face, her neck, her shoulders, her tits, small and sudden, like new plums, her belly, lower. Rice. The familiar dawn began to rise again. He knelt over her and aimed, striking her belly. She took hold of him and guided him, and threw her hips up at him. His strength died. He collapsed on her, ramming himself full into her. She gave a moan and threw her arms around his neck and her legs around his and she squirmed and wiggled under him. Her tightness, her hotness, her velvety moistness numbed him. The electric fire in his toes shot through him and exploded in his eyes. It was over for him. When he did not move, she pressed against his shoulders, lifting him, and she moved from under him. He fell prone on the bed, his face buried in the pillow.

It was the bleakest moment in his life. Every pore of him ached. He felt humiliated and disgraced and junked. He wished she would leave so that he could cry. When he did not move for a long time, he heard her get up and gather her clothes and leave the room. But he could not cry. He could not think. He was a void.

At five in the morning, Shad came into the room, clicked on the overhead light and proclaimed, "Come on, Mr. President, we have to get to work early." He waited. "Ron?"

Ron was still prone on the bed, his face still buried in the pillow.

Shad said, "Hey, Ron."

Ron rolled over and stared at the ceiling.

Shad said, "Jesus, kid, you look fucked out."

Ron said, "I'm not fucked out. I'm fucked up. It was a mess."

"Don't worry about it. It'll get better. You just need some practice."

"Then get it for me."

"You'll get it."

He got it.

About three months after that night, Ron went aboard another Transcontinental giant for another check-out. The co-pilot handed him the packet of documents, then said, "I was told to give you this letter."

It was on Transcontinental stationery, and it said:

> *On Thursday, the fourteenth of this month, Mr. Alex Miller, of our staff, will arrive at Saigon to succeed you as the supervisor of our project there. Mr. Miller is well acquainted with this type of work, having performed it for us excellently in other parts of the world.*
>
> *We will appreciate it if you will assist Mr. Miller for a few days to familiarize him with your procedures and help him find a place to live. We are grateful for your cooperation in the past, and we are pleased that so many of your men have agreed to stay on the job.*
>
> *We wish you and your company good luck on your future ventures.*

Ron stuffed the letter into a pocket and checked out the plane. When Shad returned from another military delivery, Ron showed him the letter.

Shad said, "We go home?"

"Yes. Shad, I want you to take over my job for a couple of days. I have to write up a report."

"Okay."

"And don't tell anybody about this letter."

At home that night, after the Vietnamese couple had left, Ron locked himself in his office and settled down at a typewriter. He was a two-finger typist; his progress was slow and he made many mistakes. Annoyed, he tore up the pages he had typed and burned them in an ash tray. Then he got a yellow pad of notepaper and wrote the report in longhand. It took him all night.

Around seven in the morning, the cook knocked on the door. "You want breakfast, sir?"

"Just bring me a cup of coffee," Ron said.

A few minutes later, the cook knocked again. Ron unlocked the door and opened it slightly. He took the cup. He said, "Listen, I have a lot of paperwork to do today and I don't want to be disturbed. You and your husband can have the day off."

"Yes, sir. Your lunch, sir?"

"I'll fix lunch myself, and I'll have dinner out."

"Nothing wrong, sir?"

"No. I just don't want to be disturbed."

He shut the door and locked it and went back to his desk, sipping the coffee as he edited his handwritten report. He heard the Vietnamese couple leave on their bicycles.

Then he went to the typewriter and began to copy the report, slowly and carefully, making some minor changes as he went along. He skipped lunch.

Around five, he called the shack at the airfield. When Shad answered, Ron asked, "Are you just about finished out there?"

"Just about. I'm waiting for Reilly to get back."

"When he gets back call me. I want you to pick me up. We'll have dinner in town."

"Oh? Want me to make some calls, you ole muffdiver you?"

"No. Not tonight. Call me."

Ron read over his report. Then he got a plain, business-size envelope, put it in the typewriter, took out his wallet and found the piece of hotel notepaper he had been carrying around for a long time. He addressed the envelope, folded up the several pages of his report, inserted them into the envelope and sealed it. He left his office, the envelope in hand.

Relieved and exhausted, yet strangely exhilarated, his first thought was for what was usually the last thought on his mind. A drink. He went to the liquor cabinet and poured himself an inch of scotch. Envelope in hand, he went into the kitchen, added two inches of Coke to the glass, and added some ice. It wasn't so bad this way. Sipping it, he looked around the kitchen as though he was seeing it for the first time, knowing that soon he would be seeing it for the last time. Envelope in hand, he went up to his room and undressed. Envelope in hand, he went into the bathroom, took a bath, shaved, and then, envelope in hand, he went back to his room and dressed, putting on a suit. He slipped the envelope into his breast pocket. Downstairs, he was heading for the liquor cabinet again when the phone rang.

Shad said, "I'm leaving now."

"Reilly okay?"

"Fine. He had trouble finding the place."

"I'll meet you out front."

Shad was at the door in ten minutes. Ron got in the front seat with him. Shad asked, "How come we're dolled up?"

"We're celebrating tonight. You get dolled up, too."

"What are we celebrating?"

"You're going home tomorrow."

"Tomorrow?"

"Yes. Aren't you glad?"

"Sure. What's up?"

"I'll tell you on the way back to my place. This car isn't bugged, is it?"

"I hope not."

"So do I. Have you got a lot of luggage or anything?"

"No. I got here with one suitcase and I'm going home with one suitcase."

"Good. Let's go to your place and dress you up and then let's go someplace elegant for dinner and then we'll go back to your place and you can pack."

"Why the big show?"

"I want us to look like the situation is perfectly normal, like we're just having a night on the town. One thing."

"Yeah?"

"Until we're alone again, don't say a word about going home. If we run into any of your friends, don't mention it. We're just having a night on the town."

"You're being very mysterious. Everybody knows Transcontinental is taking over and we'll be leaving. So what's the act?"

"I'll tell you later."

So they went to Shad's place and he changed clothes. They drove to an elegant restaurant in what remained of the French community. During the long meal a few of Shad's friends came to the table and joked with him. He accepted invitations for later in the week. One of them, Ron accepted. Finished, Ron paid the bill and left a good tip. Farewell.

They returned to Shad's apartment and he packed. Ron said, "Put in a set of work clothes."

"What for?"

"I'll tell you later."

Shad packed the work clothes.

When they were ready, Ron said, "Can you get out of here with that suitcase without being noticed?"

Shad said, "At this hour, everybody in this building is either sleeping or fucking."

"Let's go then."

"What about my rent?"

"I'll pay that before I go. Come on."

Shad looked around. "I'm going to miss this place. There's been a lot of fucking in here."

"And not a cherry in the bunch," Ron said.

"Just yours."

"Bastard."

In the car, Shad said, "Okay. Let's have it."

Ron glanced around the car, hoping against a bug. He said, "I've spent the past couple of days writing a report on something that's going on around here. I've got it in my pocket. I'll give it to you tomorrow when we leave the house. Tonight, I'm sleeping on it."

"I dig," Shad said.

"Tomorrow morning when we leave for work, put on your work clothes and do your regular job when we get there. I don't want the guys to think there's anything different going on. No goodbyes."

"Okay."

"When you get to Oakland, don't go through the gate with the other pasengers. The civilians have to go through Customs. Go with the crew into the office. You're an employee. There won't be any problems. Just outside, you'll find cabs. Go into San Francisco and check into the St. Francis Hotel. Don't use your right name."

"What name will I use?"

"What's your wife's maiden name?"

"Saskovitch."

"A Pole?"

"Lithuanian. She was a great lay."

"So you're Herman Saskovitch. There can't be two people with a name like that."

"Herman Saskovitch."

"Right. The first thing I want you to do is get some stamps and go to a post office and mail the envelope. Don't let anybody see it."

"Okay."

"Then go back to the hotel and stay there. Don't contact anybody you know. Not Morley or Dave or my folks. Nobody. Stay in your room. Have your meals brought in. Pay for everything in cash. Watch the newspapers and keep up with the news on television. Don't leave your room until you hear from me."

"When will that be?"

"I don't know. Miller gets here Thursday. I'll have to work with him for a few days. And then I have to wait until the cook has some news for me."

"Oh?"

"Yes. I'll make the pick-up myself and I'll fly back with it."

"It's risky."

"I've done it before."

"How come you never told me?"

"I'm telling you now."

"Anything else?"

"That's it, Herman."

When they got to Ron's house, they went upstairs to the room Shad would use. Shad took off his suit and packed it in his suitcase. He laid out his work clothes for morning.

Ron said, "Let's pack my suit, too. I'm not taking anything with me." Ron stripped to his shorts and packed the suit.

Shad glanced at Ron's crotch. "So that's the thing that's driving all the women in Saigon crazy."

"Yeah. Like it?"

"You're not in San Francisco yet."

They went downstairs and drank scotch, Ron diluted his with Coke. The envelope was on his lap. When they went up to their rooms, that night, Ron kept the envelope under his pillow. They got up early and left the house before the Vietnamese couple arrived so that they would not see Shad's suitcase. At the shack, Ron hid Shad's suitcase under his desk, keeping the envelope on him. They had breakfast at the officers' mess. On their way back to the shack, Ron stopped at the military office in the terminal and had Shad's name put on the passenger list for the eleven o'clock Transcontinental flight. They went to work. The seven o'clock giant came on time, and Ron was busy over an hour supervising the unloading. The R.O.K.—now Transcontinental—pilots came in; Shad gave them their assignments.

He said, "Joe, when you get back from your first trip, take this one, too."

Joe Reily said "Aren't you going up?"

"No. I'm not feeling well today. Probably something I ate."

By nine o'clock, Ron was supervising the loading of the giant. Passengers began to arrive around ten. At ten thirty, Ron checked them against his list and told them to get aboard. There were seven, including Shad.

He said to Shad, "I think you'd better change into a suit. You'll be less noticeable. Everybody else is in civvies. Wait in the shack for me."

Shad went into the shack and put on a suit, shirt and tie. A few minutes before eleven, Ron came in and took a look at him.

Ron said, "I think you'll pass."

"Pass for what?"

Ron unbuttoned his shirt and extracted the envelope from inside. He handed it to Shad. "Put that inside your shirt."

As Shad unbuttoned his shirt, he glanced at the envelope. His eyes shot a question at Ron.

Ron said, "You didn't see that."

"I didn't see what?"

Ron said, "Now, listen. Don't fall asleep on the plane. Don't get off at Guam or Hawaii. Don't talk to anybody unless you have to. Okay?"

"Okay."

Ron extended his hand. "Good luck, Herman."

Shad took the hand. "Good luck to you. You're going to need it more than I will."

They boarded the plane together. Ron took a head count in his preoccupied way. He gave the papers to the co-pilot. Then he left the plane and stood nearby as the stairs were pulled away, the cabin door closed, and the plane moved away. He watched it as it taxied to the end of the runway and took off.

Suddenly he felt very lonely.

And very afraid.

For the next few days, Ron added another chore to his job and Shad's. He went through his files, at the shack and at his house, removing all the papers pertaining to R.O.K. He packed them in a box addressed to Morley Covington at the San Francisco bank, and the Saigon office as the return.

Alex Miller arrived on the fourteenth. He was an older man, serious and quiet. Ron said, "You must be tired after the long trip. Let's go over to the house so you can freshen up."

"You got a house?"

"Yes. It'll be your house when I check out."

"My wife will be glad to hear that."

"Your wife coming over?"

"Yes. I may be here a long time."

"You probably will."

At the house, Miller took a bath and freshened up. When he came downstairs, Ron offered him a drink. Ron said, "Well, let's get you settled at the B.O.Q. until I get out of here."

Miller asked, "When do you think that will be?"

"That's up to you. The sooner the better."

"I've done this work before. I should be ready to take over in a few days."

"Good." They left the house and Ron noticed Shad's car. He said, "By the way, that car goes with the house. The keys should be in the ignition. Why don't you take it now so you have wheels?"

"Good idea. I was wondering how I was going to get around."

Ron pointed to his own car. "You get this one, too, when I leave. Your wife can use it."

"She'll be happy to hear that."

"You can get gas free at the motor pool."

"Great."

Ron got into his car and Miller got into Shad's, and Ron led the way to the Bachelor Officers' Quarters. He waited until Miller signed in and took his luggage to his room.

When Miler returned, Ron said, "The officers' club is just down the road, the mess next door. Why don't I take you over and show you around?"

"Good idea."

They had a drink at the club, then went next door for dinner. Miller had a lot of questions, and from them Ron could tell that Miller was a highly experienced man.

Miller asked, "When do I meet the men?"

"A couple of them usually drift over to the club late at night before they sack in. You must be too tired to wait around for that."

"Yes. I've got jet lag, I guess."

"Okay. Well, they usually show up at the shack between seven and eight in the morning for their assignments. You can meet them then."

"Okay."

"And I'll tell you what. I've got the use of a friend's apartment in town for a few days. Why don't we invite the guys up there for a party tomorrow night?"

"Good idea."

"Those parties sometimes get a little rough, but maybe the guys will behave themselves until they get the feel of the new boss."

"They won't have anything to worry about."

The party at Shad's that night was the most subdued the walls had ever heard. There were perhaps thirty people there, several of them women, a few military officers connected with the R.O.K.—now Transcontinental—project, a couple of civilians from the American Embassy, and a Vietnamese businessman who seemed to know no language at all and just stood there grinning at everybody. Without being told, the guests somehow knew they were inheriting an entirely different kind of boss. Most of the men wore suits, with shirt and tie; some wore sports clothes; the military were in dress uniforms. The women, in gowns, behaved more like nuns than the nymphos they were. There was only moderate drinking and no drugs. Ron had arranged with a G.I. cook to lay out a buffet but it looked more like a snack table at a tea for San Francisco poets than a chow spread for rugged men whose horizon of appetites was insatiable.

But it had been like this all day. From the beginning the men had always addressed Ron as Ron or Kaz. Alex Miller was Mr. Miller. Even when he had told them to call him Alex, the men compromised by calling him sir. His bearing somehow intimidated them. Besides being the scene of frequent orgies, Shad's apartment had also been a popular gambling den. Whatever else was going on, there was usually a poker game in force somewhere in the apartment. Cutthroat pinochle was particularly brutal. Usually one crapgame was going on against the floorboards in one room or another. After Ron had left his girfriend's bed, he would occasionally drop by Shad's place to gamble. He preferred craps. He rarely took the dice, preferring side bets, where winning was mostly a matter of intuition. He usually won, but he never let himself win too heavily because it made him uneasy to take back the money he had just paid the men as salary. The only mention of games at the party was made by Alex Miller. He said his wife had won several amateur bridge championships, and that he wasn't bad at it himself. He invited everybody to come by the house any evening for a game. Everybody said they would, but Ron knew none of them would. It was a good thing Miller's wife was coming over, otherwise, he'd have to learn to enjoy solitaire.

People began to leave early, around eleven. By midnight, most guests were gone. Miller, as the guest of honor, felt he should stay to the end, but he acquired the yawns.

Ron said to him, "Alex, you've had a long day. Why don't you shove off? I have to stay around for the cleanup."

Ron had a couple of cigarettes and another scotch as the Vietnamese help cleaned up, a few of them veterans of Shad's parties and wondering why the party had been so somber. Alone, Ron gave the apartment a final check. There was still evidence of Shad around, and Ron knew it would be there when the next tenant moved in. Just before leaving, Ron went into the kitchen and left the apartment keys on the table. Not knowing what Shad's rent had been, Ron placed two one-hundred-dollar bills on the table. He left.

It was one thirty when Ron reached the house, and he was surprised to see the two bicycles still in the driveway. He went through the house to the kitchen and found the Vietnamese couple sitting there, not speaking to each other.

Ron asked, "What are you doing here so late?"

The cook said, "Man come. He give me this. We wait."

He took the envelope. "Thank you for waiting. Take tomorrow off."

"Sir?"

"Take tomorrow off. You're off Sunday, anyway. I'll see you Monday."

"Yes, sir. Thank you, sir." They left.

Alone, Ron opened the envelope: "Monday, 17, same time, same place."

At last.

He put the paper in his wallet and went to bed.

Saturday was a busy day at the airfield. Four giants arrived. Ron supervised one of them; Miller the other three. Miller also gave the pilots their assignments that morning, his voice firm, his manner brisk, his decisions unyielding.

At the end of the day, he said to Ron, "Is there any way I can get the pilots out here earlier in the morning? I see on the map that some of these trips are getting pretty long."

"Just tell them," Ron said. "They're a good bunch. They know how to take orders."

"I'll have to do that. No sense paying them all that money for one trip a day. Another thing, I notice that people start drinking pretty early around here. This morning, a couple of the men smelled like sewers."

Ron said, "Don't give them any assignments. They'll lose their flight pay. That'll sober them up."

"Good idea. And I want to jazz up the ground crew. They got a little sloppy today."

"You're the boss," Ron said, and he thought to himself: I wonder how long it will be before my boys find themselves back in Kansas dusting wheat?

Ron spent Saturday night alone at home. On Sunday there was only one arrival. Ron went to the airfield for appearance's sake and to make his move. After the giant was secured and the pilots had returned from their deliveries, Ron went into the shack and took a chair opposite Miller behind the desk.

Ron said, "Well, Alex, you seem to have everything under control."

"I believe so."

"Transcontinental sent out a good man."

"Thanks." He was lapping it up.

Ron asked, "What's the departure schedule for tomorrow?"

Miller checked his clipboard. "The bird out there now heads back at nine in the morning. Another one comes in around ten and leaves at four. Nothing else so far."

Ron cleared his throat. "How about if I go back on the four o'clock?"

"Oh?"

"Yes. You don't need me around here any more. You heard about my FreytFlite deal?"

"Yes, I have."

"I'm itchy to get at that. I've got a lot of money tied up in it."

"So I've heard. I'd be itchy myself. Okay, Ron, if you want. I'll put you on the passenger list for the four o'clock."

"Thanks. One more thing. I've got a good buddy at a station hospital upcountry. He's from home. Who knows when I'll ever see him again? How about if I take a chopper the first thing in the morning and go up and say goodbye?"

"Sure thing. Any time."

The last time. Drop it. Ron said, "When is your wife coming over?"

"I'll put a note in the nine o'clock pouch. She should be here by the end of the week. She'll be glad to hear about the house."

"Right. I'll pay the servants off tomorrow. You want to keep them?"

"For a while. Are they expensive?"

"No. You bill the company for them, anyway. When will you be moving in?"

"Tomorrow night. I'm getting stir crazy in that cubbyhole they gave me at the B.O.Q."

"I don't blame you. I lived there myself when I first got here. I'll tell the servants."

"Thanks."

"I've been meaning to ask you. Have you got any kids?"

"Two. A boy seventeen and a girl fourteen."

"How's the boy stand with the draft?"

"No problem. I used my pull with our Congressman and got him an appointment to West Point. He'll be tied up for four years. The war won't last that long."

"I hope not." It was to last much longer. "See you tomorrow."

Ron went to the officers' club and joined a couple of his— Miller's—pilots and had a few of his Coke and scotches with them, a drink that made scotch lovers wince. He had dinner with them at the mess. He did not mention his departure.

At home, Ron set his alarm clock for five and went to bed early. In his anxiety, he awoke before the clock went off. It was still dark when he reached the copter hangar at the airfield. He chose the first one at the door, got in, eased it out to the ramp and took off.

As before, the armed Vietnamese came out of the woods as soon as he landed. As before, the man who had come to his house approached him, carrying two packages wrapped in brown paper, one smaller than the other.

He handed them to Ron. "When go?"

"Today. Four o'clock."

"When States?"

"Tomorrow. Around noon."

"Where other man?"

"He's sick. I sent him to a hospital in Guam."

"Who new man?"

Christ, they knew everything. "I'm going on vacation for a couple of weeks. He's taking my place."

"He okay?"

"I don't think so. I wouldn't try it."

"You come back?"

"Yes."

"We wait then." He almost smiled.

"Do that."

Ron put the smaller package in his pocket; the larger package seemed heavier than before. He got into the helicopter and flew back. At the shack, he tossed the larger package into the back seat of his car, as though it was his laundry. He went into the shack.

"Everything okay, Alex?"

"Just fine. No sweat. Anyway, you're fired." He laughed at his own joke.

Ron said, "I'm going back to the house for a few minutes. See you later."

"Roger."

"Yeah."

At the house, he took the large package inside with him, to his office, and he locked the door. He took the smaller package from his pocket and opened it, something he had not done before, always sending it wrapped to Morley. It contained two hundred and twenty-five one-thousand-dollar bills, wrapped in five twenty-five bill packets. He had no idea the payments had been in such a high denomination. Now, how to get them into the States? He could not trust the inside of his shirt. The lump would have been too obvious. He broke open the five packets, put one of the bills into his pocket, and then removed his shoes and tried to put the remaining bills in them. He could not get his shoes back on. He took out the excess bills, opened his pants, and stuffed the bills into the crotch of his jockey shorts.

He went out to the kitchen and told the cook: "I'm going away for a few days."

"Yes, sir."

"Another man will move in here tonight."

"Yes, sir."

"You take good care of him."

"Yes, sir."

He took the bill out of his pocket. "Here's your pay."

"Thank you, sir." She put it in her apron pocket without looking at it. He wondered what she would think when she tried to spend it.

He said, "Thanks for everything. I'll see you later."

"Yes, sir."

Ron went back to his office, limping slightly, got the large package, tossed it into the back seat of the car, and drove away from the house for the last time. To kill time, he drove into the city and spent a long time driving around on what he hoped was his last look at the place. Then he went out to the officers' club and had two farewell drinks for himself. He lunched at the mess. He was at the shack at three thirty.

The large package under his arm, he went into the shack and said, "Alex, here's the keys to the car. One of the guys will drive it back for you."

"Okay. Here are your travel orders. We'll be boarding in a few minutes. Why don't you go on now and get yourself a good seat?"

"I'll do that." He extended his hand. "I've enjoyed meeting you, Alex."

Miller took the hand. "I've enjoyed meeting you, Ron. Good luck with FreytFlite."

"Thanks." Ron turned to leave.

Miller asked, "What's in the package?"

"My laundry."

Miller grinned. "Well, I guess we don't have to put your laundry on the invoice."

"I guess not." Ron took a few steps.

Miller asked, "What's wrong with your leg?"

"What?"

"You're limping."

"Oh. The shoes are new. I haven't broken them in yet."

"You can take them off on the plane."

"I'll do that."

The small passenger section was empty when Ron entered it. He paused at the galley and slipped the package into the oven. He took a seat where he could watch the galley, although he knew nobody would look into the oven unless the procedure had been changed. The rest of the passengers came aboard. Then Alex Miller came aboard. He checked all the travel orders again. He stopped at Ron and extended his hand. They shook hands again. Then Miller went forward and gave the Transcontinental pouch to the co-pilot and left the plane, standing alongside, watching as the cabin door was closed and the stairs were pulled away. As the plane began to move, Miller saluted it. Christ.

As before, Ron did not get off the plane at Guam or Hawaii, this time because he didn't want anybody to notice his limp. As he saw the Golden Gate Bridge pass under the plane, he grew very tense. The plane slowly moved up to the Transcontinental hangar, and Ron saw five men waiting there. When the cabin door was open and the stairs rolled into place, two of the men came aboard.

One of them said to the passengers: "Your attention, please, gentlemen. For those of you who are making this arrival for the second time or more, we have instituted a new procedure. Everybody must pass through Customs and all luggage must be opened for inspection. Will you please disembark now and show your travel orders to Mr. Stern at the door?"

Ron let a few of the other passengers precede him, then got up and joined the line. He showed his orders to Mr. Stern. He limped down the stairs and followed the line to the inspection area.

When it was his turn, the inspector asked, "Any luggage, sir?"

"No. I'm going back in a few days."

"I noticed that you're limping. Do you need any help?"

"Just a flesh wound. I can manage. Thank you."

Ron limped out to the sidewalk and got into a cab and was driven to the St. Francis Hotel in San Francisco. On the house phone in the lobby, he asked for Mr. Saskovich.

Shad answered on the first ring. "Yes?"

"Herman?"

"Yes?"

"It's me, honey. I'm here."

"Ron?"

"Whatever you want. What room are you in, sweetheart? I'm coming up."

Shad told him. As Ron limped across the lobby, the number of the room seemed familiar to him. On an upper floor, Ron was limping along the corridor when he saw Shad open a door and take a few quick steps toward him. They went into a hug.

They went inside and shut the door. Ron glanced around. It was the same suite Morley Covington had reserved for him.

He asked, "How come you got this place?"

"It was all they had. There's a convention in town. Are you okay?"

"These shoes are killing me," Ron said. He limped to a chair and sat down and took off his shoes. He turned them upside down, and the money began to fall out.

Shad gasped. "Christ, what's this?"

"The kiss-off. Wait. There's more." Ron stood and opened his pants.

Shad said, "Hold it, buddy. You're in the right town, but you've got the wrong man."

Ron said, "You'll love this." He put his thumbs into the waistband of his shorts and pushed down. More money fell to the floor.

Shad said, "So that's how you did so good in Saigon."

They laughed and Ron fixed his clothes and they picked up all the money.

Ron asked, "Anything happening here?"

"Nothing."

"The papers? TV?"

"Nothing."

"Well, something will be happening soon. The F.B.I. is checking out the planes as they come in. Today they'll find a nice surprise for themselves in the oven."

"You had a shipment with you?"

"Yeah."

"Jesus Christ, Ron, you're crazy."

"I've been planning this for months. Either we break them first or they break us sooner or later."

"That letter to the F.B.I.?"

"Right."

"You took an awful chance, Mr. President."

"Well, we'll see soon if it paid off."

When it was time for the evening network television news, they turned on all three sets in the suite, Shad watching CBS in the living room, Ron in the bedroom watching NBC on the set there, keeping one eye on ABC on the set in the john. Nothing. They had dinner brought up, scotch for Shad, shake for Ron. They kept all three sets on, alert for news bulletins. Nothing. The late news, network or local, nothing. In the morning, they watched the talk shows on all three networks. Nothing. Nothing in the papers. All day: game shows and soaps and news capsules. Nothing. The network evening news.

Shad hollered from the living room: "Ron! Quick!" Ron ran into the living room. Walter Cronkite was saying:

In Washington today, agents for the F.B.I. and the Federal Narcotics Bureau jointly announced that they have broken up probably the biggest international ring of dope smugglers. In Oakland, California, yesterday, agents found a cache of four kilos of pure heroin that had just arrived aboard a Transcontinental Air Cargo plane from Vietnam. Officials of Transcontinental in Los Angeles said they knew nothing about the shipment, adding that their representatives in Saigon could not explain how the drugs had gotten on to the closely guarded cargo giants.

A spokesman for the F.B.I. in San Francisco said the agency had received a tip about the shipment from an anonymous informant about a week ago, and that the agency has been going over each arriving Transcontinental plane since with a fine-tooth comb. It was not revealed where on this particular plane the cache was found.

The spokesman said that the tipster had also revealed several sites within Vietnam where shipments changed hands and somehow found their way onto the big planes. Minutes after the Oakland discovery, C.I.A. agents in Vietnam descended on these remote areas, but nothing was found. However, the agencies had also been told about a powerful radio transmitter near the Saigon area. The C.I.A. was able to get a radio fix on the hideout by radios on military aircraft. These pictures have just arrived by satellite of Vietnamese arrested at the radio station...."

As Cronkite talked on, Ron and Shad leaned forward and stared at the television screen.

Shad whispered, "I knew that son of a bitch."

Then there was a close-up of the man who had come to Ron's house and had been present at every pick-up by him or Shad. Ron shouted, "There's the lousy cocksucker!"

Shad jumped to his feet and grabbed his crotch and thrust his hips at the set and shouted, "Suck this!"

Now Ron was on his feet.

The narcotics bureau in Washington said it had also been informed that a Florida-based private plane was somehow involved in the smuggling but has not been located as yet. It may be out of the country. In Saigon, government officials said that the captured smugglers would most likely receive long prison sentences and could even face execution. Meanwhile, nobody could identify the origin of the narcotics. It could be the Far East, the Middle East, or even South America. Because of the high profits on drugs in this country, the roundabout subterfuge makes the effort worthwhile.

In other news...

Ron and Shad were dancing around the room, waving their arms, laughing and shouting. They maneuvered into a hug.

Ron said, "We're free, buddyboy! We made it! We're home free!"

But they were not.

III
Patricia and Ron

Chapter Eighteen

Pat's telephone was ringing as she entered her apartment, but she did not answer it. She put down her luggage in the middle of the living room and stood there, her mind a blank. The ringing stopped: the answering service had presumably cut in. Pat stood there, waiting for the pain. It did not come. Waiting for the tears. They did not come. In a few minutes, the phone started ringing again. Pat picked up her purse and left the apartment and went to her car.

Stubby was gone. She had walked past him without a word, letting the door swing shut on him, shutting him out, shutting the world out. For her, there was no world.

She got in her car and began to drive, and, without deciding on it, she drove to Steve's place, letting herself in the apartment with the key Steve had given her months before. She saw on the stripped bed five large cardboard boxes. On the enamel breakfast table was a shoe box, a note beside it: "Pat, I've packed all of Steve's things. Let me know what you want me to do with them. Check out the shoe box. Business papers. Stubby."

She did not touch the box. She did not touch anything. She stood there, stunned and insentient.

Twilight touched the window.

There was a knock on the door. She opened it. Stubby.

"I thought you'd be here," he said. "Are you all right?"

"Yes."

"Can I do anything?"

"No. Stubby, where is he?"

"In Africa."

"In Africa?"

"Yes. What's left of him."

"God. What happened?"

"I'm not sure. Nobody seems to be sure. The papers were vague about it."

"Doesn't anybody know anything?"

"All people seem to know was that Steve was driving alone one morning on an unpaved mountain road, early, on his way to do some location shots. There was a heavy fog that morning, people say. He went over the side."

"God."

"They didn't find him for two days. They didn't think that anybody would try to make the drive through the mountains on such a morning. They say the car must have burst into flames when it hit the ground. It was still smoldering when they spotted it."

"God. When did it happen?"

"About a week ago, I guess. It took a few days for the people to reach a place where they could notify the television company. The company notified the union. When the union couldn't find you, they called me. I tried to reach you in Sun Valley, but they said you had left."

"Yes."

"All the studio knew was that you were driving back with Ted, but they didn't know when you'd get here. That's when I started hanging around your door."

"We stopped off in San Francisco."

"And you heard nothing?"

"No."

"Well, then I'm glad you heard it from me first."

Pat asked, "What do we do now, Stubby?"

"Did you look in the shoe box?"

"No."

"I did. Some insurance policies. Savings bonds. Three bank books. The title to his car. Looks like he owned some property somewhere, too. There's a will. Everything goes to you."

"I don't want anything. Stubby, do you know where his ex-wife is?"

Wife? Wife. "There's something in the box about her. From some lawyer who sends her the alimony every month."

"He had some kids, didn't he?"

"Two."

"I want everything to go to them. Can that be done?"

"I suppose so. You'll probably have to sign some papers."

"All right. Can you arrange it?"

"I guess so. What do you want to do with his things?"

"I don't know. Is there anything you want?"

"No."

"Then why don't we give it all away? The Salvation Army. Good Will Industries."

"All right. and what about..." He could not bring himself to say it.

"Steve: Why don't we leave him where he is? It doesn't make any difference, does it?"

"I guess not. I'll take care of it."

"Thanks. Here." She handed him the key to the apartment. "Thanks Stubby. I'll keep in touch."

She left. She didn't want to go home so she drove around, not knowing where she was or where she was going. It was around two in the morning when she caught herself dozing at the wheel. Then she went home.

Her telephone was ringing as she walked in. She wasn't going to answer it, but maybe it was Stubby with something important. She picked up the phone. Before she could say anything she heard Ted's voice.

"God damn you, Patricia! Where the hell have you been? I've been calling ever since you dropped me off this afternoon. Pat, we're so sorry."

"Thanks, Ted."

"Joel Steirman called just after we got in. He told us. I was shocked."

"Thanks, Ted."

"Hold it." He said something aside, to Buzz, probably. Then: "Buzz is on his way over to pick you up. I want you to stay with us for a few days."

"No, Ted. I'm all right."

"Well, I'm not. I want you here. You don't even have to bring a toothbrush. Buzz has the bathroom stocked like a drugstore."

"Please, Ted, I'd rather—"

"Don't hand me any of that lonely widow shit. Buzz should be there in ten minutes." He hung up.

She did not want to go. She did not want to see anybody. The reality of what had happened had not sunk in yet, and she wanted to be alone when it did. But when, in a few minutes, Buzz rang her bell in the lobby, she left her apartment meekly.

Colby opened his door as Buzz pulled the car into the driveway. He greeted her with a hug. "I'm glad you're here." He kept an arm around her as he led her into the living room. "Want a drink?"

"No thanks."

"Buzz, why don't you fix us some sandwiches and coffee?"

Buzz asked, "Pat, do you want a malted?"

"No, thanks. I don't want anything, really."

Colby said, "Now, don't make me sound like a Jewish mother.

You've got to eat something." When Buzz was gone, Colby said, "Okay, Patricia. I know all I have to know about Steve. Let's not discuss it. But tell me. Do you have any plans?"

"No."

"Why don't you go home for a few days, to Wyoming or Utah or wherever the hell you come from?"

"I don't want to."

"Does your family know?"

"My family doesn't even know I was married."

"What are you, the black lamb or something?"

"I guess so."

"Well, we'll keep you busy."

She shook her head. "I'm all right, Ted. I'll be all right. I just need to be alone for a few days."

"That's exactly what you don't need, young lady," Ted said, loud, sharp, and demanding.

She shook her head. "Don't fret about me, Ted. I've got my acorns."

For a moment he wasn't sure what she meant. And then he looked away and said to the ceiling, "Jesus Christ, this broad remembers everything you tell her." He looked at her. "Darling, do you think I give a fuck about your acorns? I'm worried about my own. Go home to the family hearth for a few days and get the sorrow out of your system, then I'm going to put you to work. I need you very much, and I don't want you to lie yourself off to a nunnery for the rest of your life."

She listened to him, waiting.

Ted said, "After Joel Steirman gave me that dreadful news about poor Steve, he said he hoped you'd be all right because something has come up that's going to have us all working our butts off, with no time out for tears."

"What's come up?"

"We're going to New York, my dove."

"New York? What for?"

"The Radio City Music Hall."

"What for?"

"We're the Christmas show, my dear, we're the Christmas show. Big hoopla. Flash! Hold the presses. We're the Christmas show at Radio City Music Hall. The great Thelma Thwift, on thcreen and on thtage, two for the prithe of one."

Pat said, "I don't get it."

Buzz came in from the kitchen. "Chow in a five minutes." He looked at Pat. "Did Mother here tell you that we're all going to

New York?''

Pat said, "He's been talking about Radio City, but he's not making sense."

Buzz said, "He made me promise not to say anything about it on the way over here." He sat down on the sofa next to Ted, patted him patiently on the leg, then said, "Calm down now, dear, and tell us all about it."

Ted put a hand on Buzz's hand. "All right," he said. "I'll try." He looked at Pat. "As you know, my dear, the Thelma Swift fiasco should have been finished months ago." Pat nodded. Ted said, "What you don't know—and what Joel just told me—is that the Music Hall wanted the picture for a summer run—you know, the G-rating, family crap, all those tourists. Well, we didn't make it. Well, child, what Joel just told me is that while the three of us were setting San Francisco ablaze all over again, people from the Music Hall were out here and saw some of the footage we've done, and they want us for their Christmas show."

Pat asked, "Can that be done? The picture hasn't been edited yet."

Ted said, "I know that, love. Joel has put the editing department on twenty-four-hour duty. They've got five weeks to do the job. And so have we."

Pat said, "This scares me. Tell me about it."

Ted said, "Every year, the Music Hall does a big Christmas pageant—the manger, the virgin birth, a big parade, camel shit all over the stage. They've got that part all set. Then they go into their regular show—the Rockettes, the ballet, the stage going ape and dwarfs running up and down the aisles. This year they want to do something special, a tie-in with a movie. Right behind the Music Hall is an open-air ice-skating rink for the public. The Music Hall wants to build a set that looks like that rink and do a finale with a lot of people skating on stage. Thelma Swift herself—in person, no less—comes on for the big finish. And we've got five weeks to get that ready."

"Oh God," Pat said. "Thelma Swift could never learn a new routine in five weeks."

"I know that," Ted said. "I've solved the problem. We'll let her do her Lord's-Prayer dirge. She knows that already."

Pat said, "We?"

"Of course," Ted said. "You don't think I'm going into the Music Hall and risk my ass without you there to do the dirty work? How soon can you be ready to depart for the Big Apple?"

Pat shook her head. "I can't, Ted. I can't go just now. I have too much to wind up."

"How long will it take you to finish?"

"I don't know," Pat said. "Actually, Stubby is handling everything. I don't have to do anything."

"Very well, then."

Buzz said, "Come on, Pat, come with us. Now that we've ruined San Francisco, let's go and destroy New York."

Ted said, "It would be the best thing for you."

Pat said, "I just can't."

Ted said, "You've got to. There's something I haven't told you."

"Oh God. What?"

"The Music Hall wants to book the show for ten weeks. We can get Thelma only for the four weeks in December. Then she has to go back on the road with her ice show. Apres Thelma, vous, chickadee."

Pat shot to her feet. "Oh no!"

"Oh oui,"

"But I can't do her Lord's-Prayer routine."

"I don't care if you do a routine to Jingle Bells. I need you. You're coming with us."

Buzz said, "Great. That settles it."

Ted gave him a shriveling glance. "Not quite. There's something even you don't know."

Buzz said, "Do I become one of the Rockettes?"

"You're close. While you were on your errand of mercy I went through the mail that got here while we were setting San Francisco aflame. Just a minute." He got up and went into the den and came back carrying an envelope. He extracted the letter, handed it to Buzz, and said, "Read this out loud."

Buzz looked at the letterhead. "Who's John Davidson?"

"Who's John Davidson, she asks," Ted scoffed. "Honey, you've been spending too much time in sandtraps. John Davidson is merely the Florenz Ziegfeld of Fire Island, that's all. Read the letter."

Buzz read:

Dear Tessie, ole girl:
I was at the Rockefellers' the other night and heard you are going to do the Christmas show at the Music Hall. Is this true? I've been trying to call you but there's been nobody home at your place for days. How like you. Please let me know as soon as possible because I don't want to miss the chance of watching you undergo the virgin birth on the Music Hall stage at four performances a day. I always knew you had it in you.

Something else. Don George let me hear the score for his new musical. It's charming. I sent the script to Buddy West and he wants to do the show, but only provided that you do the choreography—and only then provided you bring along your assistant, somebody named Pat. Who's he? And what happened to that sexy little Italian you had the last time you were here? Buddy is doing the Palladium in January and should be back from London at the end of the month. Say the word and we can start production on Valentine's Day. Don't you love it? And say the word fast or I am going after Bob Fosse, who is better than you are although not as cheap.

 Love,
 Jessie

P.S. I hear your new boyfriend is a professional golfer. See if you can get him to bring some of his chums along. I have had the hots for Arnold Palmer for years.

Buzz looked at Ted. Pat looked at Ted. Ted looked at the two of them.

Ted said to Pat, "I can't say the word unless you do."

Pat said, "The word."

Chapter Nineteen

New York worked its miracles. For Pat, the miracle was work. Preparing for the stage show at the Music Hall meant a constant rush of auditions, casting, rehearsals, leaving her no time to think, to remember, to mourn. When "Heaven On Ice"—on screen and on stage—opened, Pat had to be at the theater all day, four performances, in case, in a fit of temperament, Thelma Swift decided not to go on. And when Thelma Swift left to rejoin her ice show, four times a day, waiting in the wings, Pat heard: "And now, in Thelma Swift's Olympics Gold Medal performance, Radio City Music Hall proudly presents Ms Patricia Purney, direct from the LPM Studios in Hollywood." Four times a day, seven days a week, for six weeks, Pat heard the smattering of applause as she glided on stage, then the tidal wave of applause as she finished the routine.

Without a break, the Music Hall over, there was the Buddy West musical: more auditions, casting, rehearsals for two months. Work day and night. And there was something else that was also a miracle.

One morning, over breakfast and the *Times* in her hotel suite, Pat came upon an ad that brought a happy yelp from her. She picked up her telephone and asked for Mr. Colby's suite. "Ted are you two busy tonight?"

Ted said, "We're always busy every night. You know that. Why?"

"I want you to take me to a nightclub tonight," Pat said.

Ted moaned. "Nightclub? Ugh. Nightclubs are for tourists."

"Well, I'm a tourist," Pat said. "If you don't think so, ask any of your fancy friends at the party tonight. Ted, I want to go to this nightclub and I don't want to go alone."

"Which nightclub?"

"Rodney Dangerfield's."

"Who's he?"

"The comedian. We saw him once on television at your place.

He's the one who 'don't get no respect.'"

"The one whose eyes look as though they're about to fall out of his head?"

"Yes.

"Oh. Well, I don't think he's very funny. I certainly wouldn't want to sit through an evening of him."

"You don't have to," Pat said. "It's his nightclub, but he's not working there right now. I want to catch the comedian who is."

"Who?"

"Fats Mulligan."

"Never heard of him."

"A lot of people haven't, but they will. He's hilarious. I rehearsed him for a bit he did at LPM some time back, and he had me on the floor. Unfortunately, that's where most of his number ended up—the cutting room floor."

"Then he couldn't have been very good."

"He's very good. Ted, if you won't take me to see Fats tonight, I won't go with you to one of those parties when you need a woman along to make you look straight."

"Cunt. Can't we make it some other night? Buzz and I are due at Harry Houghton's place for dinner, and you know how upset she gets when anybody disturbs her table settings."

"If it's just dinner," Pat said, "we can catch the second show."

Ted submitted. "Oh Jesus. All right. Make the reservation. Do you want a lift to the Music Hall this morning?"

"No. I'll walk it."

"I hope you get mugged."

That midnight, as Fats Mulligan paused to let another burst of laughter subside, he looked over to one side of the room and said, "I think I recognize the laugh of my favorite fan, the only laugh I ever got while I was doing hard labor at LPM during my brief Hollywood career. Is that you, Pat?"

Pat called out, "Yes, Fats, your greatest fan."

Fats said, "Stand up, honey, and let the people get a look at the only genius in Hollywood."

Pat stood, there was a smattering of applause, and when she sat down, Ted said to her, "Now I know why you wanted to come here tonight—you ham. Some people will do anything to get a hand."

Pat said, "You're jealous."

After his act, Fats joined Pat's table and, after an update of personal news, he asked, "Have you seen much of New York?"

Pat said, "Mostly rehearsal halls."

"That's not New York," Fats said. "Let me show you New York. I'll take you over to Brooklyn, where I was born and raised. That's New York."

So Pat saw Brooklyn, and there was the healing of distraction in it.

And there was more healing. Gwen's daughter Vicki was in New York, studying at the American Ballet Theatre School, sharing a small apartment with two other students near Lincoln Center. When Pat had time, there were late night suppers at the apartment: dance talk.

The Buddy West musical was a smash, as everybody knew it would be. Suddenly the pressures were over and Pat said to Ted Colby, "Let's go home. I'm tired."

Colby said, "We're going home, all right, but don't expect any rest. John Davidson wants to send out a road company of the show and we'll be putting it together right away in Los Angeles."

"Oh Jesus."

Buzz said, "Bless his Holy name."

When Pat entered her apartment on Mariposa for the first time in five months, the place seemed smaller to her than she remembered. It was when she was putting her clothes away that she saw Steve's suit in the closet. She felt a bang.

Ted Colby said, "Patricia, can you swim?"

"Of course I can swim," Pat said. "How many times have you watched me swimming in your pool?"

"I don't mean that," Ted said. "I mean on your back and on your head and underwater and whatever."

"I can swim any way you like."

"Can you dive?"

"How many times have you seen me dive off your board?"

"I don't mean that. I mean dive, really dive, high dive, miles high?"

"Off the moon. Why?"

"How would you like to make a picture with another Olympic champion?"

"Not Thelma Swift, I hope."

"No, dear, not Thelma Thwift, thank Jethuth."

"Who?"

"Judy Wallace."

"She's a swimmer?"

"She won two gold medals in the backstroke and a silver in the free-style."

"And now she's going to become a movie star."

"Yes. LPM is making so much money on 'Heaven On Ice' that now they want to try it again with 'Trouble in Tahiti.'"

"And I'll bet I do her swimming for her."

"No. She can do her own swimming, but she can't dive."

"Not at all?"

"Not from anything higher than three feet. It's in her insurance policy. And I've got a production number in mind where she jumps off the top of Mount Everest. Only, you're going to do that for her."

"Oh God! Where do we do this? LPM built a winter wonderland on the lot for Thelma. Are they going to build a tropical paradise for Judy Wallace?"

"No, dear. I've already taken care of that. I tried to get the pool at MGM, but they wanted to sign up Judy and LPM beat them out of it, so they're mad. We're going to shot the production numbers at our second home. Vegas."

"Where in Vegas?"

"Caesar's Palace. We're going to turn their pool into a tropical lagoon. Mr. Kaz made the deal. He owns a hotel there, you know."

"No, I didn't know. I don't even know Mr. Kaz."

"Nobody does. He's a real mystery man. Anyway, he made the deal."

"When do we leave?"

"Well, first, we've got to hire some swimmers. UCLA is letting us rent their pool for the auditions. With any luck, we may be able to do some of the rehearsals there. We go to Vegas as soon as the set department builds us a Mount Everest. Don't you *love* it?"

Pat said, "I'll let you know after I get a look at Mount Everest."

Pat hated Mount Everest while it was still a knoll.

One night she said to Gwen, "The way they're going, the damned thing is going to be as high as the Empire State Building."

Gwen tested, "Are you scared?"

"Of course I'm scared," Pat said. "The highest dive I've ever done was about twenty feet. This thing looks like it's going up to a hundred. And that's not the worst of it. The dive is in the finale, and Ted has gone out of his mind. He's had underwater spigots installed all over the pool that shoot up umbrellas of different color water, and he's going to have platforms of flowers at the surface that are held in place by weights at the bottom. I've got to make the dive without impaling myself on a spigot and then swim to my place underwater for the number without getting tangled up the weights. One way or the other, I could kill myself."

Gwen said, "Good luck, dear."

Pat said, "The show biz expression is break a leg."

Gwen said, "Drown yourself."

Pat prepared herself for the dive by making practice dives from lower levels as Mount Everest was gradually built higher and higher. When the mountain was finished, there was a niche about fifty feet above the pool where Pat was to appear on cue—in a wig, costume and made up to look like Judy Wallace—and then wait for a few seconds for the musical cue that would send her into the dive. Just as Pat was adjusting to her practice dives, the underwater spigots were installed, giving her a target five feet in diameter where she could hit the water without being impaled. This required more practice dives, higher and higher up the mountain, until Pat could make the dive with some sense of safety. Then the floating flower beds, held by chains to weights at the bottom, presented problems. Pat had to make more practice dives as she figured out her route underwater to her place without getting tangled up in the chains.

Pat used three weeks to the practice dives, diving from the niche three and four times a day. There was then a week of rehearsals of the water ballet, two days of practice dives while the cameramen rehearsed their camera work for the dive, and, finally, filming the dive, as much as four or five times a day. Throughout all this, Pat lived in gnawing fear that haunted her day and night.

She was greatly relieved when she climbed out of the pool and heard Ted Colby say, "That was perfect, darling. It's a wrap."

But it wasn't perfect. A look at the rushes the next day showed that one of Pat's tits had slipped out of her bra halfway through the dive, and all the cameras caught it. She would have to dive again. At first she refused, but the bait of an additional week's pay to do the dive one more time, the next day, soothed her.

At the end of her day, Pat went into the casino to pick up Gwen for the drive home, but Gwen said, "I have to work late. We're shorthanded tonight. The floor manager has asked me to put in some extra time."

"Will you be long?" Pat asked. "I can wait for you."

"I have no idea. You might as well go home."

"How will you get home?"

"If I can't get a lift, I'll take a cab."

"I won't mind waiting, you know."

"No. I'll be all right. There's a casserole in the refrigerator. Just stick it in the microwave oven for a few minutes. I'll warm it up whenever I get home."

"All right, then."

Pat headed for the parking lot, when she noticed the coffee shop. She told herself she wasn't hungry enough to go through the ordeal in Gwen's kitchen, so she went into the shop and ordered a chicken sandwich and a malted. The place was crowded; the line at the cashier's desk was long. Pat signaled the waitress, whom she knew, and paid for her food.

She went into the parking lot, heading to her car. Off to her right she heard some noise, a scuffling, and she stopped to look. There was a fight going on. Two men attacking a third. On impulse, Pat went quickly to the fight. She pulled off one of the attackers, spun him around, and when he was facing her, she sent a knee with full force into the man's crotch. His eyes bulged, in pain and surprise. He grabbed himself by the crotch and hobbled away. The second attacker was still pummeling the victim. Pat brought her right arm around with all her strength and gave the man a karate chop on the side of his neck. He dropped to his knees. He looked over his shoulder at her. Then he collapsed on all fours and crawled away.

The victim had fallen to the ground, on his back. Pat bent over and peered at him. He didn't seem to be breathing. She saw the blood oozing out of his nose and mouth. She felt his pulse. Slight. She saw a breast wallet on the ground nearby. The victim's. She picked it up and inserted it into the inside pocket of the man's dinner jacket.

Then she went quickly back into the hotel, to the bell captain in the lobby. And she said, "My husband has just been mugged in the parking lot. He needs a doctor. Call an ambulance, quick. Hurry."

The bell captain reached for the telephone on the podium in front of him. Pat turned and went back to the parking lot. She glanced over at the fallen man. He was still there, not moving.

Pat went to her car and got in and she drove home.

Chapter Twenty

When he awoke the next morning there was a blank moment when Ron Kazurian could not understand why he ached all over. Then he remembered. He lay in bed, thinking about it. What little he remembered of it was chaotic. Why had they so savagely beaten the shit out him? Why hadn't they just cornered him and, threatening, told him to fork over his wallet and his Rolex? Why hadn't they just stuck a gun or a knife in his ribs? He would have given them whatever they wanted, even the keys to his car. Why had they beaten him up so relentlessly? Was their motive more than robbery? Who were the bastards? Why had they stopped short of killing him? And who was the blonde?

Patricia Purney sat in a canvasback chair in the long trailer the swimmer/dancers used as a dressing room. She was wearing a cotton robe. Under it was the bathing suit that was her costume for the dive. She was smoking cigarette after cigarette, a fire burning inside her as well as in her fingertips. Ted Colby had told her to be at the pool early, and she had got there at seven o'clock. He told her he was just going to shoot the dive, and that he would shoot it just once. Bullshit. Colby himself had not arrived at the pool until almost nine.

"I'm sorry," he announced to the world. "I had to drive Buzz to the airport to get the dailies in Hollywood, and my damned car broke down. I'm sorry, but it was an act of God. And I don't want to hear any crap about it from anybody."

But there was other crap. For infuriating reasons of his own, Ted Colby decided that shooting the dive itself would not be enough. He wanted everybody in the pool that was supposed to be there. This meant rounding up the swimmer/dancers, putting them into costume, and placing them in the pool in their places for the last moments of the production number. Then the morning became overcast, and the weather bureau had no idea how long the clouds would last. This meant racing around Las Vegas for more lights and more reflectors. And then the volume on the playback machine dwindled to a whisper and nobody could hear it. The soundmen gathered around the machine and stared at it in profound puzzlement.

Pat knew that waiting around and waiting around was an integral part of the motion picture industry. She always hated it. She especially hated it this morning. She dreaded the dive and feared it. Waiting around for it increased her dread and fear. Just thinking about it had given her a restless night. She had been restless, too, because of what had happened in the parking lot. She had acted on impulse, she knew that, but the impulse had blasted in her like a volcanic eruption and left her with locked brakes emotionally. She could not unwind.

She glanced at her wristwatch on the dressing table. Damn! For a moment, she considered quitting the picture and quitting the picture business and going back to Colorado and spending the rest of her life breeding horses. She reached for another cigarette.

In Houston, Texas, a middle-aged, short, stocky, swarthy man held a telephone to his ear and waited for the call to New York to be answered.

When it was, and he recognized the familiar voice, he said, "Where the hell have you been? The phone rang a dozen times."

"I was in the john, Uncle."

"You shouldn't spend so much time staring at that big cock of yours. Hones was on the box first thing this morning. He wants to know how did it go in Las Vegas last night."

"The boys took good care of him, Uncle. The bastard should be in the hospital for six months."

"He's in the hospital?"

"I think so. The guys said they heard an ambulance when they ran away."

"An ambulance? Who sent for an ambulance?"

"I don't know."

"Did somebody see them? Why did they have to run away?"

"I don't know, Uncle. They called me right after they got back to their hotel. It was the middle of the night here, and I couldn't make much sense out of them. They said they were both going to see a doctor themselves."

"What for?"

"I'm not sure. Artie said he thinks he's got a broken neck, and Joe said he's got a double hernia."

"Christ! That bastard must have put up a real fight."

"It wasn't him, Uncle. The guys said they had him unconscious in two minutes."

"What happened, then?"

"It was a dame."

"What?!"

"A dame. A broad. A woman."

"What about a woman?"

"Some woman beat up on them when they were beating up on the Greek."

"What the hell are you talking about? Anyway, he's Armenian."

"Uncle, all I know is what the guys told me, and as I told you they didn't make much sense. They said that when they were beating the shit out of the Greek some broad came along and attacked them. She almost knocked them out and they were lucky they got away before she killed them."

"How the hell could a woman knock out two big apes like those guys?"

"I don't know, Uncle, but she did it."

"Who was she?"

"I don't know that, either. Maybe she was his wife."

"He's not married. In fact, there was some talk around Vietnam that maybe he was a fairy. Who knows? Now, listen to me. You have really fucked this up, but good. I'm not going to tell Hones about it, and you'd better have some good answers for him if he hears about it from anybody else. Christ, you can't even hire a couple of hoods."

"I'm sorry, Uncle. They looked okay to me."

"Well, you can't do anything about it now. I don't know how I'm going to get you off the hook on this one. So tell me, how's the stock?"

"I'm moving on it, Uncle. I've got to be careful. If I move too fast, they'll catch on out in Hollywood, and they'll start buying up the stock themselves. I'm using the scattershot approach."

"What's that?"

"Well, Uncle, if I buy too much stock off the board, the price will go up. So I'm going after the stockholders one at a time, one here, one there, one someplace else. I tell them what lousy shape the movie business is in, but I give them a little profit and they're glad to get rid of the stock. This way, the brokers don't wise up and start snooping around."

"Do what you think is best. But I remind you: Hones is losing his patience. That Armenian bastard cost Hones a lot of money, and Hones wants that guy's ass."

"I'll get it, Uncle. I'll get that Greek's movie studio and his hotel and his airline, and then I'll deliver his ass to Hones personally."

"You'd better, or it'll be your ass."

"Don't worry."

"I'll worry. Something else. Hones says the plane will get to Tampa late Wednesday night. Be there yourself and take care of everything. And f'Chrissake, keep your mind on business and off your goddamn big prick."

"I'll pretend I don't even have one."

"You won't, if you keep this shit up."

The phone started ringing. Ron forced himself to get up. His steps were unsteady as he crossed the room to the telephone.

He said, "Yeah?"

"Ron?"

"Yeah."

"It's Morley."

"G'morning, Morley. How are you?"

"I'm fine. Did I wake you up?"

"No. I'm up."

"Ron, I just got a call from your broker in New York."

"Yes?"

"There've been some more stock transfers."

"How much this time?"

"Well, it's in bits and pieces from all over the country, and it adds up to about nine thousand shares."

"Who's buying?"

"It's the same pattern, Ron. Different buyers. A construction company in Houston. Some law firm in New York. A woman in Florida. Some student group at Harvard. It goes like that again."

"What do you make of it?"

"I don't know what to make of it. I could understand if stocks were moving at all the studios here in Hollywood; but from what I can find out, they can't give their stock away. You know what the picture business is like these days. It's just LPM stock that's showing any action."

"There must be a reason for it."

"I think so, too, Ron."

"Let's keep an eye on it. If it keeps going on, we'll have to dig into it and find out what's going on. Do you think there's a chance that somebody is trying to get control of the studio?"

"Well, Ron, there's always that possibility; but nobody with any sense would try that now, with the whole industry in a slump."

"You're right. Let's watch it for a while."

"Okay. When are you coming back?"

"In a few days. There are a couple of problems at the hotel I want to clear up. And the picture we're shooting here is way over budget. I want to look into that, too. I'll let you know."

"All right. See you."

Up now, Ron decided to stay up. He went into the bathroom. His left eye was still dark purple. Some blood had escaped from his nose during the night and had caked on his upper lip. He washed it off. The bruises on his chin and on his cheek were already beginning to fade. There were a few bruises on his chest; his ribs still ached, and his belly was sensitive. He freshened up and dressed. As he was leaving the apartment, he picked up his soiled tuxedo from the chair in the living room where he had deposited it when he returned home the night before, dazed and exhausted.

In his car, he took a pair of sunglasses from the glove compartment and put them on. He drove to the LPM Stars Hotel. He used the employees' entrance and rode the employees' elevator up to the executive suite on the fourth floor.

As he passed the receptionist, he dropped his tux on a chair and said, "Will you have the valet service take care of that?"

"Yes, Mr. Kaz." She looked at the suit. "Good heavens, you must have fallen into a puddle of mud."

"How did you guess?" Ron was at the door of his office. "Will you tell Milton that I want to see him?"

"Yes, sir. He's already put yesterday's figures on your desk. Do you want some coffee? I've just made fresh."

"All right."

Ron went to his desk and looked over the figures on yesterday's business. The casino was holding up. Business in the lounge was pretty good. But things were dropping off in the Hollywood Room for the third week in a row. Reservations were down, too, and so was the house take on the high rollers who used their suites for endless poker games.

Milton Graham came in. Graham had owned a small hotel-casino on a Caribbean island and had sold it in order to buy forty-eight percent of the casino at the LPM Stars. He was also on the payroll as general manager of the hotel. The receptionist brought in two cups of coffee.

Ron and Graham exchanged a nod. Ron asked, "What's wrong with the Hollywood Room? It's down again."

"That New York comic," Graham said. "He's too highbrow for the people we get this time of the year. I caught his second show last night. He's starting to give all his punchlines in French."

"Christ. How long is he signed for?"

"Three more weeks."

"We'll go broke."

"Do you want me to cancel him?"

"Who can you get?"

"I hear that Carl Ballantine is doing good business in Atlantic City."

"Can you get him?"

"I can ask."

"Do that. And how come the reservations are down again? I looked in at Caesar's Palace last night and the place was jammed."

"I don't know. We're getting some competition from Atlantic City, of course, but we expected that."

"Get together with the people in advertising and sales and work out some kind of package deal. Y'know—the plane, the hotel, meals, shows: the usual deal. It worked okay last year. See what you can do."

"Okay. I should have something to show you in a couple of days."

"Make it soon. I have to get back to the studio. Is Eddie Jaffe in town?"

"I saw him a couple of days ago. If he isn't here, he's back in New York."

"See what he can do about some publicity for us. What about that singer in the lounge? She's doing okay. Can Eddie get her on the Johnny Carson show?"

"He can, if anybody can."

"Ask him to try it. We need the plug. How long have we got her for?"

"She's week-to-week, as long as she draws. Her manager said the other night that she's got an open bid for Miami."

"Probably bullshit. Sign her up for another six weeks. If her manager wants a raise, give him half of whatever he asks for."

"Okay. I told the chef what you said yesterday about his budget. He says he can't help it if the price of everything is going up."

"Maybe I can help. I'll talk to him on my next trip."

"Right. I don't know what to do about the high rollers. I think Atlantic City is giving us trouble there, too."

"Shake the bushes. Tell them our freebies now include all the money they want. That might help."

"It might."

"I'm glad the casino is holding up. See to it that the entertainers spend more time in there. It draws crowds."

"Okay, Kaz."

Kaz.

That was one of Shad Grady's jokes. When they were in privacy and Shad wanted to express an appraisal, good or bad, he addressed Ron as Mr. President; and, good or bad, there was always affection in it. In public, however, Mr. President could sound obsequious or sarcastic, so Shad resorted to Kaz; and, whether the appraisal was good or bad, there was always affection in it. Others, assuming that Kaz was a nickname he enjoyed, picked up the habit. With time, then, Ron became Kaz to close associates at the studio, the hotel, the airline; he became Mr. Kaz with associates who were not so close; he was Mr. Kazurian with those more remote; to his friends he was Ron.

It was Shad who infected Ron with Las Vegas. When FreytFlyte was ready to open an office in Vegas, Shad moved there for a month to set it up. In that month, he got hooked on roulette. Even after the office was running on its own, Shad continued to fly out to Vegas on weekends. Gregarious and a good loser, he became a favorite of hotel managers and croupiers. At the same time, his social life in Los Angeles grew as it had in Saigon. For the fun of it, he began using FreytFlyte planes to fly his friends to Las Vegas for weekends, which made him even more popular in both cities. One weekend he enticed Ron to go along. That weekend Ron got hooked on baccarat. He also got hooked on the ease with which he could find women to spend a night with him—his place or theirs. On the weekends when Ron did not fly back to the farm, he flew to Vegas. One result: the LPM Stars Hotel.

And it was Morley Covington who put Ron into the motion picture business. On one of his flights back from the farm, Ron stopped off in San Francisco for a business meeting with Morley. Morley was concerned about the twenty million dollars in the safe deposit box down in the bank's basement, and he urged Ron to invest it to earn an income from it. Ron flatly refused and would say no more.

Then Morley suggested: "Why not use it as collateral for a bank loan? You know the bank will let you have all you want."

"I know," Ron said, "but what business should I invest in?"

"I've been thinking about that," Morley said. "How about the motion picture business?"

"The movies? I don't know anything about the movies."

"Nobody does," Morley said. "Hollywood is in another of its

slumps. Stocks are low. This is a good time to buy."

"So why buy into a failing business?"

Morley said, "Hollywood will come back. It always does, more so this time because television needs so many pictures. I've checked this out, Ron. LPM Studios is in trouble. I know the treasurer there. I don't think we'd have any problems getting major control. Want me to look into it?"

"Do· what you want," Ron said. "On one condition. I don't know anything about movies, but I'll go into the business provided you take over the business side and Dave French takes over the legal department."

"You've got me," Morley said, "but you'll never get Dave to leave San Francisco. His wife is too happy there: she's the Queen of the Jewish High Society. How about Bert Bernstein?"

"He'll leave Dave's law firm?"

"In a flash. Bert and Dave's daughter just got a divorce. He's finished in the company. He'll take any job he can get."

"Do what you want."

Ron was surprised. Shad didn't want to go in on the LPM deal. Ron asked, "What's the matter? Don't you think it's a good idea?"

Shad said, "Mr. President, I'd go in on a deal to buy horseshit if Morley Covington said it was a good idea. It's not that. I just think it's time for me to start slowing down. I've even been thinking maybe you should find somebody to take over my job at Freyt-Flyte."

Ron couldn't believe it. "You want out?"

"Of course not. But I want off. Ron, I'm thinking of getting married."

"Jesus Christ. When did this happen?"

"A few months ago."

"Who is she? Do I know her?"

"You don't know her. She went on one of the Vegas weekends with some friends from her church. That's how I met her."

"Church? Shad, that doesn't sound like your type."

"I know. That's what I can't figure out. She's a widow. She's got a couple of kids."

"Shad, I hope you know what you're doing. Have you asked her yet?"

"No. But I think she knows. I've been seeing her pretty steady."

"Well, now," Ron said, settling back in his chair, "this changes things. What do you want to do about the Vietnam money? Morley says it's about twenty million now."

"You hang on to it, Ron. You may need it for the LPM deal."

"Half of it is yours."

"I know. Well, Ron, if anything happens to me, give my half to Nora."

"Are you planning on getting married or buried?"

"I'd want Nora to be taken care of."

"That's her name?"

"Yeah."

"When do I get to meet her?"

"After she says yes. No sense stirring up a lot of shit until I'm sure."

"Let's leave it where it is. I don't need it now. If you don't, let's let it ride. Something will come up."

Something did.

The LPM Stars Hotel and Casino came up out of a bad hangover Ron suffered on one of his weekends in Las Vegas. Friday evening, as soon as Ron entered the casino at the Desert Inn, a local realtor recognized him from the pictures that got into the papers when Ron took over the LPM Studios in Hollywood. The man stepped in front of Ron as Ron was on his way to a craps table.

The man said, "Congratulations on the LPM deal, Mr. Kazurian. I'm sure you'll make a lot of money."

Ron didn't even look at the man. "Thanks."

Ron moved on, but the man stayed with him. "Mr. Kazurian, if you'll take my advice, you'll buy some land here in Vegas as soon as you can, before the prices go sky high."

Ron said, "I don't need any more land." He got to a table and watched.

A waitress passed with a tray of drinks. The man took two and shoved one into Ron's hand. "You ought to build a hotel out here, Mr. Kazurian. It'd be a natural—LPM stars appearing at the LPM hotel in Vegas. You'd be the King of the Strip."

"I don't want to be the king of anything," Ron said. "Now, if you don't mind...."

Mind or not mind, the man stayed glued to Ron all evening, even sitting down uninvited at Ron's table when Ron broke for dinner. The drinks kept coming. Ron was beginning to feel a little drunk and a little testy. The incessant buzzing in his ear ruined his concentration and his intuition betrayed him. But he could not shake the man, could not shut him up.

At three o'clock in the morning, the man was at Ron's side as Ron walked down the corridor to his room, the man jabbering away. At the door, Ron said, "There's my phone. You'll have to excuse me." Ron got into the room and just managed to slam the door in the man's face and get across to the bed and collapse on it, exhausted and defeated.

In the morning, when Ron stepped off the elevator to go to the coffee shop for breakfast, the man was there, waiting for him. He accompanied Ron into the coffee shop, and when they were seated at a table, he said, "Mr. Kazurian, you look like you need a hair of the dog. Waitress, two Bloody Marys. And keep them coming."

It went on like that all day. And all day at the tables, Ron kept losing and losing.

Sunday morning at noon, Ron had just about enough strength to raise himself on an elbow to answer the phone when it rang.

He heard, "Good morning, Mr. Kazurian. It's Mel. You told me to pick you up at noon so you could take a look at the property I've been telling you about."

"I can't make it," Ron said. "I'm not feeling well."

"You'll feel better when you see this piece of land, Mr. Kazurian. It's a beauty. Why don't I bring up a couple of Bloody Marys to get you started?"

"No, don't," Ron almost pleaded. "I'll be right down."

It took Ron half an hour to maneuver himself through a shower and a shave and get dressed. A jackhammer roared in his head. In the lobby, the man greeted Ron with a big smile that was nauseating.

"My car's right out front, Mr. Kazurian," the man said, and he took Ron by the arm. Ron submitted numbly. In the car, the man said, "This ought to fix you up." He held up a thermos bottle. "Bloody Marys. Ice cold."

Ron reached for the jug.

They drove only a few minutes when the man stopped his car at the edge of the Strip, almost beyond the Strip itself. The man said, "There it is, Mr. Kazurian. Isn't it beautiful?"

Ron looked. He saw only miles and miles of sand.

The man said, "As I told you, Mr. Kazurian, this property is owned by an elderly couple in Pasadena. It's been in the family for generations. They probably got it dirt cheap, but this dirt is getting more expensive every day. I called them this morning. I caught them just as they were leaving for church. They're very religious people. I told them you were very religious yourself and that you were thinking of building a church here. They were very happy about that, and I think I can chew them down on their price if they think you are going to build a church on the property. Of course, I didn't tell them who you were, or they probably would have doubled their price. Now, as I see it—"

Ron took a swig from the thermos bottle. "Buy it," he said.

"What?"

"Buy it."

"You want me to buy it?"

"Buy the fucken land and shut up."

"You want me to buy it for you no matter how much they want?"

"Buy the fucken land for whatever they want for it and shut up and take me back to the hotel. I'm sick."

Ron got back to his room just in time to rush into the bathroom and vomit himself into total exhaustion.

In the New York apartment, the man was undressing for the second time that night. Stripped, he was reaching for his pajamas when he caught a glimpse of himself in the full-length mirror. He studied himself. Beautiful. Gorgeous. Fantastic. Incredible. He thought of the woman he had just left. He had, he knew, given her the screw of her life. It was probably also the last screw of her life. He was sure she was fifty years old—at least fifty, and a withered fifty. For three hours, he had drilled himself into her, not missing a beat. For three hours, she lay beneath him, her fists clenched at her flat chest, her eyes closed, tears making rivulets in her makeup. Now and then she coughed a small bark. Now and then he asked her if he should stop. She shook her head a small no. When he'd had enough of her limp body, he withdrew.

He lied: "That's the best I've had in a long time, Mrs. Malone."

She knew better. She sat up and reached for a Kleenex and dried her face.

He said, "I'd like to see you again, Mrs. Malone. I'll come back whenever you say."

She stood up, her loose skin dangling at her neck, her breasts, her arms, her belly, like a withered balloon. She said softly but firmly, "I never want to see you again. You're a monster."

He took it as a compliment and laughed. "Remember what you promised me."

"I remember," she said, defeat and regret in her tone. She went across the bedroom to a small desk, took a folder out of a drawer, fished through some papers, and extracted a document. With that, she signed over to him her two thousand shares of LPM Studio stock. What a fool she had been. But she had been flattered by the attention he swamped upon her all evening, impressed by the elegant restaurant, weakened by all the wine he poured into her; and when, in his limousine on the way to her place, he took her hand and put it between his legs, she was staggered by what she felt, destroyed by a surge of passion she had never experienced before, and, not having been screwed since her husband died fifteen years before, she not only thereupon agreed to sell him the LPM stock she had inherited from her husband—she offered to give it to him if he would fuck her. Well, he had fucked her, all right. How she despised his brutality, she loathed his pompous amusement, she detested his taunting offers to stop if it was too much for her, she seethed at knowing that, in three hours, he had not emptied into her once. She went to him and handed him the document.

He said, "Thanks a lot, Mrs. Malone. I enjoyed myself so much I hate taking it."

She said, "Bullshit!"

He shrugged. As he moved to his clothes, he caught her hidden glance at him. He said, "Do you want to suck on it for a while, Mrs. Malone? Take your dentures out. I'll bet you're great at that."

She said, "Please go. Please get dressed and go."

He got dressed and left. She did not accompany him to the door; but when she heard the door close, she went to it and double locked it against him. Against the world. Against herself.

Standing naked in front of the full-length mirror in the bedroom of the apartment he kept in the city, the man was smiling, smiling not only at what he beheld but smiling at the thought of that dried-out old cunt he had pulverized. He was sure she would never forget it; he was sure he would never remember it.

The phone rang. At four in the morning, it could only be one person. The man picked up the phone. "Hello, Uncle. What are you doing up at this hour?"

The man in Houston said, "Hello, Uncle, he says, like I was in the next room. Where the hell have you been all night?"

"I was with a client."

"Like hell you were with a client. I called your office a dozen times. Nobody was there."

"I was at her place."

"A her? Were you banging somebody again?"

"What else? It was worth it, Uncle. I picked up two thousand shares of LPM."

"Yeah? At what price?"

"She gave it to me free, Uncle. I gave her the screw of her life."

"Has she got any more stock?"

"No. I took her for all she had."

"Maybe you should do business only with women from now on. You'd save Hones a lot of money."

"I do what I can, Uncle."

"Yeah? Well, there's something else you can do something about."

"What?"

"Hones has been on the box all night. He wants to know what the hell is happening in Las Vegas."

"I don't know what's going on in Las Vegas, Uncle. I haven't been there for a long time."

"What about those bums you got on the payroll out there?"

"I haven't heard from them in a few weeks. What is going on, Uncle?"

"Hones found out that the Armenian is building a hotel on the Strip."

"That's the first I've heard about it."

"Don't let Hones hear you say that. You're supposed to be the first person to find out about these things."

"Okay, so this got by me somehow. What does Hones want me to do about it."

"For one thing, he wants you to find out where the money is coming from to build it."

"That shouldn't be difficult. What else?"

"He wants you to get the word out that anybody who works in the new hotel can't work at any of the other hotels in Vegas or any place else."

"Like in the shows?"

"Yeah. The same goes for the high rollers. Hones said keep them out of the Armenian's place if they want to play at the other spots."

"Okay."

"And the same with the whores."

"That won't be easy. There are so many whores in Vegas."

"You just follow orders."

"Okay, Uncle. But, Uncle, I thought the property along the Strip was all tied up. How did the boys let this piece get away from them?"

"Nobody could get it. It's owned by some religious nuts in Pasadena. They would only sell to somebody who would build a church on it."

"Ha! A church. That's funny. The Strip could do with a church."

"So will you, if you don't stop fucking around."

Chapter Twenty-one

S had Grady was dead.

It was a shock.

After Shad withdrew from FreytFlyte, Ron put Joe Reilly in charge of the company, Reilly replacing Shad as Ron's frequent contact with the firm. With LPM, the hotel and R.O.K., now run by Stewart, Ron saw less and less of Shad. When he did, though, he noticed that Shad wasn't looking well. The doctors could not figure it out. Then, on his occasional visits to Shad's home, Ron noticed the Oriental houseboy who seemed always to be hovering about. Norah explained, "He's a Godsend. He takes care of Shad so well. I don't have to do a thing." She sounded relieved.

Joe Reilly kept up the contact with Shad by taking his check to him each month, and it was Reilly who told Ron that Shad was in the hospital. He said, "Did you know that Shad gave up drinking the day he got married?"

Ron said, "No, I didn't."

Reilly said, "You know the way some people get when they drink too much? That's the way Shad got when he didn't drink enough. He should never have married a Baptist. There's no fun in them."

Ron visited Shad in the hospital. The houseboy stepped out into the hall.

Then Shad died.

Ron flew his family down from the farm. The Frenches came down from San Francisco. The Covingtons. Milton Graham. The Reillys. After the funeral, they all went to Shad's house—Norah's house now—for refreshments. Cheese and crackers and fruit punch, served by the houseboy.

Ron went to Norah and said, "We're all going to miss him so much."

"I know," she said. "I had no idea Shad had so many Jewish friends."

As they were leaving, Reilly asked Ron: "Do they have any idea what Shad died from?"

Ron said, "Norah said the doctors told her it must have been some bug Shad picked up in Vietnam."

Reilly said, "No. A bug was the only thing Shad didn't pick up in Vietnam."

But Shad was gone.

It was understandable, then, that Ron should think about Shad the moment he looked into the mirror and saw the blood and bruises after the mugging in the parking lot. Shad would have gotten a big laugh out of it, however serious, whatever the reasons for it. And Ron would have laughed, too. There wasn't anybody around any more with whom Ron could share a laugh over something like that. There wasn't anybody around to whom Ron could open himself completely, trust utterly, rely on totally.

He learned to live with this, at first by choice, eventually by nature. At LPM Studios, only a few top executives knew him by sight. When he wanted to visit a sound stage to check on anything, he showed his pass to the guard, and rarely did anybody on the set know who he was. When the LPM Stars was ready, somebody suggested that Ron take for himself one of the elegant suites on an upper floor. He didn't. He didn't want the employees to think the boss was hanging around to keep an eye on them. He rented a furnished apartment two miles away. He never gambled at the Stars, avoiding the risk of having some floor manager recognize him and send out the word to let the boss win some of his own money. He gambled at other casinos where his face was familiar to only a few people, and familiar because they had seen it a few times. The women Ron occasionally took to his apartment or joined in their rooms in some other hotel were little more than silhouettes to him, out of mind as soon as they were out of sight. He never wondered if he would ever marry. He never thought of it at all.

But on the morning after the mugging, Ron had other things to think about. Business things. Ron already knew that the axiom for a successful hotel-casino in Las Vegas was to keep the hotel prices low in order to attract tourists who were going to lose all their money in the casino, anyway. This meant offering good rooms, good shows and good meals that were usually below their actual cost. And, with time, the costs kept going up. Even the chef was complaining that it wasn't his fault if the costs of running his kitchen had soared to an unacceptable high. Of course it wasn't. The fault was with the cost of getting the foodstuffs from the farm to the kitchen. In between was a network of buyers, shippers, brokers, wholesalers and distributors, all of whom needed profits to stay in business. As a result, the hotels were paying more for the handling of the foodstuffs than for the foods themselves. And obviously things were going to get worse.

Ron considered this: Stewart's pilots worked in the agricultural areas of the country, coast to coast, and usually they became friendly with their steady customers. Why not have Stewart's pilots buy directly from the farmers? They could fly their purchases to the nearest FreytFlyte center, which most of them used for home base, anyway. The FreytFlyte centers could then transship the purchases to Vegas, and, from the farmers to the chefs, the delivery could be made overnight—without the time and money lost to all the middlemen. If other hotels could be persuaded to come in on the deal, the procedure could develop into a very profitable sideline. Ron made a mental note to discuss this with Stewart on his next weekend at home.

Ron's other major business problem could not be resolved so easily. Ever since he had become the major stockholder—and thus virtually the owner, he had made a pracatice of examining the weekly financial statements on pictures LPM had in production on the lot and on location. Each statement staggered him. Although each picture had a set budget before production began, nobody seemed able to stay within the budget, especially on location. Since Ron's arrival, three or four of the pictures had been box-office successes, but most of them barely showed a profit. Whenever Ron visited a set, it was mostly to see where the money was going. Time and again, he observed that precious minutes—even hours—were lost to rehearsals, to take after take, to just sitting around as scenery was adjusted and lightings were tested. When he complained about it, people told him that there was no way to get around the time-consuming and money-consuming preparations. What LPM needed, Ron gradually realized, was a topnotch production manager, somebody who could figure out the way to get around the costly preparations. The individual producers at LPM didn't seem to know, all of them soon succumbing to the deadweight of old habits that seemed an inescapable part of the motion picture industry. Now and then, Ron heard about some clever producer at another studio who seemed able to stay within budget, even come in below it, and Ron would try to tempt the man over to LPM with better deals. Nobody took the bait or, if they were tempted, they stayed where they were because their own studios matched Ron's offers.

Shad Grady could have done the job, Shad with his joking, teasing, light-hearted way of goading people into doing more than they thought they could do. Shad could have done it. But Shad was gone. The situation was hopeless, so hopeless that it could wreck the studio unless the right person would come along.

Ron got up from his desk at the LPM Stars and headed for the door, unaware that the right woman was just about to take a dive right in front of his eyes.

Chapter Twenty-two

It was eleven o'clock in the morning. For four hours, Pat Purney had been sitting in a robe in the dressing room van used by the swimmer/dancers, waiting, waiting and fuming. Her ash tray was a mountain of cigarette butts. Strewn on the table in front of her were a dozen paper cups with the remains of cold coffee. Other swimmer/dancers had arrived, changed, checked in at make-up, and gone to the pool, to wait and to fume.

Finally somebody poked a head into the van and said, "Pat, we're ready for you now."

Pat snuffed out another cigarette. She stood, took off the robe, let it drop on a chair, left the van and strolled slowly to the pool and to Ted Colby.

He glanced at her. "So. There you are."

"Yeah," Pat said, her tone acid. "Remember me?"

Another glance, and a raised left brow. "Careful, darling. Mother's in a foul mood this morning. Everything is going wrong."

"Tough shit."

He looked at her now, studying her, his examination focusing on her hair. He said, "Your flowers are drooping."

She said, "So's my ass."

Colby said aside to a waiting go-fer, "Tell makeup to bring some fresh flowers for Pat's hair." The go-fer fled. Ted looked up at the sky. "I wish the damned sun would come out."

"I don't," Pat said, still acid. "Then you'll have to set the lights all over again, and there goes the day."

"It isn't your money."

"It isn't yours, either."

A makeup man arrived with several fresh flowers. He examined Pat critically, and began plucking wilted flowers from her wig and replacing them with fresh ones.

Colby took a microphone from another waiting go-fer. "Larry," he called, "have you people got the sound machine repaired yet?"

Over the P.A. system: "We think so, Mr. Colby."

"Let me hear it."

Over the loudspeaker came a blast of Hawaiian-type music.

Colby: "All right, all right. Move it up to the last sixteen bars and stand by."

Along the sides of the pool, decorated to look like a tropical lagoon, were the forty swimmer/dancers.

Colby: "All right, girls. We're going to shoot just the last sixteen bars. Everybody into the pool. Last one in is a dyke."

Carefully the swimmer/dancers slid over the edge of the pool into the water, heads high to protect their wigs and makeup, and they made their way to their positions for the last sixteen bars of the water ballet.

Colby turned to Pat. "Is Your Highness ready to do or die?"

"Yes," said Pat. "And remember what I told you. I'm going to do this just one more time. So it is a do-or-die."

Colby gave her a bittersweet smile. "With any luck, maybe it'll be both." *

Pat turned her back on him. She made her way along the edge of the pool, through the foliage there, to the back of the set, to the flight of stairs that led up to her niche. She stepped into view and looked at Ted Colby at the far end of the pool.

At his mike, Colby called, "Everybody ready?" There were murmurs. "Ready, Pat?" She nodded at him. "All right, let's have some lights." The lights went on. "Roll the cameras." The several cameras began to purr. "Larry, the music." On blasted the music. "Action!"

The swimmer/dancers began to move in their long-rehearsed formations. Pat stood in the niche, looking straight ahead, listening to the music. On cue, she brought her arms up and out, like a blessing. On cue, she leaped, stiff legged, up and out, rising a few feet into the air, her feet coming up behind her, her arms up and out, her back in a deep arch. She hung there a moment and then began to drop, holding the swan dive, ten feet, fifteen, twenty. She brought her head down, her arms together, her feet up and straight, and she cut into the water like a blade. As soon as the water closed over her, she brought her legs around, under her, bending her knees. She felt her feet touch the bottom of the pool. She opened her eyes and swam under water, dodging the obstructions, to her place for the final bars of the ballet. She surfaced, heard the music, and performed the final backstrokes of the ballet. The music stopped. Everybody held their positions and their breath.

At last, Colby: "That's a wrap."

Great sighs of relief.

The swimmer/dancers moved to the sides of the pool and hoisted themselves out of the water. Pat swam the length of the pool into the shallow water and got out on the ladder that was there. A go-fer was waiting with her robe. She slipped it over her shoulders and went around to Ted Colby.

Colby was talking to the head of the set crew, saying, "Yes, you can strike the set. And you can burn it. I'm sick of the sight of it." Then he turned to Pat. "Beautiful, my dear."

She said, "Then it was a do?"

"A perfect do."

"How about my tits?"

He looked at them and commented, "How about your tits." He smiled at her frown and said, "No, dear. It was fine."

Despite the Nevada heat, Pat shivered. "You going to need me any more today?"

"No, love. Our leading lady gets in from Hollywood this afternoon and I'll be spending the rest of the day with her. Won't that be charming?"

"Lucky you. How about tomorrow?"

"I want to start shooting the ballroom number tomorrow, providing our leading lady knows her left foot from her right. Why don't you look in sometime after lunch in case she needs some rehearsal?"

Pat moved in close and kissed Colby on the cheek. She said, "Sometimes I hate you."

"I know, dear," he said, "Sometimes I hate myself."

In the van, Pat removed her wig and let her golden hair hang full. She took off her wet costume and changed into street clothes— slacks, man's shirt, high heels. She considered removing her heavy makeup, but she wanted to get away before Ted Colby changed his mind for some reason, so she picked up her purse and left the van. As she rounded the swimming pool on the way to the parking lot, she saw that the set crew was dismantling the scenery with a happy viciousness. The tourists who had watched the filming were gone, except for one man who was watching the set crew. Pat noticed that the man was wearing a business suit, which was unusual for Las Vegas at that time of the day, and he had on dark sunglasses, which would have been usual for Las Vegas at the time of the day except for the fact that the sky was overcast and sunglasses weren't necessary. Pat noticed how intently the man was looking at her. As she passed him, she pulled her shoulders back. In her car, she still felt the tensions of the morning of waiting for the dreaded dive.

She decided that after lunch with Gwen she'd go to the gym and unwind.

As Ron Kazurian was leaving his office at the Stars, he noticed his soiled suit on a chair in the reception room. He pointed at it and asked the receptionist, "Can you take care of that for me?"

She glanced at the suit and then looked at Ron. "Yes, sir. I'll call the valet right now." She reached for her phone. "Will we be seeing you any more today?"

"I don't know," he said. "I'm going over to Caesar's Palace now and try to find out what the hell is holding up that picture. Then I expect I'll go back to the apartment. I'll check with you later."

"Yes, sir. Shall I have the suit taken over to your apartment?"

"No. I'll pick it up later."

Ron left the hotel as he had entered it—on the employees' elevator and through the employees' door. He went to his car and drove the short distance to Caesar's Palace. As he entered the parking lot, he saw that the space he had occupied the night before was vacant. He looked away from it and drove deeper into the lot. Parking, he walked around to the swimming pool. He had seen the set before, while it was being built, but this was the first time he saw it completed and in daylight. It looked effective enough. He joined a group of some fifty people—tourists, by the looks of them, and stood there with them, watching. Nothing seemed to be happening. Several men in work clothes wandered aimlessly through the set. Here and there at the cameras were a few other men, looking through eye pieces, turning knobs, aiming the lens at nothing in particular. Here and there small groups of girl swimmers loitered, chatting, some smoking, a few sitting on the edge of the pool, legs dangling in the water. At the shallow end of the pool was an older man, in a T-shirt and khakis, a clipboard in hand. Buzzing around him were three or four much younger men, busy as gnats, but at nothing, one or the other of them suddenly dashing off urgently.

Ron turned to the man standing next to him. "Have they started shooting yet?"

"Not that I know of," the man said. "I've been here over an hour, and nothing has happened."

Ron shook his head, annoyed. He resumed watching. A half-hour passed. Then the older man took a microphone from a younger man and said something Ron could not hear. Bang! came a brief burst of music. The tourists jumped. Then the older man said some more inaudible things into the microphone, and finally the place came alive. Girl swimmers began to emerge from the phony foliage; more came from the long van beyond the pool; others came out of parked cars. They all gathered at poolside and, on some signal from the older man, they lowered themselves into the water and swam to various positions, heads held high like kittens. Suddenly the men at the cameras were surgeons battling fiercely to save a life, all of them bent over their equipment and passing small tools back and forth. Then another girl swimmer came from the van, a tall and lean girl, her costume gaudier than the others, flowers in her black hair. As she slowly approached the older man, Ron appraised her. His eyes moved no lower than her tits. No tits could naturally be that perfect. She went to the older man and they talked for a few moments. Then she turned and made her way toward the opposite end of the pool, now and then disappearing behind the phony foliage. She went out of sight. The next time Ron saw her, she was high on the phony mountain, standing alone in a shallow niche. Then huge banks of lights went on, turning the overcast morning into a brittle Nevada noon. Then, like artillery loaded with celluloid, the cameras aimed at targets. Suddenly the bang of music. From the murmurs among the tourists, Ron assumed the swimmers in the pool were moving about. He could not see them. He kept his eyes on the girl in the niche. He saw her bring her arms over her head. He saw her step out into space, floating there, a rising swan, bold and stunning and aloof. Then she began to drop, unfolding her body into a sleek arrow, entering the water with a small sigh. Then he could not see her. A few seconds later, and the music stopped and the lights went off, and the swimmers began to hoist themselves up the sides of the pool. Ron did not see the diver again until she emerged from the shallow end of the pool, climbing up a metal ladder, her back to him, her wet costume gripping at the firm mounds of her. One of the younger men slipped a robe over her shoulders. She went to the older man and talked with him briefly. Then she turned and went to the long van and up the few stairs and inside. Ron wondered who she was.

The party was over. The tourists drifted away. Camera crews pulled their equipment back from the pool's edge and began to dismantle it. Electricians turned the towering banks of lights into Tinker Toys. Workmen went at the set like a hurricane, pulling up shrubbery, knocking down trees, and the mountain collapsed. Ron watched, wondering what all this destruction was costing him.

He saw a blonde woman come out of the van, hair full and long, her gait firm and specific. She was wearing slacks and a man's shirt and shoes that seemed to be just a high heel and straps. She came around the pool and passed several yards away from him. It wasn't until he looked at her breasts that he recognized who it was. He watched her go to a car, get in, and drive away. Then he gave his attention back to the havoc growing in front of him. Trucks arrived, and workers began loading the trash onto them.

Having stood still for so long, Ron felt stiff, and the aches of the night seeped back into him. He went to his car and drove to his apartment. A hot shower did him little good. He checked the fridge and saw nothing that gave him an appetite. He made himself a malted. What he needed, he decided as he sipped the drink, was a good workout, a good sweat. He went to a closet that was lined with shelves and chose a sweatshirt, a pair of linen shorts, a jockstrap, and a pair of tennis shoes. He put everything into a canvas bag, dressed in some old clothes, and he drove to the health club he had joined a couple of years before when he decided that his sedentary life was making him go flabby and that he could use some exercise.

Pat waited until Gwen had gone shopping before she prepared her hot bath. The water was close to boiling, and she settled in it slowly. She soaked a long time; she lathered up with a sudsy oil. She did stretch exercises under water. Nothing helped. She was still tight with tension. She dried herself and went into her room and tried to take a nap. Hopeless. She tried several positions, but nothing worked. When she lay on her side, she could hear her hearbeat in the pillowed ear. Surrendering, she got up, dressed, threw some work clothes in a small canvas bag, and she drove to the health club where many Vegas dancers went from time to time to limber up from the strain of the daily dance routines.

Arriving at the club, Pat paid her fee at the office, then went down a corridor to the women's locker room. She changed, then went down another corridor, through the double doors to the vast exercise room. She was relieved to see that the place was not crowded. At this hour, most Vegas dancers were still asleep in their beds—or the beds of lovers, or strangers.

Pat knew which exercise she wanted to do first. The teeter board in the room over which the exerciser had control. Once on the board, Pat could maneuver at her own speed, picking up speed as she went along, concentrating on her balance so intently that her legs relaxed and loosened up, the kinks diminishing. On many of the other exercise machines, you pushed a button, and parts began to move and you grabbed onto something and the machine literally put you through the exercise at its own speed. Pat usually saved those machines for later, when she was ready to be pushed around.

But when Pat approached the teeter board she saw that it was being used. A man. He was going at a good clip. She watched him. Nice legs. Nice head. But why the hell was he wearing sunglasses indoors? She watched him for another minute, then decided he was going to be there for a while. She went to the rowing machine and worked the kinks out of her legs for several minutes. Then she went back to the balance board. The man was still on it.

Pat asked, "Are you going to be using the board much longer?"

He stopped and looked at her. "Do you want it?"

"Yes," Pat said. "I like to start out on it. But I'll do something else."

He stepped off. "No. Go ahead. It's yours. I'll try something else. You'd think they'd have more than one of these things."

"You would," Pat said. She stepped toward the board. "Thanks."

He asked, "How's the rowing machine?"

"A bit stiff," Pat said. "But so am I."

He grinned and walked away from her. "See you later."

Pat wondered who he was. Even with his sunglasses on, Pat could sense he was looking her over. She began working the board.

Ron was on the rowing machine.

Pat worked the board for fifteen minutes, her speed gradually increasing until the board scarcely left the floor. Enough. She headed for the treadmill. Mr. Sunglasses was on it, and at top speed.

Ron saw her coming. "You want this now?"

She laughed. "No. I've bothered you enough. I'll try something else."

"You can have it," Ron said, stepping off. "I'm just about worn out, anyway."

"How do I slow it down? I can't manage this speed."

"I'll do it for you," Ron offered. He went to the controls, turned a knob, and slowed the machine. "How's that?"

It was hardly moving. Pat said, "That would be fine for my grandmother. Can you jazz it up a little?" Ron turned a knob. Pat said, "There. That's fine. Thanks."

The two of them went on like that for more than an hour, one or the other of them at a device the other wanted to use. For Pat, this was just coincidence. For Ron, it was deliberate.

Finally, Ron said, "I'm just about bushed. How about you?"

"Yes, I think so."

"Can I give you a lift?"

"No, thanks. I have my car."

"Have you had lunch?"

"I usually don't eat lunch."

"Neither do I. I suppose it's too early for a drink?"

"It usually is. I don't drink much."

"Neither do I. What, then? We must have something more in common than liking exercise. How about dinner?"

She thought about it. He was cute. "All right. Where?"

"How about Caesar's Palace?"

"I'm sick of that place. How about the LPM Stars?"

"I'm sick of that place. The Riviera?"

"All right. Show time?"

"Okay. Where do I find you?"

"I'll meet you there."

"All right. You got a name?"

"Patricia. Pat."

He nodded at it. "Ronald. Ron."

"Purney."

"Grady."

"Show time."

"Show time."

Driving home, Ron thought about her perfect boobs. What a shame if they were silicone.

Driving home, Pat thought about his legs and what presumably was between them in a bulging jockstrap. What a shame that men went to such extremes to look sexy.

Chapter Twenty-three

P at recognized Ron by his sunglasses as she approached the
entrance to the Riviera's Starlite Theatre. She recognized too,
that he had been the man in the business suit at the poolside
that morning. Small world.

He greeted her with: "You look very nice."

"Thank you," Pat said. "So do you."

They moved toward the door. The maitre d' had already been
tipped, the fifty-dollar bill in his pocket. "Ready, Mr. Grady?" Ron
nodded. They were led to their table.

As it happened, their waiter had worked at Caesar's Palace for a
while and knew Pat. He gave her a smile and a nod. "The usual?"

"Yes, Charlie."

Ron looked at her. "What's the usual?"

"A malted shake with pralines."

"That's your drink?"

"Most of the time."

Ron looked at the waiter. "I'll have a shake, too, but no pralines." The waiter nodded and left.

Pat said, "Is that your drink?"

"Most of the time. In moments of joy or despair I drink scotch
and Coke."

"Disgusting."

"That's what they tell me. But it's the only way I can drink booze
without getting sick. How come the waiter knew you?"

"He used to work at Caesar's Palace when I was there."

"What did you do at Caesar's Palace?"

"I was the assistant to the guest choreographer."

"Who was that?"

"Ted Colby."

"I thought he made movies."

"He does. But he does nightclubs and television and Broadway.
Everything."

"How'd you get the job?"

"A few years ago, Ted hired me for the chorus in a movie he was making at LPM. Then his assistant quit. Ted gave me the job."

"Just like that?"

"Just like that."

"You were lucky."

"A little luck. A little talent."

The waiter brought the shakes.

Ron asked: "When did you start diving off mountains?"

She looked at him. "How'd you know that?"

"I saw you this morning."

"How did you know me? I was wearing a black wig."

Ron looked blatantly at her. "There are ways."

She said, "Mr. Grady, I think there's something I ought to tell you right now."

"What's that?"

"I don't give up on the first date."

"Oh. What are you doing tomorrow night?"

"That depends on what you try tonight."

"Your move."

"How come you're wearing sunglasses in here? It's pitch dark."

"I've got bad eyes."

"You had them on in the gym. Do you wear them all the time?"

"Except when I'm in bed with a woman."

"What else do you do?"

"Like what?"

"Do you live here?"

"I'm here on business."

"What business are you in?"

"I work for an airline."

"You're not a pilot, I hope."

"I'm on the business side."

"What are you doing here?"

"Drumming up trade."

"Are you married?"

"No. Are you?"

"No."

"Ever?"

"Never."

"What would you like to eat? I think the waiter wants us to order."

"I'll have the coq au vin. It's usually good here."

"Then I'll have that, too. Waiter?" He ordered. "Do you spend much time here in Vegas?"

"Only when there's work to do."

"And what do you do when there is no work?"

"There's always something to do."

"Here?"

"Sure."

"Like what?"

"I hit the spots and see the shows."

"Have you seen the show at the Stars?"

"Yes."

"Is is any good?"

"The show is all right. It's the comic that's wrong."

"What's the matter with him?"

"He's just the wrong comic for a Las Vegas audience, that's all."

"I read somewhere that he did good business in New York."

"New York is different. New York has those small clubs that attract a sophisticated, international, chic audience. Put the same comic in a club like that and he can still do all his punchlines in French and be a smash. Vegas audiences are television-watchers. They want belly-laughs, not intellectual giggles. The comic at the Stars is too subtle. A room that big needs somebody who works even bigger."

"Like who?"

"Fats Mulligan."

"I never heard of him."

"He had a bit in an LPM musical a few years ago. I rehearsed him. He's hilarious. But when they put the picture together, they kept cutting away from him to get on with the plot. People didn't get a chance to see how funny he is."

"What's so special about him?"

"He's out of vaudeville. He's used to an audience of two or three thousand people. He's a Jackie Gleason who hasn't had his big break. I saw him in a club in New York. He's strictly from Brooklyn, and that's the kind of people who packed the place every night, the kind of people who come to Vegas."

Ron said, "Here comes our cock."

Pat looked around, startled. The waiter was bringing their dinner.

Throughout the meal, Ron kept picking Pat's brains, digging for her ideas about show business, all angles of it. At one point, he asked, "I suppose you want to be a big movie star someday?"

"No," she said. "I don't know what I want, but I know I don't want that. Somebody once accused me of not knowing what I want, of shopping around too much, trying too many different things, spreading myself too thin. Maybe he was right. I may not know what I want, but I'll know it when I see it."

Ron asked, "Do you enjoy what you're doing now?"

"Yes. Yes, I do," and she sounded a bit surprised to hear herself say so. "In the first place, I don't do the same thing every day. I dance, I sing, I ski, I play musical instruments, I jump off mountains. It's fun. And I love working with Ted Colby. I have a lot of respect for that man. I'd never tell him that—he's conceited enough as he is. But I get a big kick out of the way he puts together a whole production number before he hires his first dancer or swimmer or whatever. He sketches out the whole thing on a big pad. Then it's my job to take those sketches and make them come to life. I love rehearsals. But when we start shooting the thing, it becomes routine for me, boring and hard work." She thought about it. "I guess I'm like a cook who gets more fun out of putting a meal together than eating it."

Ron asked, "Do you fuck much?"

She said, "I have my good days and I have my bad days."

"What's today been like?"

"Lousy. Up to now."

"I'm glad you're feeling better."

They finished their dinner before the show began and they ordered fresh malteds to sip during it. Throughout the show, Pat kept making side remarks to Ron—why this production number was so good, why that one was not so good, why Mitzi Gaynor could draw crowds, why Shecky Greene could draw laughs. When the show was over and the waiter brought the check, Ron placed three fifty-dollar bills on it without looking at it. Pat saw and decided not to be impressed.

As they walked slowly to the main door of the hotel, Ron asked, "Your place or mine?"

"Your place for you and my place for me."

"Oh, yes. Our first date. Dinner tomorrow night?"

"I can't say yet. Our leading lady got in today, and I'll have to work with her tomorrow. I don't know how long that will take."

"Can I call you?"

"Why don't I call you?"

"I'm staying with a friend. I don't know the number offhand."

"Then I'll see you at the gym."

"You're cruel."

She moved in quickly and kissed him on the cheek. She said, "See an eye doctor." And she went quickly to her car.

As Ron entered his apartment, the telephone was ringing. He

hurried to it. "Yes?"

"Kaz?"

"Yes."

"It's Milton. Has Bert Bernstein talked to you yet?"

"No. Not today. Why?"

"He's called here three times, looking for you. I was about to send out the bloodhounds."

"I've been moving around all day. What's up?"

"I don't know. He didn't say. But he wants you to call him. Have you got his home phone number?"

"Yes."

"You'd better call him. It sounded urgent."

"All right."

"And if it's any of my business, let me know."

"All right. Milton, I was just going to call you. I want you to call those people you know in New York, the talent agency. Tell them to track down a comedian by the name of Fats Mulligan."

"Fritz Mulligan?"

"Fats."

"I never heard of him."

"I'm told he's terrific. Anyway, find him and see how soon he can move into the Stars."

"You want me to book him?"

"Yes. Get him into the big room as soon as you can and pay him whatever he wants. Tell him it's an open contract and he can stay as long as he does business."

"Okay, Kaz. Where did you hear about him?"

"A friend of mine told me about him today. We need him fast, the sooner the better."

"What do I do with the Frenchman?"

"Pay him off."

"Okay. Let me know what Bert wants."

"I'll call you back."

Ron seldom called Bert Bernstein at home, so he looked up the number in the address book he carried in the attache case he rarely opened. Bert's phone rang several times before Ron heard:

"Hullo?"

"Bert, it's Ron. What's up?"

"Oh, yes. Ron, I've got bad news for you."

"Let's have it."

"Your grandfather died this afternoon."

"Oh God. What happened?"

"I don't have all the details. Your father called and talked to Morley, trying to find you. Morley told me."

"What happened?"

"Well, as I understand it, the family was out on the porch having drinks."

"They do that every day."

"Anyway, your grandfather put his drink down and closed his eyes. Everybody thought he'd fallen asleep. It wasn't until they tried to wake him up for dinner that they saw he was gone."

"God. I'll get right up there. Where's Morley?"

"He left for the farm right away. He's driving."

"Why the hell didn't he take a plane?"

"You'll never get Morley up in a plane. You know that."

"Yes. All right. I'm on my way."

"Ron, do you want me to go with you?"

"No. You'd better stay and mind the store."

"All right. I'm very sorry, Ron."

"Me, too. Thanks. I'll keep in touch. You have the number at the farm if you need me?"

"Yes."

"Okay. Now, Bert, there's something else I want you to do for me."

"What, Ron?"

"That agency that checks out people for us?"

"Yes?"

"Get them to do a check on a woman named Patricia Purney."

"Okay. How do you spell Purney?"

"I think it's P-u-r-n-e-y. I'm not sure."

"Where's she now?"

"She's here. She's working in the picture we're doing at Caesar's Palace. So those people of yours can start at LPM personnel. I want everything on her, all the way back, just like those other people they've checked out for me."

"Right. How urgent is this?"

"It's urgent. Get them on it right away."

"Okay."

"I'll keep in touch."

Ron hung up. He called Milton at the hotel and told him about Omar. Milton was sorry. Ron asked, "Are there any FreytFlytes heading into Los Angeles tonight?"

"No. The last one left a couple of hours ago."

"What about the other airlines?"

"Nothing at this hour, Kaz."

"Then I'll have to call Joe Reilly. You got the number up at the farm?"

"I've got it around here somewhere. I'm sure the receptionist has it."

"Okay. Call me if you need me. And follow through on that comedian."

"I will."

Ron called Joe Reilly at home, and Reilly answered on the first ring. Ron: "Joe, it's Ron. I'm in Vegas."

"Yes, Ron. What's up?"

"Joe, I just got the news that my grandfather died this afternoon."

"Christ, I'm sorry, Ron. I never met the man but Shad talked about him a lot. Shad thought the world of him."

"I know. My grandfather thought the world of Shad, too. Joe, there aren't any more flights out of here tonight. I'll need my plane. It's at FreytFlyte. Can you get somebody to bring it over here right away?"

"I'll bring it myself."

"Good. When do you think you can get here?"

"Let's see. It's midnight now."

"Just about."

"I should be there sometime between two and three."

"All right. I'll meet you at the field."

"Right. I'm sorry, Ron."

"Thanks."

Ron called the farm. Stewart answered: "Jeez, Ron, we've been looking for you for hours."

"I know. I just heard. How's Grandma?"

"She's all right. It's Mama that's taking it bad."

"She would. Is Morley Covington there?"

"No. They just called from Sacramento. They're going to spend the night and come out in the morning."

"Who's they?"

"Morley and his wife. Dave French and his wife."

"Okay. Now listen. Joe Reilly is flying my plane over here from L.A. He should be here in a couple of hours. As soon as he gets here, I'll take off for the farm."

"Okay."

"I'll buzz the house when I get there."

"Okay. I'll pick you up at the airstrip."

"Yes. And if it's still dark, you'd better take a couple more cars with you to throw some light on the strip so I can see it."

"Right. You want to talk to Mama?"

"I'd better not. It's going to be rough enough when I get up there. How's Papa?"

"He's okay. Want to talk to him?"

"No. Just tell him I'm on the way." He hung up.

The man in the New York apartment was getting head. He said, "Take more of it. Take more of it baby."

The young hustler said, "I'm taking all of it that I can. You'll have to settle."

"You said you like 'em big."

"I like 'em big all right, but not this big. It's vulgar."

"That's the trouble with you faggots. You don't know nothing."

"I've never had any complaints before. What you need with this thing is a suction pump."

"Forget it, then. Lay down."

"Like hell I will. What do you want to do, ruin me for life? I'm getting my ass out of here."

"Get your ass out of here, then. And don't expect to get paid. You didn't earn it."

"Listen, honey, find me a gay on this planet who can accommodate that monstrosity of yours, and I'll pay to watch."

Chapter Twenty-four

Pat got up to an empty house. Gwen had left a note on the kitchen table. Something was wrong with her car and she had taken it to a repair shop: if she had to wait too long for it, she'd have lunch at the hotel and go to work early. Pat warmed up the coffee and toasted an English muffin and paged through a magazine as she had breakfast. Then she bathed and dressed and drove to Caesar's Palace. The swimming pool was a swimming pool again; the LPM vans were still parked a short distance away. Pat entered the van that served as Ted Colby's office, Colby at the desk over a sketching pad, Buzz nearby at *Sports Illustrated*.

Pat asked, "How did our leading lady do yesterday?"

Colby said, "She's been spending too much time in the water. She's gone duck-bottom. I can't get her to tuck her ass under. She alway's looks like she's about to squat."

Buzz said, "With an ass like that, a duck would sink."

Pat asked, "So are you going to need me today?"

Colby said, "It turns out that our leading lady can't stand air conditioning, and I can't ask the kids to rehearse this afternoon in a stifling jai-alai oven without some air. We'll try tonight, when the temperature comes down a little."

Pat said, "I think I've got a date tonight."

"We'll, think again, dear," Colby said. "I'm going to need you tonight."

Damn!

Buzz stood up. "I'm for lunch. Pat?"

Pat said, "I just had breakfast."

Buzz said, "I hate to eat alone, and Fatso here is on a diet again. Come with me and have one of your malteds."

There was nothing else to do.

After the lunch, Pat drove to the health club and wasted over an hour loitering at the exercise machines, eyes alert for Ron Grady. No Ron Grady.

The rehearsal that evening was brutal. With no air conditioning and the indoor set mobbed with dancers and extras and crews and glazing lights, the jai-alai court was a furnace. Colby's only solution was to let the leading lady wait outside until she was needed, then turn off the air conditioning and let the place warm up enough for her and too much for everybody else. After four frustrating hours, Colby called it a night.

He took Pat aside. "It's hopeless, dear. You'll have to do the dances, and we can fake her into the shots when we get back to Hollywood. I can't throw away any more time or money. I'm catching enough hell now from the front office on the budget."

Pat asked, "How long do you think this will take?"

"With her in there, an eternity. With you in there, three or four days."

Pat shrugged. "You're the boss."

Colby said, "Pass the word."

The next three days were meshed into one for Pat Purney. She was at the set by seven every morning for makeup. Shooting began around nine. There was a short break for lunch and a short break for dinner, then work until midnight. Pat managed to survive long enough to drive home and fall into bed and sleep like the drugged until the alarm clock stunned her at six in the morning. Even so, two or three times every afternoon she telephoned the health club and asked for Mr. Grady. No Mr. Grady.

Mid-morning on the fourth day, Ted Colby took a microphone from a go-fer and announced, "That's it, children. Your purgatory has come to an end. We're finished here. You've all been absolutely divine and I'm very grateful to each of you, as you will see when you pick up your paychecks next week. You can head home whenever you like, wherever home might be. If you haven't got a home, keep in touch with LPM in case we need you. Otherwise, see you next time. God bless, and all that shit."

Pat changed in the dancers' van and went to Colby's office. "You got anyting to drink around here?"

Buzz said, "Nothing non-alcoholic."

"I don't want anything non-alcoholic. Give me some scotch."

Buzz filled a tumbler with ice cubes and poured in an inch of scotch.

Pat asked, "Got some Coke for it?"

Colby said, "I won't have you insult my good scotch with that piss. Drink it the way it is or suffer."

Pat took a sip and shuddered. "When are you two heading back?"

"Right after lunch," Colby said. "This town depresses me when

I have to stay here too long. I can't wait to get away. What about you?"

"I'm going to sleep for a couple of days. I guess I'll drive back over the weekend."

Colby said, "Call us when you get in. I'll want you to look at the rushes and help me decide where to stick in close-ups of Madame Duck-ass."

Pat did not sleep for a couple of days, but she slept through most of them, napping often, reading, watching television, taking short walks. It was on her third day off, when she was thinking of driving back to Los Angeles, when she saw a newspaper ad that made her gasp. It was:

BY POPULAR DEMAND!!!
The LPM Stars Presents
FATS MULLIGAN
(Direct from N.Y. Triumphs)
Limited Engagement

At the bottom of the ad was a number to call for reservations. Pat called. She was told that Mr. Mulligan was rehearsing and could not come to the phone. She left her name and number. When her phone rang an hour later, she lunged at it. She heard:

"Pat?"

"Yes, Fats," Pat almost screamed. "What happened? What are you doing out here?"

"I don't know," Fats said, almost screaming, too. "Last night I was working in this dive in Hoboken when I got this call from this talent agency and they told me to get my ass out here right away and that I was opening tonight. I can't believe it."

"It's amazing," Pat said, still screaming. "I was talking to somebody about you just the other night. And here you are. The ad says a limited engagement. How long are you booked for?"

"Honey, they gave me an open contract. I can stay here as long as I do business. And you wouldn't believe what they're paying me. I'm taking them for a royal fucking."

"You might as well make it while you can. It's high time."

"I know. I can't believe it. Pat, I hope you can make the opening tonight."

"I'll be there. Don't worry. I'll be there for both shows."

"Ain't this the wildest thing you ever heard? I'll get you the best table in the house. Wish me luck, honey."

"Break a leg."

That evening, sitting alone at the best table in the house, Pat watched Fats Mulligan cavort on stage for over an hour, the packed audience exploding repeatedly with laughter, and she had to admit to herself that this was the wildest thing she had ever heard. And yet wondered just how wild it really was, indeed.

It went without question: it would be done the Armenian way. Omar in the living room three days, the foreigners pushed aside to make room for the mourners, the air thick with the scents of flowers and burning candles. Neighbors coming and going all day, bringing food. Each night the priest: the rosary. The Reillys, Catholics, kneeling in the living room, praying for the repose of the soul of a man they never knew. Out on the porch, the Covingtons, Unitarians, the Frenches, Jews, outlanders, quiet and uncomfortable, wondering what the prayers were supposed to achieve. Then the Mass in the Armenian church, packed, the long cortege to the cemetery. Suddenly it was over and everybody was gone, the living room furniture back in place, the house silent and, in a strange way, vacant.

Ron said to Stewart, "Let's go for a walk. I want to talk to you."

Stewart said, "I've been waiting for this. The Big Brother Bit."

"That's right," Ron said. "And it's about time. C'mon."

They walked for three hours, Ron doing most of the talking. He told Stewart about Vietnam, all about Vietnam.

Stewart kept saying, "Jesus Christ. Jesus Christ." And finally he said, "You and Shad were crazy to get mixed up in that crap."

"We had no choice," Ron said. "By the time we figured out the scoop, we knew too much. If we'd said no, that would have been the end for both of us. We had to go along with it."

"But you did eventually say no," Steward pointed out.

"Yes, in a way."

"And do you think that was the end of *them*?"

"I don't know. That's really why I wanted to talk to you about the whole mess."

"Go ahead."

"Well," Ron said, "I'm still not happy about the reasons the doctors gave for Shad's death—some tropical disease. Why did it take so long to hit him? I wish Shad's wife had allowed an autopsy. Then maybe I could shake the feeling that there was something more to it."

"You think somebody helped Shad on the way out?"

"If somebody did, then I could understand other things that are happening," Ron said. He told Stewart about the unusual activity with the LPM stock and the sharp decline in business at the hotel.

Ron said, "Joe hasn't said anything about problems at FreytFlite as yet. What about you?"

Stewart thought about it, then: "Christ, you're spooking me. I was going to talk to you about it sooner or later. I didn't think it was that important."

"What?"

"Two things. Over the past few months some of our big jobs back East have been canceling out. The food companies that buy from huge commercial farms. Either they've decided to do their own spraying or they're signing up with some other outfit."

"Who?"

"I don't know. I can't find out."

"What else?"

"The Gulf States. We just don't seem able to break into that part of the country. I've been trying for over a year. I go down there, I pick up a few good jobs; but when I get back here and send off the contracts, they tell me the outfit they're with has cut the prices and they want to stand pat."

"So what does it look like to you?"

Stewart said, "It didn't look like anything to me, until you just opened your big mouth. Looks like you're being attacked on all sides, Mr. President. I wish you hadn't told me."

"I'm glad I did."

"Yeah?"

"Yeah. Stewart, if anything happens to me, anything smelly, if it looks like somebody has helped *me* to go out, I want you to get a lawyer and go to the authorities and tell them everything I've told you. There must be some way to stop those bastards."

Stewart said, "Jesus, Ron, why don't you just give them their money back?"

"I don't think they'd settle for that," Ron said. "If they got Shad's ass they'll want mine."

"Then why don't they just knock you off?"

"That's what I'd like to know. Let's go back to the house."

On the way, Stewart said, "I don't suppose you'll ever settle down on the farm again?"

Ron said, "No, I don't suppose I will. And I wish you wouldn't travel so much yourself, any more. One of us should stay closer to the folks."

Stewart said, "You're next in line, when Papa dies. What then?"

"The place is yours."

"I've been thinking about that. What if you have a son?"

"I've been thinking about that, too."

Ron said, "Then one of us ought to get busy."

Monday morning, Stewart drove Ron to Sacramento to catch a commercial flight to Los Angeles. At the airport, Ron said, "Can you meet me in Vegas in a couple of weeks?"

"Sure. What's up?"

"I'd like to get everybody together for a business meeting."

"Okay. Say when."

"I'll let you know. And find somebody to do your traveling for you. You should be able to run the company from home."

"Yes, Mr. President."

"And get married."

"You too, Mr. President."

"I'm thinking about it."

At Los Angeles, Ron took a cab to the studio. His desk was a heap of business papers, scripts, memos and telephone messages. The young woman who considered herself his secretary, but whom he considered his first line of defense, came into his office.

"I'm sorry, Mr. Kaz," she said. "but I didn't know what to do with all that mess, and I didn't want to bother you at the farm, with the funeral and everything."

He said, "Pack it all in a box. I'll take it home."

She said, "Every department head wants to see you."

He said, "Tell them to send me a memo."

"They have," she said, pointing at the desk. "But they want to talk to you."

"Tell them I'll get back to them. Is Bert Bernstein in?"

"He was. He had to go out. He gave me this for you." She held up a manila envelope.

"Put it in the box with the rest of the stuff. When Bert comes back, tell him I'm home. And tell Morley Covington. I don't want to hear from anybody else."

"Yes, sir."

At home, Ron took time only to change his clothes and make himself a malted, and then he settled at the desk in his den and tackled the box of papers. As he worked his way through the pile, he becamed annoyed with the petty decisions that were being left up to him. Nobody in Hollywood seemed willing to make a decision, everybody so insecure in the job, so everything was left to the boss, especially the boss who owned the outfit and couldn't be fired. Shit. Where were the people with balls? Brains? He was surrounded by brains; he could hire all the brains he wanted. But where were the balls?

Late afternoon, his phone rang, and he assumed it was Bert or Morley. It was Milton Graham.

Graham said, "I know I'm not supposed to bother you at home today, but I thought you'd like to know what's happening?"

"All right, Milton. What's happening."

"Well, I've got some good news and some bad news."

"What's the good news?"

"My people in New York found that Fats Mulligan guy. He was working in some dive in Hoboken."

"Good. Can you get him?"

"I already got him. He opened here Thursday night."

"How's he doing?"

"Terrific. The word must have got out before the ads did. He's packing them in every night, both shows, and we're turning people away."

"That's good news. Is he happy?"

"He's ready to stay here the rest of his life."

"Good. Give him anything that he wants."

"I am. And you should see his girl friend."

"Oh, yeah?"

"A beauty. Maybe you should hire her as a showgirl. With those knockers, she'd draw crowds on her own."

"Talk to the choreographer about it. What's the bad news?"

"The chef. I had another battle with him about his budget. He's threatening to quit. How about if we raise the price of the meals a buck or two to get the kitchen out of the red?"

"No, don't do that. I've got some ideas for the kitchen, but I haven't had time to do anything about it. Go down to the kitchen and give the chef a kiss for me and tell him I want to have a long talk with him when I get back. I think I know a way to put an end to all his problems."

"Like cutting his throat?"

"Something like that."

"When are you coming back here?"

"As soon as I can."

"Okay."

"Milton, what's Fats Mulligan's girl friend's name?"

"I forget. He just introduced me to her. I think it's Betty Furness."

"Oh. Okay. Keep in touch."

Around midnight, the words on the pages in front of him began a jittery ballet. Ron knew he could not work any longer. He realized, too, that he had eaten nothing since Natalie's breakfast that morning. He went out to the kitchen, inspected the refrigerator, vetoed everything with a glance, mixed another malted and settled for crackers and cheese at the kitchen table.

The phone rang. Ron took it on the kitchen extension and heard: "Ron?"

"Yes."

"Bert Bernstein. Did I wake you?"

"No. I'm just having a snack before turning in. What's up?"

"I've been over at ABC all day, working on the contract for the TV rights for the films they want to rent, so I didn't get to see you at the office."

"How does it look?"

"Okay, but I may have to go to New York before this is settled."

"Okay."

"The reason I called, Ron—did you get the report?"

"What report is that, Bert?"

"The report on the broad you wanted me to have checked out. You called me from Vegas about her. What's her name?"

"Oh. Oh, yes. Patricia Purney."

"Yeah, that's the one. The report came in this morning and I dropped it off at your office on my way out. Did you get it?"

Ron remembered. "Minnie did give me something she said was from you. I guess it's in the box of work I brought home. I'll find it. Thanks, Bert."

"Any time. How are things with the family?"

"Everything's okay, considering."

"Of course. Will you be coming in tomorrow?"

"I'll have to. Minnie says all the department heads have problems for me."

Bert said, "Those bastards shouldn't bother you with all their bullshit. It isn't as though the studio was the only thing you had to worry about."

Ron said, "I wish it were, Bert. I wish it were. Good night."

Hanging up, Ron returned to the den, dug through the box of work and found the Patricia Purney report near the bottom of it. He read the report, and as he read a grin brightened his face, then a smile. He read the report again. Again. He said to himself, "Young lady, you are a liar. You are a goddamn liar. You are a beautiful goddamn liar. You are the most beautiful goddamn liar in the world. And with a little practice, you may become almost as good a liar as I am."

And he laughed out loud.

He was wide awake now, and he decided to get something else

off his mind. He rolled a sheet of paper into his typewriter and, using his pointer fingers, wrote:

To Stewart, Joe and Milton—Get on this right away.

1. Stewart's pilots, being closest to the growers, will make deals to buy up quantities of surplus fruit and vegetable crops.
2. Stewart's pilots will airlift stuff to nearest Freytflyte depots.
3. Joe's pilots will airlift stuff to Vegas.
4. Milton will make deals with Vegas hotel managers to buy our stuff at prices well below L.A. wholesalers and brokers.
5. If this works in Vegas, Milton will spread out to Reno and Tahoe. Maybe later Atlantic City, Miami and other resort areas. Maybe later we can add meats and seafood.
6. Everybody get your ass moving and keep me informed.

Satisfied and relaxed, Ron went back to the kitchen and finished the malted and the cheese and crackers. Then he went to bed. In the darkness, he saw Patricia Purney hovering over his bed, and he said to her, "Lady, I know you've got the tits for it. Looks like you've got the brains. I just hope you've got the balls."

Next morning at the studio he gave the project outline to Minnie and told her to get it to Stewart and Joe and Milton as fast as possible. And he said, "Tell the department heads I'm ready to listen to their bullshit now, and they'd better make it brief."

Even brief, the bullshit kept him in Hollywood for almost three weeks.

At about the same time, the man in Houston heard his call letters summoning him on the radio receiver in the back of his house. He went to the machine and identified himself.

He heard: "That's you?"

"Yes."

"The boss wants to talk to you." The voice was deep and guttural and very Spanish. "No names."

"No names."

A silence. Then another voice, deeper, more guttural, more Spanish. "What the hell is going on up there?"

"Up where?"

"The Strip."

"I don't know what you're talking about."

"The son of a bitch is going into the grocery business."

"Hones, I—"

"No names!"

"Sorry, boss. I don't know what you're talking about."

"The son of a bitch with the hotel. He's going into the grocery business. He's flying in the shit from all over the country. He's trying to get the other hotels to buy from him for next to nothing. The wholesalers on the Coast are getting very mad. The son of a bitch could·wreck the whole organization."

"Honest, boss. This is the first I've heard about it."

"What about the big dick in New York? He is supposed to be watching everything."

"If he knew anything, he would tell me."

"Kick his ass or get rid of him."

"I'll get right on him."

"You'd better. And keep that goddam grocery man out of our territory. How the hell can we get our own planes in and out of there with those bastards buzzing all over the place?"

"I'm keeping them out, boss. I don't answer their letters, and we're practically doing the dusting for free."

"Well, shoot 'em down if you have to. That son of a bitch fucked us once; I'm not gonna let him do it twice. I want his ass."

"You'll get it, boss."

"I'll get yours, too."

Chapter Twenty-five

It was almost five in the morning. The Nevada sun was already warming the strip. After Fats Mulligan's second show the night before he had asked Pat to accompany him to a party Sammy Davis Jr. was giving at Caesar's Palace as a farewell gesture after his final performance of his current run there.

"Around four-thirty, Fats said to Pat, "I've had enough. Shall we go?"

Pat said, "I had enough before we came here. Yes, let's go."

Fats looked around for Sammy Davis, to say good night, but Davis was already gone. It took a few minutes of good nights as they worked their way to the door, and so it was almost five when Pat dropped Fats off at the main door of the LPM Stars. As Pat eased her car away from the entrance, she saw a man come out of the employees' door of the hotel. She recognized him. On impulse, she tooted the horn.

Ron Kazurian stopped and looked at the car. His first thought was that the driver just wanted him to get out of the way, so he stepped back. Then the horn was sounded again. A bit annoyed, he sent the driver a questioning stare. And then he recognized the car. He went to it as casually as he could.

He tried to sound as though they had just seen each other a few minutes ago. "What are you doing up at this hour?"

"Delivering the milk," Pat said. "What are you doing up at this hour?"

"I just put the cows out to pasture. Want a nightcap?"

"I've had enough caps for tonight."

"How about some breakfast?"

"It's too early for breakfast."

"Will you be at the gym this afternoon?"

"I might. Will you?"

"If you are."

"I'll think about it."

"Same time. Same teeter board."

"I'll think about it."

"You owe me a second date, you know."

"I don't know that I owe you anything."

"You get bitchier with age, don't you?"

"Yes. And I'm still young yet."

"God help me." He stepped back from the car and watched as she drove away. And he wondered if she had just gotten out of bed with Fats Mulligan.

Driving away, Pat glanced at him in the rearview mirror. And she wondered in which room of the hotel was the woman who was still smiling at the fresh memory of Ron Grady in her.

Mid-afternoon, Pat called the Stars and asked for Fats Mulligan. The hotel operator said, "Sorry, but Mr. Mulligan left instructions not to be disturbed."

Probably still asleep. "Will you leave a message that Pat Purney called? I'll see him this evening."

"Yes, Miss Guernsey."

Pat took a long bath, then dressed in slacks, a shirt, the spiked sandals. She put fresh gym clothes into the canvas bag and drove to the health club. She could hear the teeter board before she entered the vast exercise room. The place was practically deserted, everybody probably sleeping off the Sammy Davis party. She made her way through the labyrinth of exercise equipment until Ron was in view, and she stood a short distance from him, watching him. Nice legs. She knew he was aware of her, but he kept looking at the floor as he worked the board at top speed.

Finally she raised her voice and asked, "Excuse me, mister, but are you going to use that thing all afternoon?"

He gave her a glance. "I'm thinking about it."

"Well, when do you think you'll make up your mind?"

"Why?"

"Because I'd like to use it myself."

He kept pumping. "Why don't you join me?"

"There's not room."

"Sure there is. You work one side and I'll work the other."

"How do I know you'll stay on your side?"

"How do I know you want me to?" He stepped off the board and went to her. "Listen," he said. "I'm sorry about disappearing like I did. I had to leave town in a hurry."

"Your kind usually does."

"No. Really. It was something important. How about some breakfast?"

"I've had breakfast."

"Oh. And you don't eat lunch, do you?"

"No. I'm surprised you remembered."

"I remember a lot of things about you." He glanced at her chest. "You don't drink either, do you?"

"On occasions."

"Is this an occasion?"

"I don't think so."

"How about a malted?"

"I don't think so."

"I'm running out of ideas. Is it too early to start on our second date?"

She was enjoying this. "It may be too late."

"Then tell me something. Did you come here to work out or to work on me?"

"I come here all the time."

"Then let me tell you something else. When I checked in here today, the receptionist gave me a dozen messages. Somebody has been calling this place practically every day and asking for me. There was no name."

"What makes you think I called you?"

"Because you're the only person in Las Vegas who knows that I come to this place."

"Maybe you have a secret admirer."

He had enough. "Listen, lady, if you had given me a telephone number when I asked for it, I could have called you and told you that I had to leave town. So this mix-up is your fault as well as mine."

She could see that he'd had enough. "Well," she said, weakening, "if you had given me a number when I asked for it, I could have called your friend and left word where you could find me when you got back."

"So we both made a mistake. Do you still want this damned board?"

"No."

"Then let's get out of here."

They went to their separate locker rooms and changed and met in the reception room. He opened the outer door for her and they stepped out into the Nevada afternoon furnace. He asked, "What do you want to do?"

"I don't care."

"Let's go up to the lake. It's cooler there. And there's a restaurant that has good malteds. With pralines."

"You remember everything."

"An Armenian never forgets."

"Armenian? I thought Grady was Irish."

"My mother is Armenian." At least it wasn't another lie.

He led her toward his car, and she followed without a glance at hers. On the drive to Lake Mead, they kept their conversation casual and indirect, both of them still parrying a little. At the restaurant, they took a table at the large windows that overlooked the lake and the dam, and they ordered. Cookies came with the malteds, but they both ignored them.

He asked, "How long have you been in the movies?" He knew perfectly well.

"I'm not really in the movies," she said. "Most of my work is off-camera. I'm only in front of a camera when the leading lady is supposed to do something she can't do or won't do."

"Like jumping off a mountain?"

"Things like that."

"What else?"

"Oh, dancing. Skiing. Ice-skating. They use me for the long shots. Or close-ups of my feet when there's something intricate. Or my hands, when the leading lady is supposed to be a concert pianist."

"Do you enjoy it?"

"Most of it. I like off-camera. The putting things together. The rehearsal. Once they start filming, it can get boring."

"Why? I'd think the filming would be the most interesting part."

"That shows how much you know about making movies. Believe me, it's boring."

"Why?"

"Well, if you ask me, there are a lot of people in Hollywood who don't know what they're doing. They don't want anybody to find out, so they lose a lot of time trying to decide what they want to do. They keep making changes."

"Who makes changes?"

"Everybody. The producer. The director. The stars. From what I've seen, the writers do more writing after the picture gets going than they do before they get started in the first place. So they end up with a different picture than they started with, and often it's a mess and it loses a lot of money."

"Whose fault is that?"

"Whose fault is it in any business? The man at the top. In any business, somebody has to be the boss. Somebody has to say, 'I put up the money and this is the way we're doing things and the rest of you can do it my way or get your ass out of here.'"

"And that doesn't happen?"

"Not as much as it should. It used to. At least, the oldtimers tell me that it used to. Every studio had a boss—a czar—and you did things his way or you didn't work. Usually everybody hated him, but he got things done and the studio made a lot of money."

Ron offered Pat a cigarette and took one himself and lighted both. "I don't think I'd like a job like that. Would you?"

"I'd love it. Sometimes when I have to sit around a set for hours while people argue over a line or a scene or a gesture or a camera angle, I'd like to take a horse whip to all of them."

"Oh, you're mean."

"I can be. I hate waste."

"But how would you prevent waste?"

"Preparation. That's why I like working with Ted Colby. He's got the whole routine sketched out before he looks at the first dancer. That's way Ted almost always comes in at budget or under budget. Maybe it's something he learned in television. In television, you don't have any time to fool around. In movies, people think they've got all the time in the world. If movie people prepared everything in advance, if everything was agreed upon beforehand, from the script to the props, you wouldn't have to waste so much time on the set trying to figure out what to do next, and you could make movies faster and cheaper. Do you still want to go to bed with me?"

"I'm thinking about it. But don't you have any questions you want to ask me?"

"About what?"

"About me."

"What do I have to know about you? Your name is Ron Grady, your mother is Armenian, you work for an airline and you're in the sales department and you've got sexy legs."

"I don't work for an airline. I own one."

"You're a liar."

"Yes, I am."

"I've never lied to you."

"You worked at the Radio City Music Hall for a few weeks skating in an ice show. You didn't meet Ted Colby backstage anywhere. You met him on a sound stage at LPM when you sneaked into a callback because you missed the auditions his little Italian sweetheart had held earlier. Your mother comes from a wealthy family in Texas. Cattle. Your father was a pilot in Korea and he became a lawyer and is now a judge in Colorado. He turned down a chance to become a member of the Supreme Court."

"You son of a bitch."

"You got started in the movies when you fell into a job playing Geronimo in a western on location near your home in Colorado. The stuntman got hurt and you did his bit for him. The two of you got to be very chummy. I don't know how chummy, but he married a girl friend of yours here in Las Vegas. You stay at her place when you're here."

"You bastard!"

"I wish you would stop making those nasty remarks about my mother."

"Is she Armenian?"

"She is. And so's my father."

"With a name like Grady?"

"His name isn't Grady."

"And neither is yours?"

"No. And your name isn't Purney. You told me you were never married. You were married. He was a stuntman on a television series and he got killed on location in Africa. You turned down his insurance and had it sent to his first wife in Kansas or Nebraska or someplace out there."

"Who the hell are you?"

"I'm not through with you yet. How do you think your friend Fats Mulligan got his job at the Stars?"

"The manager knew about him and called him and booked him."

"And who do you think told the manager to book him?"

"Don't tell me you did."

"I did."

"What have you got to say about who works at the Stars?"

"I own the place."

"Jesus Christ."

"Does the name Kazurian mean anything to you?"

"What?"

"Kazurian."

"I'm not sure."

"What about Kaz?"

A light went on. "Mr. Kaz?"

"Some people say that."

"The head of LPM Studios?"

"That's right."

She needed to fight back. "I get it. Your uncle is the head of LPM Studios, and if I play my cards right you'll get him to make a movie star out of me."

"Bullshit. If I thought you wanted to become a movie star, I wouldn't be sitting here talking to you about the movie business. I'm up to my ass in movie stars, and they're bankrupting me. The only uncles I've got are farmers in Northern California. I'm Mr. Kaz. And I'm offering you a job whether or not I ever get to kiss those tits of yours."

"What job?"

"The job we've been talking about. The czar. I need somebody who can horsewhip people. I can't find anybody. You're the first person I've met who might be able to do it."

"What makes you think so?"

"Because you were right about Fats Mulligan. That's why I hired him. I wanted to find out if you're as smart as you think you are."

"He's doing great business."

"I know that. I see the accounts every day. If you're right about him, you could be right about other things. I'm willing to take the chance. Are you?"

"I don't know." And she didn't know. "This sounds like so much bullshit. Mr. Grady, you don't have to go through all this just to chew on my tits."

"Oh Jesus. What do I have to do to make you believe me? Here." He took his wallet out of his breast pocket and flipped it open. "There. There's my driver's license."

She looked. Ronald Kazurian. She asked, "Why Grady, then?"

"Because Mr. Kaz meets too many women who want to become movie stars."

"This woman doesn't."

"I know. Will you take the job?"

"I'll think about it."

"Do you still want me to fuck you?"

"I think you already have."

IV
The Godmother

Chapter Twenty-six

Overnight, she became the talk of Hollywood. Overnight, she became, in fact, the talk of the papier-mache world of entertainment. People who knew Pat Purney and liked her were delighted with her double-barreled conquests: marrying one of the most important men in the motion picture industry and landing the most important job that man could give anyone. People who knew Pat and didn't like her remarked wryly among themselves that evidently the altar had replaced the casting couch. People who didn't know Pat Purney but who knew that their lives and their work would be affected by her, had the eerie feeling of suddenly finding themselves on another planet and not being sure whether the experience was going to be good or bad for them..

Actually, there had not been an altar. Pat and Ron remained in Las Vegas until Gwen and Stubby returned from New York, sometimes sleeping at Ron's apartment, other times sleeping at Gwen's house. They did not get much rest. Within a few hours, they both discovered the arrogant pleasure of both being total aggressors. Within a few hours, Ron had experienced every inch of Pat Purney. Within a few hours, Pat had tasted every pore of Ron Kazurian that her tongue could reach. Their aggressiveness was matched by their insatiable endurance. They touched each other while they ate, even when they had baths together. Evenings at the Stars, while they were laughing at Fats Mulligan again, their hands were busy under the table. They drove back to Los Angeles in Pat's car, taking turns at the wheel, taking turns at each other. For appearances' sake—in a town where everybody saw through appearances—Pat kept her apartment until their affair could be legalized.

The waiting went to the preparations. The license. The blood tests. The required three days. For the sake of their families they arranged to have the ceremony held in the garden of Ron's rented house in Bel Air, performed jointly by an Armenian Catholic priest and a Roman Catholic priest. On the day before the wedding, Ron sent a FreytFlyte plane to the farm to pick up his family. He sent another plane to Denver to pick up Pat's family. On the day of the wedding he sent a plane to San Francisco to pick up the Frenches. Another plane went to Las Vegas for Gwen and Stubby and Fats Mulligan and Milton Graham. The Covingtons drove in from Malibu. The Reillys came up from La Jolla. Ron sent a limousine for Shad Grady's widow, this way making Shad a part of the event. Ted Colby and Buzz hired a chauffered limousine for the event. Bert Bernstein arrived late, an LPM starlet on his arm.

Bert Bernstein was wearing a black Homburg, and, as the ceremony began, he inched close to Colby and whispered, "Do I keep my hat on?"

Colby glanced at the hat. "If it was a prettier hat, I'd say keep it on. Seeing what it is, I'd say take if off. Take it off and throw it away."

The ceremony was brief. Immediately after it, waiters came pouring from the house with champagne, while other waiters quickly loaded a long table with enough food to feed the entire S.A.G. membership. Martha Grady broke her lifelong abstinence from alcohol with determined sips of her champagne, hoping to find in it an escape from her discomfort on being surrounded by so many Catholics and Jews. Gwen went around the garden, showing off the diamond brooch Pat had given her for being matron of honor. Stewart, the best man, showed everybody the gold watch Ron had given him. Gifts from the hastily summoned guests kept arriving for over a week.

As the reception was breaking up, Buzz wandered over to Pat. "Where are you two going on your honeymoon?"

Pat said, "We've already had the honeymoon, in Las Vegas."

"I figured that. But aren't you going to go somewhere to rest up for a few days?"

"Who needs a rest? This man is fabulous."

Buzz sighed and shook his head. "Lucky you. Apparently you've married a better man than I did. These days, I have to show Ted dirty pictures, just to turn his motor on."

They were driving to work. Ron asked, "By the way, how much do you want to get paid?"

Pat asked, "For what?"

"For your job at the studio."

"I don't have to get paid for that. After all, I'm married to the boss."

"But I want you to get paid."

"What for?"

"So I can fire you if you don't do a good job."

"If I don't do a good job, I'll fire myself."

"Remember that. And remember something else."

"What?"

"When we're home, it's even-steven."

"That's the way I like it."

He had expected her to work out of his own office, but she refused. "It's too big," she said. "I'd feel like I'm working in the middle of a sound stage. Besides, I don't want to have you looking over my shoulder every minute. Just get me a little room down the hall with a telephone."

"All right." He found her a small office down the hall. He tried the telephone. "It works." He asked, "Do you want a secretary?"

"Not yet," she said. "First I want to find out everything that's going on around here."

"Like what?"

"I want to see the scripts of every picture you've got in the works, both on the lot and on location. I want to see the budgets and the payrolls. I want to see the receipts of what's running now. I want to see the deals you've got with the television producers. I want—"

"Hold it!" Ron held up both hands. "If you keep going at this rate, there won't be time for even-stevens."

"I'll pencil you in."

Ron looked up into the air, "Christ, her first day on the job, and already she's power crazy."

She was. And she loved it. Power in itself was not what drove her; her impatience with waste did. Over the years she had been in the picture business she had quietly seethed inside over the waste of time and talent and equipment while this producer or that director debated with himself about what to do next. Now that she had the power, she had the determination to change all that.

Later that day, at home, while they were on their bed and the tip of Ron's tongue was at her clitoris, she said, "Do I have the authority to make some personal changes at the studio? I think I know a few people who can do a better—"

He bit her thigh. He said, "Listen, lady, we talk business at the office. When I'm slurping your pussy, the least you can do is catch your breath."

She faked a gasp. "Like that?"

He shoved two fingers into her and she yelped. "Like that," he said.

She laughed and put her hands on the back of his head and guided his tongue back into her. A few moments later, she gasped. For real.

Next morning, as Ron was guiding his car into his parking space at the studio, he said, "You can make any personal changes that you want."

"I intended to, anyway."

She was having the time of her life. Her marriage was going as well as she could hope. Her job was going better than she had expected. For her, the two were inseparable. The success of each made the success of both more exquisite, even when one intruded upon the other. Despite Ron's rule that she keep business out of the home, there were evenings when she brought home scripts and schedules and budgets, sitting up late over them before she joined Ron in bed. There were times at the office when the sight of him passing her door made her nipples harden for him, making her more eager for an early trip to the house.

The intrusions enhanced both spheres of her. On the job, she soon observed that conferences in the office were often stiff and guarded, people sensitive about each other's sensitivities, people made cautious by the affluence of the executive suite. But she observed, too, that when she gathered five or six people at a dinner table and got a few drinks into them they became more confident, more aggressive, more creative. She knew that Ron did not want people at the house every night, so she became a regular at Chasen's, a good table was reserved for her every night, even when she wasn't there. Her casual remark around the office—"Let's talk about it at Chasen's tonight"—was an invitation, not an order, and an invitation which others enjoyed even when they weren't invited. Uninvited guests were at Pat's table often just long enough to have a drink, the chitchat before the shop talk. When Pat was not there, the table was still used for her regulars. No check was ever presented. Pat or no Pat, the bill was simply sent to the studio and paid promptly.

Ron could always tell when a Chasen's session had gone well. Pat returned home more girlish, more playful, more demanding, more insatiable. For Ron life became exciting. He still disliked the confines of an office and he still did not have a secretary, but he spent more time at the studio now and became interested in more than earnings. He learned more about his own business. With just a few words, going to the studio in the morning or going home at night, Pat could tell him about some studio problem or her resolution of it. Sometimes he would just listen and nod; sometimes he would ask a few questions. He was learning more about his wife. She could be a tough cookie. He wondered if she were tough enough to take on his own studio problems? He was worried about the continuing stock purchases. He never mentioned it.

Ron also had his other business interests: FreytFlyte, the hotel, the grocery business, Stewart's cropdusting, the family farm. These took him away from the studio, away from home, sometimes for just a night, sometimes for a few days. But he never had the feeling of being away from the studio or home or Pat. They were a telephone call away.

Pat, also, began to travel more, especially to locations, when the daily reports or the rushes indicated schedule problems. Usually a few days on location were enough for Pat to calm a temperamental director or actor or writer into compromise and cooperation. When that didn't work, she was ready to reach for the ax, firing people even when it meant having to pay them off for incomplete work. Gradually word went throughout the studio: "Watch out for Madame Titshit. She can be mean." The word got back to Pat. She shrugged it off. It was the picture that mattered. The studio. And if getting rid of the troublesome gnats on a production meant a better picture and better profits, then let the end justify the means. The hell with the rest of it.

And this happened. The unions of their marriage and their work somehow made both Pat and Ron feel closer to their families and want to be with them more. Once a month, the two of them would fly up to the Kazurian farm for a weekend. Every couple of months, they would fly to Denver for a long weekend with Pat's family. The visits were always casual, unplanned and unscheduled. They were family, enough in themselves.

At Evergreen, she usually set up her archery target and, after a little practice, she was as good at it as she had been when she won the Colorado junior championship two years running. Ron couldn't hit the target from more than twenty feet. On one visit, Pat's father, feeling chipper, suggested that they hunt up their old Karate suits and try a few movements. Ron watched, amused by Pat's frown, her pretended anger, her grunts as she swung her arms and legs. Amused, he challenged her. She threw him in ten seconds.

That night in bed, Ron deep in her, said, "Let's see you throw me now."

She squirmed a little under him, then, coy: "Now I don't want to."

She was having the time of her life.

She walked into the middle of things, pictures that others had already started on, pictures that others were in the middle of, pictures that others were winding up. She wanted something of her own, her own from start to finish, and she found what she wanted in a thick file of story outlines various writers had submitted, which had either been rejected or shelved for one reason or another. It was the story of an immigrant Irishman who had settled in Brooklyn and gotten a job as a waiter in an Irish pub. He was a lousy waiter, which gave the story much of its humor, and he was so naive that he didn't realize his friends were pulling a prank on him when they urged him to become a candidate for Mayor of New York. What happened along the way provided more humor, a lot of pathos, and a touching love story—the daughter of his opponent fell in love with him, and the big finish was that, although he could have won the election on his own, he acknowledged on election eve that he wasn't qualified, he stepped aside in favor of his opponent, married the man's daughter, and became owner of the Irish pub where he once worked. For the lead, the owner/writer had suggested Jackie Gleason.

Pat read the outline a dozen times, loved it, and one day she picked up her telephone and called Ted Colby. She asked, "Do you still want to direct a musical?"

Colby said, "I want to direct a musical so much that I'd go straight just for a chance at it."

Pat said, "I wouldn't ask that much of anybody. Ted, I found a synopsis in the inventory that I like. It isn't a musical now, but I'm sure it can be made into one. I'll send it over to you. Let me know what you think of it, and I'll tell you now that I want Fats Mulligan for the lead."

"I love it already," Ted said. And he did.

Pat tracked down the writer who had submitted the outline. Rejected once too often, he had quit show business and was teaching zoology at Burbank High. Pat put him back on the LPM payroll and, working with Ted, the three of them working evenings and weekends, they had a shooting script in two months. Only then did she tell Ron what was going on.

He said, "I have a question. How the hell is Fats Mulligan going to be able to keep working at the hotel in Las Vegas every night and make a movie in Hollywood at the same time? When does he get any sleep? Or is death the price he has to pay for fame?"

"Don't worry about Fats Mulligan," Pat assured him. "He has already told me that for years the only sleep he ever got was on buses going from one town to another on one-nighters. He can sleep just as well on the airplane you are going to provide for him. Anyway, a lot of the scenes take place in smoke-filled hotel rooms, so all Fats will have to do is get out of bed and walk down the hall."

Ron said, "You fuck up my hotel and I'll sue you."

"Sue away," Pat said. "I'll send the bill to LPM Studio."

"Shit," Ron said, "that's me, too."

Pat said, "You catch on quick."

Pat was catching on quick. This was the first production that was totally her own, and she mother-henned it, demanding in her quiet and calm, yet forceful and unbending, way in control of everything—the music, the sets, the costumes, the cast, the crew, the works. Without neglecting her other chores, without neglecting Ron, she was the first person on the set in the morning, the last to leave at night, and the talk at her table at Chasen's was mostly about the next day's work. When the time came for location work at the Stars, Pat arrived with the advance team, overseeing everything, even the rooms the company would occupy when they arrived. She stayed at Gwen's herself, where she knew she would have privacy for her homework when she wanted it but still have Gwen's company when she wanted that. And when Ron came to Las Vegas on one of his fast trips, to check the hotel or have meetings with Milton on the new business of food-supplying, Pat stayed with him at his apartment where, night or day, they took time to fill in the gaps in their lovemaking. At the same time, Pat kept in touch with pictures on location elsewhere, promptly getting on a plane to fly somewhere whenever problems developed. She quickly acquired a dislike for yes-men, and yet she would never take no for an answer from anybody. She was thriving on her authority and her responsibilities, but she was not swept away by them. From time to time, at some quiet moment in the middle of some quiet night, she would step away from herself and take a look at herself, and she recognized the woman she had become: she had become Ellece, her mother, a queen who ruled with sugar in one hand and an ax in the other, a pussycat with quick claws, and this view of herself made her laugh, laugh with pleasure and with satisfaction. She had, as she had once assured Stubby, found what she wanted, found herself, and, now that she had, she knew she would never dilute the discovery. Never.

One four a.m., another siege at the hotel coming to a pause, Pat got a call from her assistant in charge of an LPM production on location in Louisiana. Problems. Problems. Could Pat get there right away?

Pat hunted down Milton Graham. "I've got to get to New

Orleans right away," she said. "How soon can I get a plane?"

Graham asked, "How soon is right away?"

"Right now."

"There're no planes at this hour. But I'll check."

"What about FreytFlyte?"

"I don't know about FreytFlyte, but I'll check there, too."

"Call me at Gwen's, will you? I'll have to pack some things."

"Yes. Soon as I can."

The parking lot was still in darkness. Pat drove to Gwen's house, the phone ringing as she entered.

Milton Graham said: "Pat, there's no plane to New Orleans until one this afternoon. And you'll have to change at Dallas."

"What about FreytFlyte?"

"I called there. No answer. I guess they're not expecting anything."

"I'll have to call Ron, then."

"Okay. When will you be back?"

"I don't know. Tell Ted, will you?"

"Yes. Keep in touch."

"I will."

Having grown immune to time, Pat dialed the house in Los Angeles without giving thought to what time it was. The phone rang a dozen times before Ron managed: "Hullo?"

"Ron?"

"Yes."

"It's Pat, darling. Did I wake you?"

"What do you think? What time is it?"

"Around five."

"What are you doing up so early?"

"I just got back from work."

"How come?"

"I told you. We're working day and night. I left the hotel ten minutes ago."

"You shouldn't be running around Las Vegas by yourself at this time of the night. What's up?"

"Ron, Tom called just a while ago from New Orleans. They're having lots of problems. I have to go there right away."

"So go."

"I need a plane. There's no commercial flight until this afternoon, and I don't want to lose the whole day. Do you know if FreytFlyte has anything coming through?"

"No, I don't. You should have called Joe Reilly."

"I don't have his number. Ron, could you call him for me? If there's nothing coming into Vegas soon, maybe he can divert something for me. It's important."

"All right. I'll have him call you. But you listen to me, Patricia. I don't want you gallivanting around Las Vegas in the middle of the night. It's too dangerous."

"I just drive from the Stars' parking lot to Gwen's."

"Stay out of parking lots at this hour. I once got mugged in the parking lot at Caesar's Palace, and it was only midnight."

Jolt. Beat. "You never told me this."

"It happened before I met you. Those bastards beat the shit out of me."

"My God! How come you never mentioned this before?"

"I guess I forgot about it. Never mind. Those bastards almost killed me, and I don't want that to happen to you."

"I'll be careful. Pity I wasn't there."

"What could you have done, even with your fucken Karate? Just stay out of the parking lots."

"Yes, dear."

"I'll have Joe Reilly call you."

"Yes, dear."

Ron hung up the phone. He was about to reach for it again to call Joe Reilly when his arm stopped in midair. A dim memory suddenly went bright. The parking lot. Those two bastards. The woman. Remote. In a fog. Her arms flailing. No. No. It couldn't be. The world was not that fucken small.

Pat replaced the phone and headed for her bedroom to pack. She stopped in her tracks. Caesar's Palace. Gwen working late. The parking lot. The two men battling another man. Her attack. The two men fleeing. The man on the ground, on his back, unconscious, his face all blood, the thick wallet nearby. No. No. It couldn't be. The world was not that fucken small.

Morley Covington was paging through some papers on his desk. "There it is, Ron," he said. "Twenty thousand more shares changed hands last week. It's stepping up."

"Why?"

"I wish I knew. Is there something going on around here you haven't told me about?"

"You're the treasurer. You know as much as I do."

"I've been nosing around," Morley said. "I hear that Twentieth is thinking of selling a big chunk of their place. Real estate interests. I think they're putting up a swanky condo. And some oil people are scouting a couple of the studios. That can mean some more deals if there's oil. But we're the only ones that seem to have this stock hankypanky."

"How's the price holding?"

"Okay. It goes up and down from day to day, but we're holding."

"And you don't know who's doing the buying?"

"I've tried to trace it, but I keep running into dummy corporations or people I can't locate."

"Do you think somebody is trying to get control of the studio?"

"This is one way to do it. It's a long detour, but it could work. Either buying up the loose ends or getting the proxies."

"But why?"

"You tell me."

"You tell me what we can do about it."

"Okay, Ron. Let's say somebody—or some group—is trying to get control of the studio by sneaking around the country and buying out the small holders. Fight fire with fire."

"Start buying?"

"Right."

"But you told me some time back that taking that route could cause a panic, one way or another."

"It could. So we play the same game somebody else seems to be playing. We get sneaky."

"How do we do that."

"We set up our own dummy corporations and send somebody on the road making house calls. Buy a little here. Buy a little there. Gradually you go from forty-eight percent control to forty-nine, to fifty, fifty-one, as far as you want to go, and then maybe your worries can be over."

"Yeah, but how much will that cost?"

"Millions."

"We've got millions to play around with?"

"I don't think it's a matter of playing around, my friend. It could be a matter of survival. If the price stays where it is, we can manage. If it goes up, I'll have to call my old buddies at the bank in San Francisco. It's up to you."

"And if this doesn't work?"

"Back you go to milking cows."

"You get somebody to make the house calls?"

"Just a minute." Morley touched the button on his squawkbox. "Millie, will you ask Brad Cunningham to come in, please?"

Ron asked, "Who's Brad Cunningham?"

"I hired him about a year ago. He's a master's in economics from

Harvard Business. Bright kid. He's an expert on the market. In fact, he's been keeping track of our stock for us, so he knows all about this crap."

"Can he be sneaky?"

"What do you think Harvard turns out? Nuns?"

"Yeah, but can he be trusted?"

"Wait till you see his seraphic face. You'd trust him in bed with your sister."

"Is he gay?"

"I don't know. We don't have that question on our employment application."

"Maybe we should have Bert run a check on him."

"I don't think that will be necessary." There was a knock on the door. Covington said, "Come in, Brad."

In came a young man in his mid-twenties. His blonde hair was almost pink. Deep tan. Boy-next-door face. A bit tall. Muscular but not macho. Expensive suit. Jockey-shorts model.

Morley said, "Brad, have you met Ron Kazurian?"

"No, I haven't," Cunningham said. He turned to Ron, smiled, and extended his hand. "Glad to meet you, sir."

Morley said, "You should have met the boss before, but we don't see much of him around here. He hates movies."

Ron stood and shook the hand. "Good to meet you, Brad."

Morley said, "Sit down, Brad. This may take some time." Morley cleared his throat. "Brad, Ron and I have been discussing the company's stock situation."

"Yes, Morley."

"I've told Ron that you've been keeping an eye on the problem for us."

"Yes, Morley."

"We feel that the time has come for us to find out what the hell is going on and to put a stop to it before it gets out of control. And we feel you can be of a great help to us."

Brad Cunningham looked at Ron. "I'll do anything I can, sir."

Ron said, "The first thing you can do is stop calling me sir. Go ahead, Morley. I wanted to get started on this as soon as possible."

They talked for three hours, discussing the project from every angle, putting out ideas, exploring them, discarding them or building on them, planning their assault step by step, each taking on responsibilities and agreeing on how to pursue them.

On his way back to his office, Ron stopped off at the legal department and said to Bert Bernstein, "Bert, I want you to have that outfit run a check on a man named Brad Cunningham. He works here."

Bernstein said, "You mean Pretty Boy?"

"Is that what you call him?"

"Yeah. The horny son of a bitch is stealing all my starlets on me."

"Keep him away from my wife."

"You'd better keep your wife away from him."

Chapter Twenty-seven

On the day of the drug bust in Oakland, California, the drug bust that had been effected by Ron Kazurian after he had tipped off the Feds, across the country, in New York City, a man by the name of Sergio Carlotti was suffering through the worst day of his life. All day, his telephones kept ringing—the telephone in his Fifth Avenue condominium, the telephone in his limousine, the telephone in his Wall Street office—all of them private phones with unlisted numbers that were known only to a few people. One of the few people who knew the numbers was Sergio Carlotti's uncle in Houston, Texas. Uncle Julio. Sergio Carlotti's mentor. The reason Uncle Julio kept calling was that he kept getting radio messages from Colombia, South America, from a man named Hones Martinez Velasquez.

On his first call, Uncle Julio had said, "Hones is having a fit. Hones is out for blood. He wants to know who did this. He wants to know who tipped the Feds. He wants to know what happened to those fucken cocksuckers on the payroll in Washington. You'd better find out all the crap on this or it's your ass. And mine."

For the rest of the day, Uncle Julio's calls were variations on the same theme. Finally, for peace and time to think, Sergio Carlotti took all his phones off their hooks.

But Sergio continued to be worried. He continued to be scared. He was afraid of Hones, and he had a right to be. Hones was a killer. Everybody knew that. But Sergio was terrified of Uncle Julio. Uncle Julio had made Sergio what he was. Uncle Julio could destroy him. And Hones could destroy Uncle Julio.

On the night Sergio Carlotti was born in Houston, Texas, the obstetrician smiled as he eased the perfect male infant out of its mother's body. Then the smile turned to a frown, and the frown turned into a stare of horrified astonishment. The doctor said aloud, "Where the hell is the end of this kid?"

Later, the doctor thought of writing an article for the medical journal about the incredible birth he had witnessed. But all he did was talk about it to his peers at the country club. He said, "This kid was born with a cock bigger than my hard-on."

And one of his peers said, "That isn't saying much for you."

But it was true. To the Carlotti family and their wide variety of relatives in the city and across the country, it was an act of God. They were very proud, and they showed Sergio's cock to everybody who came to see the baby and bring him gifts. Sergio's grandmother said, "Mother of God, the thing is down to his ankles."

Uncle Julio's first visit to his new nephew was an event. But Uncle Julio's visits were always events. He arrived in a chauffeured limousine; he entered the house with his arms loaded with gifts; the chauffeur then emptied the trunk of the car and brought in more gifts, usually food, enough food and enough different kinds of food to feed all the Mexicans Uncle Julio was illegally importing into the state of Texas.

Uncle Julio took one look at the naked Sergio and said, "Any kid with a cock like that has to have brains to match. I'll be his godfather. I'll raise him like one of my own."

Sergio's parents did not object. They could not object. They knew they could not. They knew that everything they had they had acquired through Uncle Julio's generosities. They had, in fact, made the move from Brooklyn to Houston at Uncle Julio's request—his orders, actually—shortly after he had made the move himself. The family knew that Uncle Julio had gone as far as he could in the Italian hierarchy that ruled most of the backstreet rackets in Brooklyn. They knew that it was out of generosity that one of Uncle Julio's own uncles, recognizing Julio's limits for achievement within the Brooklyn hierarchy, assigned him to represent the extended-family's business interest in the virgin territory of Houston, Texas. Once settled there, Uncle Julio summoned his own immediate family from Brooklyn—his brothers and their families.

In a few years, the Carlotti family was a hierarchy of its own in Houston. In a short time, they soon had control of the linen service for most of the restaurants and hotels in Greater Houston. Next, they took over the commercial garbage collection business. They opened a temporary office help agency which fronted for prostitution. They established after-hours clubs for gambling. They organized an independent union of migrant farmworkers, importing them by boat from Mexico, issuing phony work permits to them, assigning them to farmers pressured into contracts, then ordering the workers to go on strike. They bought into a trucking company, then put other truckers out of business by undercutting them until the competition was nil, then sending their rates up. They made loans, loans to everybody from migrant workers to unemployed Blacks, to the struggling middle class, always at interest rates that made paying off the principal impossible. They also made loans to going concerns that needed expansion or modernization, extending the loan for a piece of the business, taking piece after piece, until they had it all.

Although he had it all, Uncle Julio nevertheless lacked the one thing he wanted most: an heir. His wife had presented him with three daughters, and with that he gave up on her. Now he had one, if only by osmosis, and he raised Sergio as his own.

Uncle Julio turned out to be wrong about Sergio's brains. From his first days in school, Sergio proved to be totally incapable of absorbing knowledge. The boy never would have gotten beyond first grade had not Uncle Julio resorted to devices by which he got most things done: expensive gifts to the schools and the teachers. And when the gifts didn't work, there were always threats. And when the threats didn't work, Sergio had his own device for getting passing grades: his dick. Time and again, teachers, both men and women, were willing to give Sergio an "A" for the astonishing adventure of getting the kid into bed.

Uncle Julio was determined to get Sergio into the Harvard Business School, and he had a reason for this. The Brooklyn hierarchy of the Carlotti Family always considered the Houston branch third rate because Uncle Julio's rackets were at the bottom of the social scale, and Uncle Julio knew this and suffered from it. He needed some class. At Harvard, Sergio could meet some wealthy Easterners, seep into their social circles, make important business contacts where Uncle Julio could launder some of his dirty money, thus giving Uncle Julio some status of his own, and the Brooklyn relatives could go fuck themselves. Uncle Julio got Sergio into Harvard.

Sergio's apartment quickly became a private club for any of his classmates who spoke with a broad "A" and whose families had been checked out by Uncle Julio in Dun & Bradstreet. Within a few months, his new friends drunk and sexed enough, Sergio was able to worm out of them investment tips they had heard their fathers mention to each other at cocktail parties and dinner parties on the occasional weekends home. Sergio telephoned the tips to Uncle Julio, who first made his own investments, and then tipped off his elders in Brooklyn in order to impress them. Before long, the entire Carlotti dynasty, coast to coast, was bragging about the inside track they had in Wall Street. On his subsequent trips to Brooklyn, Uncle Julio was welcomed with a red carpet.

Of Sergio's new friends at Harvard, two were closest. One was

Andrew Robinson, Jr., son of Andrew Robinson, Sr., the Robinson of Robinson, Sayer, one of the largest investment houses in Wall Street, with branches in twenty-three cities. The other was Eric Russell, son of Morton Russell, of Morton Russell & Associates, one of the biggest law firms in Wall Street, specializing in investments and securities and ready for anything else. On occasional weekends and during vacations, Sergio was a frequent guest at the Robinson homes in Beekman Place or at Southampton or Palm Beach or at the Russell home on Park Avenue or at Bar Harbor or Hilton Head or Bermuda. Everybody like him, men and women, saying among themselves, "Italian and Catholic, you know, but a charming young scoundrel, extremely generous, well connected it seems, and, good Lord, have you ever seen what he's got in his pants?" Many of the women—and some of the men—had.

The day eventually came when the three of them—Sergio, Andy, Eric—got into Sergio's Mercedes and drove out of Cambridge for the last time as students, all three of them now masters of Business Administration, and headed for New York and their new lives, each with his new life all set for him. Andy to join Robinson, Sayer, with a senior partnership definitely in his future; Eric to become already a junior partner with Morton Russell & Associates, having brought into the firm with him a nice chunk of the Robinson, Sayer legal account; and Sergio to have offices at Robinson, Sayer as a personal investment counselor, his clients all being named Carlotti.

Uncle Julio had bought Sergio a six-room condominium on Fifth Avenue, all windows overlooking Central Park, and from his temporary employment agency supplied Sergio with a secretary for his office and a maid and cook for his condo, all three doubling as playmates whenever any of Sergio's friends wanted one. Uncle Julio also supplied Sergio with a private telephone that rang simultaneously in his office, his car and his apartment, and with severe instructions that only Sergio should answer it. Uncle Julio insisted that all of Sergio's contacts with the Carlotti clan, in Brooklyn and across the country, should be made through Uncle Julio himself, thus defending, protecting and strengthening Uncle Julio's ascending role within the Carlotti hierarchy. Sergio visited his relatives in Brooklyn only when one of them got married or died. Otherwise, his business and social lives were confined to the swells he came to know up and down the Eastern coast and in the Caribbean, enchanting them with his generosity, picking their brains, and screwing them in one way or another.

Thus five years passed blissfully.

And then there was a change.

This was what happened:

One day, two Spanish-looking men had arrived at Uncle Julio's house in the country, about twenty miles outside of Houston. Uncle Julio thought they were Mexicans, there to arrange for the smuggling of more Mexican workers into the States. But they were Colombians. Without revealing who they were, they revealed to Uncle Julio everything they knew about him. The businesses he was in in Greater Houston, both legitimate and illegitimate, and everything about the Carlotti family, coast to coast, some of which Uncle Julio didn't even know himself, including Sergio's bisexual tendencies.

They told Uncle Julio that there was a man in Colombia who wanted to go into business with him. The man's name: Hones Martinez Velasquez. Uncle Julio knew the name, the way he knew the names of all the giants in the international network of organized crime. In the international network of drug traffic, Hones Martinez Velasquez was the greatest giant of all. Hones Martinez Velasquez was a man of mystery. It was generally know that he operated a drug refinery in southeastern Colombia that rivaled General Motors in size and technology, but few of his peers in the various realms of organized crime could ever say that they had met him. He rarely left his compound, and he conducted his business, mostly by short wave radio, to his clients around the world. In Colombia itself, he operated quite openly, with most of the government officials on his payroll. It was the government officials of other countries with whom he sometimes ran into obstacles.

The two Colombians told Uncle Julio that Hones Martinez Velasquez wanted to have a meeting with him and Sergio. It was a command performance. With no idea what was going on, Sergio obediently went to a small airport at White Plains, New York, where he was put aboard a six-passenger turbo jet and flown to Houston. At Houston, Uncle Julio came aboard. They were flown across the Gulf of Mexico to Barranquilla where they were transferred to a helicopter. Two hours later, they landed at a mountaintop heliport and were transferred to a limousine. As they were driven down the mountain road, they saw in the valley below them Hones's sprawling refinery, and Uncle Julio said, "Jesus Christ, it's General Motors."

Hones was waiting for them on the veranda of his plantation-type house at the far end of the compound. He was a short, stocky man, but he seemed huge for two reasons. One, his reputation.

Two, his bald head was enormous and he looked like a barrel from his neck to his knees. He wasted no words.

As soon as drinks were served by a small girl, Hones announced, "Wars are ruining my business. Because of Vietnam, there is so much shipping going through the Panama Canal that the Gulf of Mexico is like Times Square. And now that Cuba is trying to stir up some shit in Central America, your American Intelligence plans have turned the air over the Gulf into a beehive. I'm having trouble getting my products into your country."

Uncle Julio sipped his drink. "You think we can help you, Hones?"

"Why do you think you're here?" Hones said. He told them this: He had found out that an American air cargo company had acquired a government contract to fly supplies to Saigon where they would be put on helicopters for delivery to fighting units in the bush.

He said, "I won't have any problems getting my own supplies into Vietnam. I am sure my people in Vietnam won't have any problem persuading the air cargo company to get my supplies to California. That's where you come in."

"Where?" Sergio asked, looking around.

Hones said, "For years, I have been using Colombians to distribute my merchandise in your country. But they keep trying to sell my products to narcotics agents and are always getting arrested. I need a new outlet. The Carlotti family. Coast to coast."

Uncle Julio said, "Oh, Hones, I don't know if my family wants to get into this business."

Hones sent Uncle Julio a shriveling look that resolved the matter. He said, "When the entire operation is set up, I will be notified by radio when a shipment is to arrive in California." He turned to Uncle Julio. "At this moment, my people are installing radio equipment in your house. Your code name will be your call letters. I will let you know when a shipment is due and where it is to be distributed in the United States through your relatives." He turned to Sergio. "You are in Wall Street; you know a lot of rich people. When the payment for my products comes in, I want you to invest it for me. I've got a warehouse full of world currency and I want to put it to work. Your code name is Big Dick."

Sergio grinned at that, pleased.

Hones said, "One more thing. It is a good diversionary tactic for me to let the American authorities intercept a delivery of mine into Florida now and then. It makes them feel smug and they get careless." He looked at Sergio. "I want you to establish a base of some kind in Florida. I will put you in touch with a narcotics agent who is on my payroll. You can work together on this. Now, if you will excuse me, it is time for me to say the Rosary. I will see you at dinner.''

Everything had been going so well. Once the transshipments had been arranged, Hones put up the money to buy the plane to pick them up at Oakland, the plane registered in the name of Bicho Realtors, Palm Beach, Florida, a convenient front for Sergio, who kept a hotel apartment there for his frequent visits with the Robinsons. Hones also supplied the plane's two-man crew. All Sergio had to do was learn from Uncle Julio (who learned it from Hones) when a shipment was arriving at Oakland, notify the crew, then decide which branch of the Carlotti clan in which city would meet the plane at some small airport somewhere, pick up the delivery, then arrange to turn it over to Hones's people, and accept the payment in cash. The cash was sent by ordinary mail to Sergio's Fifth Avenue apartment, and, after sending a commission to the local Carlotti clan involved, Sergio sent Uncle Julio his commission, took his own commission, and then invested the remainder on Hones's behalf under the cover of several dummy corporations. Everything had been going so well.

And then came the shock of the drug bust in Oakland. On his several calls that day, Uncle Julio told Sergio, ''Hones wants to find out who tipped off the Feds. He's putting his people on it. You put your people on it.''

Another three years passed before anybody uncovered a clue, and Hones's people had done it. Again the call came from Uncle Julio for Sergio to fly to Houston. Uncle Julio met Sergio at the Houston airport and they drove to Galveston, then along the beach road to a deserted area. A seaplane was waiting for them. They boarded it, the pilot coaxed the plane into the water, took off, and flew low over the Gulf for almost an hour. They saw the big yacht at anchor ahead. The pilot landed the plane and inched it close, and deckhands fastened it to the gangway and helped Julio and Sergio step across. Hones was waiting for them in the lounge.

He said, ''I found out who set up the bust in Oakland. I did not want to talk about it on the radio, so I bring you here.''

Julio leaned forward. ''Who was it, Hones?''

''The son of a bitch who ran the ferrying service in Saigon. Him and his Irish friend. The two of them took me for twenty million dollars.''

''Jesus! What's his name?''

"Ronald Kazurian."

"Is he Jewish?"

"He is Armenian."

"How did you find him?"

"I have my ways."

"Where is he now?"

"He owns a cargo airline in Los Angeles. He's got a movie studio in Hollywood. He built a hotel in Las Vegas. All on my money."

"Jesus. You're not going to let him get away with it, are you?"

"No. I am not." Hones said, his face both fire and ice. "I am going to get his ass."

"I don't blame you."

"His ass and the Irishman's ass and anybody else's who was in on this."

"I don't blame you."

"But first I want him to suffer. I want him to find out what it feels like to throw away twenty million dollars." Hones looked at Sergio. "And you will do it."

Sergio came in. "Who, me?"

"Yes. I want to break him. I want to put him out of business. Every business he is in. I want him to watch everything crumble, everything he has built on my twenty million dollars."

"How do I do that?" Sergio asked.

"You better figure it out, or I get your ass, too," Hones said. "I don't care how much it costs. I don't care how long it takes. Crush him. And then I will get his ass."

Chapter Twenty-eight

I t took time.
It took planning.
And, now and then, it required a bit of deception.

But it was working.

One day, Brad Cunningham telephoned Ron from Omaha and said, "There's a pattern emerging from all this, but I haven't been able to pin it down yet."

Ron asked, "What does it look like?"

"It depends," Brad said. "Some of the people I've met are individual investors, the kind that do their own buying and selling, more for the fun of it than for a killing. It's a hobby, I suppose."

"Okay."

"But the others have brokers, and they let the brokers decide how to manage their portfolios."

"Okay."

"Well, I've been staying away from the brokers, like Morley suggested. You know the way rumors fly in this business."

"Yes, I know."

"But I've been talking to some of the people who have brokers, and they tell me they sold their LPM stock because their brokers tell them the company's in trouble. Your creditors are supposed to be hounding you, and you may have to declare bankruptcy."

"That's bullshit."

"I know that and you know that, but Ron, these people have to trust their brokers. Brokers are supposed to protect people."

"I know. Who's doing the buying?"

"Well, that's where I run into brick walls. It looks like there are four steady buyers, but I'm pretty sure that three of them are dummies. They all have post-office addresses. One in Houston, one in New York and one in Bar Harbor."

"Where the money is."

"Looks like it."

"Who's the fourth one?"

"A real estate outfit in Palm Beach. I haven't been able to find out much about them yet. Maybe I ought to go there."

"Yes. Check it out."

"There's one more thing, Ron."

"What's that?"

"Well, when I was finishing up at Harvard, a lot of the big Wall Street houses sent agents up to Cambridge to do some recruiting among the top graduates. They do that every year."

"Yeah?"

"I had a couple of interviews with a man from Robinson, Sayer."

"Robinson who?"

"Robinson, Sayer. It's Robinson and Sayer. A very big house. Sayer is dead now, I think, and Robinson runs the show. He's on the board, he gives the school a lot of money, and he walks off with the cream of the crop every graduation."

"Yeah?"

"I almost went to work for them, except that I didn't want to live in New York, and I wasn't happy with the deal they offered at their Los Angeles branch. Anyway, I got a couple of follow-up letters from them, nibbling around, but by then I was working for you, so I told them no."

"And?"

"Well, I'm not sure about this, Ron. I'll have to get home and check my files on it. But I have a sneaky feeling that the post-office box Robinson, Sayer uses for its mail is the same box number for one of those dummy corporations."

Ron measured it. "How do you read that, Brad?"

"I don't read it, yet. I'd have to be sure. But if it's true, we could be up against some very big money."

"Is this a kosher outfit?"

"A hundred percent."

"Why would they be buying up our stock on the sly?"

"Maybe because one of their customers is telling them to. I'll have to check that out, too."

"Do that, Brad. I talked to Morley this morning. He says you're doing a great job. Keep buying up everything you can and tying up as much of the rest as you can."

"I will."

"Let me know when you're coming back. Morley tells me you'd make a terrific spy. I want to know how you do it."

"It's my baby-blue eyes."

But other events were not going so well.

Each month, Ron's world seemed to be growing smaller, as though it were evaporating or an invisible cancer was gnawing at it, devouring itself. Maybe it was the economy. Maybe it was the lingering Vietnam, a gloom over the country. Maybe it was the college kids, rebels with a cause. The moon had been conquered and turned off, and you could feel the turn-off everywhere.

Ron said to Pat: "I'm going to Vegas for a few days. Want to come along?" .

"Yes," she said. "In fact, I've been thinking of going over myself. Is this a vacation?"

"Who takes vacations? I've got meetings. Is it a vacation for you?"

"Who takes vacations? I want to find out what Fats wants to do next."

"Fats is staying at the hotel."

"I know that. But we ought to talk about another picture. Or maybe a television series. He's hot now, and we should make some plans. And I want to talk to Stubby, too. I'm going to try to get him to take a job at the studio."

"As what?"

"My trouble shooter. I'm getting too old to go flying all over the country whenever something breaks down on some location somewhere. Stubby has spent most of his life on location. He knows all the traps and all the tricks. He could do the job."

"Have you talked to him about it?"

"No. I talked to Gwen the other day. Stubby's got some time off coming, and his contract on the TV series is up for renewal. Gwen isn't too sure he wants to renew. So I want to offer him this job."

"Does Gwen know?"

"No. But I'm sure she'd want him to take it and settle down. The other day, she complained that she has never seen enough of Stubby, he's on the go all the time. I think she's getting a little fed up with his flying fucks."

Ron said, "Well, at least you don't have that complaint."

"No, I don't," Pat said, a tease. "In fact, I wish you'd find something else to do with your time."

Everything had been going so well. Then, suddenly everything seemed to go wrong. It looked as though Fats Mulligan was the only person in the Kazurian Empire bringing in any money. Reservations at the hotel were down. The casino was off. No high rollers in sight. Stewart couldn't explain why the cropdusting business had sunk. Customers were leaving, especially the large commercial farmers. Entire sections of the country were hopeless, mostly the South and Southeast. The grocery business went in the red, as one Vegas hotel manager after another canceled contracts.

Morley Covington said to Ron, "I wish I could figure out what the fuck is going on."

Ron said, "That's what I think is going on. A fucking."

Stubby was elated. "Thank God," he said. "I've been going nuts trying to decide what to do. I hated the idea of giving up the series: the pay is so good. But I'm fed up with the road. I'm ready to settle down."

Pat said, "There'll be some travel. You'll be working with the location companies, so you'll have to go on the road once in a while."

"Yeah," Stubby said, "but it won't be all the time, like it is now."

Gwen said, "And you won't be risking your neck every day. That's the part I love."

Stubby smiled at her. "You ready to give up Vegas?"

"Hell, I've been ready to give up Vegas for years. I've only kept this house so that my daughter could feel she had a home."

Stubby waved it off. "Vicky will never live in Las Vegas again, unless she's here in a show. She loves New York too much."

Pat said, "Why don't you keep the house, Gwen? We'll all be coming back here from time to time."

"I'll have to think about it," Gwen said. "After all, I just found out ten minutes ago that I'm going to be moving to Hollywood."

Stubby got to his feet. "Let's celebrate tonight."

"Let's," Gwen said. "Where do you want to go?"

"I don't want to go anywhere," Stubby said, demanding it. "I'm sick of restaurants and hotels. I want a home-cooked dinner for a change. Let's eat in."

Gwen glanced toward the kitchen. "I don't think I have anything for a dinner."

"Then I'll go out and buy something," Stubby announced. "Pat, do you think Ron can join us? We can make it a real party."

"I don't know. I'll have to call him."

"Okay. I'll buy enough, anyway, just in case."

Gwen asked, "What are you going to buy?"

"I'll surprise you." Stubby walked across the room to Pat and kissed her on the cheek. He said, "Young lady, I wonder where the hell we would be tonight if, that day in Colorado, I knew how to ride that fucken horse."

Pat laughed. "I don't know where you'd be, but where the hell would I be if you didn't break your goddam leg?"

When they were alone, Gwen lighted a cigarette and sent Pat a long look. "Well, young lady, how do I say thanks?"

"You don't say thanks. I say thanks to you. I need Stubby."

"He'll do a good job for you."

"I know he will. But I'm not doing anybody any favors. The studio has become too important to me to play games. If I knew somebody else who could do the job better than Stubby, I'd offer the job to somebody else. I'm not making the job for Stubby: I need Stubby for the job."

"I've noticed that, Pat. You've changed. Sometimes I wonder if the studio has become the most important thing in your life."

"If it has, it's because the studio is another Ron for me. It's my life because that beautiful bastard is my life. If he'd asked me to fly one of those damned planes for him or spray poison on cabbages in Oregon, I'd feel the same way."

Gwen said, "You make it sound like you two had a baby."

Pat reached for her cigarettes, lit a tube, exhaled a large cloud, then said, "Okay, smart ass, let's talk about babies."

Gwen waited.

Pat waited: Bette Davis about to blow the lid off Joan Crawford. "I'm knocked up."

"Pat!"

"At least I think so."

"How long has it been?"

"The second moon went dark a few days ago."

"Have you seen a doctor?"

"No. If I saw a doctor in Hollywood just to get a wart off my ass, it would be in all the papers tomorrow. The price of fame. That's the main reason I'm here. Have you got a doctor?"

"Yes. Fred Fisher."

"Does he know about these things?"

"I hope so. He took care of me for Vicky."

"Can you get an appointment for me?"

"Of course. I'll call him now."

"No. Wait. Ron said something about going back to Los Angeles tomorrow. Something about a stockholder's meeting. I'll stay here for a couple of days. We'll make the appointment after he goes."

"You haven't told him?"

"No. I want to be sure."

"How do you think he'll take it?"

"I don't know."

"Have you talked about having children?"

"No. But he's Armenian. Armenians like kids. His parents are probably wondering when we're going to get started."

"They'll find out soon enough."

"But not too soon. Not Ron, either. Don't say anything about it tonight, not even a joke."

"Of course not."

"And not Stubby. Not yet."

"All right." Gwen stood up. "Well, we're full of surprises today, aren't we? Why don't us two gals have a little party of our own? How about a drink?"

Later that evening, while they were driving back to the apartment, Ron said to Pat: "You sure made them happy today. I've never seen them in such a giddy mood."

Pat said, "Gwen is ecstatic. Stubby won't be doing those dangerous stunts anymore."

"Is that why you gave him the job?"

"You thinking of Steve? No. Steve couldn't do the job. Stubby can. That's why he's got it. Nothing else."

He glanced at her. "You can be a coldhearted bitch, can't you?"

"When I have to."

"Well, anyway, you made them happy. They acted like a couple of love birds who just found out they're going to have a kid."

"Maybe they are. There's nothing wrong with having kids, is there?"

"No."

"After all, that's why some people get married."

"Not me. When I'm in bed screwing you, dear wife, the idea of going halfsies with you on a baby is the farthest thing from my mind."

She let it go. But she thought: "Get ready for a short trip."

Chapter Twenty-nine

The call came at two o'clock in the morning. Pat stirred in her sleep, one hand going instinctively to her belly, now slightly distended. Still half asleep, she reached for Ron and touched his back. "Honey? Ron? Ron, the phone, Get the phone."

He gave a low moan. "Shit. You get it. It's probably for you."

She pressed against his back. "Come on, Ron."

He moaned again and sat up and reached for the telephone. "Yeah? Yeah. Who? Milt? What's up? Oh Jesus! Hold it." He turned to Pat. "Pat, wake up. It's Milt Graham. The hotel is on fire."

"Oh God."

"Milt? Hold it. I want to switch on the squawker. There. Go ahead. What happened?"

They both listened:

"I don't know what happened, Ron. I was in the casino, Fats was just finishing his second show, and the crowd was coming out. All of a sudden the lobby filled up with smoke and somebody hollered fire and all hell broke loose."

"When was this?"

"About a half hour ago."

Pat called to the machine: "Has anybody been hurt?"

"I don't know Pat. I can't tell. The ambulances are here, but I haven't seen them bring anybody out yet."

Ron: "How did it start?"

"I don't know, Ron. Nobody knows. The third and fourth floors are on fire, maybe more. It's hard to tell. The fire chief just told me that the elevators are out and the stairwells are full of smoke. The firemen are having trouble getting to the fire."

"Jesus! What about the people on the upper floors?"

"I don't know. Thank God we don't have much of a house. We just about emptied out yesterday, and we weren't expecting the tours until tomorrow. But if there's anybody up there…"

Pat called: "Are you all right, Milt? Where's Fats?"

"I'm okay, Pat. I'm at the Plaza, across the road. And I just saw

Fats in the parking lot, helping to hold back the people. It's a mess here, Ron. The place is mobbed. Everybody is running over to rubberneck. I'd gotta get back."

Ron said, "Okay, Milt."

"You coming out?"

"Yes. I'll take my plane. Listen, if I can't find you around the hotel, keep trying the apartment. I'll be there."

"Okay, Ron. I've never seen anything like this."

"Milt? Hang up. I want to call Morley."

"All right, Ron. Jesus, I'm sorry."

The squawker went dead. Ron dialed.

"Hullo?"

"Morley?"

"Yes, Ron."

"Morley, Milt just called from Vegas. The hotel is on fire."

"God Almighty!"

"Morley, I'm heading right over there. I want you with me."

"Of course."

"How soon can you get to the hangar?"

"The hangar?"

"FreytFlyte."

"You're flying out?"

"Certainly."

"Ron, you know I don't fly."

"Well, you can fly *this* time, dammit."

"Ron, I can leave here right now and drive to Vegas and see you there in the morning."

"Godammit, Morley, you're my business manager. You got *any* idea what trouble we're in? I need you now, not tomorrow. You get your ass over to FreytFlyte as soon as you can. That's an order."

A pause. "Okay, Ron. I'll get there as soon as I can."

Ron banged the receiver down. Immediately he picked it up and dialed again. Then: "Joe, this is Ron. I don't have time to talk. The hotel in Vegas is on fire. Who's on duty at the hangar?"

"Jesus, man. What a shock. I—"

"Joe, we'll talk later. I need my plane right away. Is it ready?"

"I'm not sure, Ron."

"Why not?"

"I didn't think you'd be using it for a few days, so I had the mechanics give it a tune-up today. I don't know if they finished."

"Well, call them, Joe. Tell them I want my plane right away. If it's not ready, then get me another plane."

"Yes, Ron. Do you want me to go with you?"

"No. Morley is going with me."

"Morley is flying?"

"Yeah. I'll call you, Joe."

Ron hung up and, as he headed for his closet, he saw Pat get out of bed. "Where are you going?"

"With you."

"No, you're not."

"I want to, Ron."

He was dressing. "What can you do, baby? It'll be a mess."

"I want to be with you, Ron."

He pointed at her belly. "You stay here and take care of that little bastard. I'll send for you later."

She went to the door with him and had time only to kiss him on the cheek as he hurried out of the house and across the driveway to the garage. She watched him pull away, down the driveway to the street, then turn, and, wheels screeching, go out of sight.

She closed the door and went into the living room and stretched out on the sofa, too dazed to think. She put her hands on her abdomen, hoping to feel the life there. She felt nothing.

He knew.

He had guessed.

He was pleased.

He called it a little bastard. He called it our kid.

He was pleased.

She lay there all night, awake, waiting for morning, waiting for his call, waiting for the smoke to clear so that she could go to him and help him clean up the mess and put the pieces together, the two of them together, the three of them now.

She waited.

And she waited.

And she waited.

Chapter Thirty

Walter Cronkite was saying:

Ronald Kazurian, head of the LPM movie studios in Hollywood, was killed early today when his private plane crashed in the California mountains near the Nevada border. Also killed in the accident was Morley Covington, Kazurian's long-time friend and business associate. Kazurian, an experienced pilot, was at the controls. The two men were on their way to Las Vegas, where the LPM Stars Hotel, owned by Kazurian, caught fire last night. Las Vegas fire officials said that eleven people died in the blaze, with dozens more taken to local hospitals for treatment for smoke inhalation, including several firemen. In Hollywood, a spokesman for LPM disclosed today that Kazurian's widow, the former Patricia Purney, a movie figure in her own right, was rushed to Los Angeles General Hospital, where she had a miscarriage.

In other news...

Chapter Thirty-one

She did not mourn.

She was so stunned by the barrage of shocks that she was too numb to feel sorrow or pain or loss or self-pity. She did not weep. Gwen moved in with her, but they scarcely spoke. It was Gwen who answered the constantly ringing telephone, Gwen who went to the door to sign for the stream of telegrams. On the day of Ron's funeral, Pat flew alone to Sacramento, where Stewart met her and drove her to the farm. Five hours later, she was on a plane again. That evening, she was at her table at Chasen's. Strangers who recognized her were dismayed by her composure: the woman had no heart. But the people who knew her and loved her and understood her were expecting her. Gwen and Stubby were already there. Ted Colby and Buzz came in as Pat was lighting her first cigarette. Then the others arrived. Fats Mulligan and Milton Graham. Joe Reilly and his wife. Bert Bernstein and a starlet. Nobody said they were sorry. They knew she knew they were. Nobody tried to comfort her. They knew she knew they couldn't. Nobody mentioned Ron. They knew she was thinking only about him, as she had always thought about him and always would.

Bert Bernstein and the starlet stayed just for a drink. As they were leaving, Bernstein went around to Pat and kissed her cheek.

Pat asked, "Aren't you staying for dinner?"

Bernstein glanced at the starlet. "That's my dinner. See you in the morning?"

"Yes."

And when the group broke up, nobody gave any suggestion of going home with Pat so that she would not be alone. They knew she would never be alone. Never. And she knew they knew it.

Bert Bernstein looked up from his desk. "You get everything, of course, but Ron did make some suggestions for you in case you decided to dispose of any of his ventures."

"Like what?" Pat asked.

"FreytFlyte, for one thing. If you decide to get rid of it, Ron wanted you to give Joe Reilly first bid on it."

"Why should Joe bid on it? He's been doing most of the work for years, anyway. Can't we just transfer the ownership to him?"

"I suppose so. But I'll have to talk to somebody who knows more about taxes than I do. There could be some complications. Maybe you could sell it to him for a dollar, something like that. I'll check it out."

"All right. Anything else?"

"The cropdusting business. If you don't want it, it's Stewart's."

"It's Stewart's."

"Same deal?"

"Yes."

"Okay. Then there's the hotel. But I think we'd better let that stand for a while. There's bound to be lawsuits. We may be tied up in the courts for years."

"Lawsuits?"

"Yes. Remember that eleven people died. People are bound to sue. And a lot of people lost their clothes and everything. More litigation."

"Isn't the hotel insured?"

"Oh, yes. Completely. But insurance companies don't like to pay out quickly. They'll be a part of the litigation, too. It's going to be a mess."

"Can't we settle out of court?"

"That depends on what we get hit with. I've been thinking, Pat. Maybe we ought to turn this whole thing over to Dave French's outfit up in San Francisco? They've got the staff for something this big, and they're more experienced than anybody else I can think of. How about it?"

"Do whatever you think is best, Bert. Just one thing. When the legal stuff starts, if it turns out that there are any real hardship cases—I mean, people who have been seriously hurt by this in any way—I want you to try to work out a settlement with them as quickly and as generously as you can. I don't want to fight anybody who's been hurt."

Bernstein glanced at her. "Look who's talking."

She asked, "Who gets the hotel?"

"Milton."

"Okay. What about the studio?"

"Well, the studio is a public corporation, of course. I do know that Ron was the biggest stockholder, but I don't know how much that is. You'll have to talk to Morley about it."

"Morley?"

"Ooops. Sorry. Habit."

"I know. Bert, what are we going to do about Morley's department? We need somebody to run it."

"I know. Want me to scout around town? Maybe we can get somebody from another studio."

"Don't we have anybody in the house that can do it?"

"I don't know. There's a kid in Finance that Morley seemed to like."

"Kid?"

"Well, in his twenties. Brad Cunningham. Ron had me do a check on him, something to do with the studio's stock."

"What did you find out?"

"Very proper. Papa is Navy; three stars, retired. Mama is Old California, which means money, lots of money. Santa Barbara stuff. Brad did prep school in the East. Groton, I think. He got his bachelor's in business from UCLA. Two years in the Navy. Then a master's from Harvard."

"What did he do in the Navy?"

"Intelligence. Also flyboy."

"How'd he land here?"

"He applied. Morley hired him. I think they knew some of the same people."

"Do you think he can do the job?"

"I have no idea. Do you want to talk to him?"

"Bring him around to Chasen's tonight. Get him a date with one of your starlets."

"Let him get his own date. He doesn't need any help from me when it comes to the starlets."

"Oh?"

"Jesus. He's worse than I am."

"Maybe he's better."

Uncle Julio was saying, "Jesus Christ, what the hell did you do?"

Sergio held the telephone away from his ear. "Don't holler, Uncle. What do you mean, what did I do?"

"All you were supposed to do was get a little fire started at the hotel. You weren't supposed to kill off the son of a bitch at the same time."

"I didn't kill off the son of a bitch. You told me to plant a mechanic at his airline company, and I did. But I didn't tell him to fuck up the plane yet."

"Well, he sure did. Have you talked to him since?"

"I can't find him. He took off. I don't know where he is."

"Where did you find him in the first place?"

"He was working for Don Antonio in Chicago."

"Doing what?"

"Stripping down stolen cars."

"That's an airplane mechanic?"

"You didn't say airplane mechanic. You just said mechanic."

"Jesus Christ. Hones is having a fucking fit."

"What for? He wanted the guy's ass, didn't he?"

"Yeah, but he wanted the guy's money first. Where's the money?"

"Uncle, I've been telling you all along: I'll bet the bastard sank the money into the studio to buy the stock. That's why Hones wanted to get the studio away from the guy, isn't it, to break the bastard's bankroll before breaking his back?"

"Yeah, but now it's happened the other way around."

"So what does Hones want me to do now?"

"Go after the bankroll."

"How?"

"Are you still thick with that crooked lawyer from Havard?"

"Yes."

"Hones wants you to tell him to get in touch with the relatives of all the people who died in the fire."

"What for?"

"To start a lawsuit, stupid. What else do lawyers do?"

"But Uncle, lawsuits can take years. And it will cost a load."

"It ain't your money, so don't worry about it."

"All right. And what do I do about the studio stock?"

"Keep buying it. If we don't have control in six months, you can tell those two soldiers of yours to set fire to the place."

"Not those two, Uncle. Those guys will be out of action for a lot longer than six months."

"What happened to them?"

"Well, after they set fire to the hotel, they got trapped in it. They're both in intensive care. One guy is practically burned to a crisp, and the other guy swallowed so much smoke he'll never be able to take a deep breath for the rest of his life."

"Jesus Christ, can't you get nothing done right?"

She saw him come into the restaurant out of the corner of her eye. Her subliminal thought was: "A beauty. Too pretty to be straight." And she gave her attention back to Fats Mulligan.

Fats was saying, "Pat, I don't really want to get tied up in a series.

I'm a live-audience man: you know that. I can't work against a clock. Send me back to the Stars and I'll be happy."

She said, "Fats, face it. It'll take months to put the hotel back in business. That will give us plenty of time to get the series rolling. I've seen the scripts and I like them, and if you say yes we can start shooting in two weeks. We can always shoot around you later when—"

She heard, "Mrs. Kazurian?"

She looked up. The beauty. "Yes?"

"I'm Brad Cunningham. Bert Bernstein suggested that I join you tonight."

She smiled. "Oh, yes. Bert mentioned it." She offered her hand. "I guess you know everybody here. Have a seat and order a drink."

She gave her attention back to Fats, but all evening she was focused on Brad Cunningham.

He was a dazzler. No question about it. Everybody felt it. He had a quiet, easygoing way about him, smiling quickly, laughing easily, submitting warmly and intently to the chitchat offered to him, listening, nodding, laughing. He might have been part of the group from the first night. He had one drink. Vodka. He smoked a small pipe. He ordered the sole. With coffee, he had a stinger.

Around eleven, she saw him get up and come around to her, he smiled, the quiet way. He said, "Thanks for letting me come, Mrs. Kazurian. I really enjoyed myself."

"Come back any time," she said. "We're usually here every night. Must you leave so soon?"

"I'd better. I want to get to the office early. Without Morley, things are a bit upset."

"I guess so. I wanted to talk to you about that." She wished he would pull up a chair.

But he stood there, looking down at her, his blue eyes warm, searching, waiting. He said, "Yes?"

"Bert and I discussed a bit this morning. Would you mind taking over Morley's department for a while? It would be a great help."

"Certainly. I'll be glad to do anything I can."

"Good. We can talk about it in the morning."

"Just let me know. Good night. And thanks again."

She watched him go. He made brief stops for good-nights around the table and at another table with people she did not know. And then he was gone. But she kept thinking about him.

Chapter Thirty-two

The next morning, they had a brief meeting in Pat's office. She admitted: "I don't know anything about the business side of the studio. That was Ron's department. And Morley's. I know about production costs and budgets and profit and loss, but the rest of it is a mystery to me. I'm sure there's a lot more going on."

"There is," Brad said.

"Then that's where you can be a great help."

"Anything."

She nodded at that. "Why don't you take as much time as you need to get a good overlook at the entire business side of the studio? When you've got some idea about what's going on around here, let's try to figure them out. Let's talk about it. If there are any problems, if there aren't, then all I ask is that you keep things running smoothly."

"I'll do my best."

"Do you have any questions?"

"Not at this point."

"Come and see me whenever you do."

"I will."

For the next two weeks she saw little of him. She knew he was busy. Every couple of days a memo from him would reach her desk, details about some investment or obligation, about taxes and inventories, about FreytFlyte or the Stars Hotel and Casino and R.O.K. Airlines. Little of it made any sense to her. The first week he had appeared at Chasen's only once, arriving late and sitting too far down the table to chat with her.

The second week he did not show at Chasen's at all. Thursday night, Bert Bernstein, sitting next to Pat, said "The kid must be working his ass off."

"What kid?"

"Cunningham. Last night, after we had dinner here, I went back to the studio to sign some papers. I saw him in Morley's office, in his shirtsleeves, papers piled up on the desk all around him. I saw him when I went in and I saw him when I went out, and he didn't even look up."

"What do you think of the job he's doing?"

"I just see copies of the memos he sends to you. He seems to know his way around. Have you given him the job yet?"

"No. I haven't had a chance. I'm not even sure that he wants it. If it weren't for his memos, I wouldn't know he was alive."

"A couple of the starlets aren't sure about that, either. I'm getting complaints."

"I'll send him a memo."

The next day, Friday, Brad Cunningham arrived around three in the afternoon. He was carrying a bulging attache case. He looked very tired.

She felt an impulse to be annoyed. But the first sight of him always startled her a little. She tried to be calm. "You leaving us already?"

"Yes," he said, the small smile. "They turn off the air-conditioning in this building after office hours. It gets too hot to work here nights. I'm going to work at home."

"You shouldn't be working nights," she said.

"I want to get things cleared up for you."

"There's no great rush."

"Well, the more I get done, the less the new man will have to do."

"What new man?"

"Whoever gets Morley's job."

"I thought you wanted it?"

He stepped back. "Me?"

"Yes. You."

"I didn't know I was even being considered for it."

"Well, you are."

"Don't you want an older man?"

"What for?"

"I know that I'm being called 'The Kid' around here. And 'Pretty Boy.' An older man would command more respect."

"Nothing commands respect except talent. Besides, what's wrong with being called Pretty Boy? You are a pretty boy. You're doing a good job. I've talked to Bert about you. The job is yours, if you want it."

"My God. Let me think about it. I'll have to get used to the idea."

"Take all the time you want. And stop working nights. The starlets are complaining."

He laughed. "Some people talk too much."

"Some people don't talk enough. Next week, I want you to take over Morley's department. Tonight I want you to go out and celebrate."

He smiled. "All right. This is amazing. I'll see you." He took a step away, then caught himself. "I forgot." He reached into his breast pocket and extracted a business envelope. "I found this in Morley's personal file. It's for you." He moved to the desk and handed her the envelope.

She took it without looking at it. "Have a great celebration."

"Yes. Good night."

She watched him go.

She shook her head to get rid of the picture of him. Okay. She'd work at home, too. She had three new scripts for the Fats Mulligan series to read. Scooping them up, she put them in her briefcase. She put the envelope Brad had given her in the case, too.

As she passed her secretary, she said, "Tell the building people to keep the air-conditioning on until midnight."

"What for? You coming back?"

"No. Every midnight."

"What for? There's nobody here but the cleaning people."

"Button your lip, young lady, or you'll be one of them."

"I'm glad I work for such a sweet person."

They both laughed.

Driving home, Pat decided against going to Chasen's for dinner. Friday nights were usually quiet at Chasen's. Besides, the attache case in the car with her was heavy with homework. She didn't want to return to the studio on Monday with the burden of it still hanging over her head.

At home, Pat changed into shorts, a blouse and sandals, took two lobster tails out of the freezer to thaw, fixed herself a malted, then headed for the den and her homework. She sorted the work on the desk in front of her, and it was then that she noticed the envelope Brad Cunningham had given her. She glanced at it and recognized the handwriting across the front of it. Ron's. A chill went through her. Then she read it.

Ron had written: "Morley, to be opened in the event of my death. RK."

Pat stared at the envelope a long time before she could bring herself to pick it up and slit it open. She read:

Dear Morley—
I know that many times over the years when we have been

together you have wanted to ask me about the money in the safe deposit box in the bank. I have always trusted you and I never wanted to keep anything from you, but I felt it was for your own good not to know about where that money came from. Now that Shad is gone and I am gone, you have a right to know. Shad and I earned that money by helping to smuggle dope into this country while we were in Vietnam...

On and on it went, six pages, typed, single-spaced, errors ignored, errors typed over. On and on. All of it. How it began. Why it began. How long it went on. The people involved. How it was hidden about the Transcontinentals. How it was apparently picked up in Oakland. How it had been stopped. Pat read:

I won't bullshit you, Morley. Shad and I went along on this deal because we had no choice. We were scared about it and we never stopped being scared, but even so we liked the idea of all that money piling up for us in your bank. But the fun soon went out of that. I could see what dope was doing to our guys in Nam, and I could imagine what it was doing to the kids here. I knew I had to get out of it, but I also knew this was something I just couldn't walk away from. I had to figure out a way to bust the thing up. What made me more determined to do this was when I heard that the bastards were even shipping dope to the States inside the bodies of the dead GI's...

On and on. The decision. The plan. The quick trip to San Francisco. The pick-up plane at Oakland. The letter to the FBI. Getting Shad out of Vietnam. Getting out himself with the last shipment. The bust. Walter Cronkite. The TV pictures of the bastards in Saigon getting busted. The sudden joy of freedom. And the realization of the not so free freedom. Pat read:

I have never really felt off the hook. I know the game these bastards play, and they are not good losers. They know everything or they can find out everything and they do not give up until they have at least evened the score. That is the main reason I have always tried to stay out of the limelight. I didn't want them to find me or anybody connected with me, and that includes you. Even if I gave those guys their money back, they wouldn't stop there. Too many things have been going wrong with our business deals—at the hotel, the studio, Freyt-Flyte, cropdusting. I don't believe it is a coincidence. I don't think even Shad's death was from natural causes, like the doctors said. Well, he is gone now and, I guess, so am I or you wouldn't be reading this. Morley, I want you to do something for me. Go to the Feds and tell them about the 20 million bucks in the bank. Show them the papers to prove that I never used that money for anything but collateral for loans you arranged for me. If Uncle Sam wants the money, give it to him. If not, use it to set up some kind of a program in this country to get people off drugs. Then dump everything else—the studio, the hotel, everything. You know the people I love. Use this money to see to it that none of them will have to worry about money for the rest of their lives. If anything is left over, put it into the drug program. The way I see it, Morley, is that if there is nothing left of me, then whoever is after my ass will forget about it and leave everybody else's ass alone. Thanks for everything, Morley. I love you. I'll put in a good word for you with St. Peter, if I manage to get past him myself.

She read the letter several times.

She was reaching for the telephone when she realized she did not know Brad Cunningham's number. She did not even know where he lived. She telephoned the studio and asked the night operator if there was still anybody in Personnel. There wasn't. Pat identified herself and asked if the operator had the directory of the home numbers of studio executives. She did, but Brad was not listed; he was not an executive yet. Pat asked for Bert Bernstein's home number.

She called. Bernstein said, "You just caught me at the door. What's up?"

She said, "I've been going over Brad's memos, and there's something I want to talk to him about. Do you know his home phone number?"

"No, I don't. Can't it wait until Monday?"

"I'd like to clear it up now. Do you know where he lives?"

"No, I don't. But just a minute. There's somebody here who might know." His voice faded, but Pat heard: "Honey?"

A voice: "Yes, dear?"

"You've been to Brad Cunningham's place, haven't you?"

"Oh, yes."

"Do you know where he lives?"

"In Hollywood Hills."

"Do you know the address?"

"No. He drives me there."

"Do you know his telephone number?"

The starlet rattled it off. Pat heard and jotted it down.

Bert said, "Pat, it's—"

Pat said, "I heard. Are you going over to Chasen's?"

"No. The bitch has a cottage at Arrowhead. We're going there for the weekend."

"Oh? I heard the fishing's good this time of the year."

"I've already caught mine. See you Monday."

Pat called Brad's house. The phone rang several times, and she supposed he was, indeed, celebrating.

Then: "Brad Cunningham."

She said, "Brad?"

"Yes."

"It's Pat."

"Pat who?"

"Pat Kazurian."

"Oh. What a surprise. How did you get my number? It's unlisted."

"Every starlet in town knows it by heart."

"I'll have it changed. What's up, Pat?"

"Brad, remember that envelope you gave me this afternoon?"

"Yes."

"Did you read the envelope?"

"Yes, I did. Well, with Morley gone, I thought I'd better give it to you. It was personal."

"It is. Brad, can you come over?"

"Now?"

"Yes. I want you to read what Ron wrote. I need some advice about it."

"Okay. Sure. Where do I go?"

She told him. "How soon can you be here?"

"About an hour. I'll have to dress."

"You're naked?"

"I'm in a pair of shorts."

"So am I. Come as you are."

He laughed. "I'll be there as soon as I can."

She took the letter into the living room and put it on the coffee table in front of the long sofa. She turned on a couple of lamps. In the kitchen, the lobster tails were thawing. She took a few more out of the freezer and put them all in the refrigerator, slowing the process. She checked the liquor cabinet. There was an unopened half-gallon of vodka. She filled a small decanter and put it and a couple of glasses on a tray and carried it to the coffee table.

Brad was there in half an hour. She heard his car and opened the door, watching him as he approached. He was wearing beige slacks and a brown knit sportshirt, short sleeves and open at the collar. Good arms. Trim waist. Boyish. She caught his glance at her opened shirt.

As he came in he said, "You told me to celebrate, but I didn't expect to be celebrating with the boss."

She closed the door and guided him to the sofa. "We can celebrate later. For now, it's work." She pointed to the letter on the coffee table. "Read that. I'll get some ice." When she returned with a Coke for herself and the ice bucket, she could see he was already on the fourth page. She took the chair opposite him and waited.

He finished the letter, looked back at a couple of pages, then placed the letter on the coffee table. He saw the vodka and poured himself a drink, popping some cubes into the glass. He sipped and put the glass on the table. "I forgot my pipe," he said. "Have you got any cigarettes?" She pointed to the box on the table. He lit up and leaned back on the sofa and looked at her.

She asked, "What do you think?"

"I'm in shock."

"So am I."

"You knew nothing of this?"

"Nothing at all."

"It must have been terrible to live with. It explains a lot."

"Like what?" She took a cigarette for herself, lighted it, then, leaning back, brought her feet up on the chair, the shirt opening more.

He looked. "Pat, button your shirt."

She was surprised. "Sorry." She reached for the buttons.

"I'm not." He sipped his drink and took a drag. He said, "Several months ago, I got called into a meeting with Ron and Morley. Part of my job was keeping an eye on the studio's stock. Something fishy was going on, and Ron wanted me to check it out."

"What was going on?"

So he told her what he knew about it and about what he had found out—or almost found out—when he went on the road to buy what LPM he could and find out why shareholders had sold and to whom. He told her about the dummy corporations and Robinson, Sayer. He said, "There was no pattern to it, and yet it was too fishy to be coincidence."

"Do you know how Ron felt about it?"

He pointed to the letter. "In light of this, he probably thought the dopers were trying to get control of the studio and run him out. Did he ever talk business with you? FreytFlyte, the hotel, anything?"

"Never. He didn't even want to discuss the studio with me outside the office. Brad, did you notice that the letter isn't dated?"

"No." He picked up the envelope and the pages and flipped through them. "No. No date."

"Was there anything in Morley's file?"

"No. Just some personal letters, bank statements, some stocks and bonds. I sent everything to Morley's wife. Except this."

"Ron left a will."

"I'm sure he did."

"He left everything to me."

"Of course."

"The will says that if I don't want any of Ron's businesses—the hotel or FreytFlyte or anything—I was to turn it over to the person who's running it now."

"So?"

"The letter doesn't say that."

"No, it doesn't. You're right."

"Well, Brad, if Morley hadn't been on that plane or if he had lived and Ron died and Morley opened that letter, what would have happened?"

"Legally?"

"Yes."

"I don't know. Who prepared the will?"

"Bert Bernstein."

"Then you can bet everything's in order, dates and all."

"I think so, too. That's why I asked you to come here tonight."

"I was wondering why."

She gave him a long look. Her Coke was half gone. She leaned to the coffee table, put an inch of Coke into the glass, three ice cubes, and then she filled it with vodka. She took another cigarette. Then she leaned back and took a deep drag, her breasts pressing against her shirt. She let loose the big cloud, her eyes meeting his.

She said, "Bradford, that letter you just read: it doesn't exist."

He waited.

"I'm going to keep everything."

He waited.

"I want those bastards to come after my ass."

He waited.

"But I'm going to get their ass."

He waited.

"I don't know who they are or what they are where they are. I'm going to find them. I'm going to do to them what they did to my husband. I'm going to kill them."

He waited.

"And you're going to help me."

He waited.

She unbuttoned the shirt and spread the tablecloth. "Are you hungry?"

"Starving."

"Want some tail?"

"I'd love it."

She got up. "I'll put the water on."

"Water?"

"You're getting lobster tail."

"Oh."

Chapter Thirty-three

They talked all night. They knew they were trying to put together a jigsaw puzzle without having all the pieces. Brad told Pat about his stock-buying trips for Ron. He said, "Every time I thought I saw a pattern developing, I'd run into a brick wall. I now know what was wrong: I didn't know what I was looking for." He pointed to Ron's letter on the coffee table. "I didn't know about this."

"Neither did I," Pat said. "I don't think anybody knew except Ron and Shad."

"I suppose so," Brad conceded. "But somebody else knew. The people they were working for knew."

"And who were they?"

"Who are they, you mean. Whoever they are, they don't give up. They play for keeps."

"Who runs the narcotics rackets these days?"

He shook his head. "Oh, Christ, everybody. The stuff is coming into the country every day from all over the world."

"The Mafia?"

"Which Mafia? The Italian Mafia? The Jewish Mafia? The Spanish Mafia? The Irish Mafia? There are all kinds of Mafias."

"What about the Vietnamese Mafia?"

"I suppose there is one. But I don't think they'd go to the trouble to get back at Ron. They would have knocked him off as soon as they found him."

"But the stuff was coming in from Vietnam."

"Let's say it was coming via Vietnam. It could have come from anywhere. Vietnam could just have been convenient. There was American air traffic going back and forth all the time."

"Then how do we find out who we're looking for?"

"Find out who was looking for Ron."

"Where do we start?"

"With the LPM stock. I can understand now why Ron was so concerned about it. He probably figured that whoever was after the stock, he was the target. If he could find out who was buying, he could find out if they were involved with drug smuggling. Once he knew that, he could plan his strategy."

Pat shook her head. "How the hell did Ron think he could take on the whole Mafia?"

Brad pointed at the letter. "He turned them over to the F.B.I. once. He could have done it again. But first he had to find out who they were."

"And he never did."

"Maybe he was beginning to see a pattern."

"The pattern you saw?"

"No. Much broader. I was only working on the studio stock. But there was the hotel fire and FreytFlyte and the cropdusting." He pointed to the letter again. "According to that, all of Ron's businesses were in trouble. Maybe Ron felt that somebody was closing in on him."

"Maybe."

"Has the Vegas fire department reached a conclusion on the cause of the fire? Was it arson?"

"Bert Bernstein hasn't reported anything about it. They'd notify him."

"Yes."

"Bert told me several lawsuits have been filed. His father-in-law's law firm in San Francisco is representing the studio."

"Bert is married?"

"*Former* father-in-law. Bert's divorced."

"I was curious. I know some of Bert's starlets."

"So he tells me. But arson or not, these legal things can go on forever and cost a fortune. I'll bet every ambulance chaser in the country is rushing in to sue."

"No," Pat said. "That's the funny thing. There are minor cases scattered across the country—people who lost their luggage or their jewelry or something or people who had to be hospitalized for a couple of days. But the families of the people who died in the fire, all have the same lawyer."

"Really? Who?"

"Some law firm in New York, Bert told me, a very big firm."

"I wonder who put it together? It's no coincidence."

"I have no idea. Talk to Bert."

Brad reached for the cigarettes, saw that the pack was empty, and crumpled it. "We're fresh out."

"I'll get some." Pat stood. "How's the vodka?"

"I don't wany any more. Do you?"

"No. What time is it?"

He glanced at his watch. "Christ, it's after five. I'd better go."

"Please don't. I want to talk some more. Are you hungry?"

His glance was a tease. "More lobster tails?"

"I'm great at scrambled eggs."

"If you want."

"Come on. Bring the vodka."

She led him into the kitchen, and he sat down at the table. From a cabinet, she took a carton of cigarettes, extracted a pack and handed it to him. He opened it and lit up.

Pat cracked five eggs into a bowl, then added a pinch of garlic salt and pepper, a tablespoon of grated cheese and half a tomato, diced, and stirred it all into a smooth blend. As the eggs were cooking slowly, she put on water for coffee.

While they were eating, Pat said, "There's one thing we'll probably never know about."

"What's that?"

"Morley. Were they after him, too, or was it just coincidence that he was on the plane with Ron?"

"Morley didn't know about the dope," Brad pointed out.

"No, but he knew about the money. And everybody knew that Morley handled all of Ron's finances."

Brad nodded at that. "Even so, everybody also knew that Morley never flew."

"Yes. Ron had to order him to make the flight with him."

"I guess we'll never know."

"How's Morley's wife?"

"I talked to her Thursday. She's moving back to San Francisco. They've got kids there."

"I'll have to call her. I was never close to her. Not Shad's wife, either."

"I wonder if Shad ever said anything to her about the dope."

"I doubt it. Martha lives in her own little world, unaware of what the world is really like because she'd rather not know. I expect Shad married her in his old age because he'd had enough of the world he had known and wanted to get away from it. He couldn't have picked a safer fortress if he had entered a monastery."

"Ron seemed to think that Shad didn't die of natural causes."

"I know."

"It might be worth finding out."

"Now? Martha wouldn't allow an autopsy. I don't think Ron ever got over that, even though he kept in touch with her. And she certainly wouldn't allow an exhumation at this late stage."

Brad shrugged. "Probably not. But Shad was into the dope thing as much as Ron was. If the dopers were after Ron, they sure as hell wouldn't let Shad go scot free. Have you heard from Martha since the accident?"

"I got a letter from her. Condolences. Want some more coffee?"

They had second coffees in the living room, Brad this time stretching out on the sofa, Pat in her usual chair on the opposite side of the coffee table. They talked on and on.

At one point, Pat asked, "This pattern that you sometimes saw when you were on the road for Ron—what was it?"

"That's just it. Every time I thought I saw a pattern, it fizzled out."

"What was it, anyway?"

"Okay. Ron wanted me to do two things: buy up as much stock as I could and find out who else was buying it. Well, not everybody I talked to wanted to sell their stock, but they did tell me they were getting offers from other buyers either through their brokers or in the mail. Some of the people had saved the mail, and that's how I got a look at it."

"What did you find out?"

"Not much. As far as I could see, there have been four principal buyers. A brokerage in Maine, another one in New York, an import-export company in Texas and a real estate outfit in Florida."

"Real estate?"

"Yes. Why not? Realtors make a lot of money. They make investments as a company. A lot of companies do. LPM does."

"All right. Then what?"

"Well, when I tried to run these buyers down, I ran into brick walls. The only one with an address was the real estate outfit in Palm Beach. The others all had post office-box addresses. I couldn't locate them."

"Couldn't you ask the post office?"

"They wouldn't give it out. Anybody can rent a post-office box and use it for anything they want, as many different names as they want. If you want to find out who's paying the rent on the box, you have to get a court order. Morley felt that if we did that, we'd be showing our hand. But there was one thing."

"What?"

He told her about the job offers he had received from Robinson, Sayer when he was graduated from Harvard Business School and the subsequent correspondence, which he had kept.

He said, "I wasn't sure at first, but four or five stockholders I interviewed told me they had received offers from a New York brokerage, and they showed me the mail. I thought the address was familiar, and I was pretty sure why. When I got home and checked my files, I found out why. The return address on the offers was one of the post-office boxes used by Robinson, Sayer."

She watched him, waiting.

"That means," he said, "that either Robinson, Sayer is letting some offshoot company use its mailing facilities or somebody at Robinson, Sayer is playing games."

"What do you think?"

"I think it's games."

"Why?"

"The name of the company making the offers is Sheepshead Bay Holdings, Inc."

"Sheepshead Bay?"

"That's someplace in Brooklyn."

"So?"

"There is no Sheepshead Bay Holdings, Inc. If there is, it's not incorporated, it doesn't pay taxes, and it isn't a member of the stock exchange. I've checked that out with New York and Albany and Washington."

"Did you tell Ron this?"

"I only had a chance to tell him about my suspicions about the post-office boxes. I didn't get the legwork done until just a few weeks ago. I did tell Morley."

"What did he say?"

"He said he'd talk to Ron about it the next day."

"Do you know if he did?"

"No. That night the hotel caught on fire."

"Damn! What do we do now?"

"That's up to you."

"What do you think we should do?"

He adjusted himself on the sofa, making himself more comfortable. Peripherally, she saw his right hand take a quick pass at his crotch to ease the tightness there.

He said, "In the first place, I am surprised to find myself part of the 'we.' Okay, I am. In the second place, I never really knew why Ron was so upset about the sneaky stock transfers. Now I do know. Ron probably wasn't as worried about the company as he must have been about the people who were after it. They stop at nothing, and he must have known that."

"What a thing to live with," Pat said.

"In the third place," Brad went on, "I assumed that you would inherit everything; but I figured that if you decided to dump everything and go home to Mama, all the stock shit would be over and what happened to the company wouldn't make any difference. Now I know what you are going to do about everything, and I know why. I am glad I am part of your 'we' and I'll do anything you want."

"I'm glad," she said.

He closed his eyes and was mumbling. "And in the fourth place, if you don't let me go home now and get some sleep, I am going to pass out right here on your sofa and in full view of your beautiful breasts."

"Pass out." She got up. "I'll get you a blanket."

He was already asleep as she placed the blanket over him. Ever so briefly and ever so lightly, she let her fingers pause at his crotch. Then she went into the bedroom and stripped and lay down and was immediately asleep.

The bedroom was twilight dim when Pat awoke. For a moment, she wasn't sure if it was dusk or dawn. Then she remembered. And she remembered Brad. Was he still there? She lay there, eyes open, looking at the ceiling, feeling the sleep seep out of her, feeling a warmth seep into her. She got up and went into the living room.

Brad was still there, still asleep. The blanket had slipped off him and was on the floor beside the sofa. She went to the sofa and bent to pick up the blanket so that she could put it back on him, but as she bent she noticed that his clothes had climbed up on him and grabbed at his crotch. She looked at the bulge of his balls, gripped tight, at the soft tube along his left thigh. She looked at it and looked at it.

She knelt on the blanket. Slowly she lowered her face to the tube and kissed it. She kissed it again. Her tongue came out of her mouth and licked where she had kissed, moisture flowing from her. Her head began to move back and forth, the tongue licking, the moisture flooding. Her tongue felt the tube harden and lengthen.

Was he still asleep? How could he still be asleep? When would he respond? Would he respond? Then she knew. It was up to her. The Boss. It was up to her to fulfill the 'we.'

Still licking, she reached for his belt and undid it, and undid the button there, and lowered the zipper and spread the fly wide. She found the button on his shorts, undid it, and spread the fly wide. Her fingers went into the hairs, searching, probing, reaching, until they touched the tube. She backed away slightly. Then, slowly, gently, carefully, she extracted it and could see the silhouette of it in the darkening room. She bent and took the top of it into her mouth.

It was then that his left hand moved to her left breast and cupped it, gently, firmly, fully.

She continued at him, lips tight, tongue loose, each time lower and lower, until she could feel his hairs against her cheeks. She reached for his hips and he lifted himself as she drew his clothes down to his knees. She took his balls into her hand and kissed them and licked them and took them into her mouth, one at a time and then both. He gasped and stiffened. She returned to his tube and, with it in her mouth, she got on the sofa with him, straddling his legs. He sent his hands to both of his tits. She left his tube and went to his hips and belly, and she pushed his shirt aside to get to his belly button, moving herself up along his body. And when she felt his tube at the right place on her, she guided him inside and lowered herself upon him until he was in full. His hands left her tits and moved down her naked back to her buttocks. He gripped them, pressing her down on him, and she begin to grind herself on him.

Uncle Julio was saying, "Has the crooked lawyer gone to work yet?"

Sergio said, "Oh, yes, Uncle. He's got everybody signed up and he's already filed the papers in court."

"How much is he after?"

"All together, a hundred and fifty big ones."

"What's a big one?"

"A million."

"That sounds good."

"It will take a long time, Uncle."

"Hones waited this long. He can wait some more."

"But, Uncle," Sergio said, "why are we doing this? The bastard is dead. Why keep it up?"

"Hones wants his money back. That's why."

"Does he want me to keep going after the stock?"

"He says to take it easy for a while. He wants to see what's going to happen at the studio. If you can pick up some stock without any trouble, buy it. But you don't have to go all out for a while."

"Okay, Uncle."

"One thing more."

"Yes?"

"Hones told me last night that he's going to have a big crop of poppies this season."

"Good."

"He says he wants to start making shipments in two or three weeks. I will take care of things at this end, but Hones wants you to get your ass down to Florida to take care of things at that end."

"Okay. When will this be?"

"In two or three weeks."

"I'm not sure I can make that, Uncle."

"How come you're not sure?"

"I have to go back to Harvard."

"You're going back to school?"

"Not school, Uncle. The Alumni Association is having a big blowout."

"What's a lumnie?"

"It's somebody who graduated from college."

"They got an association for that?"

"It's more like a club. A lot of people get together once a year and get drunk and screw around and have a wild time."

"And that's more important than going to Florida like Hones says?"

"Well, no. But I meet a lot of rich people at these things. Customers."

"You just worry about Hones's customers. He is going to a lot of trouble for this new assignment."

"Like what?"

"He is going to play the same trick. He is going to have it leaked to the Feds that a big shipment is coming into Miami by plane and into Savannah by boat. All the Feds will go running there, and they won't be watching you and me. You fuck this up, and Hones will bury you at Harvard."

"All right. I'll do what I can, Uncle."

"You'll do what you're told. You want to live, you do what you're told."

Chapter Thirty-four

There must have been a hundred people in the apartment, and they were all naked. They were all naked and they were all smashed and they were all stoned. Out of the haze, Brad saw a man approaching him. The man seemed to have three legs.

The man let himself drop on a mound of pillows next to Brad. He asked, "You having a good time?"

Brad managed, "I'm having a great time."

The man said, "It looks like it. I just watched you bang that broad."

Brad said, "You watched it? I didn't think anybody around here was sober enough to watch anything."

"I watch everything," the man said. "I like to know what's going on around me. This is my place, and I want to know what everybody is doing."

Brad said, "Thanks for the party."

The man said, "You're welcome. I've got a good friend down in Key West. He writes plays for a living. He's a junkie. I keep him supplied with stuff, and when I'm in Florida he keeps me supplied with sailors."

"I'll bet you spend a lot of time in Florida."

"Now and then. I'm down there now for a few weeks." Then the man said, "Listen, Andy Robinson tells me you were a class-mate of his kid brother's."

"That's right. Mark was the president of the class and I was the vice president."

"How come you didn't get president?"

"Because my father couldn't afford to give as much money to Harvard as Mark's father did."

"Mark is working for me now."

"He is?"

"Yeah. I've got a little business up in Bar Harbor. Mark fronts it for me."

"What kind of business?"

"Stocks. I'm in the stock market."

"That must be interesting."

"It's okay. I'm in a lot of businesses. Down in Florida, I'm in the real estate business."

"That must be interesting."

"It's okay. I've got a lot going for me in Florida. I spend a lot of time there."

"Lots of sailors in Florida."

"That, too. Andy says you're from Hollywood."

"That's right."

"Andy says you work at one of the movie studios. He says you work at Paramount."

"That's right. I work at Paramount."

"What do you do there?"

"I'm a casting director. I bang all the starlets."

"That's a good job. Do you know anybody at LPM?"

"Yeah. I know a few people at LPM."

"Who's running the outfit, now that that Greek son of a bitch is dead?"

"What Greek son of a bitch?"

"That guy who was killed in the airplane crash."

"He was Armenian."

"Whatever. Who's running the outfit, now that he's dead?"

"His wife. His widow."

"Do you know her?"

"I've met her."

"Is she smart?"

"People say she is."

"Did she get all the money?"

"People says she did."

"One of these days, I'm gonna push her off a cliff."

"What for?"

"I've got my reasons."

"Push her off a cliff?"

"Well, in a way. I know some people who want that company. We've got a lot of stock. When we get enough, we'll push that cunt off a cliff and bankrupt her."

"Why?"

"We've got our reasons. You keep in touch with me. Once we take over the outfit, I'll make you casting director of the whole place. Then you can bang everybody."

"I'd like that. Where can I find you?"

"Didn't Mark tell you? I work for his old man. Robinson, Sayer.

I've got my own company there, too."

"Your own company at Robinson, Sayer? You must be a big shot."

The man moved his head, disclaiming. "Some people think so. But it's a small operation. I make investments for a bunch of my uncles over in Sheepshead Bay. You want a snort?"

"Not now," Brad said. "I'm still glowing from the last line. It's good stuff."

"The best. I get it directly from the manufacturer."

"Oh, really? Where is he?"

"South America. Colombia. A very wealthy man. I make investments for him, too."

"You've got a lot going. Maybe I can stop off in New York and see you on my way back to the Coast."

"I'm not in New York these days. I'm down at my place in Florida for the next few weeks. I got some big deals coming up."

"I see. Maybe next time."

"Any time. Keep in touch with me. When I'm not in New York, I'm usually in Florida."

"Where in Florida?"

"Palm Beach."

"Are you in the book?"

"No, but my company is."

"What's it called?"

"Bicho Properties."

"Bicho?"

"Yeah. It's Spanish. My backer wanted me to call it that. I don't know what it means."

"Bicho."

"Yeah. Look me up whenever you're in the neighborhood. I'll get you some sailors."

"Aren't there any women around Palm Beach?"

"Sure, but they're all shits. They've got pussies like egg cups. When I fuck 'em, most of me is on the outside."

Brad glanced at the man' schlong. "I'm not surprised."

With Brad away at the Harvard reunion, Pat devoted time and thought to the Fats Mulligan television series. She met with Ted Colby every day, going over scripts, discussing casts, sets, scenery, costs. She met with department heads who would be involved— discussing the costs.

One morning at the studio, Pat got a call from Joe Reilly. "I don't know if you want to get mixed up in all the paperwork, Pat, but

Ron used to come over to the FreytFlyte office around once a month to take a look at the books, just to see how we were doing and make some plans. Do you want to keep this up?"

Pat wasn't sure. "Do you think I should?"

"Well," Joe said, "until you decide what you want to do with the company, I think you ought to have some idea about what's going on around here."

Pat said, "I've already decided what I'm going to do with the company, but that will have to wait until Ron's will is probated. When do you want me to come out?"

"Whenever's convenient for you."

"Tomorrow morning?"

"Okay. What time?"

"How much time will I need?"

"A couple hours, I guess."

"I'll be there around ten. You can buy me lunch. That's a joke, Joe."

The next day, after going over the FreytFlyte books with Joe Reilly and having lunch with him, Pat drove to the home of Martha Grady, a ten-thousand-dollar check for Martha in her purse. She had tea with Martha, and then she drove home.

She went directly into the den, inserted a piece of paper into the typewriter, and she wrote a memo to herself, a memo about what she had found out that day, something she felt was so important that she wanted to put it into writing quickly so that she would have the facts straight when she told it to Brad Cunningham. As she typed, she thought this was probably the same typewriter Ron has used when he wrote his letter to Morley Covington.

Her fingers flew at the keys and she said aloud, "It's all right, Ron darling. Everything is going to be all right. This time, *I'll* fuck them for you."

Chapter Thirty-five

Thursday night, Pat's telephone rang at ten-thirty. Brad said, "I'm home. I can be over in a half hour. Okay?"

"Why didn't you call me? I could have had you picked up."

"There wasn't time for that," Brad said. "Anyway, I wanted to pick up some papers to bring along."

"Have you eaten?"

"I ate on the plane. That's why I'm air sick. Just have plenty of vodka on tap."

"That I've got."

"Boss Lady, you're in trouble. See you."

Pat took a quick bath, then put on a pale blue jumpsuit. She prepared the coffee table: vodka, Coke, ice, glasses, and filled the cigarette box. She heard his car pull up and went to the door and opened it. He was wearing a three-piece suit and carrying a briefcase. He gave her a peck on the cheek.

"Where's your secretary?"

"What for?"

"This has the earmarks of a business meeting."

He went into the living room and sat at his usual place on the sofa at the coffee table. He placed his briefcase on the table, opened it, and extracted some papers. They fixed drinks for themselves. Pat lit a cigarette, Brad his pipe.

He took a sip, sank back, then said, "Well, I'm pretty sure now that Ron was right. They were after him."

"The drug conection?"

"Yes."

"What did you find out?"

He took a drag on his pipe and a sip of his drink. "When I was at Harvard, a classmate of mine was a guy named Mark Robinson. That's Robinson of Robinson, Sayer. Veddy veddy big in Wall Street. Mark was at the reunion. We were pretty close at school, and we hit it off again at the reunion. Anyway, Mark has an older brother, Matthew, who went through Harvard five or six years before we did. Matthew was very close to a guy named Sergio Carlotti. Mr. Carlotti has got a cock like a stallion."

"How do you know that?"

"Because I saw it."

"That must have been quite a reunion."

"Most reunions are."

"How come you saw it?"

"I'll tell you."

He told her about the orgy at Sergio Carlotti's apartment in Cambridge. Then he said, "I don't know how good my math is these days, but here's the way it all adds up to me. I'm sure this guy Carlotti doesn't have the brains to orchestrate the vendetta that reached Ron and Shad and now you, but he is somehow the connecting link in the problems Ron was having with every business he was in. The only way we'll find out who the real power is is through this shithead."

"How do we do that?" Pat asked.

"Through his love for his enormous root."

"And how do we do that?"

Brad said, "I don't know. Got any ideas?"

"I'll try to think." she said. Then: "Let me tell you something I found out."

"Shoot."

"Last Monday I had lunch with Joe Reilly. He wanted to go over the FreytFlyte books with me. We talked about the crash. He said the man who was working on Ron's plane was new and had been with the company only a couple of weeks. He seemed to know what he was doing, so when the foreman of the shop assigned him to Ron's plane, Joe felt it was all right. The day after the crash, the man vanished."

"Completely?"

"Yes."

"A plant?"

"Could be?"

"Didn't Joe check out the man's references?"

"Yes, but too late. They were phony."

"Damn. Anything else?"

"Monday afternoon, I went to see Martha Grady."

"You did? I didn't know you two were chummy."

"We're not. Martha Grady is a sanctimonious bitch."

"Why did you go see her?"

"Brad, Ron never talked to me much about any of his businesses, except the studio. I don't think he mentioned Vietnam at all. I thought maybe Shad had been more open with Martha about it, and I wanted to find out, especially after that letter of Ron's."

"Was she surprised to see you?"

"Yes. I brought along her check as a pretext for the visit. I was surprised she didn't sprinkle holy water before she let me in."

"And did you find out anything?"

"No. She told me Shad had never spoken of Vietnam, and that if he had tried she wouldn't have listened to him. She was sure it would have been sinful. So she knew nothing. But she did tell me something that struck me as odd."

"What was that?"

"At lunch, Joe Reilly mentioned that the Gradys had a Japanese houseboy who hovered over Shad throughout his illness. When I didn't see him the other day, I asked Martha about him."

"What did she say?"

"She said that Thene was—"

"Who?"

"Thene. That was his name. Martha said he was only half Japanese. His father. I gather that his father was a Japanese army officer and impregnated his mother during the Japanese occupation in the Second War. Thene was raised in Vietnam by his mother after the Japanese went home after the war."

"How did he get over here?"

"Martha's church brought him over in a group of refugees. A lot of churches did that, you know."

"No, I don't know. How did he get the job as houseboy?"

"Martha told me that one day when Shad was away on a long business trip, Thene showed up at the door. He said that his grandparents had been Ron's housekeepers in Saigon and when they heard that Thene was coming over here they told him to look up Shad or Ron and maybe they could help him get a job. Shad wasn't there to make the decision, so Martha, out of the goodness of her Christian heart, just let Thene move in. Shortly after Shad got back, he started getting sick. Martha said she's no good around sick people, so she let Thene take over. She said he was a godsend. He shaved Shad, bathed him, fed him, gave him his medicine and injections, even when he was in the hospital."

"Injections!"

"Yes. Martha didn't know of what. She left it to Thene."

"What happened to him?"

"Martha said that a day or two after Shad was buried, Thene just packed and left without a word."

"With a well-worn needle in his suitcase, I'll bet."

They studied each other. Pat asked, "Are you thinking what I'm thinking?"

"What else is there to think?" Brad said, reaching for the vodka. "The way our picture is shaping up, Ron was right about everything. They were after him and Shad."

"And you say they're now after me."

"Yes."

"But why? Ron and Shad are dead, probably both murdered. Isn't that revenge enough for those bastards?"

"They want the money in the San Francisco bank. The money they paid Ron and Shad for their part in the smuggling. The money they used as collateral for the companies they started. Even with Ron and Shad out of the way, the Connection knows they can't get their money until they get control of everything Ron owned. All of a sudden all this bullshit about the stock accumulation makes sense. Even the hotel fire. They wanted to make Ron watch his empire crumble before they crumbled him. Something must have gone wrong. They decided not to wait. But they still want their money, with interest."

Pat closed her eyes. "So they're after me."

"They know that everything of Ron's goes to you. They're not going to stop now. You're in trouble."

She looked at him. "So what do we do?"

"What do you think we should do?"

"There must be a boss, somebody with enough patience to go through all the costly detours to get the only revenge that will satisfy him: the crushing of the Kazurian Empire."

"And how do we find out who he is?"

He shrugged. "If you want, I'll go to Palm Beach and butter up Carlotti enough to make him blabbermouth to me some more."

"That would be sexually dangerous."

Brad frowned. "I know. Boss Lady, I don't think I'm ready to pay that price, even to save your life. Maybe we can think of something else. Get your sketchbook. Let's dance it around."

V
Big Dick Carlotti

Chapter Thirty-six

They worked all night.

By three in the morning, page after page of the sketch-book was filled with arcs, arrows, circles, triangles, and rectangles.

Pat sank back in her chair. "We aren't getting anywhere," she said. "Too many loose ends."

Brad emptied the vodka jug into his glass. "So okay. What have we got?" He counted on his fingers. "We've got a missing house-boy, a missing mechanic. We have a suspicious fire at the hotel and a big lawsuit brought by a New York outfit where one of the big-shots is a buddy of Carlotti. And we can almost be sure that Big Dick Carlotti has been buying up LPM stock under a bunch of fake names."

"And we know that Big Dick has another buddy in the dope business somewhere in South America."

"Colombia."

"So now what have we got?"

"I don't know what we've got," Brad said, "but I know what we need."

"What?"

"Sherlock Holmes."

Pat sat up. "Jesus Christ, we've got a Sherlock Holmes. You just reminded me."

"Who?"

"Bert Bernstein."

"Bert?"

"No, but he knows an agency that is," Pat said. "I only discovered it recently. When Ron first met me, he had Bert's agency run a check on me. He knew more about me than I knew about myself. I'll talk to Bert about it in the office."

Brad glanced at his watch. "It's time to go to the office now."

"I know. Are you hungry?"

"Not really."

"Do you want to go to bed."

"Yes. But I'd better warn you. Boston left me limp."

"Then you'd better go home to your own bed."

Brad looked at the ceiling. "How do you like that? I make love to a state of sheer exhaustion just to be able to save her life, and now she won't even give me a place to rest my head."

Pat said, "When your head is rested, you can bring it back."

A month later, Bert Bernstein came into Pat's office and handed her a large brown envelope. He said, "I'm not doing a hatchet job on anybody these days, so I think this is yours. Your opera star?"

Pat took the envelope without looking at it. "Opera star?"

"Whoever it was, that guinea you told me to have checked out."

She remembered her fib. "Oh, yes." She glanced at the return address: "Continental Personnel Investigations, Inc." The return address was the Century Plaza. She said, "Thanks, Bert. I hear he goes heavy on the sauce and screws up a lot. This will probably decide whether we risk signing him up for the *Traviata* picture Ted Colby wants to make."

Bert pointed to the envelope. "Well, that report should tell you all you have to know about the guy. That outfit finds out everything."

"Yes, I know," Pat said. "They checked me out."

"Warts and all," Bert said, and he laughed. Then: "Please notice. I didn't open it. For your eyes only."

She said, "Thanks, Bert. It took a long time."

"Yes," Bert said. "Your boy must be leading quite a life."

"I hope so," she said. "Thanks, Bert."

He nodded to her and left. She opened the envelope. It was all there. She put the report back into the envelope and took it home with her. That evening, smoking a cigarette in her favorite chair, she watched as Brad read the report at the coffee table. He read it three times. Then he put it down and looked at her.

She said, "Is that our man or is that our man?"

"Sure sounds like it," he said. He helped himself to the vodka. "I still can't believe it."

"You still can't believe what?"

"I still can't believe that the bullshitter I met in Cambridge has the brains to pull off everything that's been going on."

"It's all there," Pat said, pointing at the report. "It all ties in."

"I know," Brad said, "but I wouldn't want to go to court on evidence like this. It's circumstantial. You know what they say about scorpions."

"No, I don't," Pat said. "What do they say about scorpions?"

"The tail has the sting, but the head tells the tail what to do."

"Who, then? The uncle in Houston?"

"Maybe. But I'm not too sure. Look at the rackets they're in. Garbage collection? Run-of-the-mill small-time Mafia crap. The question this report doesn't address is why is Big Dick Carlotti interested in LPM and Ron?"

"Drugs?"

"Yes. Drugs."

"Carlotti is a user."

"Honey, LPM Studios is full of users. It doesn't prove anything."

"The report says the family has been suspected of dealing in drugs."

"Take a walk on Hollywood Boulevard. You'll find dealers on every corner."

"Carlotti told you that he knows the source."

"He did. But it could be bullshit."

"We'll never find out sitting here."

"Okay," Brad said, a challenge in his voice. "When do you want me to go to Palm Beach?"

"To do what?"

He said, "We know from the report, and I know first hand, that Big Dick Carlotti shoots his mouth off on two subjects. Sex and drugs."

"You're going to get him high and make him confess to you?"

"I don't know what I'll do. I'll have to play it by ear. And I'll do anything I have to, to get him talking. We have to make him cut his own throat."

"But you don't even know where he is in Palm Beach."

He shrugged. "I'll find him. Mark Robinson will know where he is."

And then what? Do you know anybody there?"

"I have an aunt who lives in Palm Beach. I used to visit her when I was at Harvard."

Pat said, "The report says that Carlotti moves in pretty fancy circles. Does one of them include your aunt?"

"I don't know if my aunt can circle at all. She's pushing eighty."

"Is she fancy?"

"She lives on the same road as the Kennedys. And she won't talk to them because they're Democrats."

"That sounds toney enough. Where do we go from there?"

They could not figure out where to go from there. They talked about it for hours. Around eleven, Brad announced that he was going home, she walked him to his car, and they did not kiss good night. They had not taken time to eat. Alone, she went into the kitchen and opened the refrigerator door and stared at its contents. Nothing interested her. She went to bed.

In the middle of the night, she awoke with a start, as though she had been touched. She said aloud, "Of course." She clicked on the lamp on her night table and she reached for the telephone. She dialed Brad's number.

His phone rang a dozen times before he answered with a muffled, "Hullo?"

"Brad?"

"Yes?"

"It's Pat."

"What time is it?"

She glanced at her alarm clock. "It's five after three."

"This is a helluva time to call."

"I just thought of something."

"Are you still up?"

"No. I was asleep. But I just thought of something."

"It better be good. What is it?"

"Brad, do you happen to know a nymphomaniac with brains?"

"Yeah. You."

"Be serious. Do you know one?"

"Jesus, Pat. What a question."

"It's important."

"What's important?"

"You said we've got to get Big Dick Carlotti to cut his own throat. How about if we get him to cut his throat on his own words?"

"How do we do that?"

"Do you remember the television show *Candid Camera*?"

"I never watch television. I don't own a set."

"Well, it was a show about people who didn't know they were being photographed. They said and did a lot of funny things. It was a big hit."

"So?"

"Before television, it was a radio show, called *Candid Microphone*. It was even funnier beacause it was easier to hide a microphone than a television camera."

He sighed. "Patricia, what the hell are you getting at?"

"All right," she said. "Suppose we find a nymphomaniac who can take on Big Dick and can wear him out? She can razz him and tease him and get him bragging and maybe get him to run his mouth.''

"You're still confusing me."

"Brad, we can plant a microphone on the girl. We can bug her. We can tape record everything he says. Maybe we can get him to convict himself."

He was quiet for a moment. Then: "Where are we going to plant a bug on a naked broad? Up her twat?"

"I haven't figured that out yet," Pat said. "But do you think it's a good idea?"

"I've got a better idea."

"What?"

"Go to sleep." He hung up.

She hung up. She turned off the lamp. She lay awake a long time, thinking about it, and gradually she fell into a deep sleep.

When her phone rang, Pat thought it was the alarm clock, and she grabbed at it in the darkness. Then she realized what it was, and she reached for the telephone. "Yes?"

"Pat?" It was a woman.

"Yes?"

"Pat, we don't know each other but a mutual friend of ours called me a few minutes ago and said it would be okay to call you?"

"Who?"

"Brad Cunningham."

"You know Brad?"

"Very well. I didn't want to call you at four o'clock in the morning, but Brad said you'd probably be awake."

"That's okay. Why did Brad tell you to call me?"

"He said you were looking for pussy."

"What? Yes, as a matter of fact, I am. What's your name?"

"Mandy. Look, Pat, Brad wasn't clear about all this, but I think I'd better make something clear right away."

"What's that, Mandy?"

"I'm not a dyke."

"Did Brad tell you anything at all?"

"He just said that you could line me up with the thrill of my life."

"Mandy, I need a woman who will take on a really huge man."

"I haven't had any problems so far."

"What's your background?"

She laughed. "Honey, when I've got less than ten inches in me, I might as well masturbate."

"I'm sure this one is more than ten inches."

"I'm already getting horny. Who belongs to it."

Pat changed. "Mandy, do you know who I am?"

"Yeah. Brad told me. I've seen you around the studio a few times, but we never got a chance to talk."

"You work at LPM"

"Yeah. Once in a while I get bit parts."

"Are you doing anything now?"

"Casting called me yesterday. They want me to go over to Vegas for a bit in the Fats Mulligan series."

"Well, Mandy, I'd rather not have anybody at the studio know about your project."

"You don't have to worry, Mrs. Kazurian. The only time I open up my big mouth is when I've got something in it."

"Good. Can you come to the studio tomorrow?"

"Tomorrow or today?"

"Today, I mean."

"Sure. What time?"

"Noon."

"I'll be there."

"Ask for Brad. I'll tell him to expect you."

Pat couldn't resist it. She dialed Brad's number again, and from the several rings of his phone, she said, "I hope you're having a good night's sleep."

"No, I'm not," he said. "And I hope you're not."

"I'm not," she said. "Your girl friend just called. She'll be at your office around noon."

"Did you tell her the assignment?"

"No. I'll tell her in your office. Call me when she gets there."

"Okay."

"Tell me something?"

"What?"

"You don't have ten inches. How do you satisfy Mandy?"

"I use a fist," he said. He laughed and hung up.

In the morning, Pat spent a few minutes at her desk. Then she told her secretary, "I'm going over to Props, if you need me."

She walked over to the Property Department and she found Max, the man who ran it, and she said, "Max, do you remember a television show called *Candid Camera*?"

"Of course," he said. "I worked on it when they were shooting in New York."

"I want to have some fun," she said. And she told him what she wanted. An hour later, she was back in her office. She put a small plastic box in her purse about the size of a pack of cigarettes. A smile kept tugging at her lips.

Around noon, her secretary announced on the squawk box, "It's Brad Cunningham. He says to tell you that she's here."

"Thank you."

Pat opened her purse and touched a button on the plastic device and put it back inside. She tucked the purse under her arm and walked down the hall to Brad's office. Just inside the door was a small table. Pat put her purse on it and walked across the room to meet Mandy. Brad introduced them. Pat took a chair.

She said, "Mandy, why don't you tell us about yourself?"

Mandy was a large redhead, with big breasts. She was wearing a sunflower dress. It was blinding. "What do you want to know?" she asked.

Pat said, "Tell us how you lost your virginity."

Mandy said, "I didn't lose it, Mrs. Kazurian. I gave it away when I was eight years old."

"Tell us." Pat said. Her voice was sweet and patient.

Mandy talked for ten minutes. Out of the corner of her eye, Pat caught Brad's puzzled glances.

Finally Brad said, "Pat, when are we going to get down to business?"

"Right away," Pat said. She looked at Mandy. "Mandy, do you fuck with your shoes on?"

Mandy said, "Mrs. Kazurian, I once got laid fully dressed on the corner of Hollywood and Vine, waiting for a traffic light. Why?"

"Just a minute." Pat got up and went for her purse and brought it back to her chair. She opened the purse and took out the plastic box and pushed a button. Mandy heard her entire conversation.

Mandy said, "Amazing. How did you do that."

"A small microphone."

Brad said, "Where's the mike?"

Pat took off a shoe and held it up and pointed at the heel.

Pat talked to Mandy for over an hour, saying just enough, telling her what she was supposed to find out, where and how and with whom.

Mandy said, "But, Mrs. Kazurian, I'm supposed to report to Las Vegas next week. I've got a bit in the Fats Mulligan series."

Pat said, "You go to Palm Beach and find out what I want to know, and I'll see to it that you get a series of your own."

Pat looked at Brad. She said, "I think the time has come for you to call Mark Robinson and find out where Big Dick Canotti lives in Palm Beach and who his friends are. Then call your aunt and tell her she'll be visited by a sex-starved California widow."

Brad said, "This is very evil."

Chapter Thirty-seven

The garden party was held on a Sunday afternoon. It was a hot day, a muggy breeze coming in off the sea. Under a palm tree near the tall wall that shut off the beach road, Mandy was saying, "Mr. Carlotti, I hear you're in the real estate business."

"I dabble in real estate," he said.

"Maybe you can help me."

"What's your problem?"

"My husband left me some Florida property. I live in California. What do I want with Florida property?"

"Why don't you sell it?"

"That's exactly why I'm here."

"Where is your property?"

"Is there a place called Tampa?"

"Yes. It's on the west coast."

"In California?"

"The west coast of Florida. How much land do you have?"

"A thousand acres, I think."

"That's a nice piece of land."

"But I understand it's just swamp land."

"Once you get rid of the water and the alligators, it could be worth a lot of money."

"How much, do you think?"

"I'd have to check it out."

"May I come to your office and talk to you about it?"

"Sure. Are you staying here with Miss Cunningham?"

"No. I'm staying at a hotel."

"Which one?"

She told him.

"I live there, he said.

She said, "How convenient. Are you a Floridian?"

"No. New York. I come down here on business."

"New York? Do you know anybody in Wall Street?"

"I happen to be in the Street myself. Why?"

"My husband left me some stock. I don't know nothing about the stock market."

"You own stock?"

"Yes."

"In what?"

"A movie studio."

"Really? Which one?"

"LPM."

"You own some LPM?"

"Yes. My husband owned it for years."

"How many shares?"

"I think it's twenty thousand."

Carlotti sent his gaze up to the palm tree. "Have you got a dinner date tonight?"

"No. I don't know anybody here except Miss Cunningham. I just came east to sell the property."

"How come you know Miss Cunningham?"

"I know her brother in California."

"How come you know her brother?"

"We're neighbors in Santa Barbara."

"What does he do?"

"He's retired. He was an admiral in the Navy."

"I know a lot of Navy people."

"Do you?"

"You want to have dinner with me?"

"All right," she said. "But, Mr. Carlotti, I've got to ask you a personal question."

"Go ahead."

"Do you have a gourd in your pocket? Or is that you?"

He laughed. "It's me.'

She said, "I find it very upsetting. My husband was sick for years before he passed away. I can't remember the last time I had a man. Oh, I'm sorry to be so indiscreet, Mr. Carlotti."

He laughed. "So we'll have dinner and then we'll straighten you out."

Her look was searching. "Do you like to get head?"

"I love it," he said. "But I never met anybody who could take what I've got."

"You just have."

He searched her face. "Do you take it other ways?"

"What do you think I did with the admiral?"

He said, "Let's eat."

Later, on her bed, her purse on the night table, he said, "Why don't you take your shoes off?"

She said, "If I do, my toes will fall off."

He laughed. "You like it, huh?"

"Give me a rest. Let me give you head."

"I'll drown you."

"Try me."

Later, when he was gone, she dialed an Area Code 213 number. "Mrs. Kazurian?"

"Mandy, are you all right?"

"Holy shit! I've never seen such a root."

"Are you all right?"

"He almost blew my head off."

"Uncut?"

"I ate him. He comes on like Niagara Falls."

"Are you okay?"

"So far. I don't know how much more I can take. He wants to back door me."

"He goes that way?"

"I'll probably never use it again."

"Did he tell you anything?"

"No. I couldn't speak much. Are you sure I'm going to get my own TV series out of this?"

"I'll make you the next Marilyn Monroe."

"I've heard about her. The Kennedys live just up the street. I don't want to take on that tribe."

"Did you tape anything?"

"Yes. Are you hooked up?"

"Give me a moment. I'll have Brad get on the extension."

"Brad is there?" She heard the click. "Brad?"

He said, "Yes, honey?"

She said, "Brad, I'll never complain about you again."

"Okay, honey. Take care of yourself."

Pat said, "Okay, Mandy, play the tape."

Mandy played the tape. They could hear it as they recorded it, and they kept shaking their heads.

Pat said, "He didn't say anything about drugs. Didn't you two snort?"

"No. He didn't mention the stuff at all."

"That's what we want him to talk about. You'll have to bring it up. When do you meet again?"

"Tomorrow afternoon. He wants to see me in his office."

"Do you know what for?"

"The property. He wants to locate it on a map."

"You know what to say?"

"Yes. The deed is in California. I'll have to send for it."

"Yes. Ditto the stock certificates, if he brings them up."

"I know."

"All right, then. Keep in touch. And be careful."

Mandy gave a weak laugh. "Yeah."

Uncle Julio was saying, "So what? You call me up at this hour to tell me you've met a woman who's got a pussy like the Lincoln Tunnel? Are you high again? I told you not to use that stuff. Just peddle it."

Sergio said, "She's amazing, Uncle. She can take all I've got."

"So what? So can a cow."

"But I told you, Uncle. She owns a thousand acres over at Tampa. Do you know what kind of an airstrip we can build on that? It could take Seven-Forty-Sevens."

"So what? If Hones wanted us to use Seven-Forty-Sevens, we'd have them. We're doing all right with what we've got."

"But what about her stock? She's got twenty thousand shares."

"That, maybe Hones will be interested in. I'll have to ask him."

"It'll cost a lot of money."

"If Hones wants it, he'll send you the money on the next delivery. How did you meet this broad?"

"I met her at a party. I got the invitation last week. Some old biddy who's got a big house right on the water, right down the street from the Kennedys."

"What Kennedys?"

"The Boston Kennedys. The Kennedys Grandpa did business with during Prohibition."

"How come you got invited to something so swanky?"

"This broad knows the old lady's nephew in California. She says he knows me. He went to Harvard. I don't remember him. But it's a good connection, Uncle. These people have a lot of money. And they're into politics. They can be helpful."

"I've got half the politicians in Houston on my payroll now, and they don't do me no help."

"What do you want me to do with this broad?"

"I don't know. I'll try to get Hones on the box in the morning. I don't think he'll want the property. But he may want the stock. When do you see the broad again?"

"Tomorrow afternoon. She's coming to my office. I'm gonna fuck her blind."

"Watch your step. Goof off, and one of these days Hones will take care of yours."

Mandy paid the cab driver. Before she closed her purse, she clicked
the button on the plastic box. She got out of the cab and crossed
the sidewalk to the door of the small building. She tried the door.
It was locked. She saw the doorbell and rang it. She pressed it
again. Then, through the glass door, she saw him coming. He was
smiling. She sneaked a look at his watermelon.

When he unlocked the door to her, she said, "Why do you keep
your door locked, Mr. Carlotti? You'll discourage business."

He said, "I don't do much business here. I just keep the office
for convenience. Please come in." She entered, and he locked the
door behind her. "This way." He led her from the small outer office into an inner office. There was a desk and some furniture and
a deep rug. He indicated a chair to her, then sat behind the desk. He
asked, "How are you feeling today?"

She flashed a smile. "Considering what happened last night,"
she said, "I'm surprised I can feel anything."

"It was very enjoyable."

Then she went serious. "Mr. Carlotti, I know we're here on business, so I owe you an apology."

"What's the matter?"

"You told me last night that you wanted to know more about my
property. I thought I had the deed with me. I don't. It must be in
California. I'll have to send for it. Until it gets here, I can't really tell
you where my property is."

"That won't be necessary," he said. "I talked to my people in
Texas about it already. They're not interested. They feel they have
enough Florida property as it is. But I think I can talk them into
buying your stock."

"What stock?"

"The LPM stock."

"Oh, I forgot all about that. Good, I'd appreciate that. I've got
some Paramount stock and some Warner stock, too. Would your
friends be interested in that?"

"Just the LPM."

"If it's such good stock, shouldn't I hang on to it?"

"I've told my friends you'd sell it. You don't want to make a liar
out of me, do you?"

"I'll do whatever you say. You're the expert."

"Tell you what. You sell your stock, and I'll convince them to
buy your property."

"Your friends must really want that stock."

"They do."

"Why?"

"They have their reasons. I've been picking up LPM stock for them for a few years now."

"Why? Do your friends want to go into the movie business?"

He laughed. "No. They want to get somebody out of it."

"Why would they want to do that?"

"When I know you better, maybe I'll tell you. I had a great time last night. Did you?"

"Oh, yes. I didn't know there were men around like you."

"There aren't. We must do it again some time."

"Any time."

"Yeah? What about right now?"

"You want me right now?"

"I want it right now. Get on your hands and knees."

"Oh, Mr. Carlotti. It would hurt me that way."

"I'll put a lot of grease on it."

"I don't mean that. My husband used to like it that way. But he had to encourage me."

"How did he do that?"

"We lit up."

"You lit up what?"

"Pot. Marijuana."

He laughed. "That's kid stuff. You like smoke? I'll get you the best there is. Colombian Gold."

"What's that?"

"Hash. It's terrific."

"Why do they call it Colombian Gold?"

"Because that's where it comes from."

"Columbus, Ohio?"

He laughed. "Colombia, South America. All the best stuff comes from Colombia. I've got a good friend there who's in the business. He's got a layout like General Motors. I can get you all you want."

"Would you? How do you get it?"

"We've got our ways."

"All right. Get some; and when we light up, you can do it your way."

"Why wait? I've got something better. Do you snort?"

"What's that?"

"I'll show you."

He opened the middle drawer of the desk and took out a silver box about the size of a deck of cards. When he opened the box, she saw that one section of it contained a white powder. The other section held several small straws.

She said, "You smoke that?"

"I'll show you." He put a pinch of the powder in his left palm and his right hand brought a straw to his nose. He moved his left hand to the straw and took a sharp sniff. She saw the powder disappear up the straw. He looked at her. "Try it."

She tried it. Immediately her eyes watered and blinked. Amazement spread across her face in a silly grin. "My goodness! What's happening to me?"

"Coke."

"Coca Cola?"

"Cocaine."

"Does this come from General Motors, too?"

"Everything I handle comes from there. Only the best."

"You handle it?"

"In a way. Try some more." He watched her try some more. "It's a great high, isn't it?"

She was dazed. "I've never been so high. I'm flying."

"So does the stuff."

"What?"

"It's a joke. Your ass getting warm?"

She looked around. "We don't have a place to lie down."

"Just bend over the desk."

She moved to the desk and put her purse on it and bent. He came around behind her and began pulling up her sunflowers. He brought the silver box close to them. He said, "Help yourself whenever you want."

She said, "You help yourself whenever you want."

He began to press into her.

She let out a loud groan.

He said, "Why don't you take off your shoes?"

She said, "If I do, my toes will fall off."

They played the tape four times. Then Brad said, "Okay. What have we got?"

Pat said, "We've got Colombia, South America, Colombian Gold, coke, Texas, Florida, and a nice gal with a sore bum."

Brad said, "And we've got something about flying, too. His joke."

"Yes. They probably fly the stuff in from South America."

"To Florida or Texas. Or both."

"Or points in between. If it's a General Motors, they most likely have their own planes."

"I wonder how they get through. The Feds and the Coast Guard watch every inch of the Gulf."

Pat said, "Well, let's hope Our Gal Mandy will luck out. She will if anyone can."

Mandy was trying.

Carlotti had been out of town all day and returned late. They had dinner in the restaurant of the hotel where they were both staying, and then they went up to his penthouse suite. Entering, they were passing near the sofa when he turned and gave her a playful push. She fell on her back on the sofa. Immediately he was astride her, his zipper down, he pulling out his dong, hand over hand, and feeding it into her mouth, smiling as he watched it harden and disappear.

She couldn't breathe. She took him several full beats, and then she put her hands to his hips and pushed him away until he was out of her. "Not that way," she said.

He collapsed on his back at her side. "I thought you liked eating it."

"I do," she said. "But when you want to fuck, use my pussy, not my throat."

She slid to the floor between his legs. She took off his shoes and threw them aside. She undid his belt and the button there and pulled off his pants and threw them at the shoes. She took off his shorts. There it was, in all its glorious challenge. She moved in on it. With three or four gulps, she had it all.

She knew she had to get him to talk, and she knew what she had to get him to talk about, and this was difficult to do with her esophagus clogged. She backed off from him until he popped out.

"Pussy time," she said.

She pulled up her dress and climbed higher on him until she was positioned. Then she guided him into her, slowly, deeply, fully, until she could feel his baseball knob pressing against her pancreas.

She sighed. "I'll never get used to this."

He said, "Nobody ever has."

"It's wonderful"

"I know." He reached for her tits.

She rode him. "Mr. Carlotti, you told me something the other day, and I can't figure it out."

"What's that?"

"That Greek at LPM Studios, why do you want to put him out of business?"

"We already put him out of business."

"How?"

"Don't you read the papers?"

"Not much, I'm afraid. How did you put him out of business?"

"He was in a plane crash."

"Oh, dear. Well, you didn't have anything to do with that, did you, Mr. Carlotti? I can't believe you did. You're too nice for anything like that."

"Okay. So I didn't have anything to do with it. Shut up."

"We were fucking, Mr. Carlotti, and it's wonderful. But I was wondering."

"What?"

"Why you wanted to put him out of business in the first place."

"Because he screwed us."

"Us?"

"Me and my partners."

"Mr. Carlotti, I can't believe there's anybody in the world smart enough to take you. How did he do it?"

"He robbed us."

"He held you up."

"In a way."

"How did he do that."

"It's a long story."

"Tell it to me, Mr. Carlotti. We've got the time. I want to stay with you all night."

"Why do you want to hear it?"

"I don't know anything about the business world, Mr. Carlotti. My husband never discussed his business affairs with me. I'm fascinated by the business world. Tell me the story, Mr. Carlotti." She kept riding him.

He said, "It goes all the way back to Vietnam. That Greek bastard was working for us, but he didn't know it. We paid him good money. A lot of good money. When he decided he had enough, he broke up the connection."

"How did he do that?"

"Never mind. He broke it up. It hurt us, it really hurt us. We lost money for a long time. So we made up our minds that we were going to get his ass. It took time to track him down, but we did. And we've been on him ever since."

"But, Mr. Carlotti, he's dead now, isn't he? Isn't it settled?"

"No. We want our money back."

"How are you going to get it?"

"Everything that bastard ever owned, he bought with our money—his movie studio, his hotel, his air cargo company, even the cropdusting shit."

"What's the cropdusting shit?"

"You never heard of cropdusting?"

"I don't know. I've got a nice garden in California; sometimes in the summer it gets overrun with bugs, so I squirt a pesticide on them and kill them."

"Cropdusting does the same thing," he said, "Only you do it from an airplane on a much bigger scale. That's the best thing that's come out of all this so far."

"What do you mean?"

He opened his mouth.

A telephone rang in the bedroom.

He said, "Shit!"

She said, "Don't answer it, Mr. Carlotti."

"I have to. It's my hotline. Get off."

She went stiff-armed, lifting from him. Then she had to stand to let the last several inches escape. He got up.

"Wait here," he said. He headed for the bedroom, his shirttails low on his hips, a great protuberance extending in front of him, like a divining rod. He shut the door.

She tried to listen. She could hear his voice, but his words were lost behind the closed door. Then she noticed his clothes on the floor, where he had thrown them, and saw the bulge in a rear pocket. She reached into it and extracted his wallet. She looked into it. A wad of big bills. A cardholder containing a picture of an elderly, Italian woman, maybe his mother; his New York driver's license; membership cards to clubs in Bar Harbor, Newport, New York, East Hampton, Hilton Head, and Palm Beach; and some business cards. She flipped through them. One caught her eye and she stared at it a few seconds, memorizing it. She put the wallet back. Then she sat on the sofa, opened her purse, took a cigarette from the pack, and lit up, waiting.

He came out in a few minutes, a big smile on his face. "I've got good news for you," he said. "We're going to buy your LPM stock."

"How nice," she said. "Am I going to make a lot of money?"

"Today's closing price, plus fifteen percent. I tried to get twenty-five percent, but my uncle wouldn't agree to it. Even so, you'll make a nice profit."

"Thank you, Mr. Carlotti. What about my property?"

"We don't want that just yet. We've already got all the land we need in Tampa."

"I was hoping to get rid of that before I head home."

"Don't worry. I know some people in Brooklyn who are always looking for an investment. I'm sure I can talk them into buying the property."

"Wonderful."

"Let's go to bed," he said. "I've had enough straight stuff for tonight. I want something else."

"All right," she said. She snuffed out her cigarette, picked up her purse, and stood. They went to the bedroom.

He said, "You won't need your purse. This isn't going to cost you anything. And take off your goddam shoes."

"Roll over," he said.

She rolled over on the floor and looked at him, a small fear tugging at her eyes.

He knelt between her legs, his look a leer. He took hold of her calves and brought her legs up, bending her in half, and he placed her legs over his shoulders. His divining rod moved in, touched her, searched, discovered, pierced.

Her hands grabbed the air. "Easy."

He scolded. "You like it rough."

"I do," she said. "But I think my feet are about to fall off."

The telephone rang at two in the morning. Pat awoke on the second ring. She touched Brad. "That's Mandy. Get the tape recorder ready." She clicked on her night light and reached for the phone on the fourth ring. "Hullo?"

"Mrs. Kazurian?"

"Yes, Mandy. Are you all right?"

"I don't know. I've been standing on my head all night. I'm still dizzy. I can't go on much longer."

"I understand. Did you get anything, Mandy?"

"I think so. Ready?"

Pat looked at Brad. "Are we hooked up?"

Brad nodded.

Pat said, "Okay, Mandy. Roll it."

Pat and Brad could hear the tape on the squawk box as it was transmitted to the tape recorder. From time to time, Pat and Brad nodded at each other. They were making points. Then came the silence during the hot line call.

Mandy said, "Mrs. Kazurian, something happened at this point. I'll tell you about it later."

Then came the part about the stock and the property and cornholing. Then silence.

Pat said, "That was very good, Mandy. Did you hear him on the telephone?"

"He had the door shut. I could hear his voice, but I couldn't catch what he was saying."

"You said that something happened while he was on the phone."

"Yes. I went through his wallet. His pants were on the floor near the sofa. I took them off of him. I noticed the wallet while he was on the phone. So I took it out of the back pocket and I went through it."

"Did you find anything important?"

"I don't know. He's always talking about his partners in Texas."

"Yes."

"And when he came back from the hot line he mentioned an uncle."

"Yes."

"Well, in his wallet was a business card with the name Carlotti on it, and the address was in Houston."

"What did the card say?"

"On one line was 'Julio Carlotti, Unlimited.' On the next line was 'Imports-dash-Exports.' And at the bottom was an address. It was a post office box."

"Do you remember it?"

"Mrs. Kazurian, I am known all over Los Angeles for being the hottest ticket in town, but I'm also known as being the fastest study. Of course I remember. Got a pencil?"

"Yes."

Mandy recited the address.

Pat wrote it down. She asked, "Was there a phone number?"

"Not printed on the front of the card. But somebody wrote a number on the back. Carlotti, I suppose. Is seven-one-three the area code for Houston?"

"I don't know. I'll have to check it out. What was the number?"

Mandy recited it.

Pat said, "Great work, Mandy. We'll follow up on everything. When do you see him again?"

"Well," said Mandy, "it's five o'clock in the morning. If he runs true to form, I expect him to be banging on my door any minute. I'm not going to answer it. I gotta sleep. And I need a little vacation. When I get up, I'm driving down to Miami. My equipment needs a rest."

"Do you have another date with him?"

"He told me at dinner that the Kennedys are throwing a big bash at their place Saturday night. The Harvard crowd. He's invited, and he's taking me along. He wants me to wear a brassiere. You know the Kennedys."

"I don't," Pat said, "But I've heard. Wear a girdle."

Mandy said, "That's no way to talk to a good Democrat."

"Sorry."

Mandy said, "Mrs. Kazurian, what do I do about the stock?"

Pat looked at Brad. "Can you take care of that?" Brad nodded. Pat said, "Mandy, when he's ready to make the deal, tell him the stock certificates are here in your home and that you'll have to call your maid to have her mail them to you."

"My maid? I'm getting rich, right?"

Pat laughed. "Yes, you are. You're doing a fantastic job, Mandy. I'm grateful."

"You're paying me wonderful money, Mrs. Kazurian. I love this line of work. To tell you the truth, Mrs. Kazurian, I don't really like this guy; but if I could cast his joint for a dildo, I wouldn't need another man for the rest of my life."

She looked at Brad. "What do you think?"

Brad said, "Cropdusting."

She nodded. "Yes. What time is it?"

"Almost three."

"I'll call Stewart in the morning."

"What for?"

Pat said, "I told you what Joe Reilly told me, about a meeting Ron called in Vegas with him and Stewart and Milton. Everybody was complaining about business being so bad."

"Yes."

"And Stewart said he was unable to expand the cropdusting anywhere in the South. He said some other company seemed to have the region tied up. He said even when he cut his own prices almost down to cost, he still couldn't break through the wall. He said he even wrote the company and tried to work out a deal, but he never got an answer."

Brad said, "So?"

Pat pointed to the tape recorder. "Carlotti just told Mandy that cropdusting was the best thing to come out of all this so far."

"So?"

"Big Dick has an uncle in Houston who is in the import-export business."

"Right."

"Suppose he's also in the cropdusting business."

"Suppose he is?"

"Wouldn't that be a convenient way to get drugs into the country, especially along the Gulf of Mexico? Who'd suspect that a cropdusting plane would be carrying anything more than a load of insecticide."

Brad said, "I'm beginning to grab it."

Pat said, "I'm calling Stewart in the morning to find out the name and address of his Southern competition. If it's Julio Carlotti, we're making progress."

Brad shook his head. "If I didn't know better, I'd say you were Italian."

"Why?"

"You think like a hood."

"Not all Italians are hoods."

"The ones we're dealing with are. I wonder who the Godfather is? Uncle Julio?"

"I'm not sure. But once we find out, they're sure as hell going to find out who the Godmother is."

Chapter Thirty-eight

At seven o'clock in the morning, Pat telephoned Stewart. who said, "Of course I'm up. I've been up and hard at work for two hours. Besides being in the bug business, I'm a farmer, you know."

"I don't know how you do it," Pat said.

Stewart said, "I don't, either. Pat, maybe I ought to get out of the bug business."

"Oh?"

"Yeah. With Ron gone, y'know, I'm next in line for this place. After all, Pat, I was born and raised a farmer. I've been thinking maybe I ought to settle down and get married and start raising a few farmhands of my own."

A pause. Then Pat: "All right, Stewart, if that's what you want. I think it's wonderful. But can you hang on to the bug business until Ron's will is probated?"

"Sure. I don't have a wife lined up yet."

"Good. I'll tell you why I called. Joe Reilly told me the other day that you had problems expanding your cropdusting business in the South. Is that true?"

"Not problems. I just couldn't get in."

"Joe said you tried to reach the competition to make a deal. What's the name and address of the company?"

"I've got it around somewhere. Why do you want it, Pat?"

"Ron's will," she said. "I think I'd better have as much information as I can get concerning everything Kaz was involved in."

"Okay. Can you hold for a minute?"

"Yes." She waited.

"It's Bicho Air Services Company. Houston."

"Spell Bicho."

"B-i-c-h-o. I guess it's somebody's name."

"Sounds like it," Pat said, and she thought: *Bicho Properties, in Palm Beach.* She asked, "Got an address?"

"It's a post office box."

"What's the number?"

He gave it to her. It was identical to the number Mandy memorized from the business card.

Pat said, "Thanks, Stewart. How's the family?"

"Everybody's fine. You coming up to see us?"

"One of these days."

"We'd love it." There was a pause, and then he said, "Pat, did Ron ever talk to you about Vietnam?"

"Now and then."

"About him and Grady in Vietnam?"

"Now and then. Did he ever talk to you about it?"

"Yes, when he came home for Grandpapa's funeral. We had a long talk about it. He told me everything."

"Oh? Pat, did Ron ever say anything to you about Grady's death? That he was suspicious about it?"

"He might have."

"Pat, do you know where I'm coming from?"

"Yes."

"Then you know why I want to get out of the bug business. Maybe you ought to get out of the movie business."

"Maybe I will."

"Be careful, Pat."

"I will, Stewart."

"I love you, Kazurian."

"And I love you, Kazurian."

She looked at the clock. Seven-fifteen. Eight-fifteen at Evergreen. She was sure her father would be up. She dialed the number. She heard:

"Judge Purney's residence." It was one of the maids.

Pat asked, "Is he there."

"May I ask who is calling?"

"His daughter. Patricia."

"Oh, yes, Miss Purney. The Judge is at breakfast. I'll see if I can get him for you."

Pat waited a few minutes. Then she heard a click, and: "Well, young lady, what brings this on?"

She had to smile. "Hi, Dad."

"Since you've become a big movie mogul, I thought I'd never hear from you again."

"You know better than that. How are you, Dad?"

"Just fine."

"And Mother and Sis?"

"They're fine, too. They're still in bed, of course. Do you want to talk to your mother?"

"No. I just wanted to talk to you."

"Have you been behaving yourself?"

"No. I need some legal advice."

"I thought as much. What have you done?"

"Nothing. It's just something I have to find out."

"What is it?"

"Dad, if a person uses a post office as his address, how do I go about finding out where he really lives?"

"You don't. The post office is not required to disclose that sort of information. There are laws."

"But suppose this person is involved in some sort of crime? Couldn't the local police get the information?"

"Where is this?"

"In Houston. Couldn't the Houston police find out?"

"Not unless they got a Federal court order."

"How come?"

"Pat, the U.S. Postal Service is an independent agency within the Federal Government, and to obtain the information you want would require moving at that level. And you'd have to have plenty of evidence to get your foot in the door."

"What about the F.B.I.?"

"What about the F.B.I.?"

"Could the F.B.I. get the court order without a lot of publicity?"

"The F.B.I. is a Federal agency. I suppose so."

"And what about the Federal Bureau of Narcotics?"

"Patricia, I don't like the sound of this. What are you mixed up in?"

"Nothing, Dad. It's a technicality in a movie we're thinking of making, and I just wanted to be sure that we've got the legal side of it right."

"Don't you have any lawyers at the studio?"

"Yes. But I wanted the legal mind I know."

"Bullshit, my dear. You're up to something. What is it?"

"Dad, I just thought of something."

"I'm afraid of this. What?"

"You have friends in Washington, don't you?"

"Yes, if anybody in Washington is a friend."

"At the F.B.I.?"

"My friends are in the Justice Department. The F.B.I. is part of Justice. I suppose I know somebody there. Why?"

"And the Narcotics Bureau?"

"Same thing. Why?"

"It just occurred to me. Why don't I send copies of the script to the F.B.I. and the Narcotics Bureau and have somebody there go over the scripts to be sure we've got the technicalities right? It could save us a lot of embarrassment later, in case we've goofed on the legal aspect."

"All right. Why don't you do that?"

"Well, Dad, I wouldn't want to send them to Washington cold. Some secretary might just stick them in a bottom drawer, and that would be the end of it. How about letting me send them to your friends?"

"You want to send them to my friends?"

"Yes. Somebody I know will read the scripts and get back to me on them and be able to speak with some authority. Can you give me their names and addresses?"

"Not right now. That's in my office at the courthouse."

"Can you call me later about it?"

"I've got a busy schedule today, Pat. I'll have my secretary call you. Will you be at home or at the studio?"

"I think I'd better stay home today, Dad. I'm expecting some other calls."

"All right. I'll have Emma call you."

"One more thing, Dad."

"What?"

"Telephone numbers."

"You want their telephone numbers, too?"

"No, Dad. In the script, Dad, the hero is a private detective who is trying to track down some gangsters. He comes upon this telephone number, and he suspects that the person who has that telephone number is the same person who has the post office box. Would he need a Federal court order to find out the telephone number?"

"No. Telephone companies are usually public corporations. All he'd have to do is go to the local police and convince them that he has good reason to find out the information. The police could easily get any municipal judge to sign an order for it. Of course, he could just call the number and find out for himself."

"That's too simple, Dad."

"I suppose it is."

"Well, thanks, Dad. I know you're busy so I won't hold you up. I appreciate your help."

"Help, my ass. I'm sending you a bill."

"Do that."

"When are you coming home?"

"As soon as I can."

"Do you want me to mention this call to your mother?"

"Better not. She'd be upset because I didn't talk to her."

"She'd be even more upset if I woke her up just so you could talk to her."

"Then don't mention it."

"All right. And listen, young lady, if you feel that for one moment I believe this horseshit about a movie script, then either you are not as smart as I think you are or you think I am not as smart as I am."

"You're smart, Daddy."

"So are you. Just don't get too smart."

Judge Purney's secretary called at one. She gave Pat the names and addresses of two people: an Assistant United States Attorney General at the Justice Department, and a Deputy Director of the Federal Bureau of Investigation. The secretary said, "The Judge told me to ask you if you wanted a contact at the C.I.A."

Pat said, "Yes, all right, if he has one."

The secretary gave her the name of a Deputy Director at the Central Intelligence Agency. And she said, "The Judge said you could use his name in the event that you contact any of these people."

Pat said, "Thank him for me."

"Yes, ma'am. Will there be anything else?"

"Not at the moment, but tell the Judge I might need a good lawyer later. I hope he'll be available."

"I'll tell him."

Pat called her secretary at the studio. She said, "I've got a lot of reading to do. I can get it done better here at home without interruption, so I won't be in for the rest of the week."

"Okay, dear."

"If anything important comes up, you call me here."

"Okay."

"Have there been any calls?"

"Fats Mulligan called a few minutes ago from Miami. He's finishing up there this weekend, and he just got an offer from the Concord in the Catskills for next weekend. He wants to know if he can take it or if you want him to get his fat ass to Las Vegas."

"Call Ted Colby in Vegas and have him call Fats. The two of them can work it out. Anything else?"

"Just the usual crap."

"All right. Listen, do you know any Spanish?"

"Any Spanish what?"

"Spanish words."

"A few. I used to know a Mexican. Why?"

"Did you pick up any Spanish from him?"

"Why?"

"I've come upon a Spanish word that I don't know the meaning of, and I'm trying to find out."

"What's the word?"

"Bicho."

A big laugh. Then: "Why, Patricia Kazurian, I am shocked that a nice lady like you would use such vulgar language."

"You know the word?"

"Of course. 'Bicho' is the Spanish gutter word for 'penis.' My boyfriend used to use it as an invitation whenever he started feeling horny. 'Bicho, bicho.' The son of a bitch. Boss Lady, don't tell me you're going to Tijuana?"

"No. I just found out somebody's got a sense of humor."

"I hope that's all it is."

She called Brad on his private phone at the studio. She said, "I won't be in today."

"I've been looking for you."

"Why?"

"Nothing. What's happening?"

"I'll tell you when you get here. When can you make it?"

"I've got a budget meeting in half an hour. I'm free after that."

"Okay. And cancel anything you've got for tomorrow. I want you to stay with me for a few days."

"Okay."

"How's your bicho?"

"My what?"

"Your bicho. It's Spanish."

"The only Spanish I know is Spanish Fly."

"Isn't Spanish a lovely language? I'll be there as soon as I can."

"Bring your bicho."

"I never leave home without it."

Their lives began to center around the telephones in Pat's home, a squawk box and a tape recorder.

Mandy usually began her calls by setting the scene. Then she would attach her tape recorder to her telephone for the playback,

Pat and Brad taping on the machine in the bedroom while listening on the squawk box.

An early call:

Mandy: "Jeez, Mrs. Kazurian, this man never stops. He's got to have that thing of his in me somewhere all the time."

Brad: "Knock it off, Mandy. You love it."

Mandy: "True, Mr. Cunningham. But a girl like me has to get her rest."

Pat: "Did you get anything?"

Mandy: "A little, I think."

Pat: "Go on."

He had picked her up at ten in the morning and announced that they were going on a business trip to Tampa. She feared at first that the trip had something to do with her nonexistent property, but he did not mention it.

She said, "Mrs. Kazurian, I didn't get to see much of the scenery along the way. Mr. Carlotti kept me busy eating him. Anyway, there's not much for you to hear on the tape, so I'll put the machine on fast-forward until we pick something up. He turned off the main highway onto a country road. When I sat up, I saw that we were going through farm country. Cows and horses and silos and things. We went on for a few miles. He didn't speak. Then he pulled up at the side of the road and stopped. Across the road was an open pasture, but no cows or horses. There were three airplanes parked there. Okay, now."

Carlotti: "I see my boys made it right on time."

Mandy: "Your boys?"

Carlotti: "The pilots. They work for me."

Mandy: "You've got pilots working for you?"

Carlotti: "In a way. They fly the planes and I tell them where to go."

Mandy: "Those sure are funny-looking airplanes. I've never seen any planes like them, except in old movies. What kind of planes are they?"

Carlotti: "They're cropdusters."

Mandy: "Cropdusters?"

Carlotti: "Don't you know what cropdusting is?"

Mandy: "I'm not sure."

Carlotti: "Farmers use them. In the summer, all kinds of bugs show up and eat the farmers' crops. Farmers hire cropdusters to fly over the crops and spray poison on them to kill the bugs."

Mandy: "Oh. I have a garden at home. When the bugs show up I just use a can of Raid."

Carlotti: "Same thing. Only cropdusting is on a much bigger scale. There's more bugs to kill."

Mandy: "But doesn't that contaminate the crops?"

Carlotti: "Who cares?"

Mandy: "You're an amazing man, Mr. Carlotti. You're in real estate, you're a stockbroker, you're in cropdusting. What else do you do?"

Carlotti: "All kinds of things."

Mandy: "Is there much money in cropdusting?"

Carlotti: A laugh. "There is the way I do it."

Mandy "What way is that?"

Carlotti: "Wouldn't you like to know? You stay here. I've got to do business with the boys."

They heard the car door open and shut.

Then Mandy, low: "Mrs. Kazurian, this is Mandy. Mr. Carlotti just got out of the car. He's going across the road. It's a narrow road, country, maybe not even two lanes. He's on the other side now. There's a little hill. He's going up. There's a fence. Barbed wire. He's climbing through. Ha! He got his pants caught. I'm not surprised, with what he's carrying! There. He's out. He's heading for a small building at the far side of the field. It looks like a big tool shed. Somebody is opening the door. I see a man. I can't tell much about him. Mr. Carlotti is in the way. There's another man. Mr. Carlotti is at the shed. He's shaking hands with the men. They've gone inside. Now, I don't know anything about airplanes, so I can't tell you much about these ones. They're not jets. They've got a propeller. The wings seem too big. The bodies, are fat, squat. They've got pipes sticking out of the sides. There's something written on the sides, but I can't read it from here."

Pat looked at Brad. "Bicho Air Services, Unlimited." Brad nodded.

Mandy: "They're coming out now. There are three men. Mr. Carlotti is putting his wallet in his pocket. One of the men is holding some bags. They look like the bags of sugar you see in supermarkets. Two-pounders. Looks like five of them. The other two men have gone back into the building. Mr. Carlotti and the guy with the bags are getting near the fence. I may have to cut this off. Here come the other two out of the building. They're carrying bags. Big bags. They look heavy. They're heading for one of the planes."

Brad said, "Pesticides."

Pat nodded.

Mandy, low: "Mr. Carlotti is at the fence now. The man with the bags is helping him through. Shit. He didn't get stuck this time. Now he's taking the bags from the man. They're shaking hands. Here he comes. Hold on."

They heard the car door open.

Carlotti: "I'll just put these on the back seat."

Mandy: "What is it, Mr. Carlotti? It looks like bags of sugar."

Carlotti laughed: "It's sugar, all right. Even sweeter." They heard him settle in and turn the ignition, the engine soft and costly. "I always have trouble turning around here. There's not much space."

Mandy: "Your friend is waving at you."

Carlotti: "Where? Oh." Louder, "Take care, Mitch. You know where you go from here?"

Mitch: "The Panhandle."

Carlotti: "Right. Then Biloxi. And keep in touch with my uncle."

Mitch: "Right. See you next time."

Carlotti: "Right. And see what you can do about having this road widened. It takes all day to turn around."

Mitch: "Okay, Mr. Carlotti."

Carlotti: "All set?"

Mandy: "Yes. Where are we going?"

Carlotti: "Palm Beach."

Mandy said, "Mrs. Kazurian, that's about all there is. I had a rough trip all the way back to Palm Beach, so there's nothing on the tape. When we got here, he dropped me off at the hotel and said he had to go to his office and do some work. Did I get anything important for you?"

Pat said, "You sure did, honey."

The next day, another call

Mandy was saying, "Mrs. Kazurian, Mr. Carlotti certainly is a generous man. He invited me up to his suite last night for dinner, and when I got there he gave me a couple of presents."

Pat: "How nice. What did he give you?"

Mandy: "Some of his products."

Brad: "Mr. Carlotti is in a lot of businesses, Mandy. Which products did he give you?"

Mandy: "The products he gets from South America."

Brad: "He told you they came from South America?"

Mandy: "Yes. I've got it all on tape. I really don't need that stuff, as you know, Mr. Cunningham. All I need to get high is a hard cock, and I'm out of this world. But I was so pleased: the boxes are so nice, solid gold, both the snort and the Colombian Gold."

Pat: "He gave you some Colombian Gold?"

Mandy: "That's what he called it. It's hash, really. And it comes in the cutest box. It's got this little doodad that rolls the joints for you. We had so much fun with it. I've got it all on tape. Do you want to hear it now?"

Pat: "Yes, Mandy. Play it."

Mandy: "I turned on the machine while I was waiting for Mr. Carlotti to open the door. Are you ready?"

They listened. They heard Carlotti give Mandy the little gold boxes. They heard him teach her how to roll a joint. Then they heard her bait him, so shrewdly, making him brag. She asked him where he got the Gold, and he said, "Off the planes this morning."

And she said, "I thought those turtles were cropdusters."

He laughed. "They are. And much more. Wait till I tell you."

He chuckled as he told her about his stroke of genius. He told her how Mr. General Motors started having problems getting his products into the country because of the heavy sea and air traffic in the Gulf of Mexico. He told of how he and his partner in Texas had a meeting on Mr. General Motors' yacht in the middle of the Gulf and how he had noticed the little islands all over the place. It was later, in New York, that the idea hit him.

He said, "I remembered that Greek who was in the cropdusting business. His planes could fly wherever they wanted without any trouble. So it hit me. Why shouldn't we go into the cropdusting business? The planes can land on a dime. Hones could use Colombian fishing boats to get his products out to the islands and our planes could pick them up and bring them into the States and nobody knew what was going on."

Mandy: "And that's what happened in Tampa?"

Carlotti: "It happens at Tampa and everywhere else along the Gulf Coast. All we've had to do is keep the fucking Greek's company out of the area. We've had no trouble doing that. We practically dust crops free."

Mandy: "Hones? Is that Mr. General Motors' name?"

Carlotti: "Yeah. But don't tell anyone I told you."

They heard a knocking.

Carlotti: "That's our dinner."

Mandy came on. "Mrs. Kazurian, that's about all I got on the tape."

Another call.

Mandy was saying, "To tell you the truth, Mrs. Kazurian, I'm getting a little tired of having Mr. Carlotti send out for dinner every night. Every night, he calls a restaurant of some different nationality, and by now I figure I've serviced waiters from every country in the United Nations. But last night was too much."

Brad asked, "What happened last night?"

Mandy said, "I didn't know it, but Mr. Carlotti ordered from a placed called The Butchery. The waiter was a gay."

Brad laughed. Pat said, "Good heavens, Mandy, what did you do?"

Mandy said, "When I saw what it was, right away I told Mr. Carlotti, I said, 'I'm sorry, Mr. Carlotti, but I don't use dykes.' And Mr. Carlotti said, 'You don't have to. She wants you.' So I said, 'I'm sorry, Mr. Carlotti, but I don't mess with broads in any way whatsoever.' And Mr. Carlotti said, 'This isn't a broad. It's a faggot who went up to Baltimore and had a transsexual job. She's artificial. I couldn't believe it, so I said, 'Why should any man do anything as stupid as that?' Mr. Carlotti said, 'He figured if he had female equipment he could make out better with men than before. That's why.' So I looked at the poor thing, and I said, 'Can you make out?' And he said, 'No, but I can still get it the other way' and I said, 'Well, Mr. Carlotti, you'll have to take care of that. I can't.' And Mr. Carlotti was getting upset, and he said, 'You don't understand, Mandy. After his scars healed and he was ready for action, he found out that he didn't want men any more. He wanted women. That's why he's working at The Butchery. So you won't be playing with a dyke, Mandy, just by a gay who jumped the fence.' Well, Mrs. Kazurian, I couldn't figure that one out, but Mr. Carlotti and I had already had a couple of snorts, so I decided what the hell. And, you know, Mrs. Kazurian, he wasn't half bad."

Mandy said, "No. Anyway, I told you what happened, so there's no sense playing the tape. Besides, Mr. Carlotti didn't do much talking last night. I guess watching us turned him on, because that's what he was doing to me until four o'clock this morning. But the reason I called you, Mrs. Kazurian, is that we went on another trip today."

"Oh? Back to Tampa?"

"No. To Jacksonville this time. And you can take my word for it, Mrs. Kazurian, from Palm Beach to Jacksonville is a long time without getting a chance to come up for air."

Recovering, Brad asked, "Where did you go in Jacksonville, Mandy?"

She said, "We didn't go into the city, Mr. Cunningham. We went to another airport."

Brad asked, "Out in the country again?"

"No. This one was right on the main highway."

"Jacksonville International?"

"I don't think so. I didn't see any terminal building. Just big hangars lined up on one side. Mr. Carlotti pulled up to one that had a sign on it: Bicho Air Services."

Pat: "What happened then, Mandy?"

"Mr. Carlotti told me to wait in the car. He took a lot of packages out of the trunk and went into the hangar. He was in there maybe a half hour. When he came back to the car, he said he wanted me to meet a couple of friends of his."

Brad asked, "Did you have the machine going, Mandy?"

Mandy said, "No, Mr. Cunningham. I didn't turn it on for the drive to Jacksonville because I knew there wouldn't be much conversation. Then when Mr. Carlotti told me to get out of the car, I reached for my purse but he said I wouldn't need it. So I went with him into the hangar."

"What did you see in the hangar?"

"Just a couple of those turtle planes and two guys, the pilots, I suppose."

Pat asked, "What happened, Mandy?"

Mandy sounded impatient. "What do you think happened, Mrs. Kazurian, with people like that? For over an hour, the three of them kept rotating on me. Half the time I wasn't sure who was where and doing what. I got the feeling that we were playing musical chairs, and I was the only chair."

Pat said, "Awful!"

Mandy said, "Well, Mrs. Kazurian, with a girl like me, that sort of thing can be a lot of fun, but Mr. Carlotti didn't even introduce these guys. I walked into the hangar, and the next thing I knew they were banging away. No class."

Brad asked, "Mandy, were either of these men at Tampa when you were there the other day?"

"No, Mr. Cunningham. Mr. Carlotti must have a lot of people working for him," Mandy said. "In fact, I said something like that on the way back."

"You had a chance to talk to him?" Pat asked.

"Yes," Mandy said. "Lucky for me, Mr. Carlotti didn't get horny until we reached Daytona Beach, so I taped him."

"Let's hear it."

Mandy: "Mr. Carlotti, I'll be glad to meet everybody you've got on your payroll, but I'd like to know how many there are so I know what to expect."

Carlotti: "Baby, if you took on everybody I've got working for me, you'd never have time for anything else. I don't even know how many people we have. I just make contact with the guys who come into Florida."

Mandy: "They come into someplace else?"

Carlotti: "Anywhere along the Gulf, depending on where the pick up is on the islands and where the stuff is headed."

Mandy: "My goodness, how does anybody know where to be and what to do?"

Carlotti: "Uncle Julio takes care of that. Once he knows which island it is, he lets me know where the stuff is coming in."

Mandy: "How does he do that?"

Carlotti: "Telephone. How else?"

Mandy: "And how does he find out which island it is?"

Carlotti: "Hones lets him know."

Mandy: "By telephone?"

Carlotti: "Hell, no. Radio. Hones has got a radio network bigger than NBC. He can talk to his people anywhere in the world whenever he wants. Then you better follow his orders, or the shit flies."

Mandy: "He's mean?"

Carlotti: "Jeez. You know what his favorite sport is? Hunting down poachers with a bow and arrow."

Mandy: "What's a poacher?"

Big Dick: "I don't know, but I wouldn't want to be one."

Mandy: "Well, then Mr. Carlotti, you must do a lot of traveling back and forth along the Gulf Coast. If you ever need any company, just let me know."

Carlotti: "No. I just handle Florida. I got cousins all along the coast that take care of arrivals in their territory. Right now, the Feds are hot around Louisiana and Mississippi, so most of the stuff is coming into Florida. That's why I'm so busy. But things will calm down after a while, and I'll go back to New York."

Mandy: "I hope that's not too soon."

Carlotti: "I never know. Getting hungry?"

Mandy came on: "That was all I got, Mrs. Kazurian. There wasn't much talk for the rest of the trip."

Pat asked, "Are you seeing him tonight?"

Mandy said, "No. He said one of his friends is getting married next week, so he's going to a stag party tonight, somewhere on somebody's yacht, somebody named Ford or Dodge or Chrysler, one of those automobiles. So I won't be seeing him tonight. But Mr. Carlotti did the nicest thing. He gave me a thousand dollars."

Brad asked, "What for?"

Mandy said, "He said we're going to a party tomorrow night at the Kennedys'. It's formal, and Mr. Carlotti wants me to buy myself a new outfit. Isn't that nice of him?"

Pat said, "Yes, but I can't believe the Kennedys are in on this."

Brad said, "The Kennedys are Harvard."

Pat asked, "Well, Mandy, what are you going to do with yourself tonight?"

"Get some sleep," Mandy said. "I haven't had a good night's sleep since I got here. I'm going to put in ear plugs so I won't hear the phone or the door, and Mr. Carlotti can get off out in the hall, for all I care."

And then the call:

"Mrs. Kazurian, it's Mandy. This will have to be quick."

"What's the matter, Mandy?"

"Mrs. Kazurian, I don't know how he did it, but Mr. Carlotti got himself a key to my door. There's no chain, so I can't lock him out, and I don't know when he might walk in on me. But something happened tonight I think you should know about. Mr. Carlotti has got a narc on his payroll."

Brad said, "A narcotics agent?"

"That's what it sounded like to me, Mr. Cunningham. Listen, I hope you've got the machine on because I'm gonna have to talk fast."

Pat said, "It's on Mandy. Go ahead."

"All right. Well, this morning I went out and bought the outfit Mr. Carlotti wanted me to get for the Kennedy party tonight, and I had my hair done, etc. Well, around five o'clock I took a bath and I was sitting here relaxing because I knew it was going to be a big night, and all of a sudden I heard a key in my lock and Mr. Carlotti walked right in on me. I was so shocked. So suppose somebody else was here? So I said, 'Mr. Carlotti, we're good friends, but I think you should at least knock on the door when you want to come into this place.' And he said, 'We're better friends than that, aren't we, baby? Look, I brought you some presents.' Well, after that, I couldn't stay mad at him. He handed me a couple of boxes. In one was a pair of shoes and in the other was a purse, and I said, 'Mr. Carlotti, this is very kind of you, but I already have shoes and a purse.' And he said, 'Yes, but I'm sick of seeing you with the same shoes and purse every time. Wear this tonight.' What could I do, Mrs. Kazurian? I just thanked God that I'm a quick study because I'd have to depend on my memory to tell you anything that happened. Well, around nine o'clock Mr. Carlotti used the key again, but this time I was ready for him. As he was driving me to the party, he said, 'You are going to meet a good friend of mine tonight and I want you to be nice to him.' And I said, 'I'll be nice to anybody you say, Mr. Carlotti. Is he on your payroll?' And he said, 'Yes, but he's on Uncle Sam's payroll, too, and that's why he's important to me.' And I said, 'You never told me about your Uncle Sam.' And he said, 'The government Uncle Sam. He works for the government.' And I said, 'Well, so do the Kennedys. Is he one of the Kennedys?' And Mr. Carlotti said, 'He works for a different part of the government. He's in my business, only his job is supposed to be to put me out of business. I pay him big bucks and take good care of him. He's one reason why my business is going great.' I said, 'What does he do for you, Mr. Carlotti?' And he said, 'Smitty knows what the other Feds are up to all the time. He's one of them, and he lets me know where things are going to get hot anywhere in the Gulf of Mexico. I tell Uncle Julio and Uncle Julio tells Hones and we move our business to some other part of the Gulf until the heat is off. That's worth big money.' And I said, 'I'm sure it is, Mr. Carlotti, so I'll be real nice to your friend.' He said, 'I'm nice to him, too. Once in a while I let him know where a shipment is coming in and he tells his boss and they make a raid and a lot of arrests and the boss thinks Smitty is a hot agent and give him a promotion and Smitty finds out new ways to help me out. I pay him back by taking him to Key West with me and my friend and line him up with a lot of little sailors, and everybody is happy.'"

Brad said, "I don't, Mandy. Did you meet Smitty?"

"I sure did," Mandy said. "Now, I like black men, but I never saw a black man as beautiful as Smitty. He makes Sidney Poitier look like a misprint. I guess Mr. Carlotti tipped him off about me. Smitty didn't waste any time pressing that Zulu warrior of his against me while we were dancing. I was just about to rape him right there in front of all the Kennedys when Mr. Carlotti came up and told me that Smitty would drive me back to the hotel and that I should be nice to him. As if I had to be told."

Pat asked, "Then Carlotti didn't go with the two of you?"

"No. I think Smitty doesn't like an audience. Anyway, I asked Mr. Carlotti when I was going to see him again, and he said, 'I'm going over the The Butchery and get me that faggot.' I haven't seen him since."

Brad asked, "Did you get Smitty's full name?"

"No. We didn't talk much after we got here. And when he left here a few minutes ago, I didn't have the strength to ask him any questions. But I wanted you to know right away about him being a narc."

"Yes," Pat said. "I'm glad you did. It's very important."

"I thought it might be," Mandy said. "So what do I do now about Mr. Carlotti?"

"What do you mean?"

Mandy said, "Well, he doesn't want me to wear the shoes or the purse any more. I don't want to get him mad, so I'd better have a good lie ready when I've got them with me. And now that he's got a key to my place, I'll never know when he's going to walk in on me. I'll be afraid to call you—he might catch me playing a tape."

Brad said, "Okay, Mandy, listen. You know my Aunt Agatha, don't you?"

Mandy said, "I met her at the party you had her give for me when I got here, but I haven't seen her since. I don't think she liked me. She kept giving me dirty looks."

Brad said, "Don't worry about that. I'll call her later and tell her you might be wanting to use her telephone to call me once in a while. I'm sure she'll let you do it."

"Suppose she won't?"

"She will," Brad said. "I'll blackmail her. I'll tell her that I know she's sleeping with that cute Cuban gardener of hers, and I'm sure she wouldn't want that news to get around Palm Beach."

"All right, Mr. Cunningham," Mandy said, "but I have a question to ask you. How much longer do you want me to hang around? I never thought I'd live long enough to hear myself saying this, but, I'm sorry, Mr. Cunningham, I'm just about worn out."

Chapter Thirty-nine

They gathered together all the tapes they had recorded and took them and the machine into the living room and set up on the coffee table. They played the tapes again. And again.

Pat said, "We've got to make copies of all this."

"Yes."

"I think getting it all on cassettes would be better than this tape."

"Do you have a cassette recorder?"

"No, but I can get one at the studio."

"I don't want the studio involved. Can we buy two today?"

"It's Sunday. Stores are closed."

"What about Hollywood Boulevard? The tourist traps. They should be open."

"I'll check."

"Get four cassette players, if possible. Do you need money?"

"I've got about three hundred."

"Let me see what I've got." She went into the bedroom and checked her purse. When she came back she said, "Here's four hundred."

"I'll get as many as I can. Do you know how to edit the tapes we've got?" Pat asked.

"What do you mean?"

"I want to make a copy of Mandy's tapes isolating Carlotti's voice."

"It shouldn't be difficult. We just snip off what we don't want and then splice the loose ends. I'll get splicing tape and scissors, too."

"Call me if you have problems."

"Okay."

She watched him drive away. Then she went into the den and got paper and a pencil and a stopwatch, and she returned to the coffee table. She rewound the tapes they had just heard and got the tapes from Mandy's earlier calls, and then, in chronological order, she played them back. Whenever something should be cut, she stopped the machine, checked the watch and made a note of the time. Then she clicked the machine on again. She did this for two hours and still had gone only halfway through the tapes. The telephone rang. She went to the den. Brad? A problem?

"Yes?"

"Pat?"

"Yes."

"Jesus Christ, you've been on the phone all day."

"Who's this?"

"Stubby."

"Oh, Stubby, I was on the phone with Ron's brother about what to do with the estate when the will is probated."

"Is that still up in the air?"

"Not for much longer, I hope. What's up?"

"Where's Brad?"

"I don't know. Why?"

"I've been calling his place all day, but I don't get an answer. I thought he might be with you."

"Not at the moment. Is anything wrong?"

"Nothing his John Hancock can't solve."

"What is it, Stubby?"

"Well, I just got back from Chicago this morning and I have to go on the road tomorrow and I need some travel money. Brad has to okay the expense voucher. Is he in town?"

"Yes. In fact, I'm expecting him any moment. He should be at the studio tomorrow. What time are you taking off?"

"I'd like to get out of here in the late afternoon."

"Then you should have time to get over to the studio in the morning, won't you?"

"Sure, as long as I know he'll be there."

"He will be. Where are you headed, Stubby?"

"Houston."

"Houston?"

"Yes. Didn't you get my memo? I sent it to you from Chicago on Tuesday."

"I haven't been in the office for a few days, Stubby. I had to work on some scripts, so I stayed home for the peace and quiet. What's going on in Houston?"

"Not Houston, really. The Johnson Space Center. The Becker script."

"Oh, right."

"I told you in the memo. I got a call in Chicago from the NASA people. I've been hounding them for weeks for permission to shoot some of the interiors in the control room. Well, they finally okayed it and called me at the studio and got my number in Chicago and reached me there. Now we can skip a set at the studio. We can use the real thing. It'll save us a fortune."

"And you're off tomorrow?"

"Yes. I thought we'd fly down tomorrow and check into the Holiday Inn there and go to work the first thing Tuesday morning, finding out what we can use and what we'll need, and then everything will be all set when we send in the company in a few weeks."

"Yes. Who's we?"

"I'm taking three or four of the technicians with me. They're the ones who'll do all the work."

"Of course. Stubby, I wonder if you could do me a favor?"

"Of course."

"A friend of mine in Houston is getting married next weekend, a girl from school. I was just wrapping her present when you called. It's nothing valuable. Just something silly, but it is fragile. I'm mailing it to her, and you know what can happen in the mails."

"Yeah. It would probably arrive in pieces."

"The package would have a better chance for survival if you mailed it when you got to Houston. Could you do that?"

"Sure. But Pat, the post office will be closed by the time we get there. And we're not going into Houston, just renting cars at the airport and heading over to the space center."

Pat said, "There's a mailbox at the airport, right?"

"I think so."

"So when you get to the airport, pop it into a mailbox and I'll just pray until I hear from my friend."

"No problem."

"When you get your money from Brad, come in my office and I'll give you the package, wrapped, stamped and ready to go. Don't forget it."

"I won't."

"Love to Gwen. See you tomorrow."

"Tomorrow."

Pat replaced the telephone, then stood there for a moment, looking at it. "Sorry I had to lie, Stubby." She worked on the tapes for another hour, when she heard Brad's car come up the driveway. He came in carrying a large box, wrapped in brown paper and tied with twine.

She said, "What the hell did you do, buy another case of vodka?"

"No," he said, leading her into the living room. "I was able to get four machines, and the clerk wrapped them all in this box so I could carry them."

"I hope you bought some cassettes."

"A dozen. And a splicer."

"That should do. Sit down. I've got something to tell you." She told him about Stubby.

"What have you got in mind?"

She said, "I've been timing Mandy's tapes for cuts; I've got about an hour to go. Then let's cut and splice the tapes and get everything on the cassettes. We'll have to be careful about the fingerprints."

"Okay."

"Then why don't we make a nice little present for Uncle Julio—the cassettes and one of the machines?" She pointed to the brown paper and the twine. "We've got the wrappings. Then Stubby can mail it for us when he gets to Houston tomorrow, and Uncle Julio will have no idea where it came from."

Brad asked, "What about fingerprints on the package?"

Pat said, "A dozen people will handle the package before it gets to Uncle Julio."

"You think of everything. Who gets the other machines?"

"That's for me to know and you to find out."

Chapter Forty

Wednesday. Twilight. Houston.

In a small back room in a rather large house on a rather large estate some twenty miles out of the city, a man sat alone in the growing gloom. He was an old man, a suddenly old man, a suddenly very old man. His big black mustache, of which he had been so proud, had suddenly gone gray in moments. His mop of thick black hair, which had always made him feel so young, so virile, had gone gray, too, quickly. His face, once handsome in a rugged, peasant way, almost without lines, was suddenly furrowed with deep crevices. The tears that flowed from his eyes were caught by the ridges and held there now in tiny streams. The darkness grew on him, engulfing him, putting him into hiding, as he knew now that he must be as long as he lived.

He was sitting at a long table. He could still see the cassette machine on the table in front of him. He could see the cassettes beside it. He knew what he had to do. He moved his chair closer to the table and looked at the face of the radio antenna rise out of the ground to shoot quickly a hundred feet into the air. He clicked a switch on the transmitter and a red light went on. He knew that, hundreds of miles to the south, somewhere in the mountains of Colombia, a buzzer was sounding through a long, low plantation house. He waited. The red light went green.

He heard: "Yes?"

He said, "Hones?"

"No names."

"It doesn't matter, Hones. It is all over. We are finished."

"What are you talking about?"

"Somebody knows, Hones. Somebody knows. It is over. We are finished."

"Are you drunk?"

"Not yet. It is over, Hones, everything we have built over all these years. Somebody knows. We are ruined."

"What has happened?"

"I got a package in the mail this morning. A recording machine. Seven cassettes. It is all there, everything, everything about us. It is all there. Somebody knows everything."

"Will you make sense, you old fool?"

"Hones, is your recording equipment connected?"

"Of course it is. It always is. You know that."

"I want you to hear something."

"Can't you just tell me?"

"I want you to hear this. I want you to hear his voice. The son of a bitch."

"Make it fast. I am expecting a call from Vienna tonight."

"Listen to this, Hones."

He put the tape marked No. 1 into the machine, closed the lid, and pushed the lever marked *Forward*. Then he sank back in his chair. He listened to the tape for the third time. Then he played the second tape. The third. The fourth. And the tears flowed.

Then he heard: "Is there much more?"

"Three more tapes."

"What is on them?"

"Everything. They know about the movie stock. The cropdusting. The mechanic. The plane crash. The hotel. Vietnam. The diversionary action. Smitty. Tampa. Jacksonville. My brothers in Brooklyn. They know everything, Hones."

"How did you get this?"

"I told you. In the mail this morning."

"Where was it mailed from? Was there a postmark?"

"Yes. It was mailed from Houston."

"To what address?"

"My post office box."

"Any return address?"

"My post office box."

"Then it must be somebody in Houston."

"I guess so."

"Who is the woman?"

"I don't know."

"Can you find out?"

"I will try."

"Did anybody touch the machine or tapes besides you?"

"No."

"Check for fingerprints."

"All right."

"See if you can find out where it was purchased."

"All right."

"Where is he?"

"Palm Beach."

"At the hotel?"

"Yes. In the penthouse. He has a lease on it."

"See that he stays there."

"All right."

"And don't let him know that I know all this."

"All right. What are you going to do, Hones?"

"What do you think I am going to do?"

"I know, Hones. I suppose it must be done."

"It must be."

"I don't think I can do it, Hones."

"I will."

"What about us? What about you and me, Hones? They know about me. They know where I am. They know about you."

"But they don't know where I am."

"They will find you."

"I am not worried. They can't get near me."

"What do you want me to do, Hones?"

"Nothing."

"What about our business?"

"Do you have any more nephews?"

"I've got a lot of nephews."

"Do they all have big bichos?"

"I don't know. I don't think so. I would have heard."

"For now, we do nothing. All this may blow over. If it does, we will work out some other system. If it does not, I will have to find someone else."

"You will find someone else?"

"You think I cannot? There is always someone else. I must go now."

"All right, Hones. Let me know what happens."

"You will know what happens."

"Good night, Hones."

"Good-bye, Julio."

Saturday. Two o'clock in the morning. Los Angeles.

The telephone was ringing.

It rang several times before it penetrated Pat's deep sleep. Dazed, she fumbled for the phone, and:

"Hullo?"

"Mrs. Kazurian?"

"Yes."

"It's Mandy. Mrs. Kazurian."

Pat sat up and glanced at the clock. "What is it, Mandy? Are you all right? Where are you?"

Mandy said, "Yes, I'm all right. I'm at my place at the hotel. But, Mrs. Kazurian, the strangest thing just happened."

"What?"

"Well, I was with Mr. Carlotti, and he was in bed with me."

"Where?"

"In me, for a change."

"I mean, where were you?"

"Oh. Up at his place."

"What happened, Mandy?"

"Well, when Mr. Carlotti left my place yesterday morning he said he had to make another trip but that it wasn't important and I didn't have to go along. He was going over to Everglades City, he said, to pay off a few people, and he'd be back as soon as he could. He told me to get some rest. Well, something happened to his car along the way, and he got back very late. He ordered food in. So we ate and then we had a few drinks and smoked some Gold and snorted a little, and then we went into his bedroom and got undressed and started to make it. Mr. Carlotti sure was in a good mood, I must say that, and he was going like crazy for a long time. And then I heard a noise in the living room and I looked and I saw these three guys standing at the bedroom door."

"Had you ever seen them before?"

"No."

"What did they look like?"

"I dunno. Spanish, I'd say. Two of them were kinda short and squat and they had beards and dark skin and they wore white suits. The third man was older, and he was big, very big. He had this great big head and he was bald and he had a little mustache. Well, Mrs. Kazurian, I didn't know what to make of it. So I said, 'Mr. Carlotti, we got company.' So Mr. Carlotti looked over his shoulder and he went white, Mrs. Kazurian, he went as white as a sheet. And he said, 'Hones.' That's all he said. 'Hones.' Well, I had some idea who that was, but I didn't know which one. So the big guy said something, and the two little guys came over to the bed and they pulled Mr. Carlotti out of me and made him get dressed. And then they took him away."

"They took him away?"

"Yes. When I heard the door slam, I got up and I went into the living room and I looked around for Mr. Carlotti and he wasn't there, so I figured the three men had taken him away. Well, I didn't see any reason for sitting around there and waiting for him to come back, so I got dressed and came down to my place. I know it's late, Mrs. Kazurian, but I don't know what's going on, so I thought I'd better call you right away."

"You did the right thing, Mandy."

"What do you want me to do now, Mrs. Kazurian? Is Mr. Cunningham there? What do you people want me to do now?"

Pat said, "Brad isn't here. Now, listen carefully. Here's what I want you to do. What time is it there?"

"Around five."

"All right. Here's what I want you to do. Before you do anything, pack your things. Pack everything except what you may need for the next few days. Be sure to pack the shoes and the machine and any tapes you may have."

"Yes."

"I'll call Brad and tell him what happened. I'll have him call his aunt and tell her that you are going to show up there in a few minutes and that you are going to leave some luggage with her."

"All right."

"Have you still got the rented car?"

"Yes."

"Use that. But don't go directly to Brad's aunt. Drive around. Be sure you're not being followed. Drive back to the hotel the same way. Then stay there. Stay in your suite. Don't go out. Don't go out for any reason, unless, of course, the place catches on fire."

"That would be just my luck."

"Now, Mandy, I want you to stay there for a few more days. If nothing happens in a few days, if you don't hear from Carlotti, you can come home. Don't call me again, but keep in touch with Brad's aunt. We'll check with her. If nothing happens in a few days, we'll let you know that you can come home."

"Oh, thank God. I can't wait."

"Just a few more days."

"Yes."

"Now, do what I told you."

"I will. Right away."

Pat hung up. Immediately she dialed the number at Santa Barbara. Many rings. The Brad's "Hello?"

"Brad."

"Pat?"

"Yes."

"Are you all right? What's up? What time is it?"

"It's two o'clock. I had to call you right away. I just heard from

Mandy."

"Oh? What happened?"

"Brad, Hones has Carlotti."

"No! What happened?"

She told him. And she informed him of her instructions to Mandy.

Brad said, "Okay. I'll call my aunt."

Pat said, "Brad, it's five o'clock in the morning there."

"So what? If I know my aunt, she's probably giving her Cuban gardener his fifth delight of the night. Do you want me to come over?"

"No. There's nothing you can do. I've got everything under control."

"It sure sounds like it, Godmother. It sure sounds like it."

Thursday. Three in the afternoon. Palm Beach.

Mandy was finishing her second lunch. Having nothing to do, having run out of Gold and snort, she had little to fill her time except eating and television. She had ordered another large T-bone steak, two baked potatoes, three ears of corn, a huge salad, buckets of butter and sour cream. She'd had the waiter place the table in front of the television set, and she was watching the last minutes of a soap opera.

Suddenly there was a banging at the door. Started, she stood and looked at the door. Before she could move, the door burst open.

She said, "Mr. Carlotti, where have you been?"

He was dressed as she had last seen him, but his clothes were badly disheveled. His hair was mussed and his face was badly bruised and scarred and covered with scabs of blood. Under his arm he carried what looked like a mahogany cigar box.

He glared at her. "You rotten, bitch whore."

She said, "Mr. Carlotti, that is no way to talk to me."

His voice was low, a growl. "I'm gonna kill you."

She said, "Mr. Carlotti, now stop it. I've never done anything to you, and you have no right to threaten me."

He said, "Nothing? You ruined me. You killed me. How did you do it? How did you get it all on tape? What was the trick? The shoes?" He took some steps to her, stumbling badly.

She said, "Mr. Carlotti, you get out of here. I'm going to call the manager."

"Go ahead," he said. "Cal anybody you want. You'll be dead before anybody gets here."

She said, "Mr. Carlotti, stop it. You're scaring me."

"Oh, don't be scared," he said, his voice going saccahrine. "Don't be scared. I brought you a present. See, I brought you a present." He was approaching, stumblling, once almost dropping to his knees. He held out the mahogany box.

She said, "Mr. Carlotti, you've already given me too much. I can't accept any more presents from you."

"But I want you to have it," You'll love it. Go ahead. Take it. Look at it."

She took the box and lifted the lid. She screamed. She screamed and screamed, and she dropped the box to the floor.

He picked up the steak knife. "Now I'm gonna give you another present."

He swung the knife at her and cut a slash in her negligee.

She said, "Mr. Carlotti, stop this. Get out of here. I'll call the police." She backed away.

He moved to her, the knife held high.

She backed away.

He swung the knife and stumbled and almost fell.

She turned and ran into the bedroom. She could hear him coming after her. There was no place for her to hide. He was nearing and stumbling and tripping and dropping to his knees.

The French doors to the terrace were open. She ran out on the terrace, and she hollered for help, she hollered and hollered.

She heard him close to her. She turned. He was growling and mumbling and swinging the knife. She bolted to one side. His momentum kept him coming. He stumbled and fell on the low railing. His movement kept him coming and she watched his feet rise from the floor and the force of him sending him tumbling forward, and she watched him slip over the railing and drop twelve floors to the concrete pavement at the swimming pool. She kept looking at him, the knife still in his hand. He was not moving. People went running to him.

Mandy left the terrace and went into the bedroom, to the telephone on the night table. She dialed a number and waited. At the other end, the phone rang and rang. Mandy decided Pat was not home. She hung up and dialed another number.

She heard: "LPM Studios."

"Mrs. Kazurian, please."

"One moment."

Muzak.

A buzzing.

"Mrs. Kazurian's office."

"Is she there?"

"Yes, but she's in a meeting just now. May I ask who's calling?"

"Tell Mrs. Kazurian it's Mandy and that I must speak to her urgently."

"One moment."

Muzak.

Then: "Mandy?"

"Oh, Mrs. Kazurian!" And then she broke down, great sobs shaking her body, and she felt very cold.

Pat said, "Mandy? Mandy? What is it? Are you all right?"

Mandy said, "Oh, Mrs. Kazurian, the most awful thing just happened." And she told her.

Pat listened without a word. When she sensed Mandy had finished and seemed to be gaining control of herself, Pat asked, "Is he dead?"

"I don't know. I'm not sure. I think so. I'm on the twelfth floor."

"Have you called the police?"

"No."

"Has anybody?"

"I don't know. There are a lot of people down there, looking at him."

"All right, Mandy. Now listen to me. Listen to me very carefully. I want you to get dressed right away. Be sure to pack everything that you still have with you. Don't even leave a toothbrush behind."

"All right."

"Then leave the hotel. Don't check out. Don't pay the bill. Just walk out. Don't use your car. Take a cab over to Brad's aunt. I'll have Brad call her right away so she knows you're on the way. His aunt will take you to the Miami airport. Get the first plane you can out of Florida. Go anywhere. Don't come here. Is there any place you can go where you know someone?"

"I have a sister in Minneapolis."

"Go to Minneapolis, then, as soon as you can. Go to your sister's. If she can't put you up, ckeck into a hotel. Don't call me. Call Brad's aunt and let her know where you are. We'll keep in touch with her. As soon as I know it's all right for you to come home, I'll call you."

"All right, Mrs. Kazurian."

Pat said, "Mandy, I'm very sorry we put you through all this. But you've done something tremendously important. You may never know how important. And I'm sorry about Mr. Carlotti."

"So am I, Mrs. Kazurian," Mandy said. "He wasn't such a bad guy."

"I'll always be grateful to you, Mandy."

"Mrs. Kazurian, I hear a siren."

"You'd better get moving."

"Okay."

"Mandy, what was in that box?"

"Mr. Carlotti's watermelon."

Pat replaced the telephone and looked at the four writers gathered around her desk. She said, "Gentlemen, something has come up. We'll have to put this discussion off until next week." Then they left.

She got up from her desk, left her office, and went down the hall to Brad's office. He was dictating to his secretary. Pat said, "Can that wait until some other time?"

Brad said, "I'm not going to say no to the Boss Lady." He gave his secretary a nod and she left.

Pat told him about Mandy's call. He listened to her as though she might be giving him yesterday's headlines. Then he asked, "What next?"

She asked, "Have you got any plans for the rest of the day?"

He said, "I don't think it would make any difference if I did. What are your plans?"

"I'm going home now. I want you to pick me up in an hour and drive me out to the airport."

"Where are we going?"

"You're not going anywhere. I'm going to Washington."

"Why can't I go with you?"

"Because I've got a book to read, and I don't want you jabbering in my ear all the way."

"When are you coming back?"

"On the first flight I can get."

He knew. "See you in an hour."

She went home. In the bedroom, she put on a pair of gloves. In the kitchen, she took the rest of the brown paper and twine Brad had brought back with the cassettes he bought on Hollywood Boulevard. She made three packages, each containing a cassette player and a set of the edited cassettes. She addressed each package to one of the men whose names had been given to her by her father's secretary, using the same name and address for the return—an Assistant United States Attorney General, a director at the Federal Bureau of Investigation, a director at the Federal Bureau of Narcotics. She put the three packages into her large attache case, adding a book she had seen advertised in the papers and picked up at Dalton's a few days before. In the bedroom, she changed into comfortable jump suit, and she was checking her purse for cash when she heard Brad pull up in the driveway.

As she got into his car, she say, "We go to the post office first."

"You didn't have to tell me, he said."

At the post office, she had the packages weighed and bought sufficient. She applied them to the packages as they drove to the airport.

At the airport, Brad asked, "Which airline?"

She said, "I'll try American first. If they don't have anything, I'll work my way through the terminal."

"You have any idea when you'll be back?"

"As soon as I can."

"Call me from Washington. I'll pick you up."

"It might be very late. I'll take a cab home."

"If you prefer."

As she got out of the car, she said, "In the meantime, it might be a good idea if you learn how to ride a bicycle."

"I'll do my best."

She got a coach seat on a United flight to Washington. There, she left the plane, walked through the long corridors into the lobby, then went outside and found a mailbox and deposited the three packages. Back in the lobby, she studied the big overhead sign indicating departures. She had to wait an hour for an American flight, with stops at Denver and San Francisco. To fill the time, she went into the coffee shop and took a stool at the counter. The waitress asked her what she wanted.

She resumed reading her book, and she said to herself, "I tried, Ron darling."

She was home at two in the morning. She called Brad. "You can stop worrying. I'm home."

"How did it go?"

"Fine."

"Plan on having dinner here with me for the next few nights. We can watch the news together."

"Right."

"See you in the morning."

Walter Cronkite was saying, "In Washington today, both the Federal Bureau of Investigation and the Federal Bureau of Narcotics issued a joint statement that together they have broken up what is described as the largest dope smuggling ring bringing drugs into the United States, and probably the biggest operation of its kind in the world. Dan Rather has the story."

Dan Rather was saying, "Walter, there's been a lot of confusion around here for the past couple of hours, and details are scant and often contradictory. All we have been able to find out is that both Federal agencies received an anonymous tip concerning the smuggling operation, and that the information may have arrived in the form of cassettes sent by ordinary mail from someplace here in Washington. And we have been able to find out some fascinating information about the smuggling itself. It seems that the drugs have been coming into the country from South America, most likely Columbia. We're told that the drugs were carried out of Colombia on fishing vessels, small ones, and that the drugs were hidden in waterproof bags inserted into the bellies of gutted fish. By some sort of ingenious pre-arrangement, the drugs themselves were placed on deserted islands in the Gulf of Mexico and were picked up by American planes. Here's the amazing thing, Walter: the planes were actually cropdusters, the kind of planes used to spray pesticides on insects that attack crops on farms. We're told that the planes belonged to a company called the Bicho Air Services, Unlimited, out of Houston, Texas, but we haven't been told much about the company. A narcotics bureau official admitted that the planes were well known by government departments, including the U.S. Customs, and the agencies were so familiar with the planes that they attached no importance to them when they sometimes saw the planes far out over the Gulf. We're told that agents have moved in on Bicho terminals at Houston, New Orleans, Biloxi, Tampa and Jacksonville and that about a dozen pilots have been arrested, some of them with drugs aboard the planes. Also arrested in Florida was one Xavier Smith, known as Smitty, himself a Narcotics Agent, but who was also found to be on the Bicho payroll, evidently tipping the company off to any investigations by his agency. Smitty is said to have social contacts among high society in Florida and New York. I've just learned, Walter, that when Federal agents broke into the Bicho headquarters at Houston they arrested one Julio Carlotti, said to be the head of the American end of the operation. I've been told that seconds before the arrest, Carlotti apparently gave himself an overdose of heroin and he is now under intensive care in a Houston hospital. I'm told, too, that Carlotti is a member of the well-known Carlotti family of Brooklyn, New York, a powerful branch of organized crime, and that several Brooklyn members of the family have already been picked up for possible involvement in the smuggling, as well as involvement in a number of otherwise so-called legitimate businesses. We hear talk about a Sergio Carlotti, but little is known about his whereabouts at this time. Just a minute. What? Thanks. Walter, the State Department has called in the Colombian ambassador to this country and has insisted on Colombian cooperation in tracking down the origin of the drugs inside that country, and the ambassador tonight is flying home to confer with his government. I think that's about all we have now, Walter. Back to you."

Walter Cronkite was saying, "Colombia, South America, is also in the news tonight in a quite different area. LPM Studios in Hollywood has announced that they have just purchased movie rights to the current best-selling Louis Schreiber biography of Simon Bolivar, the Colombian patriot, and a major motion picture epic will be made later this year, shot entirely in that country.

"In other news…"

Pat clicked off the set.

Brad said, "Proud of yourself?"

"Not really," she said. "There's nothing to be proud of. Besides, the job isn't done yet." She reached for the phone on the desk.

Brad asked, "Who are you calling?"

"Mandy. She can come home now."

"That ought to make her happy."

But before Pat could pick up the telephone, it rang. She took it. "Hello?"

"Pat?"

"Yes."

"Bert Bernstein."

"Hi, Bert. What's up?"

"I'm in San Francisco. I just had dinner with my father-in-law."

"You mean your ex-father-in-law."

"No, I mean my father-in-law. Looks like my marriage is going to be patched up."

"A lot of starlets will be sorry to hear that."

"They had their chance. Pat, you know Dave's law firm is representing Ron's estate on the hotel fire case?"

"Yes."

"Well, Dave told me at dinner that he got a call this afternoon from the law firm in New York that's representing all the plaintiffs. They're dropping the case."

"What?"

"Yes. There won't be any court action. You'll have to settle with each plaintiff on an individual basis. You're going to save a lot of money."

"Good, Bert."

"Isn't it? And Dave talked to the insurance company. Now that there's not going to be any legal action, the company is ready to write the fire off to unknown causes and share in any settlements the estate has to make."

"I don't know what to say, Bert."

"Don't say anything. But save your money. At Jewish weddings, the newlyweds expect a lot of expensive gifts."

"Let me know when."

She told Brad.

He sang, "Ding dong, the witch is dead. Which old witch? The wicked old witch. Ding dong, the wicked witch is dead."

Pat called Mandy. She said, "You can come home now, Mandy. The coast is clear."

"I know," Mandy said. "I just watched the news. What a relief. I thought I'd have to spend the rest of my life in hiding."

"Well, you won't, Mandy. Come back on the next plane, if you like."

"All right, Mrs. Kazurian, but I think I'll stay up here for a while. There are lots of nice people in these parts."

"Do what you like, Mandy."

Mandy said, "You know, Mrs. Kazurian, people have been telling me for years that Swedes are coldblooded. Well, they're not when you get to know them, believe me. Mrs. Kazurian, I'm even getting to like their food."

Pat laughed and hung up.

Brad asked, "So?"

Pat said, "Mandy has discovered the wonders of smorgasbord."

Chapter Forty-one

It took time.

It took planning.

It took a lot of work.

Now and then, it required deception.

And the frustration in it was having a destination and not knowing where it was.

The deception was the Simon Bolivar movie. Pat went ahead with it even though she wasn't sure she would actually produce the picture. It was a front, a convenient front, a necessary front. She assigned a writer to prepare a scenario from the book; then she assigned three writers to do a shooting script. Older and wiser heads in Hollywood warned her that no pictures with locales south of San Diego had made any money since Wally Beery did Pancho Villa. Nobody—not Paul Muni, not Bette Davis, not even Marlon Brando—could make a movie which involved Latin-American politics that would pull a big audience. And scholars pointed out that unless the Schreiber book was fictionalized and romanticized it would turn out to be a downer, since Simon Bolivar himself turned out to be a bit of a bastard, a despot and a dictator who died broke and hated, and who himself had said you will never find an honest and democratic government below the Rio Grande. But Pat pushed on. Pat and Brad pushed on.

Pat had the LPM publicity department barrage the media with phony tips on possible stars to play Bolivar. Ricardo Montalban. Fernando Lamas. Cesar Romero. Bolivar's wife had died after a few months of marriage, so the part was small and was reportedly turned down by Rita Hayworth, Dolores del Rio and Sophia Loren. On Bolivar's birthday—July 24—LPM staged a rally at his statue in Central Park, heralding him as the Great Liberator of South America, but the only people who showed up were fifty Puerto Ricans who were members of Actors Equity and had been hired at scale to spend the day waving Colombian flags in front of the statue of a man who had been born and who had died in Venezuela. But it helped. It all helped.

It helped when Pat needed a cover for telling Stubby: "I want you to go down to Colombia and find some locations for the Bolivar picture. Have you read the script yet?"

"No, I haven't," Stubby said.

"Okay. I'll have the Story Department send you a copy. Bolivar was a revolutionist, a guerrilla leader, and a lot of the fighting took place in the mountains, so we'll need mountains.

Stubby said, "I've been to Colombia, on the TV series. The place is full of mountains. What kind of mountains do you want?"

Pat said, "That's up to you. I've talked to Joe Reilly, and he will equip one of his FreytFlyte planes in Colombia for aerial photography. Photograph the whole damned country."

Stubby said, "Why go through all that? Why don't we just use the Rockies. They're mountains. Who'll know the difference?"

Pat said, "I will. Besides, shooting the picture in Colombia is part of the hoopla."

The hoopla helped when Pat needed a cover for telling Bert Bernstein: "I don't want any trouble with the Colombian Government when we start filming down there. Can that Sherlock Holmes outfit of yours find somebody down there who can help us get around all the legal red tape that always comes up whenever we try to make a picture in a foreign country?"

Bert Bernstein said, "Money talks. Money talks all over the world. I'll get you the price list for Colombia."

And the hoopla helped when she said to Joe Reilly: "This Bolivar thing is going to cost a lot of money. Brad Cunningham handles the purse strings at the studio, and he's got veto power over me so that I don't bankrupt the company. He'll be going with me when I head down to Colombia for final estimates on the budget. We'll probably need a helicopter to get to some of the remote locations. Can we use one of FreytFlyte's choppers?"

"Sure," Joe Reilly said. "Let me know when you want it so I can assign a pilot."

Pat said, "Brad was a Navy pilot. Can't he fly us around?"

Joe asked, "Can he handle a chopper?"

"I don't know," Pat said, "but he certainly can learn, can't he?"

"I suppose," Joe said. "Have him call me. I'll have one of my men here show him how."

But there was more than hoopla.

Pat and Brad played the Mandy tapes again and again, noting clues for the whereabouts of General Motors. Frequently they stopped the machine and played a few inches of the tape over and over. They agreed that Uncle Julio and Big Dick had entered Colombia at Barranquilla and were transfered to a helicopter that took them southeast into the remote mountain district near the Venezuela border. They became more convinced of this when Stubby reported that the Colombian Government authorized him to do his aerial photography anywhere in the country except in that area. And they became even more convinced when, through the Sherlock Holmes outfit, their pigeon in the government sent word that LPM might just as well forget about that desolate region: there were no roads, no town, no electricity, and the mountains were full of bandits.

Brad said, "Boss Lady, do you think our little pigeon is shitting us?"

Pat said, "I think our little pigeon is a little worried about his little peter."

On their own, they were able to obtain maps of the area from, of all places, the National Geographic Magazine, and, from the U.S. Printing Office in Washington D.C., they received a catalog of publications by the Federal Bureau of Narcotics, listing among them a booklet entitled, "Gobal Areas of Cultivation, Confirmed and Suspected." The inaccessible southeastern zone of Colombia, South America, had been suspect for a long time but never confirmed. Good.

But there was something they had to confirm about themselves. One day, Pat asked, "Would you say that you're in good physical shape?"

Brad said, "You ought to know."

Pat said, "I mean, well, how many pushups can you do?"

Brad said, "You ought to know."

"Besides that," Pat said. "In the Navy, did you have to go through survival training?"

"Of course. It was a snap."

"Would it be a snap now?"

He frowned at her. "I think I know what's coming."

What came for both of them was a backbreaking physical fitness assault. Mornings, they jogged. After work, they spent two hours at a health club. They bought backpacks, and on weekends they went up into the Sierras, ignoring the marked hiking trails and making their way up and down mountains, across streams, eating K-rations and sleeping under the stars, sometimes under the rain-clouds. Pat located an archery range at Long Beach and practiced for hours to sharpen the old skills that had made her Colorado State Junior Champion in her teens.

At one point, near exhaustion, Brad said, "You know, we really don't have to go through all this. Big Dick is dead; Uncle Julio is dead. The worst of your problems are over."

"Are they?" Pat asked. "What about Hones? After all, it was his money. How long do you think it would take him to find somebody else to try to get it back for him?"

"Suppose we don't find Hones?"

"We'd better find him, before he finds us. Besides," Pat said, "I want to do to him what he tried to do to Ron."

"Put him out of business?"

"You can call it that."

The time had come.

The pigeon was saying, "Senora, you have been very generous with me and I am grateful. But I think I have done a good job for you. In this country, you cannot get anything done unless you know the right people in the government to pay off, and fortunately I am in a position to clear the way for your motion picture. But that is all I can do for you."

"All you have to do," Pat said, "is tell us where we can find him. We have some idea where he is, but we need to know precisely."

"Then you will have to ask someone else," the pigeon said.

Brad said, "We'll pay you well. We'll pay you all you want."

"There is not enough money in the world for me to tell you what you want to know," the pigeon said. "What good would the money do for me in this country? I would be dead in a minute."

Brad said, "We could get you out of this country in a minute. We could send you anywhere you want to go, wherever you feel you would be safe."

"And what about my wife? What about my children?"

Pat said, "We can send your wife and your children to you."

He thought about it. "My wife?" He shrugged. "But my children, I care very much about my children."

"They will be safe."

"But where? That man has long arms. He can find you no matter where you hide. Where could I go?"

Brad asked, "Don't you have any friends or relatives anywhere else in the world?"

"I have a cousin in your country, living in a place with the name Kalamazoo. Do you know it?"

Brad said, "Yes, we know it."

"Have you gone there?"

"Nobody goes to Kalamazoo."

"Will it be a safe place for me and my children?"

"Yes. For anybody. Now, tell us."

The pigeon closed his eyes, thinking, and a shudder went through him. When he opened his eyes, he looked at the map on the wall on the FreytFlyte office at the Barranquilla airport. He asked, "Will it be enough if I just point?"

The pigeon stepped to the map and placed a finger on it, just about where Pat and Brad had figured Hones would be but a bit more to the east. He asked, "How will you get there?"

Brad said, "Helicopter."

The pigeon moved his finger in a circumference about an inch away from where he had pointed. "Land no closer than that. He has an airfield with much traffic during the week. You could be seen."

Brad asked, "During the week?"

"Yes," the pigeon said. "He is a strict Catholic and will not have any work done on Sundays. Everybody is away to their homes. On Sundays, the compound is like a morgue, just the guard at the gate."

Pat said, "The gate?"

"Yes. There is a fence around the place, but just to keep out the animals. He does not have to worry about people. Everybody near there works for him. Even so, don't land too close. You will have to go the rest of the way on foot. It is very difficult. Jungle. Mountains. Rivers. It is very difficult."

Brad pointed to the circumference. "How far would this be?"

"Fifteen, twenty kilometers. Very rugged."

Brad asked, "Have you been there?"

"Once. My father worked for him, a chemist. When my father died there two years ago, I was summoned to fetch his body."

Pat said, "Tell us everything you can about the place."

The pigeon rolled his eyes and he shuddered again. "I am signing my death warrant."

Pat said, "Maybe. So are we."

It was important for them to approach General Motors on a Sunday morning. There would be no way of knowing beforehand whether Hones would be alone at the house: they would have to risk that. The entire effort was a great risk, for that matter, but they had gone too far to postpone or discard their plan, and they knew they would have no peace unless they at least tried.

On Friday, they waited until the siesta doldrums had quieted the Barranquilla airport. They boarded the helicopter, taking with them only Stubby's aerial maps, the pigeon's sketch of the compound, their backpacks, Pat's bow and arrows, Brad's pistol. As a diversion, they first headed out over the Gulf and then turned west, proceeding until they reached a desolate place along the shore and could return overland unnoticed and head southwest. With Pat tracing their route on Stubby's maps, they avoided populated areas, zigzagging, maintaining a height to dim the noise of the prop. On and on they went for almost two hours, reaching the mountains, descending, weaving their way between them. By twilight, they approached the circumference the pigeon had indicated on the map, and they landed in a quiet valley. Brad nudged the helicopter close to the trees.

They got out. They knew they faced a hike of some twenty kilometers, but as the crows flew, and they were not crows and they faced twenty kilometers of rugged mountains, across sudden valleys, wading through freezing streams. Saturday dawn, they had no way of measuring how far they had gone. They rested, they ate K-rations, they took turns napping. Pat heard a plane approaching and reached for Brad to awaken him, but it passed and she let him sleep. At least they were in the right neighborhood. At noon, they resumed their hike.

Sunday morning, the rising sun in their face, they reached a certain mountaintop and looked down at the valley below. General Motors. They compared the pigeon's sketch with what they beheld and, in whispers softened by the wind, they agreed on their strategy.

They waited and they watched. They saw no one. Nothing moved. Around ten they began to descend the mountain and make their way through the underbrush to the road; then, still in the undergrowth, along the road to the main gate.

They saw the guard there, sitting on a stool, asleep in the hot sun. Brad opened his jacket and removed the pistol from his belt and attached the silencer to it. He took aim. For a second he hesitated, his breathing quickened. It was as though he were back in Vietnam, machine-gunning the Viet Cong from his helicopter. This man was the enemy. He held his breath and slowly squeezed the trigger. There was a spit of air and a puff of smoke and the guard fell from his stool to the ground.

They waited. And then they went to the dead guard and sat him upright on his stool and they took the ring of keys from his wrist and they opened the main gate and they entered. They made their way quietly and cautiously along the narrow streets, passing the silent buildings, some small sheds, some as big as a house, some as big as a sound stage, and they came to the fence at the far end of the compound. They found the right key for the lock that was there, and they crossed the road and went again into the jungle, walking for about a mile. And then they could see the long, low plantation house.

There was a man on the porch, reclining in a canvas chaise, an old man with a huge head, bald, and a small mustache. Part of a newspaper was on his lap; the rest on the floor beside him. At his elbow was a table, with a bottle of something on it and a glass and a bowl that might earlier have contained ice cubes. The man appeared to be asleep in the hot sun. They watched him for a long time. He did not move.

Brad whispered, "Can you do it from here?"

Pat said, "I could do it from twice the distance."

Brad took a bottle out of his pocket and removed the top. Pat drew an arrow out of her container and dipped it into the jar. She placed the arrow in position, drew the bow string, and took aim. Beat. Beat. Beat. There was a twang of the bow string and a whoosh of the arrow as it soared across some fifty yards. It struck the man in the chest and sank deep. The man sat up, his eyes wide, his mouth grabbing at air, his hands pulling at the arrow. And then he sank back.

They waited.

They waited.

Brad whispered, "Do you think he's dead?"

Pat said, "I don't know. He should be. Give me the pistol."

"What are you going to do?"

"Give me the pistol."

He gave her the pistol and she stepped from the bushes into the open plane and, determined, she went firmly to the porch. Her footsteps on the wooden stairs sounded like thunder. She did not look at the man. She went behind him and pointed the pistol at the top of his head. There was a spit of air. A puff of smoke. She returned to Brad.

"Let's go."

They retraced their way through the mile of jungle to the rear gate. They entered the compound and locked the gate behind them. They went quickly through the compound to the main gate and locked it and put the ring of keys back on the dead guard's wrist. Then they entered the jungle and began to climb the mountain.

They did not stop. Knowing the way, they traveled quickly, their sense of sudden freedom making their hearts and steps light and confident. In the first hours of Monday morning, the mountain sky still full of stars, they were back at the helicopter. Pat threw her bow and arrow into the thick bushes. Brad threw the bottle. They pushed the helicopter into the clearing and they got in and they lifted off even before the motor was ready for them. In three hours they were back at Barranquilla.

They went into the FreytFlyte terminal, and Brad asked the assistant manager, "Anything going north today?"

"Yes. In about an hour. To Mexico City."

"Room for us?"

"Sure. Joe's orders: anything you want."

"Fine."

By evening, they were at Mexico City and they changed to a FreytFlyte going to Los Angeles. At Orange County they got into Brad's car and he drove Pat home. He did not get out of the car.

He said, "See you in the morning?"

"Yes. Are you going to Bert's wedding next weekend?"

"I guess so. I got an invitation. Do I have to wear a hat at a Jewish wedding?"

"I think so. I haven't thought of a gift for them."

"Neither have I."

"We'll think of something. Brad, let's drive up. There's a lovely inn in Carmel. We can stay there a few days."

"All right."

"And then let's go up to the farm for a few days. I'd love to see the folks."

"I'd love to meet them."

"It's time."

"See you in the morning."

"Yes."

Never, never did the two of them ever talk to each other about where they had been and what they had done. It was something that had to be done, and, done, was best forgotten. As far as each of them knew, the other never even thought about it again. There were too many other things for them to think about: themselves, as partners, friends, lovers. And they both hoped that they would remain as they were now for as long as they both would live.

THE END